SEAN KENNEDY

Ghost Squad

Evolution Game Book 1

This book was professionally typeset on Reedsy.
Find out more at reedsy.com

Contents

1

The Lioness & The Inventor

Kavi wheezed as air rippled below bruised ribs. He pushed himself off the sand and looked across the circle to his opponent. She was dressed in light sparring gear. Her wide-legged linen pants snapped with impossibly fast kicks and her loose fitting top allowed for full motion. Marie Stonecrest had a beauty that middle age failed to tame. Dark, short hair capped angular features that never knew indulgence. The sicari scars mapping her military history glowed white on the tight skin of her face, further narrowing cheekbones and jaw. Her amethyst eyes glowed with purpose and intensity.

She was a full head shorter than Kavi. Even so, it was obvious, even to the two barn cats lazily watching from the rafters that she was the predator and he the prey. Her bare feet floated over the sands. Her measured breathing made mockery of his deep gulps of air.

She closed, feinting with a kick to his abdomen. With a shift in her hips the same foot changed direction and darted towards his face. Kavi shifted his weight backwards and narrowed his eyes as her foot missed his nose by a hairsbreadth. Before her foot reached the ground he leaned forward and swept his foot low in an attempt to take out her standing leg.

Marie leapt over his kick and spun. She predicted where his head would be as he returned to ready position. Her legs scissored around his neck and closed with vice-like strength. She arched her back and her full weight pulled Kavi ears over knees to land flat on his back.

"Your foot work is pathetic and slow," she said as she waited for him to catch his breath.

"Yes ma'am," Kavi said. He brushed sand off his pants as his ego brushed off the comment. After a lifetime of training with her, he never once received a word of praise.

"Four years at the Bastion should have taught you to move your feet," she said.

He grabbed a small handful of sand and charged. He struck with a flurry of punches. Marie easily dodged and blocked. On his final punch, he opened his hand and the sand flew into her eyes. She closed them immediately and Kavi swept a kick at her legs. Somehow she leapt over the kick but Kavi wasn't finished. He continued the spin and caught her in the stomach with an elbow.

"You know I wasn't half bad, even against those idiots at the Bastion. I wasn't Grim's level but I was top five in every martial skill," he said.

"But never number one."

He circled as his mother wiped sand from her eyes. "Never number one," he agreed. "Shocking, considering every instructor at the Bastion told me how they could never go toe to toe with the Lioness of Valun. I wonder how they'd do now that you've lost a step."

Her eyes narrowed in anger as the barb struck. His widened in fear. She launched a series of kicks and punches that came so fast, Kavi could only react by instinct. After he blocked or dodged the first whirlwind he noticed her anger made her sloppy. She left herself open to a throw on her stronger punches to his left side. When the pattern presented itself again, he took advantage. He grabbed her arm with both hands, shifted his weight over his hips and used the extension of her own blow to send her flying.

She twisted in the air to land in a crouch. He stood in shock. They had been sparring for almost twenty years and he had never thrown her. Not once.

"Close your mouth before something flies into it," his mother said. "This should teach you a valuable lesson. Anger has no place in the circle."

He wanted to throw his tall, wiry form to the roof in celebration but knew it would further lessen her opinion of him. Instead, he ran one hand over his own angular features in a pretense of wiping sweat from his face. His fingers lingered for a moment over his own sicari scars, permanent pedigree of his time in the Bastion and the Eagles. While the Lioness' scars were sharp and accentuated her cheek bones making her look more feminine, Kavi's were ragged, less refined. Kavi thought back ruefully to the boy who so desperately wanted to coarsen his boyish jawline to better fit in with his brother warriors. A lifetime ago when petty things mattered.

They formally bowed to each other in the center of the circle.

"First thing tomorrow, take a group to patrol our eastern border. We received a couple of disturbing messages from the farmers out there. Bandits poaching the herds."

"It's not old Creb again is it?" Kavi asked. "He sees bandits in every passing cloud."

Marie nodded. "Of course it's Creb, but this time he was joined by Holden and the Freisons. Holden has never been one to jump at shadows and we haven't heard a peep from the Freisons since they settled almost five years ago."

Kavi nodded. "I'll start at the Freisons then talk to Holden."

"I also need you to scout the Mill Bridge. Those traders from Brickolage lodged a complaint with the Council in Krom. Something about bandits camped along the banks of the Rhune. They claimed that if they had a slightly smaller guard they would have been attacked."

Kavi grimaced. That's all they needed - an official patrol being sent from Krom to 'help' them secure the bridge. Krommians were not known for their subtlety. "They could have brought their concerns to us."

"Most Brickers don't know we're responsible for the security of the bridge." She held up a hand to stall his protest. "Not everybody knows your father. He may be one of the most famous Tinkerers of his time but his time is passing."

Kavi snorted. "I doubt that. They're still teaching his sulimite distillation methods at the University. Did you hear the current Cog entered a request to rename the Mill Bridge the Tribar Bridge?"

"His head is big enough already," said his mother. "Hopefully the request won't make it out of peer review. That man doesn't need anything else with his name on it. Two University buildings are more than enough."

Kavi disagreed but didn't press the point. Her Krommian up-bringing frowned at taking pride in accomplishment. She expected everyone to perform to the best of their abilities regardless of their birth talents. She was the living embodiment of this ethos. Her accomplishments in battle were legion. With sword, shield and sheer tenacity she turned the tide at Valun, earning her title of the Lioness of Valun. After the battle, the Krommian Council offered her a generalship. Each of these accomplishments were indelibly marked on her face, forearms and calves, where the sicari scars could be seen even when wearing armor. The Krommians didn't pass out medals. They cut their lauds directly into their skin using daggers dull enough to leave permanent scars.

Her budding romance with a young tinkerer taught her there

was more to life than war. Their romance became legend between the Garden Cities of Krom and Brickolage. She turned down the commission but accepted lands and the title of Baroness.

Kavi shrugged and changed the subject. "If there's trouble, I wouldn't mind having Grim with me."

A dark cloud passed over his mother's face for a fraction of a second. A lifetime of intimidation had him hyper-tuned to her moods.

"Doesn't that boy have enough to do in the forge?" she asked.

"Master Brixon is a pushover when it comes to Grim," said Kavi. "Besides, Grim can always get away with taking some of the newer weapons out for field testing."

Marie sighed. "Fine, take him. Check with your father before you head out tomorrow. He mentioned something about testing one of his devices. He might have new toys for you."

Kavi groaned. No one doubted his father's brilliance. He turned many early scientific theories, which Brickolage based its identity upon, on their heads. In the end, he almost always turned out to be right.

"Oh, don't be so dramatic," said his mother.

Kavi arched an eyebrow at her. She held the gaze until he relented. "Fine," he said. "But I'm not testing explosives or anything with the word 'aerial' in it."

* * *

Kavi walked into the beehive of activity inside the tower. His father's workshop was twice the size of the Barony's small keep. Tribar had dozens of engineers who came from Brickolage to work and learn from the famous tinkerer. Apprentices rushed about, grabbing materials and doing odd jobs for the journeymen and his father. He considered asking one of them if they knew where his father was but discounted the idea. A careless question often led to a long and fruitless conversation about some theory he had little interest in. He walked to the back of the workshop where his father kept his office and workbenches.

When he walked in Tribar held up a long, spindly finger. "What are the three principles of sulimite kinetics when applied to a spring?"

Kavi knew this one. "If the spring is imbued with sulimite the kinetics don't change. The potential energy increases by half the square of the compression distance times the density of the sulimite infusion. This turns into kinetic energy upon release that is directly proportional and often explosive."

"Wrong, when properly imbued, the sulimite is never explosive," said Tribar. His eyes never left his bench.

"Tell that to my broken hand," said Kavi.

At that, his father looked up. He had a device strapped to his head with several lenses of different magnification that could be levered over either eye to help him work with the miniature pieces strewn about his desk. He pulled the odd hat from his head and set it on his workbench.

"Kavi, my boy, come in. I thought you were one of my apprentices. How did you learn so much about spring mechanics?"

"I read," said Kavi. He faked a hurt expression.

Tribar engulfed him in a bear hug. Kavi couldn't help but breathe in his father's scent of leather, oil and the acrid stench of sulimite and melted metal. Kavi got his height from his father but he had grown taller than the tinkerer over the last couple of years.

Kavi broke the embrace. "Besides, after becoming your primary beta tester, I thought it worth learning as much about this stuff as possible."

Tribar's eyes widened at that. "You're re-considering a couple of years at the University?"

Kavi held up a hand. "That barge pushed from the bank long ago. Four years at the Bastion and another four in the Krommian Silver Eagles is enough formal education for a lifetime."

Tribar snorted. "I'll never understand why your mother thinks hitting other people with sticks qualifies as an education."

Kavi refused to take the bait. He scanned his father's office, always amazed by the organized chaos of the tinkered equipment haphazardly strewn over every flat surface.

"I'll spare you the old argument," said his father.

"Thank you. The Lioness said you had new toys for me to test?"

Tribar muttered something under his breath. Kavi knew the man hated it when Marie called his work toys. His father picked up the large metal safe under his desk and set it on the bench. The clockwork augmentation integrated into the muscles and tendons of his right arm made the motion look effortless. Tribar opened the safe and pulled out a pair of wide spectacles. Leather blinders covered the side of the eye to the ear.

"Fashion statement?" said Kavi.

The old inventor's lips almost curled into a grin before a deep sadness pulled them down into the neutral affect he showed the world. He shook his head. "I get enough of that crap from your mother. These are SUMENI goggles."

They looked at each other for a moment. Kavi waited for him to explain and finally asked. "Okay, what do they do?"

"See this lever on the side of the googles?"

Kavi nodded.

"Those are the three settings. The first, marked S, is sulimite usage. With the lever in this position, you can detect anyone using suli. They will glow with a bright red hue. I know I don't need to say it, but I will anyway. Be careful when approaching anyone under the influence of sulimite. The goggles will detect both raw and processed sulimite. Raw sulimite will have a yellow glow and processed sulimite will have a slightly orange glow."

Kavi slipped the googles over his head, the leather straps rubbing over his scars. His father tightened the strap on the back until they fit snugly then flipped the switch from off to the S setting.

"Look around the room," Tribar ordered.

Kavi saw a riot of orange and yellow lighting the room. Almost everything his father worked with these days had an element of sulimite. Only the ultra-rich could afford the accelerant. Tribar's devices and the licenses that went with them ensured he and his workshop had an unlimited supply.

"Do you invent anything without suli anymore?" said Kavi.

Tribar ignored him. "The M setting is for Mood Evaluation. When the goggles are in this position, you will be able to tell the mood of the person or people in view. Red is angry, yellow happy, blue sad, you get the idea. It's meant to be an early warning system when on patrol."

"Does it work on animals?"

Tribar looked up at the ceiling for a second as if contemplating this for the first time. "Maybe. I never thought to test it on animals. Run some tests when you're on patrol."

"What does the N setting do?" Kavi reached to flick the lever down with the goggles still on.

Tribar grabbed his hand. "Not with the lights on. That is a night illumination setting. Here, let me shut these off."

Tribar began to move around the room, his aura a deep navy blue. It was an old sadness, one Kavi shared. Losing his younger brother Brink was the most painful thing Kavi had experienced in his twenty-four years but it broke something in his father.

With each twist of Tribar's wrist a light went off until the room sunk into darkness. "Now try it."

"Oh, that is cool," Kavi whispered after flipping the lever. The lab was bathed in green monotone, but he could make out everything within it.

"Don't use that mode during the day or it'll hurt your eyes."

Kavi took the goggles off and studied them. "Let me guess, SUMENI stands for Sulimite Usage Mood Evaluating Night Illuminating goggles?"

"I must be getting predictable."

"Anything else you wanted to show me?"

"Nothing as big as the goggles. I've got a couple of wrist bows for you." He handed Kavi a small box.

Kavi frowned when he opened it. "Mini crossbows?"

His father nodded. "You pull the strap around your forearm. It adjusts so it can fit over a mail shirt. Put the bolt in like this. Pull the bow back and set it behind the lever here. Put this strap around your middle finger, like so. Then when you pull the middle finger down," Tribar pointed to a target in the far corner. "the lever releases and away it goes." The bolt flew and missed the target by several meters, skittering into a shelf of old books. "I never was much of a shot."

"Good thing I am," said Kavi. "Thanks."

"Are you taking Grim with you on patrol?" asked Tribar.

Kavi nodded. "That's not a problem is it?"

"Not for me. Tell him I've got something for him before you leave."

2

Grim

Kavi walked out of the inner gates and down the hill into town. The keep had a small anvil, a forge and a grinding wheel near the stables. Those were used primarily for horseshoes and weapon repair. Lady Stonecrest once used a farrier for these smaller tasks but he died to the pox two summers ago. Kavi fished for the farrier's name but never knew the man well. He died before Kavi returned from his last tour with the Eagles.

The real smith work took place in town at The Unbreakable Anvil. Legend had it, the Lioness saved Master Brixon's life. When Marie was granted her lands, Brixon went with her. A smith of Brixon's caliber combined with Tribar's formidable reputation brought craftsmen from Krom and Brickolage and the town at the base of the hill grew with industry.

The Baroness ordered an outer wall to surround the town but it had already been re-routed twice as new inhabitants moved in. Kavi waved at the townsfolk making their way to the keep. They bowed or tilted their heads in respect. Kavi smiled uncomfortably. The respect they showed was inherited. It made him feel like an imposter.

Kavi walked through the wide double doors of the Unbreakable

Anvil. A bored apprentice sat at the front counter. He looked up at Kavi's arrival and grinned. "They're in the back."

Kavi pushed through the smaller door that led to the forges. Through the door was a symphony of motion similar to his father's workshop. The banging of hammers hitting metal accompanied the hissing of hot iron quenched in salt water vats. The din of the smithy sounded a harmony to the shouted commands of Brixon and Grim. It was clear they had both given orders in the field. Their deep voices cut through the racket with ease. Apprentices scrambled to obey.

Kavi breathed in the heat and made his way over to Grim. Master Brixon saw him first.

"Welcome, Lord Stonecrest," said the master smith. "Here to steal Grim for another adventure?"

Kavi bit his tongue. He'd told Master Brixon enough times to use his first name instead of his title. "Do you mind if he joins me on patrol? May be a good chance to field test some of your latest gear."

The master smith snorted. "I didn't buy that excuse the first time you used it lad. All I know is if you didn't pull him out of the forge he would never leave."

Brixon aimed a critical look at Grim. "I appreciate dedication but obsession is unhealthy. Once he's completed that dagger for your father, he's all yours."

"Thank you Master Brixon. I'll let him know."

The smith nodded and went back to shouting orders.

Kavi was not a small man but he was dwarfed by Grim. The young smith stood head and shoulders over Kavi. He wore an extended leather apron that looked like a bib on his massive frame. While most apprentices struggled to lift the huge smithing hammers, the hammer looked like a toy in the big man's hands.

Grimstance Broadblade was the son of General Broadblade. The General was a rival and friend of Marie's. They came up in the

Krommian service together and Kavi and Grim had known each other since they were toddlers. If Kavi was tested at the Bastion, Grim was run through the gauntlet. And he came out on top. Every time. By their third year, there wasn't an instructor at the Bastion that could best him.

No one was surprised when Grim was appointed to the Suli Elites. Everyone *was* surprised when he received a dishonorable discharge after his third mission. The General disowned him and Grim lived homeless on the streets of Krom for a full year, drunken and sodden in his own filth. He left the city and vanished for six months before appearing at the doors of Stonecrest Keep. He was clean, composed and begging for clemency. Lady Marie granted it.

She offered him a position in her guard but he refused it. His soldiering days were over. He wanted to settle down with an honorable profession. Brixon gladly picked him up as an apprentice even though he was long past the age most apprentices started. He was a quick study and, three months ago, Brixon appointed him journeyman.

Kavi approached after one of Grim's powerful strikes on a heated piece of metal. Sparks flew. Grim was marked by the same sicari scars Kavi had, except under his service scar was another jagged scar which indicated his time in the Elites. Grim didn't look up when he approached.

"No," Grim said.

"What? I didn't even ask for anything," said Kavi.

"No," Grim repeated. "Let's just skip the part where you try to convince me. I'm not joining whatever hair-brained scheme or mission you've come up with this time. I'm not a soldier anymore Kavi."

"I'm not asking you to be a soldier. I'm asking you to watch my back."

"That's why you have guards, my lord," said Grim.

"Ooh, my lord. I like that. How about a bow? Can you manage a bow?"

The sparks from Grim's next hammer blow danced around Kavi and he jumped back which brought a smile to the big man's face.

"I've got orders piling up Kavi. I can't leave any time a fancy strikes you," said Grim.

Kavi looked up and met Brixon's eyes. The master smith had been watching the exchange and gently shook his head. "Master Brixon just called bullshit on you Grim," said Kavi, slipping in to the common tongue to swear. "Besides, this isn't a fancy, this is an order from the Baroness."

"Soldiers take those kind of orders, not smiths," said Grim.

"Fine, I didn't want to have to do this but you forced me into it. My first stop is the Freison farmstead."

At this, Grim did look up. "Not funny Kavi. Did something happen to Fallon?"

"Her father reported bandits in the area. As far as I know, everyone is fine but you couldn't ask for a better excuse to visit."

Grim grunted.

Kavi swept his arms up, painting a picture. "Just think of it Master Grim. You come prancing in on horseback, or whatever you call that gigantic bull you ride. You survey the scene, make sure everyone is ok then make an oath. 'These bandits will never trouble you again milady.' I wouldn't be surprised if she asked you to help plow her fields right then and there."

The two apprentices helping Grim chuckled. The laughing stopped with a glare from the huge journeyman. "Fine, I'll go," Grim said. "No picking on Big Blue though. I wish you had half the personality that horse has."

"See, I knew there was still fun in you Grimmy. We just need to invent new ways of ripping it out. Maybe I'm taking the wrong approach. Since you seem to share such a bond with that monster you call a horse, maybe an apple would help." He clicked his tongue twice in the back of his cheek as if calling a horse. "Or a sugar cube, you want a sugar cube Grimmy?"

Grim showered him with sparks again. "When do we leave?"

"Meet at dawn in the upper bailey. Wear your mail and bring your gear," said Kavi.

Grim nodded.

"Oh, and my father wanted to talk to you about something. Make sure to visit him before we leave."

"I need to give him this dagger anyway." Grim pointed his chin towards the mostly finished blade sitting on one of the benches. "Once the apprentices grind and wrap the blade, it'll be ready."

"Aren't you curious about what he wants?"

"Nope, but I know you are and not knowing is driving you crazy." Grim's smile was genuine this time.

"Keep your secrets Grimmy, but no sugar cube for you."

3

Missing Sheep

The day dawned crisp and cool for early autumn. Kavi stood in the upper bailey with six of his mother's guards and Stonecrest's huntsman. That was standard patrol size and they weren't expecting any real trouble. They double checked their gear before setting out. Kavi pulled the SUMENI googles out of his saddlebags and pulled them over his head to hang around his neck.

"Nice specs," said Carlin. The Baroness' huntsman had the look of a man who slept outdoors. Not dirty but weather-worn, like a well fit old cloak. "Your dad make those?"

Kavi looked awkwardly down at the specs and nodded.

Carlin looked at him warily. "They're not going to set anything on fire are they?"

"In theory, no," said Kavi. "But I'd stay out of their visual range until we make sure."

Carlin paled at the comment. The man had a wonderful vantage point when Kavi crashed into the pine trees while testing the 'Single Man Ariel Scouting Harness' which everyone happily shortened to SMASH.

Carlin was only half Krommian and never took to the scarification of gentile Krommian society so his face was strangely smooth. It looked unnatural to Kavi.

The six guards muttered about pulling dice out and starting a game. Kavi stopped them with a glance. "Where the hell is Grim?" he asked in common.

"Keep your pants on, *milord*," rumbled the huge blacksmith as he clattered through the gate on an enormous horse. "Big Blue needed two full bags of oats this morning. He must have known we were going on a trip. Besides, it gave me a chance to sharpen and put a final polish on Brodie's sword." He grabbed the blade strapped to the back of the saddle.

One of the guard's eyes lit up. "You said she wouldn't be ready until next week," said Brodie.

"Well, if you're complaining I can leave her here for when we get back," said Grim.

"Oh, hell no," said Brodie. He grabbed the sword and the other guards gathered around like children at a name day party. He pulled it out of the sheath.

Brodie looked slightly confused as he held it up. "Feels too light, will it hold up?"

Grim pulled out his own sword. "Give it a try."

Brodie took several practice swings then engaged the big man. After three strikes, he looked at Grim with awe. "I barely felt the shock of each hit. What did you do?"

"I'm working on some alloys with Master Brix and Tribar. There's some dampeners in the hilt but look at the edge where you struck my weapon."

Brodie closed his eyes as he rubbed a finger down the edge. "Not a notch." Then his eyes widened again. "It's suli-treated isn't it?" he whispered.

Grim held a finger to his lips and winked.

"Any chance I could get one of those Master Smith?" asked one of the other guards.

Grim snorted. "Oh, it's Master Smith now, Jax? Ass kisser. Brodie here's the only one worthy of holding a sword of that caliber. If the rest of you scrubs show me solid improvement on your forms tonight, I might put your names on the list."

Kavi sidled next to Grim. "Lioness already put an order in to outfit all the guards with those didn't she?" he asked out of the side of his mouth.

"Yep," Grim responded just as quietly. "No reason to let them know that though."

* * *

The ride to Freison Farm took most of the morning. The Stonecrest lands were gentle hills with wide valleys formed millennia ago by ancient tributaries of the Rhune. This made for fertile land. Lacking protection from natural predators and enterprising bandits, farming attempts in the area had failed. Once the Lioness took over the lands, the attacks stopped. Over the past several years the farmlands thrived. They now provided all the food for the Stonecrest community with some left over to sell in the markets of Krom and Brickolage.

The farmhouse was quaint. Wooden fences to the east of the house held chickens. Smoke rose from the chimney and Kavi's stomach grumbled. One of Goodwoman Freison's meat pies would be far better than the hardtack they kept in their bags.

The scouting party reined in outside of the small fence surrounding the house. Kavi had the group dismount. "Brodie, you're in charge while we find out what happened," said Kavi.

Grim and Carlin followed Kavi to the front door. Goodwoman Freison heard them coming and swung the door open before they reached it. "Milord Stonecrest, please come in."

The home was well kept. The moment they walked past the threshold, Kavi's mouth watered. A stew pot hung on a metal hook over the fire and a younger woman stood in the kitchen kneading dough. Grim's eyes darted in her direction. Goodwoman saw the look and scowled.

"You have a lovely house Goodwoman," said Kavi to pull her attention from Grim.

"I forget you've never been here milord."

"Everyone knows the Freisons are wonderful tenants. There's been no need. Please, tell me what you'd like us to investigate."

At the compliments, her scowl lessened to a slightly smaller scowl. Kavi didn't know if he'd ever seen the woman smile, even at celebrations. Farming was a tough life.

"Harold is preparing the harvest in the southern fields with the boys," she said. "But Fallon and I heard them tell the story a hundred times. Reckon we can tell the tale."

"Grim, would you ask Fallon to join us?" asked Kavi, tone innocent.

The Goodwoman growled as she said. "No need, milord. Fallon, get in here girl!" she yelled.

Fallon was a beauty. Her long raven hair was swept back in a ponytail. When she entered the room, it brightened with her presence. She had two needle thin scars under each eye that made her large, beautiful eyes even more gorgeous. Her smile eclipsed her mother's frown and she nodded to their visitors. "Milord Kavi, Smith Grim, Huntsman Carlin, what can we do for you gentlemen today?"

"We're here to root out the bandit threat, milady," Grim said.

Kavi hid his smile. If Grim wanted to lead the discussion with Fallon, he wasn't going to stop it.

Fallon blushed at the title. It didn't distract her though. "That's the thing milords, we're not sure the threat is bandits." She looked straight at Grim. "Or just bandits."

"What does that mean?" asked Kavi after a second, realizing her look had frozen Grim.

"I'll start at the beginning. My three brothers were repairing a fence up in the far northern field after four goats went missing. Buttersnap pushed through the fence again. She's the oldest female."

"What did I tell you about naming the animals Fallon?" interrupted her mother.

"There's no harm in it mother! Especially the ones that give milk. I know you're not going to turn *them* into meat pies."

Her mother grunted.

"Anyway, Mikel and Declan continued to fix the fence while Tomas went to gather the goats that went missing. They're not very smart. The goats, I mean. They normally follow the old game trail along the edge of Draydale Woods," said Fallon.

"I know the one," said Carlin.

"Of course you do. I've seen you scouting up there." She smiled at the huntsman rendering him speechless.

"Did Tomas find the goats?" prompted Kavi.

Fallon turned back to him. "Three of them, milord, though all three were in a bad way. Poor Buttersnap was covered in blood and shaking when Tomas found her. The other two had passed out from fright. Buttersnap hasn't produced milk since the incident."

"That poor goat," said Grim.

Kavi gave him a flat look before turning back to Fallon. "I'm sorry to hear that. If it were bandits, wouldn't they have taken all four animals?"

"That's just the thing milord, Tomas found several arrows on the ground. They were all bloodied. He also found ripped clothing and tracks he'd never seen before. From something big. If bandits were trying to take the goats, maybe they got interrupted by something."

"All three of those boys know how to track," said Carlin. "So it probably isn't a bear or boar. What I don't get is why you didn't send word about the beast when you sent word for help?"

"After we penned the goats back up, Da took the boys to visit Holden to see if he had seen anything strange in the area," Fallon said. "Holden was also missing some livestock. When we went to visit, Old Creb was already there. Well, as he does, Creb blew the whole story out of proportion and made it sound like the beast was a demon. If we sent word that demons were attacking, how seriously do you think the Lioness would have taken the news?"

She had a point. The Lioness had no patience for fools. "We were going to go visit Holden next to get his take on the whole thing," Kavi said. "Now, I'm thinking we should go straight to the site where the goat was taken."

"No use going to see Holden anyway. He decided to follow the tracks into the wood after we sent word to the Keep."

"And?" asked Carlin.

"He's not back yet," said Fallon. "That was four days ago."

* * *

When they arrived at the site, Carlin kept the guards away to avoid disturbing the tracks. Tomas met them and corroborated Fallon's story.

"Nothing else you can remember lad?" asked Carlin.

"T'only other thing was a bit strange Carlin. Sir," said Tomas. "My brothers asked me not to say nothing so I don't become the next Old

Creb, but it seems important."

"Out with it then," said Carlin.

"Well, other than the smell of blood, I also smelt burnt butter." He held up a hand. "I know it sounds odd-like and I wouldn't have mentioned it if the smell wasn't so strong."

"You ever hear anything like that?" asked Kavi.

"Not outside a kitchen," said Grim.

Carlin crouched around the site where Tomas found the goats. He walked through the site twice, moved some leaves and twigs then crouched again. After several long minutes, he stood up.

"From what I can tell, it looks like it was only two men," said Carlin. "Best guess, they were only going to take one of the goats so the Freisons wouldn't get suspicious. They killed the goat with an arrow and came down to take their prize when they were interrupted by this beast."

"That poor goat," said Kavi, looking straight at Grim.

Grim ignored him. "Then what happened?" asked Grim.

"The blood on the ground smells human," said Carlin. "There. You can see the tracks of one of the men limping away. Look at these tracks here, see how deep the claws sink in? Whatever this thing is, it's big. My guess is the beast killed one of the men then took dead man and dead goat back into the forest for lunch."

"Any problem following its trail?" asked Grim.

"Naw, even you could follow this trail, Grim," said Carlin as they set off. "It's like the beast painted big red arrows to point the way. You can see where Holden picked it up, but his trail requires a good eye."

The tracks led into the woods. Even though it was midday, the woods felt dark. Knowing what they were following, the darkness seemed to thicken like soup left over a fire.

Kavi reached for his SUMENI goggles and slipped them on. He

21

flicked to the night illumination setting but there was too much ambient light and the terrain was white washed. He left them in mood enhanced mode. On the mood setting, yellow must be fear because most of the guards were rimmed in a faint golden glow.

"Sir, you want a couple of us to keep watch on this side of the woods, in case the bandits try to flank us?" asked Jax, trying not to let his voice squeak.

"You get your ass in line soldier," said Grim. "They're bandits Jax. Flank us...you're hilarious." Grim's glow was a determined purple but Kavi could see deep undertones of blue. There was an ocean of sadness there that the big man hadn't opened up about.

The trail was easier to follow in the woods. Broken branches and blood marked the passage of something big. Some of the blood stains were close to twice a man's height on the passing branches.

"I know where we're headed," said Carlin. "There's a cave farther up the path. A couple of black bears made it their home years ago. Who knows what's living there now."

"But it could still be bears. Right?" asked Jax. "Right Carlin, we're probably just dealing with a rabid bear."

The hunter held up his hand for silence. The cave mouth leered from the darkness like a scar.

In front of the cave, a man sat cross-legged, looking in.

"Is that Holden?" asked Kavi.

4

The Cave

Kavi softly called out, "Holden, what are you doing?" He still wore the SUMENI goggles. Holden had no aura. Kavi thought the goggles must be on the fritz and jostled them. But no, Grim and Carlin had auras but Holden had nothing.

Kavi made his way to the farmer sitting statue still in front of the cave. "Holden," he whispered again. He touched the man's shoulder.

Holden turned his head and Kavi staggered back. Gaping eye sockets bored into him. Jax let out a scream from behind him. Grim drew his sword and the rest of the guards followed. "Holden, what happened to you?" asked Kavi.

Blood caked the man's face around the sockets. Then he smiled and held out his hands. There was a desiccated eyeball in each hand. He pointed these towards the cave. "With my eyes out here, *now* I can see," croaked the farmer. "Because you have to be able to see to find them. I've got to find them, Patrice. They are so close. So close."

Kavi held the vomit that threatened to explode. One of the guards didn't have as strong a stomach and a wet splash hit the ground. Kavi took a deep breath before the stench could hit him.

Carlin had his bow out and an arrow knocked. He stalked silently

23

towards the cave. Kavi signaled to Grim and the two followed. Kavi flicked the setting on his goggles to night illumination and kept his focus on the cave. The cave wasn't deep, maybe thirty meters. Bones littered the ground but Kavi couldn't see anything living.

"It looks empty," he whispered.

"Predators know how to hide," said Carlin, eyes scanning the cave. "But it would be difficult to hide something big in here."

Carlin pointed. "There's the remains of our bandit." The unfortunate criminal was missing both legs and an arm. Carlin pulled the bandit's rusted sword from its sheath. He cut some cloth from the bandit's jacket and wrapped it around the hilt of the sword. "Mind your goggles," he said to Kavi.

Kavi pulled the goggles off and let them rest around his neck as Carlin used one of his father's fire starters to light the makeshift torch. He stuck the blade into the ground and continued his surveillance.

Kavi made his way up to where the beast had made a nest of sorts. Surrounding the nest was a semi-circle of neatly placed skulls. Above the nest was mounted the head of a goat.

"What could do something like this Carlin?" asked Grim. "Animals don't decorate. Maybe Old Creb isn't so crazy."

Kavi's critical mind scoffed, but it was hard to deny the evidence in front of them. There were always stories of strange beasts and monsters roaming the Reaches and the Wastes. Even more stories than usual, lately. Problem was, there was never any evidence of the creatures, not in generations. The Lioness ignored the stories and so did most of Stonecrest, but that never stopped Old Creb.

"I've heard the the rumors too, but demons?" said Kavi.

"Whatever it is, it hasn't been here for days," Carlin finally said. "I'll scout around the cave to see if I can pick up its trail."

Carlin shrugged and walked outside. After several minutes of scouting around, he came back in the cave. "There is no trail."

"What do you mean?" asked Kavi.

"It's like the beast flew away," said Carlin. "Whatever it is, it's gone now."

"Damnit!" shouted Kavi. He picked up one of the skulls in the semi-circle and threw it against the wall where it exploded into shards.

"We have to report this back to your mother Kav," said Grim.

"Report what?" asked Kavi. "We don't know anything."

"Holden is sitting out there with his eyes in his hands!" said Grim. "What we know is that nothing about this is normal. We were trained to share abnormal information. You know that."

"I do, but I'm not bringing half-baked intel back to my mother. We'll have Jax escort Holden back to the Freison homestead but we're going to ride further into the wood until we hit the Rhune. We can follow it to the bridge."

"Those guards out there, save for Brodie, are little more than kids. They're about to break. If we get thrown into a fight, we'll lose," said Grim.

"Bullshit. We've got you to turn the tide," said Kavi. He sighed as he looked at the big man. "It can't be about just doing the minimum. That reputation's followed me around for too long. You know this is the right thing to protect the people of Stonecrest."

"Sold," said Carlin from the mouth of the cave. "Should we mount up?"

Grim kept the sour expression but held his tongue.

* * *

Making their way through the forest on horseback was difficult. The game trails this deep in the forest were made by smaller animals.

25

They spent most of the time leading their horses until they reached the Rhune. This late in the year, the river ran slowly but it was still more than a hundred meters wide.

Kavi knew from experience that the water was frigid. It flowed down from the Miter Highlands which were towered over by the Icy Talons. The snow melt from the giant peaks kept the Rhune running briskly for most of the year. This early in autumn it was close to its lowest level.

They made better time riding along the river bank. Carlin scouted ahead while Kavi led the small band at a measured pace. The shadows were getting longer when the bridge came into view.

Carlin stepped out of the underbrush and held a finger to his lips. Kavi reined in his horse and heard those following do the same.

"What is it?" he whispered to Carlin.

Carlin's eyes never left the bridge. "I found a camp a little way down this path." He pointed his thumb over his shoulder deeper into the forest. "It's empty but hasn't been for long. Based on the bedrolls and shelters, I'd say there's probably eight to ten men."

"Sounds like our bandits," said Kavi.

"Maybe," said Carlin. "Something's off though. I've never seen a bandit camp look so....," he searched for the word. "precise. They have a latrine dug by somebody who's done it before. The shelters are lined up in rows. I don't know a lot of organized bandits."

Grim moved from the back to join the conversation. "Did they have a sentry posted?"

"No," said Carlin. "But if there's only eight or nine of them and they wanted to cause trouble at the bridge...."

"Better to risk somebody finding the camp then being short-handed," finished Kavi.

"Not if keeping your identity hidden is critical to the mission," said Grim. "How far is the bridge?"

"A ten-minute walk," said Carlin.

A distant scream pierced the air. It was human but would have made the raptors of the highlands proud.

"No time," said Kavi. He yelled back to the guards. "Mount up, get to the bridge now!"

The scream came again as they thundered up the riverbank. Kavi did his best to arm his wrist crossbows while riding but found the task impossible on horseback. If he had time, he'd do it when he dismounted. He reached for the goggles and pulled them over his eyes. It would be useful to know if their opponents were on sulimite. Suli made an untrained foe deadly. It made trained warriors nearly unstoppable.

As they rounded the last bend in the river before the bridge, Kavi could make out snippets of a melee taking place above. Two Brickers were surrounded by bandits. Three of the bandits were down and not moving. One of the Brickers was wounded and staggering, blood pooling beneath him. The other Bricker was a blur as she moved from foe to foe. She caused massive damage with her small dagger. The woman glowed with the faint red of one using sulimite. She was the only one of the group glowing.

Kavi urged his horse up the bank to the bridge. Wrist crossbows forgotten, he pulled his sword and waded into the fray. He struck the first bandit while the man's back was turned. His sword sliced a half moon of flesh out of the man's neck and the bandit collapsed instantly. One of the bandits turned to face Kavi but his face sprouted an arrow as Carlin's shot flew true.

"Regroup!" yelled one of the bandits. The five remaining men pulled back from the melee and formed a shield wall. The bandit who called for order pulled the wounded Bricker with them and held a knife to the injured man's throat.

"As I live and breathe," said the leader of the band. "If it isn't

Grimstance the Coward. What are you doing these days when you aren't getting good men killed, Grim?"

"Good men don't murder women and children, Roanik," said Grim.

"Aww, come on now, that part was just a bit o fun," said Roanik. "But you couldn't even finish the men we were sent to kill in the first place."

"You know this creep?" asked Brodie.

Grim nodded. "He and I served together in the Suli Elites. He was a bandit even then."

"Ha! Better a bandit than a coward!" said Roanik.

"When did they finally kick your crooked ass out of the Elites?" asked Grim.

"Shortly after you got the boot. They kicked me out for behavior unbecoming a warrior." He looked to the men still surrounding him. "You see, where Grim couldn't seem to hurt anybody, I had the opposite problem. Killing felt right to me. It was almost like I was doing the folks I killed a favor. I took away their pain. You know what I mean?"

Even his own men seemed unsettled by the comment but that didn't faze the bandit leader. "Don't know what this world is coming to when a soldier is frowned on for doing some killing. When Grim's daddy heard about our last mission, the big general gave me my walking papers without so much as a thank you." He gave an exaggerated shrug. "Good news is, somebody always needs killing and other somebodies are always willing to pay for it."

"So, who's paying for this gig?" asked Kavi.

"Little lordling's got a voice," said Roanik. "Would you believe me if I told you this is freelance work? Me and the boys thought we'd try our hands at a little free enterprise."

Grim snorted. "Mercenary scum like you don't work for scraps."

Roanik shrugged and yelled. "Shields up, forward two."

"Here they come!" yelled Grim. Kavi and the guards spread out behind the big man.

Roanik burst into motion. He pulled his knife across the injured Bricker's throat. With a spurt of arterial blood, the Bricker collapsed. The surviving Bricker screamed. Roanik charged in the other direction making his way to the horses tied up on the far side of the bridge.

The shield wall was only four men wide but it was enough to block almost the entire width of the bridge. The female Bricker vaulted over the wall and gave chase to the bandit leader. Roanik's eyes widened as the suli-enhanced Bricker closed the ground between them. The bandit leader reached for a throwing knife and flicked it towards his pursuer. She dodged fast enough for the knife to miss her throat but it still caught her upper shoulder. When she paused to pull the knife out, Roanik jumped on one of the horses. With a couple quick smacks of his hand and a slicing of rope, he scattered the other horses then galloped away.

Grim yelled at the men holding the shields. "You see that! Your leader just left you to die. Drop your shields and weapons and you might live through this."

As one of the bandits turned to look back at their fleeing leader, Grim struck. His hand whipped into motion and the flat of his blade caught the man on the side of the head, felling him instantly.

"Only three of you left. Anybody else want to try their luck?" asked Grim.

The remaining men dropped their weapons and shields.

"Now, you're going to tell us what you know about that bastard, the beast that's been plaguing this area, and how you came to be here," said Kavi. "Or your day is about to get a lot worse."

5

Threats and Consequences

They talked. They just didn't know much. They were a group of disgraced soldiers mixed with several bandits picked up along the way. They had been working for Roanik for the past half year but didn't know where their leader got his contracts. The captives were certain that harassing the folks crossing Mill Bridge was a contract. They just didn't know who placed it. They knew nothing about the beast except that one of their companions disappeared while scrounging the area for food.

"Nothing and more nothing," Kavi said.

The huntsman grunted. "We need to take em back to the Lioness. There's always a bounty for bandits posted in Krom."

"How's our Bricker doing?" asked Kavi.

"Still unconscious," said Grim.

"Didn't look like the knife hit her that hard," said Carlin.

"It wasn't the knife that knocked her out," said Kavi. "You see how fast she moved? She was flying high on suli."

Carlin frowned. "That stuff is dangerous for the untrained."

Kavi pointed to the glasses resting on top of his head. "Tribar's going to have some questions for her when we get back." Kavi turned to the guards. "Strap her to the horse. Gently!"

"How about the other bandits?" asked Brodie.

"Tie their hands and make them walk behind the horses. Be as rough with them as you want. We need to get this lot back to town and formulate a plan of how to deal with whatever did that to Holden."

* * *

Night had fallen when they finally passed through the gates of Stonecrest. The flickering of torches throughout the town cast long, unsteady shadows. Grim nudged his horse towards the smithy but Kavi caught his eye. "You know the Lioness is going to want you there for the report."

Grim grunted but turned his horse back to the keep. "Might as well get it over with."

The Lioness was in the military briefing room when Grim and Kavi arrived. She nodded to both before asking for an update.

They shared their experience at the farm, the cave and the bridge. She listened to the full story without interrupting.

"To sum up, we have two new threats." She held up one finger. "A wild creature eating men and livestock that knows how to disappear cleanly enough to shake our best tracker." She held up a second finger. "And some person or group that hired an old friend of Grim's to harass travelers over the Mill Bridge."

"That scum is no friend of mine," said Grim.

She gave the large man a cold stare that she held for an uncomfortable silence before saying, "Grim, you are dismissed. I will send Kavi or one of the guards down to the Smithy tomorrow if we have more questions for you."

Grim executed a crisp military salute. It seemed to mock in its precision. He turned and left the room.

"What was that?" asked Kavi.

She arched an eyebrow at him. "I accepted that boy under my protection only after your father badgered me into it. Not long after he moved to town, we started having bandit attacks. Now we learn the leader of the group of bandits used to be in Grim's unit?"

Kavi stared at her for a second. "This is Grim we're talking about! He's been my best friend and a third son to you since we were little kids. How could you think he has anything to do with this?"

"Don't be naïve Kavi. War changes people. Him more than most. Being a member of an elite killing squad breaks men. Not only was he kicked out of his unit, he was disowned by his father, who happens to be one of *my* close friends. I don't know all the details but we would be foolish to trust him just because you're friends."

"You're wrong," said Kavi. "And our friendship has nothing to do with it."

"Maybe," she admitted. "But I have a duty to protect the people of Stonecrest." She looked sternly at him. "As do you! That means looking at threats from every direction, whether or not they offend your delicate sensibilities."

Kavi grimaced. This was The Lioness he was talking to, not his mother. She had been planning and executing military campaigns for longer than he had been alive. "Fine, but I'm not going to spy on him. I don't have that in me."

She looked at him as one might look at an ant that had just crawled through the potato salad at a picnic. "We were too soft on you. I blame your father for that. I was harsher on your brother and..."

He clenched his fists and shook his head, but held her gaze. "Are we done?"

"We're done when I dismiss you. I don't accept insubordination

32

from my soldiers, so don't think for one second I will accept it from you."

"Yes, ma'am."

She held the stony gaze for several long breaths. "Prioritize the threats and give me a plan of action for each."

This was a test, like most things with his mother, but Kavi was prepared. "The Mill Bridge is the most common crossing of the Rhune. Harrying travelers means disrupting trade between Brickolage and Krom. This hurts both cities but since it is our responsibility to protect the bridge, it hurts us in two ways. It damages our reputation and directly impacts trade coming through the town. The removal of the bandits buys us time but does not solve the problem. We need to discover who placed the contract."

He looked to his mother who nodded for him to continue. "The beast is the more immediate problem. We don't have enough skilled farmers to lose another like Holden. Our farmers provide food for the entire town and harvest is only weeks away. The beast must be dealt with first."

"How?"

"We put Carlin to work tracking the thing. We have him set up a blind near the cave and wait. When he discovers what it is, he puts it down himself or calls for backup from the guards."

"And if it does to Carlin what it did to Holden?"

"Maybe Dad has something that could prevent that from happening."

"What if it's magical in nature?" she asked.

"We contract out help. We send for a Vonderian mage."

"It will take weeks for a mage to get our message then further weeks to travel from Vonderia."

"We send missives to the mercenary companies in Krom and Brickolage," said Kavi. "Every company worth their salt has at least one mage on staff. It will cost more but far less than losing an entire harvest."

She nodded. "What's the next step in the investigation around who's trying to disrupt trade?"

"We offer incentives to the prisoners. The carrot may help where the stick didn't."

"Waste of time," said his mother. "You won't be able to trust a damn thing those deserters say."

Kavi shrugged. "I don't think they *have* more information, but we don't have a lot of other options. It might give us a lead." He held up a hand to stall her next objection. "We also need to talk to the Bricker we rescued when she wakes. She may have seen or heard something before we got there. Who knows what her enhanced senses picked up. If that leads to nothing, I start asking Grim about other members of the Elites that might have known Roanik."

"They won't talk to Grim," said his mother.

"Maybe not, but they might talk to me."

"Doubtful, but worth a try."

He ignored her underwhelming confidence in his abilities like he always did. "Anything else I'm not thinking of?"

"There's plenty you're not thinking of," she said.

"Care to share?"

"Not yet," she said. "And probably not until we clear Grim. I don't trust you to keep anything from him. It's second nature for you two to start whispering secrets like when you were children. I need to discuss this with your father tonight and we'll put some of these plans in motion."

She looked back down at the papers on her desk and reached for a quill.

"Is that all?" asked Kavi.

"Dismissed," she said without looking up.

He saluted then added. "Good night." He didn't wait for her response as he walked out of the briefing room.

6

Nettie

After a quick meal Kavi made his way to check on their patient. "Is she awake?" he asked the physician after quietly slipping into the infirmary.

The woman looked up from one of the two other patients in the room. "The Bricker?"

Kavi nodded.

The physician pointed to a still form in the far corner of the room. The figure was lying on her side with her back to them. "She might be napping but she gained consciousness early this morning. She's got the start of a sulimite hangover and some minor cuts and bruises. Other than that she seems fine."

"Thank you," said Kavi. He made his way to the woman's bed. When he noticed her eyes were open, he grabbed a chair and pulled it next to the bed. On closer examination, her eyes were red and slightly puffy. That could be the sulimite but he doubted it. She had been crying.

"I'm sorry about your friend," said Kavi.

"He's my younger brother," she said in a soft voice. "He *was* my younger brother and now he's gone forever. I have no idea what I'm going to tell our parents. I keep hoping I'll fall asleep and wake up and find out it was all a dream."

The hurt in her voice reached into Kavi's chest like a claw. He stomped on the empathy that threatened to rise and took the coward's path. "I can't imagine the pain you must be in," said Kavi. He could imagine it. He spent the last two years running from it. Focus on the job. "What I can do is help bring the man who did this to your brother to justice. To do that, I need information. Can I ask you some questions?"

She sat up and stared at him. When the blanket fell, he gave a surreptitious scan and saw no augmentations. Not all Brickers had the means or the intelligence to afford or build the body modifications. Her face was round and clear of scars and he found himself wondering why the industrious Brickers would gladly install clockwork into their bodies yet were sickened by the natural beauty of healed skin.

Her eyes gripped his. "What you could have done was get there fifteen minutes earlier! Or appointed guards or found another way to prevent this."

Kavi let her rage wash over him. He was good at that, at being a diversion, a target. They locked eyes for several long moments. "I can't turn back time," said Kavi.

She sagged as the momentary rage left her looking more defeated. "I know," she whispered.

"Can you tell me your name and how you and your brother found yourself on the Mill Bridge?" asked Kavi.

"My name is Amelie Nettie Patching but everyone calls me Nettie. My brother is...," she swallowed a sob and continued in a shaky voice. "was, my brother was Pick Patching. We were traveling across the bridge because we were following a dream."

"A dream? Did you hope to apprentice for Tribar?"

She gave him a puzzled look. Then, realization dawned across her expressive face like petals of a flower opening at sun's first touch. "I forgot Tribar lived in Stonecrest. I wonder if he ever figured out how to turn back time. He wrote several papers on the topic."

Kavi grimaced. "I'm afraid not. He concluded time is, in fact, one-directional."

"How would you know that? You don't look Brickolage trained."

"I'm not," said Kavi. "Tribar's my father."

"Oh," she said with a quick intake of breath. "So you would know about most of his research."

"Not even close," Kavi said. "But I know about the big stuff. If he figured out how to turn back time I would have heard." He realized he just destroyed even the thinnest hope she had of saving her brother. "I'm sorry."

She stared at her hands and went silent.

After the pause went far past uncomfortable, Kavi cleared his throat. "If you were not here to apprentice for Tribar, what dream were you following?"

She stared at the ceiling for a moment, wrestling with some internal conflict. She then looked Kavi in the eye. "You're going to think it's stupid."

He nodded to her in encouragement.

She sighed. "Who cares about that now. Have you ever heard of the Korbah Conundrum?"

Kavi frowned. He heard the name somewhere. It sounded like something his father would have studied at some point. Then it struck him and he barely stifled a laugh. "You mean from the—"

"Yes, from the Triad Quest," she interrupted. "I told you, you'd think it's stupid. Everyone else does."

"It's not stupid Nettie," said Kavi. "Me and my friends took a crack at the Triad when we were kids. It's just that nobody has solved a Quest in over a hundred years."

"That we know of," said Nettie.

"What do you mean?"

"Nobody has solved a Quest in over a hundred years that we know of," she repeated. "I was looking through the Quest histories in the University Library. Did you know that each Sage left two Quests a year for as long as we have recorded history? The Quests normally begin in one of the six Garden Cities before spreading through the land. They are the primary reason why we have trade between the Cities today. Then, a hundred years ago, the Quests stop?"

"Maybe the Ancients don't release a new Quest until the old ones are solved. The Triad Quest was just too hard to solve," tried Kavi.

"I don't think so," said Nettie. "It doesn't match the pattern. In the past, there were five, sometimes even ten Quests unsolved at a time. Some of these Quests might be too difficult for one generation only to be solved by the next after an advancement in technology, art or magic."

"Huh," said Kavi. "But what if the Triad was the last Quest the Ancients left us?"

"That's the prevailing theory but I think it's wrong. What if, instead, there is a group solving these Quests without anyone's knowledge."

"Why?" said Kavi. "Quest solvers received huge prizes and the prestige that went with it. They were heroes."

"I think they still receive prizes. Solving a Quest always results in *some* reward. Not from any ruler or government but from the Sages. What if this group is quietly amassing a fortune for some grand power play?"

"Huh," said Kavi. "I guess it's...possible, but improbable. As my father likes to say, the simplest solution is usually the correct one. This explanation seems too complex. How would you keep that big a secret quiet for this many years?"

"That is the right question," said Nettie. "Think for a second. If this group already solved several Quests, chances are good they have the resources to buy influence. A lot of mouths could be kept closed with the hordes of gold and sulimite these Quests reward, don't you think?"

Kavi shook his head slowly. "Maybe, but it still seems far-fetched. What does all that have to do with a bandit attack?"

Nettie shrugged. "Because I've solved Korbah's Conundrum and I think the next step of the Triad Quest is here. Near Stonecrest."

Kavi's mouth dropped open. "Wait really? Why are you telling me? Why not solve the next step on your own?"

"You saw how well that worked out," said Nettie. "My brother paid the ultimate price. My guess is the scum who killed him was paid by this shadow group. I did some hard thinking last night and realized I was going to need help. You are trying to bring this bandit to justice. Right now, our goals align. Let's get this bastard and solve the Quest in the process."

He quickly shared the story of Holden and the cave. "Do you think the Triad Quest and this beast are linked in any way?"

She shrugged. "I haven't found anything about a beast in my research, but it's possible. In the older stories, Quests required the heroes to overcome an obstacle and sometimes that was a monster. Sounds a little ridiculous when you say it out loud. There hasn't been a verified monster sighting since before our grandparents' lifetimes."

"You don't put any stock in the rumors coming in from the Southern Reaches?"

"Always sounded like superstition to me," said Nettie. "But we're dealing with a Quest which means we can't rule anything out."

* * *

"That is quite a story," said his father. "What did your mother say?" "I haven't told her yet," said Kavi. "You know she'll tell me to drop it. That's why I came to you first. You've heard the rumors: monster sightings, large shadows appearing on the ground from a cloudless sky, new projectile weapons, five times the speed and accuracy of our flintlocks appearing in a skirmish then disappearing without a trace. The world is changing too quickly for any of it to be normal. Her explanation is better than most."

Tribar smiled. "The world is always changing my boy. The notion of a single group of Quest solving conspirators is highly improbable. Can you imagine the amount of organization and planning required? You know the old yarn: three people can keep a secret only if two of them are dead. This is too big a secret."

Kavi cocked his head. "How else can you explain the rumors?"

He gave Kavi the slightly disappointed look he gave his apprentices when they should have puzzled something out on their own. "Easy. Vonderian magic and Bricker clockwork. Excuse me, technology. That's what the University wants us to call it now. These monsters are most likely chaotic magic being released by Vonderian Mages meddling with forces they shouldn't be meddling with. And the weapons? I don't know if you remember my old assistant, Caster, but she dramatically improved on flintlock weapons in just three years of us working together."

It was Kavi's turn to look disappointed. "Too convenient. The Mage Council has only gotten more strict in locking down chaos magic. There's too many sightings for it to be a couple rogue mages. As for the clockwork, I saw Caster's flintlocks, her clockwork couldn't hold a candle to what my old unit claims they saw last month. Something else is happening."

Tribar nodded. "I appreciate your skepticism but I'll agree to disagree. Especially on the new clockwork, the new *technology.* Can't say I'm crazy about the term. Brickolage is always a couple decades ahead of the rest of the world."

"Then why aren't we seeing this new technology coming from Brickolage?"

"Maintenance, my boy. You can deliver technology but if you don't have anybody to fix it when it goes wrong, might as well be handing out lumps of pig iron."

Kavi grinned and shook his head. His dad always pulled him into long, off-topic conversations. "That's not why I'm here."

Tribar took his tinkering specs off and laid them on the table. Kavi's eyes flicked to the clockwork gears clicking and spinning on his father's right arm, as fascinated by the device as he was when he was a child. "I know. You're hoping I can validate the girl's theory. Even if she doesn't give us the solution to Korbah's Conundrum."

"She's not stupid. She knows she loses all leverage the moment she shares the solution. You have any devices that can tell us if she is lying about it?" asked Kavi.

"Yes, but that is a violation of trust. I'm not willing to cross that line with someone who hasn't wronged us. Besides, she could be telling the truth and still be wrong about her theories."

"What about questioning her about her sources? Could that give you a hint to the authenticity of her solution?"

"Maybe," said Tribar. "We could also just go see if she's right. I could fund the expedition in the name of science."

"Thanks," said Kavi. "But we need the Lioness' backing. If Nettie's right and there is a shadow group solving Quests, they have a lot of gold to spread around. If they shelled out coin to hire scum like Roanik, chances are he's not the only one they hired. We're going to need the guards and we're going to need the Lioness' expertise."

Tribar sighed. "Ok, I'll talk to the girl. I'll also get one or two of my apprentices to join me so we can do some follow up research."

Kavi stood to leave. "Thanks," he said. He turned back to look at his father. "Do you know why Mother is so sure Grim means us harm?"

Tribar shook his head. "She's not sure at all, but betrayal is her deepest fear. The thing the stories don't tell about the Lioness is the betrayal which required her to be the hero she was during the Battle of Valun."

He ran fingers through thinning hair for a moment before coming to a decision. "I don't know if it's my place to share this story but it may help you understand her a little better. On the eve of the Battle of Valun, one of her closest friends and most trusted soldiers snuck into the enemy camp and shared battle plans with the enemy."

Kavi sat down, hard. "Sold them out to the Astrans? I can't imagine a Krommian even talking to an Astran."

"Hard to believe with the amount of hate between the two peoples. The lesson your mother learned that day is - *everyone* has something to hide. No matter how much we think we know somebody, we can't know everything. We all have secrets. She's struggled with trust ever since."

"What happened to the traitor that betrayed her?"

"She executed him. She demanded to hold the sword that ended her friend's life."

"Sounds like her. She wouldn't let a crime like that go, friend or not, especially when you weigh the cost of lives to her troops."

Tribar nodded. "It's the only answer to treason on a battlefield. Her quick, personal action in dealing with the traitor solidified the respect she already garnered on the field. So, the legend of the Lioness grew," said Tribar. He sighed deeply. "It wasn't until three months later that she learned the Astrans had kidnapped her friend's two young daughters, two weeks before the fateful battle. The man was trying to protect his little girls."

Kavi's stomach turned.

"Imagine having to carry that on your conscience," said his father. "Even worse, she knew the man didn't share news about the kidnapping because he knew the Lioness would bring that information directly to command. It would have been the right thing to do but it would have cost him his girls. The man knew he couldn't trust your mother with the information because of her strict sense of duty. She had gone through her military career always doing the right thing. It became her identity."

"That's why she left the army isn't it?" asked Kavi.

Tribar nodded. "It broke who she thought she was. She followed all the rules and it cost her a close friend. And his little girls. The army deals in absolutes. Reality is never that simple. She knew she could never deal with that paradox while still in the service, so she did the brave thing and left."

"The brave thing was to leave?"

"Of course. Staying in the army would have been way easier. She would have been able to blame the system for the impossible situation she found herself in. Instead, she accepted her part in what happened and started to learn how to deal with the shades of gray life is actually made of."

"It's hard to imagine a stricter, less flexible version of my mother."

"You have no idea," said Tribar.

Kavi got up to leave before remembering the other reason he sought his father out. "Do you have any idea what could have done that to Holden?"

"Not yet," said Tribar. "I've got my apprentices doing research and I'm going to examine him today. Holden's from good Krommian stock and not one to break easy. Even after he lost his family to the pox he was strong enough to continue on. This is no ordinary beast. I spoke with your mother last night and we agreed we can't send Carlin out there without protection."

"Did she tell you about the shrine we found in the cave?"

Tribar nodded. "Even if I do come up with some protection for Carlin, we probably want to wait on assistance from a Vonderian mage. One of my apprentices shared a disturbing story this morning about an old legend from her mother's village south of Brickolage. They found a similar shrine years ago."

"What did it turn out to be?"

"They never found out," said Tribar. "A couple of days after they found the shrine, my apprentice's mother was sent to Brickolage to ask for assistance in hunting the beast. When she returned to her village with help, she found it deserted."

"Where did the people go?"

"According to legend, they were never heard from again. Nobody found any bodies, no one left any notes. They were just gone."

7

Leaving Home

"What do you mean the girl is gone?" asked Kavi, stunned. Why would Nettie leave after their conversation yesterday? His mother must have bullied her into it. Her intolerance for ideas that didn't fit hers for how the world should work was legendary. He couldn't understand how his father dealt with it all these years.

The Lioness' expression did not change. "She's not a prisoner. Your father did not find anything to support or refute her claim that she solved the first part of the Triad. She wished to leave and we have bigger problems."

Her lack of empathy was impossible to understand, especially after the loss of a son. Kavi scowled. "You're okay with letting a young Bricker who just lost her brother to bandits on the bridge, which we're supposed to protect by the way, go off on her own and jump *back* into danger? This must be what people mean when they talk about Stonecrest's legendary hospitality."

"Are you done?" asked his mother.

"Pretty close to being done with you and Stonecrest," said Kavi.

"Enough," said the Lioness. "I sent Carlin to follow her. He will

46

keep an eye on her and bail her out if she runs into any real trouble."

"Unless she's right," said Kavi.

"Oh come on. You're smarter than that. We all chased the Triad at some point until we discovered it's just another fairy tale, like the Ancients."

"You mean like the crumbling remains of the giant domes surrounding the Garden Cities?" asked Kavi. "Like those fairy tales? We ran past those giant, transparent remains every day on our way to the Rock while I was at the Bastion. You lived in Krom longer than I did. How can you pretend the Ancients and their Sages didn't exist? The domes are standing proof, as are the giant statues of the Krommian Quest solvers that stand guard over the arena."

"And you think her theory of some shadowy cabal keeping the Quests from the rest of the world has basis in fact?" asked Marie.

"Not yet, it's a theory, but how is her theory any less reasonable than the idea that the Sages just quit sending us Quests after thousands of years? What facts do we have to support that theory?"

She shrugged. "All the great minds of Krom and Brickolage, including your father's, have concluded that this is the most likely reason."

Kavi snorted. "Conventional wisdom? That's your argument? It wasn't long ago when everybody believed there was no way we could breathe under water until one of those great minds, my father, invented a way to do so."

He was so tired of being dismissed, so tired of being thought of as the disappointment son, so tired of trying to please this impossible woman. Tired enough to cross some lines. "The real problem is you and Dad got old. You got comfortable. You forgot how to dream."

Marie's eyes narrowed. "And that's all you've ever done. Dream. Having responsibility ages all of us. If you ever took any on, you would understand that."

And there it was, how little she thought of him laid bare. "That's exactly my point! The Bricker is right and you're wrong. I'm taking the responsibility of that conviction and I'm going to help her. I'm taking Grim with me. He's another example where you're wrong. It's time I took responsibility for that too."

"I knew you didn't have it in you to lead Stonecrest," she said, sadly.

He knew the ultimatum was coming. It was her favorite tool, but it still stung. He was done backing down. "Of course. We all know *I'm* not the future. That was Brink's role. I'm just a skulk in the shadows."

She slapped him. "How dare you throw that back at me."

The slap felt good, cleansing. "I lost a brother that day."

"And I lost a son! There is no comparison."

Now that the line had been crossed, he wanted it all on the table. "Of course not, nobody can ever compare to the Lioness. Even in suffering. You lost two sons that day because you could never see past your own ego to actually talk to me." He turned to leave.

"If you disobey me on this, don't expect another chance to lead."

He was sure there was regret in her somewhere but he couldn't see it. Only the rage. Rage took the place of any other emotion. He looked at her sadly, his own anger turning to pity as he saw how weak the rage made her. *Just feel, for once!* he wanted to scream at her. It would fall on deaf ears. "Leading is standing up for what's right even when other people call you a fool. The Lioness taught me that," said Kavi.

There was no salute when he left the briefing room.

* * *

Convincing Grim wasn't nearly as hard as he expected. They shared the same frustration with the Lioness and the defiance felt good.

Righteous indignation is a wonderful glue for the young and self-indulgent.

They stopped Brodie as he walked into the guardhouse.

"The Lioness still have you working with the flintlocks?" asked Kavi.

Brodie shook his head. "No, they're too damned slow. I can fire five arrows or two crossbow bolts in the same time as one flintlock shot and I don't have to worry about powder burns. What's the point of those damned things?"

Kavi shrugged. "Don't buy into that weapon of the future nonsense?"

Brodie shook his head. His eyes widened in pleasure as he patted his sheathed sword. "This though, I have to thank you again for the blade Grim," said Brodie with a smile. "I've been sparring circles around the rest of those yahoos in the barracks."

"You always sparred circles around them," said Grim.

"Yeah but with how light this thing is," he patted the sheath lovingly. "I can embarrass them for twice as long."

Grim pointed to his own blade. "Let me know when you're ready for a real challenge. Did you see which direction Carlin and the Bricker girl went?" he asked.

"Jax was on duty this morning, hang on. Hey Jax!" the guard sergeant yelled.

Jax came clattering down the stairs. He grinned when he saw Grim and Kavi. After a quick discussion with Brodie he said, "Yeah, she and Carlin left through the west gate early this morning. She was all in a huff and Carlin looked like he always does, slightly bored."

"Yeah, that's his, I don't want you to know I'm observing everyone and everything, look," said Brodie. "Those eyes don't miss anything."

Kavi nodded. "The west gate? Were they headed to Krom?"

"Don't think so," said Jax. "Me and Tris watched em for a little while and they didn't take the Council Road south. They cut north, straight towards the Draydale."

Jax shivered and Brodie fixed him with a stare.

"What?" asked Jax. "It's going to take a lot to get me back in those woods after seeing what that thing did to Holden. Don't give me that look! You didn't have to ride back through the woods with him mumbling all that creepy stuff. Man was touched by something dark. Real dark."

There was several moments of heavy silence as they reflected. Kavi broke it. "Did you hear them say where they were headed?"

"Nope, just her whining about not needing a bodyguard and Carlin agreeing with her and following anyway," said Jax.

"I hate it when he does that," said Brodie. "Makes the man impossible to argue with. You want an escort?"

"Not this time Brodie," said Kavi. "This isn't exactly a sanctioned outing."

"Great, so is the Lioness gonna chew us out for letting you leave?"

Grim patted his blade with a grin. "You could always try to stop us," said the big man.

"Yeah, try to stop them Brodie!" said Jax. "I'll tell the Lioness how bravely you fought after Grim turns you into little Brodie chunks."

Jax was still laughing as he opened the gate for Kavi and Grim. As they rode through, Kavi looked back over his shoulder. He knew the town would never feel the same again.

They rode hard for what was left of the morning. Finding the trail was easy. Carlin left clear markers behind so even an inexperienced woodsman would have no problem. The huntsman expected a tail.

They stopped for a quick lunch of jerky and hardtack. "Do you think the Lioness had Carlin leave us a trail? Could she have planned this whole thing?" asked Kavi.

"I wouldn't put it past her," said Grim. "But you tell me. Was she playacting when she kicked you out of the keep or was it the real thing?"

"It was real," said Kavi thinking back to the angry words. "Maybe Dad had something to do with Carlin leaving the trail. He probably knew I would chase Nettie."

"Your Da doesn't miss much," said Grim.

It was slower going the deeper they went into the forest. They dismounted and carefully led the horse past fallen logs and heavy underbrush. They stopped to catch their breath in an open glade. The rays from the sun ran hypnotically through the glade on near horizontal paths marking late afternoon.

"You want to push on or make camp here?" asked Grim.

"Let's go until it gets too dark to follow the markers Carlin's been leaving," said Kavi. "Once it gets dark, we may be able to see their fire."

Grim nodded and they bumbled ahead for another hour or so. After Grim's horse nearly stumbled over a fallen log he finally pulled up and turned to Kavi. "That's it," said Kavi pointing off into the distance. "That's got to be a campfire."

Grim squinted and could just make out the slightly brighter splotch in the mostly dark landscape ahead of them. They had been traveling steadily uphill for the past several hours and Kavi guessed the fire was on top of the rise they were climbing. As they made their way closer, it was obvious it was a small fire.

They both picked up the pace as stomachs realized a hot meal was close.

Then the screaming started.

8

Korbah's Conundrum

They dropped the lead ropes of the horses and ran. In their mad dash, they gave up any thoughts of stealth and exploded through the underbrush like two angry bears. An arrow whooshed over Kavi's head and he knew it was only the luck of passing under a falling tree that caused it to miss.

"Carlin!" he yelled, knowing the huntsman wouldn't miss a second time. If it *was* the huntsman.

He and Grim continued their mad dash towards the flickering flames of the campfire. The shadows on the canopy above shifted in a chaotic dance as the screeches continued. As the screams came to a crescendo, the single piercing shriek of a raptor rose over the din.

Then, silence.

When they broke into the clearing, they found Nettie and Carlin standing back to back. Carlin had his bow drawn and Nettie held what looked like a dowel or a pipe in her left hand. The only sound was the gentle crackling of the fire. After the cacophony of moments before this new silence felt menacing, as if predators were regrouping for an attack.

Then Carlin started to laugh. "You two look terrible."

The laugh was so unexpected that both men drew their swords at the sound. "Who...who was doing all the screaming?" asked Grim. Carlin pointed up. "Damned croakers. They're mimics, they pick up a sound somewhere in the forest and copy it perfectly."

"They're actually called lyrebirds since they can duplicate any type of music," said Nettie. "Back in the early three hundreds, Crazy King Bazord replaced his entire royal minstrel corps with the birds. They made beautiful music but only when they wanted to. They covered the floors of the palace with so many droppings it caused the great plague of three fifteen. The birds wiped out a quarter the population of Brickolage, including Bazord himself."

The history lesson seemed so absurd under the circumstances that Grim and Kavi stood slack-jawed and staring.

"You two want some stew?" asked Carlin.

"What was the shriek that shut them all up?" asked Grim.

"My whistle," said Nettie. She held up the small wooden tube. "I carved it years ago to emulate the hunting cry of a Gyrfalcon. You'd be amazed at how many creatures fear the strike of the Gyr. Even bigger predators will pause at the sound. And that includes men! Dad taught us the extra second can make all the difference," said Nettie. "Pick carved one that made the shriek of an eagle. He blew it in the University once and scared the pants off a...," she blinked her eyes a couple of times then went to sit back by the fire.

Grim sheathed his blade and after a moment Kavi did the same. "That screaming damn near scared my pants off," said Kavi. "Almost as much as the arrow you shot at my face."

"Sorry 'bout that, couldn't tell who or even what you were in the dark," said Carlin.

"Couldn't have been too much of a surprise someone was following with that trail you left," said Kavi.

Carlin glanced over at Nettie guiltily. "While that one was adamant about not asking for help, I'm not dumb enough to turn it down if it comes offering," said Carlin. "Go fetch your horses and I'll scoop you a bowl of stew."

"Why did you leave without me, Nettie?" asked Kavi.

"The Lioness made it clear there was no chance her son would help with my 'ridiculous Quest.' And...I just...I couldn't stay lying in that bed any longer, with nothing but my thoughts. I needed to move."

Kavi assumed as much, but the confirmation made him feel better about his own decision to leave.

With the horses cared for, Kavi leaned against his bedroll with a full stomach. His heart had finally stopped racing and he felt something he hadn't felt in a long time. Contentment. It seeped into him like the warmth from the fire. He gave a real smile at the freedom of being out on his own. For the first time in forever, he wasn't following orders. The freedom lent a sense of purpose. Now that they found Nettie and were in a position to help, that purpose turned to curiosity.

He pulled out a journal he'd grabbed before leaving. It had the notes he took when he was a kid investigating the Triad. The opening page had the three verses that started the first step of the Triad Quest. He began to read aloud, pausing at the end of each stanza.

Three hungry snakes crawl the roads of Grendar
  The first what was, a glutton of innocence
  The second what comes, consumer of pain
  The third what ends. He writes the world in blood

Your trail lies in the middle of solving this riddle
  What runs but never walks, has a mouth but never talks
  Darker in summer than winter, rooted by mighty a splinter
  Where three kings once reigned, now three kings lie slain

This is the last for some, the closer of doors
The first for others, the opener of ways
The birth of an era for all
Ware the Quint, she marks the world in night

-Augury of Korbah the Seer

"Wasn't Korbah a madman?" asked Carlin.

"Only after no one could solve the Quest he gave. He was once a powerful Sage, well respected in the highest circles," said Kavi.

"Doesn't matter," said Grim. "He had the mark. Most Quest givers were nuttier than a squirrel's wet dream but if they had the mark, the Quest was legitimate."

"Scholars in Brickolage and Vonderia believe the mark is what made them crazy," said Nettie. "Whatever the Ancients did to start a Quest rarely worked out well for the Quest giver."

"So, what are you seeing that everybody else missed Nettie?" asked Kavi.

Nettie tucked an auburn lock behind her ear and stared across the flames at Kavi. "Let's start with what you all figured out so far," she said.

"Only what the experts already know," said Kavi. "The verses before and after the rhyming section could be prophecy, could be the ravings of a madman. But the middle part is most likely the first step in the Quest. The riddle is pretty obvious - What runs but never walks, has a mouth but never talks." Kavi looked to Carlin as the older man nodded.

"Yup, even I got that one. A river," said Carlin.

"Darker in summer than winter, rooted by mighty a splinter," continued Kavi. "Grim and I figured that one out when we were kids," said Kavi.

55

"That one's easy too, a forest," said Grim. "The leaves provide cover in the summer and not in the winter. The whole root and splinter bit laid it on a little thick."

"And finally the three kings," said Kavi. "Everyone knows of the Tomb of Kings outside of Vonderia. It held the bodies of Magus the First, Second and Third. All three were assassinated."

"Then what?" asked Nettie.

"Well, the riddle passage starts with, 'your trail lies in the middle of solving this riddle," said Kavi. "The theory has it that the Quest must begin somewhere between The Amail River, the Tomb of Kings and the Night Forest. They're all pretty close to each other to the east of Vonderia."

"And what did they find?" asked Nettie.

"You know they didn't find anything!" said Grim.

"Wrong," said Nettie. "They found a deep cave that adventurers of every nationality explored for years. The Vonderians even sent a survey team. They mapped every centimeter of that cave. Nothing. No sulimite, no precious metals, nothing."

"Could this shadow group of Quest solvers beat them to it?" asked Grim.

"The thought crossed my mind," said Nettie. "But in this case, no. The cave was a red herring. The conventional wisdom was wrong."

"What did they miss?" asked Kavi.

"The answer lies in the story of the Brothers Royce," said Nettie.

"Why does that name sound familiar?" asked Kavi.

"Weren't they rebels from a long time ago out of the Miter Highlands?" asked Grim.

Nettie's eyes widened in surprise. "Not many have heard the story."

"Our history teacher at the Bastion mentioned them," continued Grim. "Something about a rebellion put down a couple hundred years ago. So, what about the Brothers Royce helps us solve this riddle?"

"We should arrive at the most likely spot sometime mid-morning tomorrow," said Nettie. "I'll share the rest then."

"Don't trust us yet?" asked Grim.

"Would you?" asked Nettie.

"We're here aren't we?" said Grim.

"The Quest hasn't been solved for over a hundred years, another night won't see the end of the world Master Grim," said Nettie. She slid into her bedroll and turned her back to them.

Grim grunted. "Fine, I'll take third watch, I'm tired."

Carlin nodded to him, "I don't mind taking middle watch, milord. You two rode a lot harder than we did."

"Just Kavi now, Carlin, and thank you. Tomorrow night, we're drawing straws."

The older huntsman grunted but made his way to his own bedroll.

Kavi sat with his back against a tree and stared out from the camp. As his eyes adjusted to the darkness his mind adjusted to his situation. The events of the last couple days flashed like lightning through clouds of thought, each memory ethereal and elusive.

He'd never cut so deep when talking to his mother but it was long past time he said something. She wasn't the only one with license to grieve.

His thoughts turned inward. The contentment in freedom turned to second guessing in the ink black of forest night. The liberty was as terrifying as it was wonderful. Following orders was stifling but carried its own freedom from responsibility. He would be fully accountable for all choices made from this point forward.

His brain ran laps as he grappled with this slice of existentialism. He was lost in a maze of repercussions - leaving against his mother's orders likely cost him the more comfortable path - when Carlin tapped him on the shoulder.

Kavi jumped. "You scared the crap out of me. Again."

"Sorry about that," said Carlin with a smile nearly imperceptible in the dark night. "I'll try to be louder next time."

Kavi looked back to the fire and frowned. "It's not mid-watch yet, what are you doing up?"

"Something about the bird cries bothered me," said Carlin. "I'm going to take a look around. I'll take watch when I get back."

Kavi nodded and the huntsman melted into the night. His earlier thoughts turned to mush as fatigue set in. He had to pinch himself to keep his eyes open. When Carlin returned, he gave Kavi a thumbs up and Kavi sank into his bedroll to fall into a dreamless sleep.

* * *

Nettie withdrew for most of the morning as they rode. She consulted her journal any time Carlin looked to her for direction. She would point one way or another as the small party made their way north. She made them stop more and more often as the terrain grew hillier.

They could hear the Rhune roaring in the distance. The water ran a lot faster as the hills got steeper. The trees of the Draydale thinned as their path got rockier. Nettie dismounted as they crested one of the hills and walked in a circle, trying to find her bearings. She flipped through a couple of pages then looked down to the trees again.

"We might actually be able to help if you let us," said Kavi.

Nettie sighed, looked down at her journal again then slapped it closed. "Fine. I'm looking for the Cairn of the Brothers Royce. I don't know how well it's marked but it's supposed to be on this side of the Rhune near the edge of the Miter Highlands."

"You mentioned the Brothers Royce last night," said Grim. "What do they have to do with any of this?"

"Do you know what Royce translates to in Krommian from the Highland dialect?" asked Nettie.

Something clicked in Kavi's head. "King. And there were three brothers weren't there?"

"And you think the Royce brothers were the three kings in the riddle?" asked Grim. "Sounds like a stretch."

"I thought so at first," said Nettie, ignoring the big man's grumpiness. "But let's look at the riddle again."

Your trail lies in the middle of solving this riddle
What runs but never walks, has a mouth but never talks
Darker in summer than winter, rooted by mighty a splinter
Where three kings once reigned, now three kings lie slain

She recited it from memory, then said, "Tell me what you know of the Royce brothers."

"Almost nothing but what we learned at the Bastion. They were rebels that got put down a couple hundred years ago," said Grim.

"Exactly, none of the Krommian histories recorded anything about them except that they were rebels. I found a book in the Brickolage archives that had a very different account from a soldier involved in putting down the rebellion." She continued to look around the hill as if trying to find a landmark.

She did this for long enough that Grim finally cleared his throat. "Are you going to keep us in suspense?"

"Right," said Nettie. "Turns out the rebellion was not minor at all. The Royce brothers came from a powerful family that left Krom years before because they believed the monarchy had become corrupt. They were the first to voice the idea of a ruling Council instead of all the power being in one person's hands."

"Isn't that what we have today in Krom?" asked Carlin. "Did they actually win?"

"Not even close," said Nettie. "Their idea won, in the end, but the Royces were obliterated, the rebellion ruthlessly destroyed. The king at the time, Creighton the Third, made sure to purge any information he could of the uprising and the battle in the hopes of killing the idea. Which only made the idea more powerful. What he did succeed in killing was almost all memory of the Royces. I'm convinced that's why this Quest was never solved!"

"How are you so sure?" asked Kavi.

"Judge for yourself once I tell you about the brothers. The eldest brother was Malcom Royce. He lost the ability to walk during a hunting accident so he traveled everywhere on horseback. He never let his disability limit him though. He embraced it. He became known as the Galloping Cripple."

She looked at them expectantly for a moment, then sighed in exasperation. "Still not getting it. Ok, let me tell you about the second brother Michael. Michael was a giant. He was said to be the fiercest of the Highland warriors, a true berserker. But he was mute. He never made a sound, even in battle. This added to his legend. Imagine a giant silently chasing you with an axe."

"Has a mouth but never talks," whispered Carlin.

"Finally!" said Nettie. "At least the huntsman has capacity for critical thought."

"Whoa," said Kavi. "That has to be more than coincidence. Runs but never walks and mouth but never talks. What about the next line? Darker in summer than winter, rooted by mighty a splinter."

"That brings us to the third brother," said Nettie. "Mitchell was the prettiest of the three and the best with a sword. Unlike most highlanders, he tanned nicely and was often called the Bronze Royce. When King Magnus sent his forces to quell the Highlanders, Mitchell offered to fight General Antonius in single combat. The Highlanders would surrender if he lost but would gain their own kingdom if he won. Though Antonius did not have the power to agree he did so anyway. He had an order from the king to destroy the Royces. He would attack whether he won the duel or not, knowing the treachery would take the rebel army off guard. Antonius easily won the duel and took Mitchell's life with his spear. Moments after the duel, the army attacked and killed all unfortunate highlanders who showed up that day."

"So that covers the darker in summer than winter, but how does the root and splinter thing fit in?" asked Carlin.

Grim looked to Kavi, both thinking the same thing.

"Antonius' spear is mounted in the Hall of Warriors at the Bastion. He named it Splinter," said Grim.

9

Withdrawal

"It would help if I knew what a cairn was," said Carlin.

They had been pushing their horses through the hills while trying to keep the Rhune and woods in sight. Nettie continued her single minded focus on the notes in her journal. She clung to the research like a shield. It was the distraction that kept her from falling too deep into the chasm of grief. As the hours of searching continued she began to fray like a knitted sweater in a field of brambles.

"It's how they bury people," she snapped. "You're old enough to be my father and you live at the edge of the Highlands. How do you not know this?"

Kavi was also growing impatient. He took a deep breath and reminded himself she just lost her brother. "A cairn is more like a pile of rocks." He noticed Nettie about to object when he quickly continued. "Based on how old the cairn is, it often gets covered by dirt and weathered down like any other hill. Over time, it can look like just another hill."

"Like a barrow," said Carlin. "I was thinking about the old Highlander stories. Nobody's lived up here for years, probably not since the Royces laid claim. It's not all rock, the farmlands from generations ago turned into moors. Only the bravest hunters range this far north and only in the day. The moors are said to be haunted."

"Superstition is the provenance of fools," said Nettie.

"Girl, you're making it hard to help you," said Carlin with a sigh. "Let me finish. Stonecrest isn't old enough to have a previous huntsman. When I entered into the Lioness' service I hunted with every woodsman who knew the land. One of the more interesting was Bram McDermott who lived closer to the moors than anyone thought sane. He called the land south of the moors the Barrow Barrens. Farmers around these parts now just call it the Barrens on account of nothing grows there. Bram told me that on particularly snowy winters or hard raining springs, the Rhune floods and human bones seep to the surface. Maybe those are the remains of highlanders who fell while fighting with the Royces. If so, there's a good chance that's where our Kings are buried."

"That sounds way better than riding around aimlessly for another couple of hours while she curses at her book," said Grim.

Nettie scowled but didn't comment.

"How far up the Rhune are the Barrens?" asked Kavi.

"Can't be more than an hour's ride," said Carlin.

"Nettie?" asked Kavi.

The Bricker nodded. "Fine."

The ride up the river was an easy one. The trees from the forest thinned considerably and they didn't need to dismount to avoid obstacles. Nettie nearly fell from her horse twice as she continued to read and ride. She scowled at any looking her way as she regained her balance.

Carlin brought them to a halt near a non-descript hill about a kilometer past where the trees of the Draydale ended and the abandoned farmlands began. "This is where Bram took me. Don't know if this was the exact hill but we're definitely in the Barrens."

Kavi looked at the hill and the one behind it and the one behind that. "We have maybe three hours before it gets too dark. There is no shortage of hills that could qualify as Barrows." He turned to the Bricker. "Nettie, anything that could point us in the right direction?"

"Most cairns will have standing stones that mark the grave. Sometimes they will be placed in a circle, or sometimes two or more will be propped up to form an arch. The Highlanders believed the structures a gateway to the afterlife."

"So, we should look for rocks," said Grim. He looked up at the hilly and rocky terrain. "Glad we could narrow it down."

Carlin snorted.

Nettie glared. "Purposefully placed rocks." She rubbed tired eyes. "Gentlemen, I can take it from here. I'll be damned if I'm going to continue to share information I gathered over the last four years with a trio of Krommian halfwits doing their best to humor me."

"It's going to get worse tonight," Grim said softly. Nettie's short temper caused something to click. "I'm not sure how much suli you took or how much tolerance you've built but when the shakes come you won't be able to protect yourself from a chipmunk."

Nettie prepared to shout but swallowed it. She shuddered and folded in on herself. She looked very small and very young. "I took it all. Everything we had left. Pick was too young and I knew that if we had any chance against those butchers on the bridge, suli was it. So I took it all."

"How much was that?" asked Grim.

"Almost a gram," she whispered.

Grim gasped. "Remind me how Brickers refine suli for consumption."

"It was unrefined, I...I didn't have any choice. It was die on the bridge or take the suli," she said. She started shaking.

"Have you ever taken suli before?" Grim asked quietly.

She shook her head.

All the contentment and excitement of the Quest disappeared. Rage took the place of fear, something Kavi learned from his mother. "You took a gram of *raw* sulimite!" yelled Kavi. "You can't be that stupid. So what was the plan? Come up here, by yourself, and die? We have two full time physicians, Loam trained, on call in Stonecrest. You only had to wait one more day and you wouldn't be in this situation."

Nettie had the decency to look ashamed. She pulled out a wool sweater and put it on. "There was no plan. I had to get away and do something," she said in a small voice. "Anything but lie in bed and think." She started shaking harder.

Carlin burst into action. "Let's head back to the edge of the forest. I'm going to grab wood for a fire. Kavi, can you set up a quick shelter? Grim-"

Grim was already moving. "I'll run to the river and grab some water. I'll also carve a basic dowel so she doesn't swallow her tongue." He turned to Nettie. "Tonight is going to be hell. The most raw suli I ever took was half a gram and I had been training with it for almost a year."

"What kind of idiot takes raw suli when you can use the refined stuff?" said Kavi, still furious.

"The Elites make us train with it so we know how to manage the withdrawal if we're forced to take it in an emergency. When it wore off, I had one of the worst nights of my life."

Kavi pulled a hatchet off his saddle and went to work chopping down some of the smaller pines that thrived in the area. The soft wood was perfect for a basic A frame. He had the ridge pole planted when Carlin walked up with several stacks of firewood.

"Might as well make a big fire," said Carlin. "She's going to need the heat to break the fever. With the amount of noise she'll be making tonight none of us will be sleeping. With any luck the noise will scare predators and bandits away."

Carlin got a small flame going as Kavi put the last of the leafy branches over the A frame. The huntsman threw on some of the bigger pieces of wood. He waved to Grim who was making his way up the hill with a small bucket and five canteens of river water. Carlin put some water to boil and Kavi pulled out the percolator his father built him a long time ago. The night ahead was going to need coffee.

"Might as well try to get some sleep before the worst of it hits," said Grim, looking at Nettie. He pulled out a small whittling knife and started slicing bark from a piece of ash he found by the river.

Nettie continued to shake but grabbed the bedroll from her mare and moved it into the A frame. She collapsed on top of it and curled into a ball.

Kavi grimaced at Grim who nodded then looked down at the piece of wood that started to take on the cylindrical shape of a chomping dowel. "What are her chances?"

"With Loam trained physicians, a hundred percent. Up here, with us? It's a coin flip," said Grim.

"She seems pretty tough," said Carlin. "She'll pull through."

Grim nodded. "It's going to be a long night."

* * *

"I honestly don't know how a girl this size is capable of creating this much vomit," said Grim as he used a wet cloth to clean the remnants of the reddish orange liquid from her mouth and nose.

"I'm happy to switch sides any time you want," said Kavi as he cut a piece of her pant leg away to drain the diarrhea that started to build up higher in her pants. He shook his hands in disgust as he realized he hadn't gotten ahead of the brown liquid. "Carlin is a coward."

After the odor from the early bouts of vomit hit Carlin, he nearly lost his own dinner and offered to do a quick patrol of the perimeter. He left before either Grim or Kavi could protest.

"You're just angry you didn't think of it first," said Grim. "Besides, he didn't go through the same training we did. One small Bricker can't make a fraction of the stench a squad of elites can after a mission." Nettie heaved again and Grim wasn't quick enough to avoid the fresh stream hitting his boots. "Although, I gotta say she's doing her best to break some records."

Nettie seized, her body contorting into a rictus of pain.

"Quick, pass me the dowel before she swallows her damn tongue," said Grim.

As Kavi passed Grim the dowel Nettie sat up and looked Kavi straight in the eye. "The Black Rose is a symbol of hope. Do not fear it. Rose brings the only chance of solace from the Collective." At that, her eyes rolled back, she let loose a tremendous fart and passed out.

Carlin chose that moment to walk back into camp. "You are not going to believe what the moonlight revealed on my walk."

10

Moonlight

I t appeared Nettie had made it through the worst of the seizures. Grim nodded to a worried Kavi. "Look at her. She's a third my size. I got this. Unless you manifested healing powers overnight?"

"Alright Carlin, lead on," said Kavi as he walked to the hobbled horses.

"Don't bother," said Carlin. "It'll be easier to show you on foot."

The two men made their way through the outskirts of the forest. Kavi kept tripping over sticks and rocks in the darkness that Carlin avoided with no effort. "I don't know how you found anything at night," said Kavi as he stubbed his toe on another rock.

"Give it a sec," said Carlin. Once they made their way out of the forest and into the Barrens, the half moon lent a metallic shine to the rocks spackling the barren hills. "Better?" he asked.

"Nothing about this night is better," muttered Kavi under his breath but he nodded to the huntsman. Kavi was furious at his mother for putting Nettie in this situation and angry at himself for not recognizing it sooner. How could he have missed something so obvious?

"Good, let's pick up the pace. The girl was on to something," said Carlin.

He led Kavi for another half kilometer until the roar of the Rhune drowned out any other sounds of night. As they topped a small hill he could see the moon dancing off the ripples of the river below.

"What do you see?" asked Carlin from their vantage point.

"Besides the river?" asked Kavi.

"In spite of the river. Come on boy, I know those idiot warriors in the Bastion taught you *some* scouting skills."

Kavi thought for a second before he realized the moonlight didn't create the glare the sun did. He ran his eyes up and down both river banks. That's when he saw a series of half buried standing stones in a half circle, with the opening facing the river. The earlier glare from the setting sun made it difficult to look towards the river. "I see the stones. How do you know it's a cairn?"

"Look at the river again," said Carlin.

Kavi saw the reflection of the stones in a calmer part of the river. In the center of the half circle of standing rocks was an opening that wavered back and forth with the ripples of the Rhune. "Did you try to go in?"

"Nope," said Carlin. "I'm not dumb enough to walk into a barrow at night on my own."

"Don't blame you," said Kavi.

"Down," said Carlin in a low, urgent voice.

Kavi dropped next to him, taking shelter behind a small boulder at the top of the hill.

"What?" whispered Kavi.

Carlin pointed and Kavi saw a giant silhouette winging through the sky. "What in the hell is that thing?" asked Kavi.

"I'm not sure," said Carlin when the silhouette finally winged out of view. "But I have some ideas. Do you smell that?"

Kavi breathed in deeply with his nose. He spent the last six hours breathing only through his mouth as he tended to Nettie. He hadn't realized he was still doing it. "Nasty. That same burnt butter smell we found at the cave."

Carlin nodded. "We know that whatever it is, it's not a natural flying predator. If it were a raptor, it would have spotted us easily. With the size of that thing, we would have been a quick meal. I have to report this back to the Lioness in the morning."

Kavi stood back up. "Understood, and I agree. Do you mind scouting the entrance to the Barrow with us before you leave?"

The older man put a hand on his shoulder. "You know how hot your mother can get, Kav. Come with me and report this new information about the beast, get back in her good graces."

"How'd you know about that? You left before our fight," said Kavi.

Carlin chuckled. "You've been dancing between angry hedgehog and kicked puppy since you caught up to us. No other person in the world gets you so worked up."

Kavi nodded. "Getting back in her good graces is not the goal anymore," said Kavi. He and the woodsman started the walk back to camp. "I have excelled at getting in everyone's good graces for as long as I remember. Because of it, I have no idea what *I* want. I keep following the path put in front of me like one of Dad's golems."

They made their way back into the trees of the Draydale. "When Nettie told us her crazy theory, it seemed like an opportunity to do something that mattered," said Kavi. "If somebody is keeping these Quests from the Ancients to themselves, that's not right. It's like they're taking the world's chance to dream again, you know?"

Carlin snorted with his usual charm.

"You don't agree?"

"You asking as a friend or a Lord of Stonecrest?" asked Carlin. The huntsman never slowed his pace through the trees.

"When have I ever pulled the Lord of Stonecrest card on you?" asked Kavi.

"Fine. You know what most people dream of? To get a position in some lord's house. To know they're going to be able to eat tomorrow, to know their children are going to be safe."

Kavi thought about Carlin's words. The simplicity of that dream sounded wonderful, but it wasn't how he was brought up. The whole world wanted more from him, expected more from him. "You're right, but don't you ever feel like you have a greater purpose to fulfill? Something that will shake the world?"

"That greater purpose nonsense is for rich kids," said Carlin. "You're Ma and Da have been wonderful to me and mine. Those boys you call city guards respect you but they worship your mother. You know why?"

"Because she's the Lioness. Everyone knows her story," said Kavi.

"Wrong." This time Carlin didn't hide the anger in his voice. "They worship her because she made them part of her dream. She expects everyone around her to be better. Not just you. Everybody. People do everything they can to live up to that expectation, partially for her, but mostly for themselves. She has a clear vision of Stonecrest becoming a major trade hub between Brickolage and Krom. She's got the steel will to make it happen. That's a dream anyone can be excited to be a part of."

"Unless you were born to it," said Kavi. He was getting heated himself. "You will leave an amazing legacy as the first Huntsman of Stonecrest. You created the position. My only option is to become a less impressive version of her. I'll always be Kavi the Cub, a footnote in the legacy of the Lioness."

Carlin stopped before they reached the camp. The sky to the east was just starting to brighten so the huntsman could look him in the eye. "You know how many people would change places with you in a heartbeat? Your problem is you've never been desperate. You haven't faced real pain." He held up a hand. "Don't start about the Bastion. I know the training is tough, but it's different than facing a decision of whether or not to steal a piece of bread so your kid doesn't starve."

"Exactly," said Kavi. "How can I know what I'm capable of until I put myself in a situation where I'm making life and death choices?"

Carlin thought for a second, then nodded. "You got a taste of that in the Eagles."

"Border skirmishes with the Astrans at the head of a squad of Silver Eagles? That's a game of posturing for Krommian officers to show off. There's no desperation. There hasn't been serious conflict for years," said Kavi.

"And that's a bad thing?" asked Carlin. He started walking towards camp again.

"I'm not saying that!" Kavi growled. He blew out a breath to release the misdirected anger. "If I don't find out what's important to me right now, I never will. If it means going against the wishes of the Lioness...so be it."

"That's—" Carlin started to respond.

"Is Kavi whining again?" interrupted Grim as they broke into the small clearing where they set up camp. The big man had made a porridge of oats and mushrooms that sat in a small pot balanced on one of the rocks next to the fire.

"The girl feeling better?" asked Carlin.

"She's sleeping at least," said Grim pointing to the mound of blankets in the A frame.

"Any more hallucinations or pronouncements about black roses or anything else?" asked Kavi.

"You know you can't read into that," said Grim. "First thing they taught us in the Elites, never believe what you see or hear in the suli fever. Believe me, I saw outrageous things when I was coming down."

"What did she say? Something about the Black Rose being good and then something about...solace from the Collective. Could that be her shadow group?" said Kavi.

"I tell you not to read anything into it and what do you do? You read into it," said Grim. He shook his head and grabbed a couple of canteen cups out of his pack. He ladled a scoop of porridge into each.

Carlin and Kavi muttered their thanks and tucked in.

"What did you find?" asked Grim.

"The girl was right. There's something down there," said Carlin. "Cairn, barrow, whatever you want to call it. The opening is visible when you're not shading your eyes from the glare off the river."

"Let's check it out then," said a small voice from the mound of blankets. "If you wouldn't mind escorting me to the river to clean myself up first."

Nettie sat up. She looked down at the mess she made of herself and back to the trio of men sitting around the fire. "I'm sorry for putting you through that. Thank you."

Grim nodded. "I've been there, it's no picnic. Refined suli is much easier, no worse than getting a hangover from too much whiskey."

Nettie gave him a shy smile. "I'll be sure to use the refined stuff next time I'm about to die."

Grim smiled back. "See that you do. If experience taught me anything, it's that you're going to be too weak to explore a barrow today."

She pulled herself out of the A frame and wrinkled her nose at her own stench. "Let's test that on the way to the river. I don't think I can handle another minute of my own stink."

Grim took the young Bricker down to the river while Carlin and Kavi broke camp. They wrapped the soiled clothes and blankets into her bedroll and slung them on to her horse to be cleaned later.

"So?" Kavi asked Grim. "Are you coming?"

Grim shrugged but it was Nettie that answered. "I'm not fit for battle but I'll be damned if I let you explore that Barrow without me."

11

The Barrow

The barrow entrance was tucked into a small valley between two larger hills. They were at least two days ride north from any major settlement. So, the chance of a boat or even a raft on the water this far north was almost zero. Kavi wasn't surprised no one had discovered it.

They dismounted and Carlin dropped to a knee near the entrance to look for tracks.

Nettie walked toward the Barrow. She had to stretch to touch the long flat stone that framed the top of the entrance. Grim would have to stoop to get through but Kavi would have no trouble walking through upright. Nettie peered into the inky darkness but couldn't make out a thing.

"We're going to need torches," said Nettie.

"Did you bring those goggles your dad made?" asked Grim.

Kavi shook his head. "No, didn't want to bring any of the latest clockwork without the Lioness signing off. I did bring a couple of his old torches. They're suli powered so we can explore without smoke. Are we ready to check this out?"

"Hold up a moment," said Carlin. He broadened his sweep of the area outside the entrance.

"Did you find something?" asked Grim.

"No," said Carlin. He wiped dirt from his knee. "That's the problem. I found absolutely nothing."

Nettie smiled. "That's good news, right? Maybe we're actually the first ones to explore this place."

"When I say nothing, I mean that I didn't find even a single animal track. We're too close to the river for that and this barrow would be a great shelter for animals. I should have seen something. There's not a damn thing here. It's almost like somebody came in and swept it of tracks." He looked at Nettie. "Or animals know to stay away from this place."

"If what we saw flying overhead last night was the beast...," said Kavi. "Do you think it claimed the barrow too?"

"Doubt it," said Carlin. "You remember the entrance to the other cave." He gave an involuntary shudder at the thought of Holden standing outside with eyeballs in hand. "Whatever that thing is, it's not hiding its tracks."

"We had a strong wind last night, could that have wiped any tracks away?" asked Nettie.

Carlin raised his eyebrows but didn't answer.

"Carlin, I promise we're not going to do anything stupid," said Kavi. "Besides, if we run into trouble, we've got Grim. Go ahead and report back to the Lioness about what we saw last night. The town needs to know that thing is still flying around out here."

"When should I tell her to expect you back?" asked the huntsman.

"Don't tell her anything," said Kavi.

Carlin looked to Grim as if expecting support. Grim shrugged. The huntsman mounted and said, "Fine, do it your way kid. If my feeling is off and this place is as abandoned as it looks, it's been so for a long time. Don't take any unnecessary risks."

"Thanks Grampa," said Nettie but her voice didn't hold the bite of the day before. She looked at the huntsman with something close to fondness. "Don't worry, I'll take care of these two idiots."

Carlin smiled at that. With a gentle heel to his mare's side, he turned the animal and rode off.

* * *

Tribar's torches worked remarkably well. A twist of the handle activated the recycled suli to create a bright ray of light shooting from one end. With a further twist, Kavi could narrow or widen the beam to illuminate most of the tunnel. The light had a reddish hue which added to the eeriness of walking into an underground tomb. The walls were stacked rock with large standing stones providing support. After several meters the hallway opened into a larger room with a series of shelves built into the rock walls. Bits of wax on the shelves showed where someone had lit candles in the past.

"I might have something over here," said Grim. He directed the light towards a section of the wall. "Look at these rocks. They're a different shade than everything else in the barrow. There's no water stains or lichen, like this wall was built long after everything else."

Kavi walked over with his torch causing Nettie to close her journal and follow. With both torches pointed at the section of wall it was obvious. "Huh," grunted Kavi. "Not sure if a regular torch would have picked that up."

Grim grabbed one of the flat stones in the wall and pulled. The weight of the stones above it required him to set his legs and strain. Kavi pulled out his belt knife and wedged it between the rock Grim was pulling and the one next to it. The sedimentary nature made it easy to flake off and allow Kavi to stick the blade in farther. Grim switched from brute force to wiggling the stone back and forth while Kavi used the knife as a lever. With a final tug the rock came free. It got easier from there. Grim and Kavi removed several other rocks from around the small hole they made.

The light from the torch revealed a hallway stretching into the dark behind the now crumbling wall. Kavi joined Grim to kick at the base of the hole they created. The rest of the wall fell quickly.

"You're turning me into a believer, Nettie," said Grim. "This wall *was* built recently and I can only think of two reasons why."

Nettie nodded. "To keep people out or to keep something in," she said.

"Let's hope it's the first. Maybe we're walking into a Quest that's already had it's teeth pulled by this shadow group of yours," said Grim.

"Only one way to find out," said Kavi.

Kavi squeezed past the big man to take the lead. The rocks lining the walls were far older than the temporary wall they broke through. After a minute of walking, the narrow hall opened into a much larger room. The stacked rocks of the hallway continued all the way up to form a well-designed dome. In the center of the room lay three stone sarcophagi. The tops of the decorated stone tombs lay on the ground next to them. The top of the middle sarcophagus lay shattered in pieces.

The three tiptoed closer to the raised dais holding the bodies of the three kings. It was obvious there had been a massive struggle in the room. Old, dried blood splattered the painted images adorning the smooth stone of each bier.

Nettie took the torch from Grim's hand and knelt to examine the painted scenes. "This is the right place," she said. She crouched then shuffled around the side of the far left coffin and pointed at one of the images. "See here? This would be Mitchell's tomb. This is the battle between him and Antonius."

She continued to scoot around the side of the coffin. She ignored what sounded like dry wood snapping as she moved until a loud crack caused her to look down. She jumped up and backed away. Human bones littered the ground on the far side of the dais. Nettie put her hand out to lean on top of the ridge of Mitchell's open tomb as the last of her strength faded. The excitement of finding the Royces' tomb had given her the strength to make it this far but the adrenaline had run out.

As she leaned against the tomb there was a slight click. The sarcophagus started to sink into the floor. Grim grabbed Nettie and joined Kavi in taking cover behind the middle coffin. They heard a large whoosh of air but nothing followed. Grim covered Nettie with his body while Kavi had his arms over his head. After a minute of claustrophobic breathing Nettie began to laugh.

"Of course!" she said. She wriggled her way out from under Grim. "The traps were sprung. That whoosh of air must have shot projectiles that killed these explorers. It's a good thing we *weren't* the first ones here. We'd be dead now."

Kavi stood up and looked inside the middle sarcophagus. "There's a staircase leading down."

"If they had the time to put that wall up, they definitely had time to clear this place of value," said Grim.

"Maybe, but-" said Kavi.

"There might be a clue to the next step of the Triad," interrupted Nettie.

"Unless this is the end of the Triad Quest," said Grim.

"Then there might be a clue to the next Quest," said Nettie. "Either way, we're obligated to find it."

Kavi looked at her critically. "Do you have the energy to make it down the stairs?"

She nodded and walked over to him, but her legs gave out as she tried to swing her right leg over the rim of the sarcophagus. The exhaustion from the withdrawal hit hard and she cursed.

"We could scout and help lower you down if we find anything," said Kavi.

She looked at him, anger battling weariness on her face. Finally, she nodded. "Grim's right, it's probably empty anyway but you carry me down there if you find anything remotely interesting!"

Kavi and Grim descended the steep stairway inside the middle tomb. The temperature dropped and moisture gathered in tear drops on the walls. When they reached the bottom of the stairs Kavi grabbed the canteen off his belt and took a long swig. The stress of exploring worked up a thirst. He offered the canteen to Grim but he shook his head.

The stairs ended in a cramped hall that led to a squat door ten paces away. Grim cursed and even Kavi had to duck to advance down the hall. Behind the door was a small room that looked like a root cellar with two notable exceptions. There was a large, empty chest lying open below a bronze placard. There were scratch marks and gouges on either side of the sign as if someone had tried, unsuccessfully, to remove it. Kavi moved closer and brought the torch up.

"Damn," said Grim. "They did a number on that thing."

The sign had been thoroughly defaced. Kavi could just make out some flowing script engraved into it. The engravings had been deeply scratched so not a single word could be read. Any doubt Kavi and Grim had about Nettie's theories evaporated. A group of people had solved this Quest and the world was none the wiser.

"This had to have been the next clue," said Kavi.

"I'm pissed and I gave up on the Quests years ago. What right do these bastards have preventing the world from chasing the elder

80

dream?" asked Grim, slipping into the common tongue.

The righteous anger simmering under the surface started to boil inside Kavi. "We can't let this stand."

The two made their way out of the small room and back up the narrow stairs. They shared what they found with Nettie.

"If it really is as unreadable as you say, there's not a whole lot we can do about it," she said.

"We can let the world know," said Kavi. "If this doesn't light a fire, I don't know what will."

"Before we go, would you mind grabbing a rubbing?" She passed Kavi a charcoal stick and some thin paper. "I doubt we'll get anything out of it, but it's worth a try."

When he climbed out of the sarcophagus for the second time, he saw Grim tending to Nettie. "She's fading fast, Kav. I'm shocked she had this much energy to begin with. We need to get her back to camp."

The large man turned to Nettie. "You have any problem with me carrying you out of here?"

She shook her head. Grim lifted her up and she nuzzled into his shirt.

It only took a couple of minutes to retrace their steps. Kavi smiled when he saw the light from the opening to the Barrow. It couldn't have been much past mid-morning. They hadn't been in there that long. Even so, the natural light was blinding and he squinted as he made his way outside.

His heart dropped when he saw what awaited them.

"It's about time. I was this close to sending the boys down there to pull you out," said Roanik, pinching his fingers together. At least thirty men stood behind him, and in front of him he held Carlin with a knife to his throat.

12

The Cage

"You're outnumbered," said the brigand captain. He took a long, dramatic sniff at the air and looked at Nettie. "And, judging by the smell, the little Bricker isn't going to surprise us with a suli rampage this time. So, I'm only going to offer this once. Throw down your weapons and we'll let you live." His lips pulled back in a sneer. His scars, which were very similar to Grim's, bunched up on the left side of his face like little inchworms.

"Or, we could back into the cave behind us," said Grim. "You know I can hold one of those narrow hallways by myself for the rest of the afternoon without breaking a sweat."

"The thought had crossed my mind," said Roanik. "We did have the same training after all, didn't we coward?" His grip tightened on the knife as he brought it closer to Carlin's throat. "That's why we brought your huntsman friend along."

"Oh, and we're supposed to believe a humanitarian like yourself is going to let him go if we surrender?" asked Grim. He took a step backwards.

Roanik laughed which caused the knife at Carlin's throat to draw a bead of blood. "Not even a little. But you can watch him ride away and know there's a chance you'll be able to free yourselves later. Or, even better, know he'll stage a dashing rescue. Hope springs eternal and all that," said Roanik with a wink.

Kavi caught Carlin's eye. There was resignation and recognition that this situation wasn't going to end well for him.

"So, we disarm and you let Carlin go. Just like that," said Kavi.

"Just like that," said Roanik.

"Not good enough," said Kavi. "Grim, set Nettie down and get back to the first defensible hallway. Roanik, take me first. You can even bind my hands. Let Carlin take Nettie and when they've ridden off, Grim will come out."

"No can do. The Bricker girl is on the list," said Roanik.

"What list?" asked Kavi.

"Well look at that. You've gotten a piece of information I wasn't planning on giving. Good for you, lordling. My employer has a list of people I'm supposed to take alive. If it were up to me, I'd kill this idiot right now," he made a slicing motion with the knife without drawing more blood. "Then send the rest of my men in after you, one at a time if needs be until the coward makes a mistake or runs out of steam."

Grim set Nettie down and looked at the men behind Roanik. He snorted. "Not likely. Let's go with your plan Kav."

"Or, I could sit out here for a couple of days until you run out of food and water. Then, I'll drag your dehydrated bodies out of there. I'm holding the cards this time," said Roanik. "Now it's a matter of whether you let your friend here live."

"And who is this employer of yours?" asked Nettie in a voice barely higher than a whisper.

"I bet you have some ideas about that, don't you girl?" said Roanik.

"He's not going t-," started Carlin before Roanik pushed the knife slowly into his skin.

"We know," said Kavi. "He's not letting you go. Even if it looks like it. If Nettie is right about who your employer is, they prefer being discrete."

"That's where you're wrong lordling," said Roanik. "My employer is changing their tune. You may have heard about some of these border skirmishes lately. They've been pulling strings for years, so why do you think you're hearing about these little incursions now?"

"You tell me," said Kavi.

"That decision isn't mine to make. However, they were very clear that *discrete* is no longer a priority. They're no longer hiding."

"Fine," said Grim. "Bind me first. Kavi, take a defensive position and I'll let *you* know when Carlin is safe."

Roanik signaled for the men behind him. Two of the men held flintlocks on Grim while two others carried their bindings. Kavi noticed Grim's eyes widen when he saw the metal anklets and bracelets linked to a slave collar. They both expected rope. Kavi shrugged. It didn't change the situation or their decision.

"Only the arms, then let the huntsman go," said Grim. He dropped his short sword on the ground next to the big knife he pulled from his belt.

Roanik removed the knife from Carlin's throat. He motioned to the huntsman's horse saddled nearby. "Your lucky day, old man."

Carlin hopped on the horse and with a couple of swift kicks to it's side, he had the mare at a canter.

"Head through the Barrens Carlin!" yelled Kavi. "You know the land better than they do."

It surprised no one when a group of horsemen wheeled out of the woods to follow. Grim glared at the brigand captain who shrugged. "At least he's got a chance." Roanik smiled and punched Grim in the face. "Wow, did *that* feel good," said Roanik. "Ok lordling. I stuck to my side of the deal. Your turn."

As soon as the restraints were on Kavi and Nettie, Roanik looked to one of the men and nodded. The man pulled out a pouch and poured a small amount of powder in his hands. He blew a little into Kavi's face and everything went dark.

* * *

Kavi woke to a jounce and a rumble. He spat something out of his mouth which didn't quite clear his lips. He started to brush it away with a hand. A clanking noise accompanied the restraint as he brought his hand to his lips. He looked at the piece of straw he pulled from his mouth then to the iron links bound to the cuffs on his hands. He lifted a foot to confirm the chain attached to the anklets and the uncomfortable metal collar around his throat. They linked to a central chain which ran under an iron ring bolted to the floor. Five others rode in the caged wagon with him.

There was no sign of Grim or Nettie.

Stupid, stupid, stupid. He followed after the girl and walked right into a trap and now he was a Krom-damned slave. He would never hear the end this when he got back home. *If* he got back home.

He looked at the scruffy man sitting next to him. He was a young Bricker, well-made clothes torn and dirty. By the bulkiness of his left shoulder under his black jacket, it looked like he had an augment on that arm but Kavi couldn't hear any whirring or clicking of gears. The man had sores at his wrists where the metal rubbed against the skin.

"Where are we?" Kavi asked in a raspy voice bereft of water.

The man looked at him but didn't answer. "Hey, I'm talking to you," said Kavi, louder now.

A loud clang resonated from one of the bars of the caged wagon near Kavi's head. Kavi shifted his head to look at a rat-faced slaver holding an iron bar. He struck the bar near Kavi's head again. "No talking," said the man in common. "That's your one warning."

Kavi pulled on the chain restraining his hands to see how it affected range of motion. He could barely raise his hands above his head. While looking at his hands, he noticed the woman sitting across from him glaring. With the chains connected, Kavi's pull had forced her legs forward. He lowered his arms and winced an apology.

He took a deep breath and let his training kick in. They traveled slowly and by the position of the sun, they headed south. There were no discernible landmarks, only dry land populated with red sandstone canyons. So, anything south of Brickolage. Some slaves walked next to the wagon. They were chained together and looked worse than those locked with him in the wagon. The walking slaves wore rags and thin sandals. Those were the lucky ones. More than half were barefoot and several were naked. The slave in front looked up for obstacles every several minutes with eyes devoid of hope.

Kavi knew of the horrific realities of slavery but only in the abstract. The firsthand experience was an atrocity. The stench was a thing of nightmares. Kavi spent time on pig farms so manure wasn't a foreign concept but pigs lacked self-awareness. As the thought crossed his mind, the woman across from him urinated. The warm liquid darkened her pants before trickling on to the wagon floor and out through the grate made for that purpose. Her face burned with shame, the scars under her eyes white against her red face.

She must be a new captive too. Those outside of the wagon were past shame, driven only by an animalistic desire to survive. Perhaps those in the wagon were a higher escape risk. His fellow passengers all looked new to their captivity.

Kavi wasn't able to answer the question for himself before the rod came banging on the bars of the cage again. This time it was on the other side and directed at a tall man who looked Vonderian.

86

"You, no fiddling with cuffs," yelled a wiry jailer with a large, unplanned scar across his neck. Scar flanked the other side of the carriage from Ratface.

The man gave the jailer an icy gaze, rubbed one of his chafed wrists but set his hands back on his lap.

Kavi looked back at the line of slaves outside of the carriage. He wondered why there was one slaver for the entire line and yet there were two guarding their cart. The six prisoners in the cart were getting special treatment. The question was why.

Kavi closed his eyes and tried to rest.

* * *

He woke to Ratface banging the bars near his head. The stench in the cabin only increased over the course of the day. Kavi was surprised he could still smell the waves of body odor pulsing from Ratface. Bathing was clearly not a priority for the man. He was thankful for the ladle of water the man held to his lips though. Kavi didn't even care the water was dirty as he gulped it down. The moving cart caused the water to slosh over his chest.

The cart slowed and he reached out with his hands to get the last bit of water at the bottom of the ladle.

"No. No touching," yelled Ratface.

He pulled the ladle from Kavi and swung it at him. Kavi saw the strike coming and caught it. He stared at Ratface. The slaver spat in Kavi's face and loosed a high pitched, weaselly laugh as he pulled the ladle back. Kavi grimaced in disgust as he wiped phlegm from cheek and lips.

The cart pulled into a canyon where a ramshackle camp was being set up for the night. This consisted of slavers pounding stakes into the ground. They hooked the chains of the slaves to the stakes and left one slaver to guard them. Other men set large cook pots over a series of campfires where they prepared a thin gruel or stew. Kavi couldn't smell what they were cooking but he could imagine it. The hunger pangs had started hours ago.

He craned his neck. He didn't see any meat but it looked like oats and maybe root vegetables were being added to the pots. Based on their treatment so far, Kavi was surprised they would be fed at all. He shrugged. Slaving was a business and slavers didn't get paid for dead slaves.

As the two slavers guarding their cart headed towards the campsite, Kavi called out to Ratface. "Will we get the chance to use a privy?"

Ratface raised the iron bar and approached the cart. "You rich boys are something else, always expecting the world to bend to you."

Kavi turned as much as the chains would allow to face the man. If Ratface swung that bar there was a good chance he would inflict serious injury. He tried for tact. "I figured taking a crap in my pants, in the cart, would be a mess you'd have to clean up later. I'm just trying to save you some work."

"And you never know when to shut your damn mouth," said Ratface. He raised the bar to strike.

"Stop," said a voice that cracked like a whip.

Ratface lowered the bar and turned to look at the newcomer. The man was large, almost as large as Grim. In the past, he must have been well-muscled. His shoulders were broad and he had the sure gait of a warrior. Most of that muscle had turned to fat. His clothes were well made, seamed with gold lace and decorated with an obscene amount of filigree, yet they fit poorly, barely covering the man's large belly. What may have looked regal on another made this man look like a down-on-his-luck circus performer.

The large man walked over to the cart and his hand stabbed like a striking adder to grab Kavi by the throat. "Rich boy causing trouble?" he asked.

Ratface nodded. "Yes Tuvani. He said he wants to use privy."

Tuvani chuckled and rotated Kavi's head as if he were examining a prized steer. "Ah, rich kids. The same the world over." He released Kavi's throat with a push. The push was strong enough to slam him back until the chains around his hands and neck went taut to catch him.

Tuvani moved around to the back of the cart where all the inhabitants had a clear view. "My name is Tuvani. Perhaps you've heard of me?" He met the eyes of each prisoner in turn then shrugged. "No matter, I was once a headliner in the southern arenas." He twirled his obnoxious mustache in a demonstration of showmanship.

"Let me guess, circus performer?" asked the Vonderian from the far side of the cart. Angry, dark eyes sat below a mop of straw colored hair.

Tuvani tilted his head back and laughed. "Oh, I like you funny wizard boy," he said. He nodded to Scar. Scar punched the man in the back of the head hard enough to rock him forward until the iron neck collar stopped his head with a jerk. Kavi winced at the whiplash the man would feel later.

"But not too far off," said Tuvani. "The gladiator pits have a circus feel to them, especially on feast days. The big difference is in the arena, the animals sometimes eat the performers." He laughed again and this time Ratface joined him.

Tuvani turned back to the wagon. "Lucky for me, I was too good to fight animals. I only fought men. And I did it well enough that I got to retire and take on this wonderful trade. You are probably wondering why you are here and why you are in the wagon? Why you sit, while those poor fools," he pointed at the slaves chained to the stakes, "have to walk. Yes?"

He raked the captives with his piercing gaze again. "My answer is: I don't care. I don't care what questions you have. I don't care who you were before you ended up with me. I don't care if you live or if you die. The only thing I care about is that you don't cause trouble for me until I deliver you to your new owners. To make sure you don't make trouble, I have come up with a list of rules."

Tuvani snapped his fingers at Scar. The wiry man pulled a dirty piece of paper out of his vest pocket and handed it to the big man.

Tuvani made a show of reaching into his own jacket pocket where he pulled on some spectacles then began to read. "Rule number one: do *not* fuck with me or any of my men." He took the spectacles off and tucked them back into his pocket. "That's really the only rule. Understood? If you cause trouble, we will beat you. Then we will whip you. Five times at least, maybe even ten."

Scar pulled the whip from his belt and gave it a dramatic crack near the cart as if subduing an unruly lion.

Tuvani laughed again. "He's very good with that. You should have seen him in the arena. The first enemy he fought used a whip. That's who gave him that beauty mark. He was dragged around by his neck until he was smart enough to play dead. When he stopped moving, his opponent came to finish him off. That's when he stabbed the man in the testicles fourteen times and took his whip. He's been using it ever since."

Scar gave them a theatrical bow.

"And, that's why I hired him. He has a way with the crowd, yes?" Tuvani looked back to the ground is if trying to remember something. "Right, where were we? Oh yes, you give me or my men trouble you will get beaten. Then we whip you, then you get to choose which slave we kill in your name." He gave a tiger's smile. "It wasn't until we added the last that we found we could keep you fools from trying to escape. For some reason, you *kurats* seem to care about lives of nobodies."

"I don't care if you stay in the cart for weeks until your legs go numb and fall off." He looked at Ratface. "Do you remember that one time? She's screaming - oh, my toes are black, my toes are black."

Ratface joined him as they laughed together. Tuvani wiped his eyes. "Good times. Big problem is it cuts into my profits and my client pays me very well for star gazers like you. So, instead of losing toes, you get to work. If you work hard enough, you get to eat."

Tuvani pointed at Kavi and the Vonderian. "Rich kid and funny wizard, you get to dig latrine. Don't worry, me and my men will be watching you." He pointed to his eyes and then to them. "As for the rest of you, you get to clean up your own filth and make lovely carriage sparkle. If you're lucky, you might even get to rub down horses. How does that sound?"

They unlocked Kavi's hands but kept the other chains in place. Kavi luxuriated in the freedom of stretching his arms as he followed after Ratface in a hobble. He joined the Vonderian and three walking slaves as they moved away from the main camp to start digging the latrine.

Ratface handed Kavi a pick and handed the Vonderian a shovel. He looked at them with a hand on the hilt of his short sword. "Please try something stupid," said Ratface with an evil smirk.

Scar unshackled the other slaves and handed them shovels. He nodded to the group of slaves before cracking his whip above their heads. "Now work, this isn't a feast day."

Kavi slammed the ground with his pick a dozen times until the ground began to loosen. He took another strike when he heard one of the slaves gasp. He looked up to see all three pointing to the sky.

The man threw down his shovel and yelled, "Ach'Su! Ach'Su!" The slave began to run as fast as the chains around his legs let him. The whip caught him in the back but it was Ratface that gave Kavi pause.

The slaver's face drained of blood as he looked up at the sky.

That's when Kavi smelt burnt butter.

13

Ach'Su

Kavi's mouth went dry but he hefted the pickaxe in front of him like a shield and set his feet. The creature flying towards them was hideous. It looked like a mixture between a lion and a vulture, a darker form of the old legends of griffons Kavi read about as a child, but the proportions were all wrong. It looked like the lion was emerging from the body of the vulture as if the vulture body was too small to contain it. The vulture wings were large but not near large enough to keep the enormous body of the emerging lion aloft. There had to be another force involved.

Kavi trembled as the creature the slave called an Ach'Su dove towards them. Time seemed to slow. The Ach'Su had four legs rather than the two of a bird. Each leg ended in a series of talons, but not the talons of a bird. There were five claws instead of the three of a raptor. In lieu of a dewclaw, the farthest talon up the leg was thumb-like. This had to be the creature that created the macabre shrine they had visited the previous week. *Was that only a week ago?* These errant thoughts fled as the whoosh of giant wings passed like a tempest overhead.

The Ach'Su's target was the running slave and Kavi didn't have time to regret the relief that flooded through him. He stared in horror as talons pierced into the slave's lashed back and picked him from the ground. The beast bit into the man's shoulder, ignoring the screams and thrashing of its victim. It gulped down the meat as it banked and flew back the way it came.

Ratface sighed in relief but the other two slaves furiously started digging. They dug as if the earth held answers. One of the slaves looked at Kavi and the Vonderian and yelled in common, "Dig! Fast, you dig."

Kavi slammed the pick down several times to broaden the hole. "Why?" he asked.

The slave didn't look at him as he shoveled dirt behind him like a badger on suli. "Ach'Su always strike twice. First time for food, second time for fun."

Ratface must have believed him. "Tuvani, bring the crossbows!" he shouted. Kavi risked a look back. The big gladiator rushed their way with two large crossbows in hand.

Kavi slammed into the earth in earnest. As the latrine trench grew, he risked a glance to the sky. The giant beast flew over one of the mesas in the distance. The body in it's front claws dangled like a perverted marionette.

The Vonderian used his shovel to remove the earth Kavi softened with the pick. They got into a rhythm and the hole grew to knee-depth.

Kavi heard Ratface whisper, "Great gods above."

He looked to the sky and saw the falling body of the slave. Even at a kilometer away, they heard the wet squelch of the body hitting the ground. Then the monster banked back towards their position.

"Slaves in front of pit," yelled Tuvani. "Wizard boy, if you have spells now is time to use them."

The two remaining slaves ignored the command and continued to dig. Even when Scar snapped the whip, they lay at the base of the hole.

Ratface drew his sword and stabbed one of the men through the back. "Tuvani said out," said Ratface. "Have chance at living in front of pit or die in hole. Your choice."

Kavi looked at the Vonderian who nodded. They stepped in front of the pit with the last remaining slave.

"Can I have a real weapon?" Kavi asked.

"That pickaxe is real enough!" yelled Tuvani.

Kavi took a deep breath and felt his pulse slow. He cycled his breath in line with his thoughts. This was a pre-battle meditation he learned as a child from his mother. *Move like wind, strike like fire, defend like earth, parry like water.* The old mantra sharpened his senses and some of the fear left him.

He felt more than heard the Vonderian match his breath. The man must have seen combat before. They breathed in unison and on the next out breath the Vonderian whispered, "I'll counter magical attacks, you cover the physical."

Kavi slapped the handle of his pickaxe in agreement.

The Ach'Su flew closer and again started its dive. This time, Kavi was certain they were the target. He gripped the pickaxe and took a two-handed axe stance Bastion warriors learned in their first year. Time slowed again and Kavi looked to their monstrous opponent. Their eyes met. He flinched at how human the Ach'Su's eyes appeared. Even at this distance, he could sense immense pain from the beast.

As the beast's dive picked up speed, it opened its mouth to roar. A cone of blackness rippled out to accompany the mind-numbing shriek. Kavi heard the twang of two crossbows. He saw the bolts disintegrate as they passed into the cone of darkness.

"That is probably not good," Tuvani boomed in common as the men reloaded.

The Vonderian stepped in front of Kavi and held his arms in front of him like a wrestler awaiting a charge. He stared down the beast. When the cone hit the Vonderian it bounced back towards the Ach'Su. Even the Ach'Su seemed surprised by this development. It pulled up from its dive at the last second to avoid its own darkness.

As the Ach'Su wheeled away for another pass Kavi heard the Vonderian gasp. He looked at the man and was shocked to see his fair skin had darkened as if he were rubbed with charcoal. His eyes were a grainy black.

"You ok?" Kavi asked.

"So strong," the man whispered. His blond hair was matted in sweat and those disconcerting black eyes sparkled like the cosmos. "But you have to be able to see. That's what we're missing. They can't see from the inside." The Vonderian reached for his eyes but passed out in a heap before his hands made it to his face.

Kavi shuddered at the similarity and tone of the Vonderian's words to Holden's. He looked to the sky and saw the Ach'Su readying for another pass.

Kavi stepped in front of the man's unconscious form and readied himself. *Move like wind, strike like fire, defend like earth, parry like water.* As the beast dove, it did not use the darkness attack. Kavi assumed it needed time to regenerate the beam of hatred. This was going to be a physical attack. His turn.

Kavi avoided the front talons with a blazingly fast sidestep. He struck and scored a hit against the beast's flank. Kavi felt grim satisfaction as the beast's blood splattered his face. He spat out the drops that landed inside his open mouth. He shifted again and avoided the back talons which struck even as the beast took to the air again.

Kavi shouted in defiance. Then the blood from the creature began to burn and his shout turned to a scream. He wiped at his face and spat but the pain magnified. He distantly heard two more crossbow bolts fire as his vision narrowed. He felt his body collapse and he fell on top of the Vonderian.

* * *

He blinked his eyes open. A half span in front of his nose the vacant recesses of a skull stared at him. Kavi sat up and shuffled backwards. The orbs were not quite vacant, candlelight flickered through the empty sockets. As Kavi continued to skitter back, his hands rubbed against other bones. The skull he faced on awakening wasn't the only one. Seven others were placed in a semicircle. Kavi woke in the middle of that circle.

He jumped to his feet and his head began to throb. Dread settled in the pit of his stomach as he realized where he was. The nest. He heard a loud rustling and looked to the cave entrance, terrified of what he would see.

It wasn't the Ach'Su though. It was a man. When the man shuffled into the candlelight Kavi had his second shock since awakening. "Holden?" he asked.

The man ignored the question and Kavi's mind raced. How could Holden be here? He should be under the care of the physicians in Stonecrest. It didn't make sense.

The man staggered towards him, his movement jerky and unnatural. Kavi looked into the vacant gaps where his eyes should be and saw candlelight there too. *How in Krom's name?* Holden held up his eyes and gave Kavi a little bow. "Hello young cub, now do you see?"

"No, I don't see anything," said Kavi. "How are you doing this? Why are there flames behind your eyes?"

Holden grinned until his mouth took up his entire face. When he opened it to laugh, Kavi saw teeth sharpened to points. There were far more teeth in his mouth than any man had the right to. When Holden stopped laughing he held his eyes to look at Kavi again. "They have to be on the outside to see. I'll tell you what I see young lion, a choice was made, a snake was played. Growth for wonder. An even trade? Perhaps. The only way to know is to see. Knowledge for happiness. Six in one, a chicken in the other. A dose of tru and you'll understand," said Holden.

"Well, I'm glad we cleared that up," said Kavi. The comment came to his lips before he could stifle it. Fear had taken control of his mouth.

Holden's shark-like mouth split into that horrible grin. "Tempering requires no understanding. The marked begat the shift, the shift begat a new era. The mewl of the cub becomes the roar of a generation. The way is open and you've already walked through it. There are no backsies. Your pace quickens and events precipitate in accordance."

Kavi rubbed his eyes with his hands trying to clear the bizarre scene. When he removed his hands, Holden still stood there. "Why must you speak in riddles?"

Holden cocked his head. "Is there another way? The change has begun young cub. I hope you're fast enough to stay ahead of this new age." Holden pointed to his temple. "The connections up here have been rewritten. Trauma and violence are the key but they are not the answer."

"I don't understand."

"Of course you don't. It's not going to be clear until you take them out. In the meantime, let me help you see."

Holden threw one of his eyes to Kavi. Kavi screamed as the disgusting thing shifted in the air to keep looking at him as it flew. Kavi had no control over his body as his hands reached out to catch the horrible missile.

14

The Southern Market

When Kavi opened his eyes it was to the familiar rumble of the caged wagon. He sat up quickly and looked around. No cave, no Holden. It must have been a dream. One of the creepiest dreams he'd ever had, but only a dream. Right?

Kavi closed his eyes to counter the wooziness caused by sitting up. The stench in the caged cart was worse than normal. He reached a hand to his cheek where the Ach'Su's blood had struck and winced at the raw skin. He rubbed gingerly at his face, neck and chest, searching for other injuries but found nothing.

He sat up straighter and pawed at his face in panic. Nothing but the fresh wounds. The scars that had been constant companions since he entered the Bastion were gone. Kavi pulled at his chains to get enough slack to continue his investigation, ignoring the scowls from the other prisoners. He probed the area below his left armpit to find the scar the pine branch gave him when he tested his father's aerial harness. Gone. *How?* He was certain the slavers hadn't healed him. Besides, he never heard of a healer that could remove a scar. Even Astrans didn't have that power.

Kavi released the slack of the chains and slumped back, exhausted.

When his hand hit the wagon bed it squelched in a reddish black liquid that pooled around him. Blood? No, the only wounds he had were the burns on his face. He noticed that his right hand, which he used for the body exploration, was covered in a thin film of the same stuff. The liquid was coming from him! The stench was horrid, a mix between sulfur and rancid meat. He rubbed a drop of the liquid between forefinger and thumb. It was syrupy in texture.

What had the Ach'Su done to him? Was he struck by that darkness attack after he passed out? That didn't make any sense. That darkness was terrifying and he was sure it wasn't a healing force. He took a deep breath and flexed against his chains. He was exhausted from the ordeal, yet he felt stronger. He flexed again. A lot stronger, like he had just done several months of Suli Elite workouts.

By Krom, that stench was awful. He didn't know how he secreted this nastiness or how the other prisoners could handle it. Kavi looked at the prisoners and noticed that they did their best to turn their heads away from him.

He looked across the wagon at the tall Vonderian. The man didn't have scars before so it was hard to tell if he was healed but there was no syrupy pool beneath him.

"Are you okay?" Kavi whispered as loudly as he thought he could get away with.

The Vonderian's head snapped up and found his eyes. "What do you think?" he whispered back.

The iron bar struck the cage next to the Vonderian's head. "The only reason that one didn't hit you is you saved us back there wizard boy," said Scar in his raspy voice. "No talking, even in whispers."

Scar pointed at Kavi. "That goes for you too rich boy." Scar wrinkled his nose. "You smell terrible."

The 'wizard boy' continued to stare at Kavi. He mouthed silent words at Kavi for several minutes. Kavi did his best to understand

and reply. He finally understood that the man's name was Pip. Other than that, very little got through and the pantomime became progressively more frustrating. Eventually, they threw their hands up in exasperation. This tugged on the chains of the other prisoners which scored them a round of ugly looks. If the mood in a slave carriage on the way to market could get darker, this was the way to do it.

The bumps in the rutted road jolted the prisoners as Kavi worked to regain his bearings. Through pantomime with the woman across from him, he learned he had been unconscious for a day and a half. The attack by the Ach'Su must have forced an abbreviated camp to get out of the beast's hunting range. It's the only way this group could have made up enough time for the red rock canyons to the east to be replaced with the dull flatness and sharp smell of the Salt Wastes.

During his time in the Eagles, he heard scouting reports which taught him the Salt Wastes were new to his generation. The Salt Flats had always been far to the east. Once, they were seen as a resource for desert travelers and chefs the world round. A visit to the Flats was an opportunity to see fascinating desert life in an otherworldly habitat. Recently, scouts raised alarms that the Flats had spread. As they spread, the exotic life they once supported disappeared. The salt pulled from the Flats was no longer edible even after refinement. A corruption had invaded.

Many of the best academic minds worked to understand the problem. Since the spread was worse far to the east, it hadn't threatened the farmland of the major Garden Cities. Since it wasn't an immediate threat, the Garden City governments chose not to get involved. Legend has it, the Salt Waste moniker was given after the Krommian General of Agriculture and Logistics said to one of his aides, 'Don't bother me about Salt, Waste someone else's time with this nonsense.'

He looked over the desolate landscape and wondered if the Garden

Cities made a big mistake.

His thoughts were interrupted by a small patrol of riders passing their slave caravan. The riders looked disdainfully at the slavers but did nothing to help. The slave trade was reviled but not outlawed. Slavery was illegal in the Garden Cities but thrived in the peripheries. As people moved from the Cities, they realized frontier work was hard labor. The ruthlessly enterprising found that getting the less fortunate to do the work made for a better lifestyle. Especially when that work was done for free.

The number of travelers passing the caravan increased throughout the day. Kavi's small hope of rescue diminished each time they were passed with nary a look in their direction. When they began to share the road with a stream of travelers Kavi knew they must be getting close to their destination.

The Southern Market sprouted around an oasis like a desert bloom. It had grown far beyond the small, spring-fed lake within it's first several years of existence. What started as a temporary settlement on trading days had become a permanent trading hub. It was roughly equidistant from Krom, Loam and Brickolage so it catered to a wide variety of cultures and tastes. It was far outside the major Garden Cities so was beholden to no official government laws or regulations. To call it lawless would have been a mistake. Violent crime was bad for business. There were strict penalties that came with banishment from the market for a period of years. Anyone caught stealing or breaking the terms of a deal was strung up. There was zero tolerance for crooked purse strings.

Kavi couldn't believe the sheer volume of noise as they neared the gates. It sounded like war being fought paces from where he sat. He supposed many considered trade as a form of battle.

Guards stopped them at the gates. They wore patchwork uniforms except for wristbands stamped with an image of the marketplace.

Tuvani brought his column of slaves to a halt as he approached the guard checking trade licenses.

The guard looked at Tuvani and his merchandise and wrinkled his nose with disgust. "Slaver," he said. "What is the purpose of your visit and how long do you expect to stay?"

Tuvani responded to the disgust with raised eyebrows. "Guard," Tuvani replied, matching tone. "I come to sell this merchandise in the stocks tomorrow." He pointed to the wagon. "The premium livestock will auction on the Titan's floor later that evening."

Tuvani passed the guard his trading token and manifest. The guard made a big show about testing their authenticity. He used two Bricker devices to scan both the token and the list. He grunted as the device showed both identifications passed and waved them through.

If the noise outside were a thunderstorm, the noise within was a hurricane. Hawkers and buskers fought over street corners. The women from the balconies of the ramshackle brothels lining the street pulled down colored blouses to extend cleavage to lewd degree. Tuvani smiled as several waved and called him by name.

The main thoroughfare was primarily used by traders of larger merchandise like animals and slaves. Kavi winced as one of the poorly clad slaves from their caravan had her foot stepped on by a goat passing the other way. She barely reacted. At least it wasn't a cow.

Other traders used the cobblestone boulevards to the east and west. They were crowded with more people, but one didn't have to worry about stepping in pig droppings. Appearance and status were important to traders. Nothing said country bumpkin like boots splashed with manure.

The caravan made it's way to an open area in the far eastern side of the marketplace. Slave pens filled the landscape and depression settled over the area in a sweat filled fog. The heat wouldn't abate until late evening but Kavi had grown used to sweat dripping off the end of his nose. He wasn't sure where the perspiration came from as they only got two ladles of water a day. The sweat bothered him only when it dripped past the raw skin on his cheeks and lips.

Tuvani moved his caravan of walking slaves into one of the pens with Ratface's help. "You sure you don't want both of us to escort this lot to the Titan with you boss?" asked the weaselly man.

"No," said Tuvani. "I need you here to keep an eye on the stock."

Ratface hung his head.

"Don't worry, once we drop this lot off at the Titan, you have first leave to visit the ladies," said Tuvani.

The weaselly smile from Ratface brought another round of deep belly laughs from Tuvani.

Titan's Square was aptly named. Not only was it an enormous stone plaza but it was towered over by a giant statue. What made the statue unique was that it was not of one of the gods or even a historical figure from the past. The subject of the statue was still alive. Azis Manari ran the auctions that took place every seven days in the middle of the square. He was the leader of one of the original four Bedouin tribes that met each year at the oasis that became the Southern Market. Azis' vision and drive turned the Southern Market into what it was today. His successor to the tribe he left behind was the first to call him the Titan of Trade. That title adorned the plaque below the enormous statue.

Carts were not allowed on Titan's Square. Neither were animals. Kavi was surprised the sale of slaves was permitted on the well kept square.

Pip kept trying to get Kavi's attention. When he did, the magicker did his best to communicate an escape plan to Kavi. When they opened the carriage to transfer them to the holding cells Pip would make his move. Kavi nodded his agreement but noticed Scar watching the exchange. The jailer smiled as he watched the Vonderian become more and more animated.

Hopes of escape were dashed as the caged wagon pulled up to a well guarded pavilion on the edge of the east side of the square. Thirty armed men and women garbed in matching black chain link armor guarded the pavilion. Half helped unload wagons while the other half kept a steely eye on the prisoners, hands resting on the hilts of weapons. They were predators waiting for prey to bolt.

Their cart joined two others in a queue. Kavi watched the guards efficiently unhook one slave at a time from each wagon. They ushered the slaves down a ramp which faded into a tunnel under Titan's Square.

When their cart was next in the queue one of the soldier's approached Tuvani. The woman moved with a deadly grace Kavi had seen in only one other woman, his mother. "Gladiator," she said with a nod of respect. "You find us any worthwhile additions?"

Tuvani returned the nod in an uncharacteristic dimming of his usual boisterousness. "Mareena," said Tuvani. "Your beauty is matched only by your deadliness in the ring."

The woman didn't react to the compliment. Her eyes moved to those chained in the cart. When her eyes met his, Kavi felt a flash of pain in his left temple. The gaze was invasive, probing. Her eyes flickered to the pool of liquid he sat in and the pain in his temple intensified. He stilled his mind. *Move like wind, strike like fire.* One of her lips twitched upwards in the hint of a smile before she moved to the Bricker sitting next to him. The man stiffened as that same probing gaze ruffled through his mind.

"A handful. I also have an interesting story to tell about a run in with an Ach'Su," said Tuvani.

That caught her attention. "You had a run in with one of the Marked?" she asked.

Tuvani spat to the side of the cart at the name. He nodded. "Too many foul creatures coming out of the Wastes these days Mareena. It's bad for business. I lost three slaves in five minutes and it would have been more if it weren't for the Vonderian and the rich kid." Tuvani pointed to Pip and Kavi.

"Tell me every detail," she said. "Even little things you don't think are important."

Tuvani launched into the tale.

"Well, that is interesting," she said when Tuvani finished his story. "How on earth did a Void Mage and a Krommian hybrid scare off one of the Marked all by themselves?"

"Come now, Mareena, me and my men fired at least twelve bolts into that damn thing," said Tuvani.

She snorted. "You might as well have thrown cabbages at it. I've seen one of the Marked eliminate half a squad of League trained soldiers using every trick to kill it. Never did it show signs of pain no matter the weapon that struck it. And you're telling me a Vonderian and a Krom spawn armed with a pickaxe caused it to scream and flee?"

"I swear it, milady," said Scar as Tuvani let his indignation leave him sputtering. "The boss has a way of...," he searched for a word that wouldn't anger either party, "...enhancing his stories, yes. But I was standing next to these two as they dug the latrine. It happened as Tuvani said."

She looked at the smaller man and nodded. She turned back to Tuvani. "Quit the offended act gladiator, your job is to a put on a show and you do it damned well. Besides, if this story is true, these two are going to make you a lot of gold."

That statement turned Tuvani's staged outrage into a grin. "How much gold is a lot of gold would you say?"

* * *

The cavernous rooms under Titan's square were chiseled directly out of the bedrock. Huge stone struts led to arches that provided the massive support needed for the square above. These underground rooms bustled with activity.

Kavi went from the tunnel to a holding room filled with at least twenty other slaves. Guards in black, wearing black whips coiled and belted to their sides, came in and told them to strip.

A small Astran monk protested at the treatment. "I will not. Lord Astra has forbidden us from baring our naked bodies before others," said the small man.

One of the guards uncoiled his whip and sent a lash at the monk's back. "Slaves are not permitted religion," said the guard. The small man screamed.

Two guards forcefully removed the man's dull gray robe, now spackled with blood. The bald man was entirely hairless. Kavi had heard the rumors. The god Astra demanded each believer perform purification rituals that stripped them of all hair. He'd never seen it until now. Kavi's eyes locked on the stark wound weeping blood down the man's back. The monk muttered to himself and Kavi's eyes widened as the lash began to close. Apparently their healing abilities weren't rumors either.

The Astran caught Kavi's look and shot him a venomous glare. "Avert your filthy eyes, heathen," said the monk.

Kavi looked away. There was enough trouble down here without looking for more.

From the holding pen, they were led one at a time to a room labeled Cleansing Chamber in the common tongue. Kavi perked up for the first time in the last week at the thought of a bath even if it was a bucket of cold water dumped over his head.

When he stepped into the Cleansing Chamber the entrance door shut behind him. Kavi found himself in a small circular room. A loud noise from several holes in the wall preceded a rush of hot air strong enough to cause Kavi to grip the metal bars placed on either side. The air was followed by a stinging wind filled with sand. Kavi shut his eyes and covered his privates as the sand scoured the dirt, blood and syrupy liquid from him. After a minute that felt like an hour, the wind was replaced with a vacuum. The sand and grime were sucked back into recessed holes below the large blowers.

Kavi felt numb. Each step of the dehumanizing transformation from human to slave was worse than the last. He knew it was intentional – a premeditated path meant to destroy defiance. He hated himself when he admitted it was working.

No! He was made of stronger stuff than that. He straightened his back.

When he left the Cleansing Chamber, a guard handed him a small set of canvas shorts which he pulled on. He was then led down a long hallway of cells. The inhabitants were from all parts of Grendar. Every Garden City was represented but the majority seemed to be from Loam, Brickolage and Krom. Most of the Krommians had been badly beaten. Kavi wasn't surprised. The warrior culture demanded men that prized fighting over thinking.

One large man was beaten within an inch of his life. He lay motionless on the floor of his cell. Kavi's eyes widened as he recognized a scar on the man's chest. Kavi pulled from the guards holding him and stepped to the cell.

"Grim?"

15

The Draft

The guard to his left kicked Kavi in the back of the knee which dropped his face into the rising knee of the guard to his right. Kavi's vision exploded into white and red stars. He stopped resisting and let the guards lead him back to the middle of the hallway.

Grim hadn't responded, still unconscious.

Kavi looked around wondering if he'd see Nettie or Carlin in one of the other cells. "Eyes forward," snapped the guard on his left.

Kavi's mind flittered over a hundred escape scenarios in a matter of seconds. Every one ended in failure. This group was too well armed and too organized. If he had a chance at escape it wouldn't come without a giant distraction. He looked at the well lit and well patrolled hallways. Not likely. Thoughts of escape would have to wait until he understood the situation a little better.

The guards dropped him off in his cell which had a small pallet and a small chair. It could have been worse, at least he didn't have to sit on bare stone.

He cooperated as the guards removed his chains and shut the cell door. Kavi sat and began to meditate. If what Tuvani said was true, the auction was tomorrow evening. With nothing else to do, Kavi resolved to understand if anything else changed since he fought the Ach'Su.

* * *

There was no visible passage of time in the underground cells. Yet Kavi knew the auction was close when a group of healers walked down the cell-lined halls. Individual healers peeled off from the group to consult with each captive.

The woman who entered Kavi's cell had done away with traditional healing robes. She wore sensible slacks and a fitted blouse with cuffs pulled back so as not to hinder examinations. Her lack of eyebrows gave her the egg-like features of the Astran at intake but she had long flowing reddish gold hair. Her clothes aligned with the black motif the soldiers employed, but her top claimed a sense of rebellion in the yellow embroidery around cuffs and lapels.

That rebellion did not make her an ally. Kavi caught her eye but saw no empathy as she approached, only clinical curiosity.

She grabbed a small stool and sat in front of him. "Do you mind if I inspect your wounds?"

Kavi fixed his eyes on her. "That's the first time someone's asked my permission for something since my capture."

"Don't get used to it," she said. "I only ask because it helps me get my job done faster." She pushed a strawberry lock out of the way and Kavi saw the whole mass of hair shift slightly. A wig then. Her fingers rubbed over the still raw wounds on his cheek where the Ach'Su's blood struck.

Kavi winced.

Her fingers turned ice cold for a moment which Kavi assumed

was healing magic. She frowned. "What did you say caused these wounds?"

Kavi scrunched up his cheek. Yep, still hurt. The healing hadn't worked. Kavi contemplated a moment of rebellion but stifled it. Regardless of motive, the healer was here to help him. "The natives called it an Ach'Su. But I heard the leader of the guards outside call it a Marked."

She pulled back for a moment and gave him a long look. "So you're the one. Marked by the Marked as it were," she said with an indulgent smile.

Kavi did not indulge. "Could the Ach'Su have healed me? When I woke up after the battle I was covered in blackish-red goo and my sicari scars were gone. I also felt stronger."

She scooted her stool back and examined him from several paces away. "I doubt the Marked healed you. I've heard rumors about what the League calls an evolution, but it only happens to their greatest warriors. I've never witnessed it and it always sounded like propaganda to me. Maybe that's what happened to you."

"Is that why your healing didn't work?" he asked moving his fingers back to his cheek.

She shrugged. "Doubtful. If you have evolved, the propaganda claims you'd heal even faster, so it more likely has to do with the beast. We know very little about the Marked. They are a new intrusion on the world and we have virtually no data." She stood up and turned to the hall. "Craig!" she shouted.

A younger healer walked in to the cell. He wore the trappings of a traditional healer, black robe swishing as he walked. He looked down his nose at the female healer, barely containing a sneer as he looked at her wig. Kavi could feel the waves of self-importance rippling off the young man. He gave her a short bow devoid of respect.

She ignored his posturing and pointed to Kavi. "This is the one that had the run in with the Marked. You worked with the wounded of Senet Company didn't you?"

He nodded.

"Did you find necrosis in the wounds?"

"I did. I had to remove the necrotic tissue entirely before I could heal anything," the man said. "One of the wounds proved impossible to heal until I realized it had infected the man's kidney. I had to remove half the kidney until any healing worked."

The woman nodded. "Thank you. That is what I assumed."

He inclined his head towards Kavi. "Would you like me to take a look at him?"

"I've got it. I figured I'd ask before torturing this young man. You know they don't allow us to numb the pain here."

The self-important man left and the woman looked at Kavi as she pulled out a small scalpel. "For whatever reason, the League believes pain builds character. I'm sorry, this is really going to hurt before I can get in there and heal it properly. Do your best not to move."

* * *

Kavi moved shaking hands over the tightened skin of his cheek and lips. The pain during the procedure was excruciating and seemed to last for hours. The physician finished over an hour ago but he still shuddered at the memory of her cutting into his face. Sicari scars hurt, but at least he got to hold the knife.

Shortly after the healers completed their rounds the cells began to empty as prisoners were led up to the auction floor. Anytime the door to the ramp to Titan's Square opened, Kavi could here amplified voices speaking followed by loud cheers and boos.

The early auctions went quickly and within an hour the cells were nearly empty. Kavi craned his head inside the bars. He couldn't see a lot of details but guessed there were only about ten prisoners left. Still no sign of Grim or the Vonderian who faced the Ach'Su with him. Based on the attention he received since Tuvani told Mareena the story of the Ach'Su, Kavi wasn't surprised to be part of the main event.

His first reaction was pride. As if fetching a good price was a measure of his own worth. He banged his head against the cell door. The thought was pathetic. He dug his fingernails into his hand until the skin threatened to draw blood. Even now, about to be sold as a slave to the highest bidder, he hoped to please. No more. No more fulfilling other people's expectations. No more playing by the rules of polite society. No more following orders.

The irony was not lost on Kavi. It took the forfeiture of all freedom to find the beginning of liberation from the velvet chains which bound him to family and station. The decision made, Kavi felt all apprehension of the auction vanish. Come what may, he would face it standing on his own two feet.

And yet, a sneaking suspicion gnawed at his consciousness. *You've made vows like this before. They held right up until you were tested.* Kavi pushed back at the ghost of Kavi past.

No more.

* * *

Seven more prisoners were pulled from their cells before the guards came for Kavi. Like the prisoners before him, they didn't bother chaining or clothing him in more than his canvas shorts.

The contingent of guards assigned to Kavi had increased. Rather than the three who escorted the previous slaves up the ramp, Kavi had six. Kavi of yesterday would have felt some level of satisfaction that he posed a threat.

All he felt now was disdain.

Kavi emerged from the ramp on to the main square and the tumult of sound hit him like a wave in rough surf. Bright lights assaulted his eyes. After the dimness of the underground cells, Kavi had to shield his eyes to make out anything more than blurry shapes.

A stage had been crafted in the center of the square with seats on all sides. Bright lights lit the stage, casting the guards who stood upon it in heroic light. The previous slave was being walked down the stairs of the stage. Kavi watched as the woman was led towards a squat building off the western edge of the square. He lost her as she passed behind the bleachers.

Two of the guards brought a podium from under the stage and placed it at the center. The motions were practiced, making it clear they had been doing it all night. A smaller man stepped to the podium and clicked a Bricker device in his hand.

"Well, that was exciting, wasn't it folks?" he asked in a voice that boomed across the square. He waited for a moment as the crowd roared. "The top ten draft picks never disappoint. When the vines burst through the stone in the center of the Square, I thought the Titan himself was going to have a fit. Good thing his sense of humor is as sharp as his business sense." He pointed at the man seated at the base of the statue.

The crowd's eyes shifted and the Titan nodded with a tight smile.

"Not to worry, Magnificence, I'm sure the League will replace that priceless stone by the end of the week. As eager as I know you all are to bid on these fine specimens, I want to remind you that the private auction for the top ten starts in Maldoy's Hall at the stroke

of midnight. Minimum bid is a thousand gold. If you don't have a
platinum chit, either get one or enjoy the rest of the night in our fine
restaurants and brothels."

Great, thought Kavi. This wasn't even the auction. Just another
show to demonstrate his value. He sighed.

"Next up, we have the half Krommian, half Bricker with the sculpted
body of a young Antonius. This young man was trained in the famed
Krommian Bastion before serving four years in the Silver Eagles where
he retired with full honors."

Boos and jeers of 'rich kid' and 'lordling' greeted this last pro-
nouncement. Even this far south, people knew the Eagles were
commissioned by those with money or station. Kavi grinned as he
realized the jeers didn't bother him.

The man held up a hand to quiet the crowd. "Yes, yes I know.
But isn't it fun to see those once so high, laid so low?" The crowd
responded with a wave of cheers. "What makes the rich kid interesting
is not that he was caught when he solved Korbah's conundrum. Which,
give credit where credit is due, is pretty impressive," he paused for
the crowd but they didn't bite. "But because he took on an Ach'Su
with a pickaxe while his legs were bound."

This time the crowd went silent. They had heard the rumors.

"And won," said the emcee, the words crushing in their volume
over the silent square. "He didn't kill the Marked," the man had to
pause as half the audience spat on whatever empty ground they could
find. Several in the crowd cursed as flecks of spittle found clothing or
skin. "But he did strike it hard enough to draw blood and cause it to
flee."

Whispers and denials replaced the spitting. The emcee held up his
hand again. "I swear it is true. There were over ten eyewitnesses and
our very own healers examined his wounds. They confirmed they
were made by the acidic blood of the Ach'Su. That's why he is our

number three candidate in the draft." The emcee's arms slid to point at Kavi.

A spotlight framed his mostly naked body. He resisted the urge to rub his hands over the tightened skin where the healer had mended those wounds. Instead, Kavi spat on the ground.

"Nice to see he still has some fire, isn't it?" asked the emcee. "Tonight, we'll test that fire. The top three candidates will show off their skills not against three of our finest...but against five."

The crowd cheered.

The guards led Kavi to the steps as others grabbed the podium and moved it under the stage. Kavi climbed the stairs and allowed himself to be led to the center of the stage. Four men and a woman spread out around him. Kavi rolled his eyes and sat down. He wasn't going to play their game.

The defiance caused the crowd to boo. The emcee stepped in front of the stage and activated his Bricker device again. "Gotta love these rich kids, don't you folks?" he said theatrically. "While they're not motivated like the rest of us, the League always has levers to pull."

Two of the guards protecting the stairs walked under the stage and dragged out a man. Kavi recognized him instantly - it was the only surviving slave that stood with him and the Vonderian against the Ach'Su. He carried the same look of abject terror on his face now as he did when they faced the beast. The knives hovering near the man's throat were cleverly obscured so Kavi could see them but the crowd couldn't.

Kavi shook his head and stood up. His defiance was not worth this man's life. The crowd cheered and the man sagged with relief. The guards dragged the slave back to where they were keeping him.

Kavi took several deep breaths and looked at the five surrounding him. Three were Krommian warriors and would fight with a style he knew well. The Bricker pulled out two devices, holding one in each hand. Kavi recognized one as an imperium trap and the other as a smoke screen. He would have to watch the woman. She was Vonderian and held a steel capped war staff like she knew how to use it. The real threat was her magic. Kavi had very little experience fighting magickers.

He didn't feel the least bit nervous. He didn't need to prove anything. He would only perform to save the slave's life. If he took a beating, so be it. He'd taken beatings before. Kavi took a deep breath and let the mantra come. *Move like wind, strike like fire, defend like earth, parry like water.* The calm swept over him and he breathed in his surroundings.

The stage was sturdy under him. He could feel the slight impact of each warrior's weight as they stood on the structure. He registered the emcee yelling, "Start the fight!" but it didn't matter.

* * *

Kavi steps out of time.

The first Krommian warrior charges exactly as Kavi knows he will. The goal is to get Kavi to step into the clutches of the second Krommian. Kavi can tell the two have been fighting together for years and this is a regular move. Kavi has seen the choreography ahead of time. This is a play that he not only stars in but also writes.

He moves exactly the correct distance to the right. He sticks out a foot to trip the charging Krommian who crashes into his partner. They roll off the stage in a heap and a crunch.

Cue the groans from the crowd, thinks Kavi. The crowd complies.

Kavi realizes he is having fun.

Next comes the Bricker with his traps. Kavi knows he will throw the imperium first and then the smoke screen to hide the motion of the

Vonderian. Kavi has no problem plucking the imperium trap from the air as if it were handed to him. With a flick of his wrist, he redirects it at the feet of the Vonderian. He knows it will go off and stun her for the duration of the fight.

With a slap, Kavi hits the smoke screen at the face of the last standing Krommian. He knows it will blow up in the man's eyes but it shouldn't blind the soldier for more than a day or two. With a sidekick, he sends the reeling Krommian off the stage to land on top of his fellow warriors.

The only warrior remaining is a pale Bricker who is quickly stepping away from Kavi. The crowd boos as the man falls off the back of the stage.

Kavi walks towards the Vonderian who's crimson eyes fill with panic. She is unable to move so Kavi lightly grabs the staff from clenched hands and uses it to gently push her off the stage. The crowd has gone silent.

Kavi bows his head and flips off the stage.

The flow of time resumes.

* * *

Soldiers in black surrounded him and he raised the staff in a defensive stance but no longer knew what would happen next. He lashed out and missed. He dodged as one of the men swung a cudgel at his hip. He didn't see the strike from the blackjack that hit him in the left temple.

The world went dark.

16

The League

The dark room had the tasteful elegance of the long time wealthy, something rarely seen near the Southern Market. The smoke of fine cigars and the clink of ice chilling twenty-year-old scotch brought a liveliness to a room used only twice a year. The Owner's Lounge above Maldoy's Hall was active tonight. Not only because of the Draft and the Auction but because the owners would be discussing rule changes.

The Majordomo of the League was a wizened woman with still-broad shoulders and the sharp wit required to wrangle the oversized personalities in the room. "If the gentleman and gentlewoman of the Risk and Mehen Companies would please find your seats, we will begin," she said in a soft voice which still carried over the conversations in the room.

Each Owner was allowed one aide for these meetings, a second in command to take notes and provide counsel. This permitted the group to fit around the large oak table which spanned half the room. The League expanded three years ago to allow two more Companies to compete. With the expansion came the predictable grumbling from the six established Companies.

The expansion was necessary with the capture of a fourth Sage. The six Companies could no longer field enough teams to successfully manage and contain all open Quests (and corresponding League competitions) the Sages produced. Even when they dug into their Triple-A squads, the Companies lost too many team members. While most of the Owners saw the sense in expansion, it took a directive from the leadership of the Collective to bully the holdouts. With the directive came the Majordomo. She was a not-so-subtle warning. While the Owners held a huge amount of power over the League, the League still answered to the Collective.

"Before the meeting begins, I'd like to lodge an official complaint about the barbaric nature in which we are still testing Candidates during the draft," said a tall man from the end of the table.

"Can it, Rowan. Three Companies tried your neuromanced simulation technology two years ago. It was an unmitigated disaster," said the woman from the Mehen Company, the tattoos around her neck and eyes flashing with each word.

"Mehen, this is your last warning," said the Majordomo. "The Collective will no longer tolerate your flippant violation of using personal names in these meetings. Your next violation will result in Team Mehen forfeiting the first Quest encounter of the season. Am I clear?"

The woman and owner of Mehen Company rolled her eyes but nodded to the Majordomo.

"Are we still that concerned with security, even here in the owner's box?" asked another man. The white ascot he wore magnified a tanned and handsome face. He held a crystal tumbler filled with three fingers of scotch.

"That is correct, Wari. Until we capture this fifth Sage, she will continue to feed information to the criminal group known as the Liberators. As far as we know, this Sage is more powerful than the other four combined and her clairvoyance hasn't driven her quite as mad as the others. We must assume anything we say has the potential of being divined and shared with our enemies," said the Majordomo.

"The fifth Sage is a woman?" said Wari with raised eyebrows that looked combed. "I hadn't heard that."

"That goes a long way to understanding why this Sage is so powerful," said a small woman with a raven embroidered in green on her black velvet jacket. "It's been what, three centuries since the last female Sage?"

"That is correct, Sugoroku," said the Majordomo. "Every female Sage is a harbinger of change. If you remember your history, it was Constance the Clear that foresaw the creation of the Collective itself."

"And with all the resources the Collective claims access to, how have we not captured this Sage yet?" asked a grossly rotund man puffing on the stub of a cigar.

"Need I spell it out for you, Ch'es? Capturing someone with the power of foresight is not trivial. Every time the Collective closes in and stages a raid, we find we just missed her," said the Majordomo.

"I assume the other Sages are no help?" asked Wari.

Mehen snorted. "Have you seen them lately? All four of 'em are crazier than a bag of cats. My five-year-old can hold a conversation better than those nut jobs."

"Mehen is correct," said an old man with a carefully trimmed goatee. His facial hair was framed by the scars of a long military career. "Even Sage Gerand has lost the ability of coherent thought." He sighed. "A shame. I once considered the man a friend."

"As did I, Lord Go," said the Majordomo. "Sadly, that is the fate of those born with the gift of Sight." She paused for a moment, remembering. "On to less maudlin thoughts. We have plenty to cover this evening. Let me start with the agenda."

The Majordomo pulled out an officious looking scroll case with gold leaf on the end caps. She removed several pieces of paper. "First, we need a plan to handle interruptions from the Liberators or any third party once a Quest has been sanctioned by the League. Especially once the location has been identified and the two Companies to compete have been determined. Second, we need to discuss when and how we start pulling the League out of the shadows. We need a plan to market to commoners and open the betting pools to larger groups. Finally, the Marked. The frequency of their interference is accelerating. We need ideas on how to mitigate the threat." She looked around the table finding eye contact with most. "Any other topics for discussion?"

Many of the owners whispered quietly to their aides affecting a sense of not paying attention to the logistics of the meeting. The Majordomo knew better, these owners were obnoxiously self-centered, but they were also ruthless and intelligent.

"I have no desire to experiment with Risk's neuromanced simulator again, but the man has a point," said Wari. "The draft grows more dangerous each year for the guards we appoint to police it. I could care less when they were cheap mercenaries hired from Azis or any of the outfits from the Markets. Even the lower tier Candidates have little problem handling the mercenaries lately. When it was clear our castoff players were no challenge for the highest draft picks we had to put double A team members on that stage to showcase the Candidate's worth. You saw what this year's crop did to the double As. Between the Krommian hybrid, the Vonderian, the Loamian hellcat and that monster of a Krommian warrior - I now have two promising development players who will never make the professional team. They have permanent injuries even the Loamians can't heal. I put a ton of gold into training those assets and those investments are gone in a single evening. I know I'm not the only one. Something has to change."

Heads nodded around the table. No one wanted to bring it up for fear of admitting weakness but they were all taking losses in the draft. The cost was too high for the potential of bidding on new players that would most likely never make the professional squads.

"Yeah, it sucks," said Ch'es in his preferred common language. "We all hate slagging gold on bad investments but have you noticed how drastically the quality has risen over the last three years? Ever since our first encounter with the Ach'Su..." He held up a hand to forestall the anger building behind the Majordomo's eyes. "My mistake, since our first encounter with the Marked. The Candidates the Collective has found are incredibly powerful."

"And what's the alternative? We don't see how these Candidates perform under pressure?" asked Mehen. "I still don't understand why you're all opposed to giving the guards suli. Yes, it's expensive, but it's a tiny fraction of the suli we pull in from a single completed Quest."

"Maybe there is another way," said the Majordomo thoughtfully. "Let us come back to this when everything else has been discussed. There may be some solutions to be found in how we start to lift the veil of secrecy around the League. Any other topics?"

"Just one," said a bespectacled man in a sharp white suit sitting next to Mehen. "Do we actually need to be here?"

"Whatever do you mean, Senet?" asked the Majordomo.

"Will these be edicts passed down by the Collective, like in our last Owner's meeting, that we need to hop to and obey? Or does our opinion matter? If it's the former, please send those decisions to me in paper form so I can go back to doing something that is not a complete and utter waste of my time."

The Majordomo held the man's gaze for a long time but he didn't flinch. The other owners watched the battle of wills between the two with the same rapt attention they gave the draft. Finally, the Majordomo nodded her head. "I will admit the last meeting was contentious but the Collective made its point. My directive in this meeting is to follow the will of the Owner's Council on all decisions made as a group. While the Collective has ideas, how the League conducts itself is up to the League."

Senet nodded his head. "That's what I needed to hear. Please continue."

"Let's start with handling interruptions by third parties while on Quests, Liberators or otherwise," said the Majordomo.

"Maybe we don't call them the Liberators, even amongst ourselves," said a spindly man who looked emaciated sitting next to the rotund Ch'es. "If we are going to come out from under the veil of secrecy, let's not give another group the moral high ground. We've all played the game in our business dealings. It should be a simple thing to paint them as villains."

"Point well taken, Ur," said Majordomo. "We can put Collective agents on the initiative as well. For now, let's refer to them as the Agitators."

"I propose that if a third player comes on the field during a sanctioned League Quest, both Companies are obligated to halt advances and form an alliance until the third party is destroyed or driven off," said Risk. "That seems to be the most logical approach."

Ch'es laughed. "And if your Company is about to solve the Quest when it happens?" asked the fat man.

"Positions will be recorded and teams will need to return to where they were before the interruption," said Risk.

"You know that is complete horseshit Row-," Mehen caught herself this time. "Risk. You know how competitive the professional players are. They'll never agree to who is where in their advancement."

"Then we'll need an Arbiter," said Go. "An independent mediator whose only job is to track progress. They can be appointed by the Collective."

"The idea has merit. I would prefer they come from a group that is also independent from the Collective," said Senet.

"It's a terrible idea," said Ch'es. "We really want that much oversight on the field of battle?"

"Don't worry greasy pants," said Mehen. "Nobody is going to stop your team's underhanded tactics, only prevent the Agitators from putting a thumb on the scale." A new thought occurred to her. "Wait a second, is that what you were doing all along? You were working with the Liberators?"

Ch'es sputtered, deeply offended.

"That's exactly what he was doing, can you believe this pastry eating son of a Harpstran whore?" Mehen asked.

"Are you upset that he cheated, or that you didn't think of it first?" asked Ur.

"Now that you mention it, a bit of both," said Mehen.

The Majordomo held up a hand. "Ok, will someone make a motion for an independent arbiter?"

Go made the motion and Risk seconded.

"All in favor, say Aye." Everyone but Ch'es and Mehen voted in the affirmative. "The Ayes have it."

"And what happens if one of the teams violates the Alliance before the threat is dealt with?" asked Ch'es.

"Immediate forfeit of the match to the other team," said Risk.

"I can live with that," said Ch'es. "Everyone else?" Nods met the query.

"Done," said Majordomo, taking notes on the official meeting ledger. She finished writing and looked at the group. "Next up, removing our veil of secrecy from the rest of the world."

"What is the outcome the Collective hopes to achieve by unveiling the League?" asked Senet.

"Legitimacy," said the Majordomo. "The League can front the

Collective as a whole."

"And why does a secret organization need legitimacy?" asked Senet.

"I thought that would be obvious," said Majordomo. "Power."

"Are we to assume the Collective has changed its mind on ruling the populace?" asked Go.

"We have no interest in controlling the population, Lord Go. We want to usher the people to a brighter future."

"That's even thicker than your normal brand of pig vomit," said Senet. "You may not want leadership responsibilities but you definitely want control. You just want to do it through entertainment."

"I'm not sure why that is a bad thing," said Ch'es. "Imagine the revenues. If my bookies could be taking odds from each of the Garden cities, we will fill lakes with the gold coming in."

"For that to work, the moral high ground becomes imperative," said Ur. "We need to eliminate the Agitators or launch a campaign that destroys their reputation."

"Or maybe we, you know, stop making slaves out of the Candidates," said Senet.

The whole table laughed.

Senet did not join in.

"Wait, you're being serious?" asked Ch'es. "Who would volunteer for something like this?"

"All the same fools who tried to solve Quests before we started kidnapping Sages," said Senet. "All we have to do is make them heroes again."

"This kinder, gentler approach has merit, Senet," added Sugoroku. "But these changes will not take place overnight. Our brutal training regimens have been crafted over decades not because they are cruel, but because they are effective."

"You misunderstand me, Sugoroku," said Senet. "I expect none of our practices to change. If anything, they will become more ruthless. The world already understands Quests are dangerous. When we go public, we need to spread the word that the benevolent League is giving Candidates a real opportunity to complete the Quests, in spite of the danger."

While Go, Sugoroku and Risk looked thoughtful, the rest of the table shook their heads. Senet sighed. Change was always difficult, especially for those that reaped the benefits from the status quo.

Senet leaned forward and tried a new approach. He found the eyes of the doubters. "Look, the only difference is the illusion of choice. The idealists will come willingly, but you're concerned that's not enough to keep our rosters filled. I get it." He held up a finger to stop Ch'es. "But. But there are desperate people the world over. We feed them, we train them and most importantly, we give them a dream of becoming a hero and we will have more volunteers than we know what to do with."

"We all know who will object to this," said Majordomo quietly.

"Which brings me back to my original question," said Senet. "If the Thin Man wants to make all the decisions for us, then we have no autonomy and this exercise of ownership is a waste of time. If the Collective is looking for incompetent lackeys, then by all means...you know how easy they are to find. I'd be happy to sell my shares of Company Senet today."

Majordomo held his stare. "Your concerns are understood Senet, but let's think for a moment about *why* he would object. Volunteers can quit when things get desperate. Desperation is the key to the Collective's success."

Senet nodded thoughtfully. "That's the current theory...but what if it's wrong? Or partially wrong? The Collective has made its disappointment with the stagnation of our advancement very clear. The recommendation from on high is always the same: be more ruthless.

Our ruthlessness has almost reached its limit. All that's left is brutally killing our candidates and we all know that is counterproductive. Isn't it time to try something new?"

"And you think the illusion of choice is the answer?" asked Wari.

"I think it's worth a try," said Senet. "After all, heroes solved Quests long before the League existed. I think it's possible our *recruitment* methods are backfiring. We're snatching idealists but our training methods rob them of those ideals. But if they sign up?"

Even the Majordomo was nodding now.

"Besides, if it appeases the Collective we can add a mandatory service period for the first year. If the militaries do it, so can we."

17

The Nest

Kavi didn't remember much about the trip except for the changes in temperature. He remembered being very hot and uncomfortable, then being very cold and uncomfortable. The beating the guards gave him after the draft broke several bones and knocked out two teeth.

When they threw him in the box, a deep voice said, "We might heal you when you arrive but I want you to remember the pain that comes from resisting the League."

And it was a box. He could almost sit up but never fully. There was enough room to turn from his back to his stomach when the mood hit him. There were air vents in the top of the box but he could see nothing but the sky for the duration of the trip. They spared him a small blanket that wasn't quite large enough to stretch over his entire body.

Most of the trip passed in a febrile fog. He swam in and out of consciousness enough times that he wouldn't have been surprised if someone told him the trip took a week or a month. He had a hard time parsing hallucination from reality. A nice man with soft eyes would sometimes come to the air vents and speak gentle words. Every time he visited, Kavi felt his fever drop. He assumed the man transferred healing energy to keep him alive.

More than once, he awoke to a small woman with almond eyes sitting in the closed box with him. He couldn't remember much of what she said except her urging him to hang on. He needed to persist and things would get better. He distinctly remembered her saying, "The Liberators work to free you all." He remembered thinking, *that's nice, at least someone is trying to help us.* When he reached out to touch her, craving any sort of human contact, his fingers passed through her.

At times, he was conscious enough to catch snippets of conversations happening outside of the box. The Auction was a huge success and he went for one of the highest prices in history. If it weren't for him fighting the guards, he would have gone even higher. He also heard they were traveling to the Nest, a camp somewhere deep in the Talons. His new captors weren't openly sharing information but they were doing nothing to hide it.

The last time the small woman appeared, he was in a lot of pain. He hadn't seen the man with soft eyes for hours, days? When she appeared, she wore a paper thin, black lace veil embroidered with roses. She stroked his face and sang him a lullaby his father sang to him when he was very little. Before she faded, she lifted her veil and kissed his forehead. "Cling to your independence, dear boy. You'll need it in the months ahead. Look to the black rose for hope."

* * *

When the trip finally ended, Kavi was helped out of the box by the man with soft eyes. His body was weak enough that he needed assistance walking into the squat building the carts pulled up to.

"At least you're real," said Kavi as he leaned on the man's shoulder as they hobbled along. The pain in his left leg was excruciating when he put weight on it.

"Few of us agree with the harsh treatment they put Candidates through," he said. He put his hand on Kavi's left leg and the pain faded. "You'll still need to be careful until we reset the bone and heal it."

Kavi nodded his thanks but felt his anger rising. "While I appreciate the help and the kindness, you're still working for them."

The man snorted which caused his bushy mustache to flare. "Before you get too self-righteous, know we are all in the same boat. I wish to be here as little as you."

"Everyone here is a slave?" asked Kavi.

"Most of us, yes. Though some have embraced their captivity. Those are the ones you have to watch out for. The more pain they had inflicted upon them, the more they wish to inflict it on others."

Kavi nodded. "I saw that at the Bastion. Those that whined the most about training as first years were the harshest to underclassmen when they had a position of power."

"You're Krommian then?" asked the man. "That will settle some of the bets the others were taking on the heritage of the barbarian in the box."

"I try to avoid labels," he said. He stopped hobbling long enough to stick out his free hand. "Kavi Stonecrest."

The man took the proffered hand. "Olsen Brand, Astran by birth, not by ideology. The moment I saw an opportunity, I ran as fast as I could from those insane zealots." He swept a hand around him. "And look how well that turned out for me."

"What's up with the facial hair?" asked Kavi. "I thought you had to be purified."

"I fled before my voice dropped. The big surprise was finding out I could still call on Astra's healing grace without the purification ritual. Left me with a lot of questions." He looked up to the sky for a moment then changed the subject. "How about you, young lion, what were you running from?"

Kavi looked at him sharply. "You know who I am?"

He smiled at Kavi's reaction. "I do now. Every Astran's heard of Marie Stonecrest," said Olsen. "You know our shared history. We lost that battle. In my city, the Lioness of Valun is the boogeyman mothers threaten children with if they don't say their prayers."

Kavi stopped and looked back. Others were unloading out of the carts. Many of them limped and shuffled like Kavi but none required assistance walking. Kavi scanned the faces but there was no sign of Grim or Nettie. A quick count put the number of new Candidates at twenty-five. Kavi smiled when he recognized the tall Vonderian. The man shrugged off the assistance the guards offered as he climbed out of his latest, celled cage.

Kavi did a quick scan to get a sense of location and potential escape routes. Snow piled high on either side of the road they had traveled. Kavi wondered how they kept the road clear of that much snow.

The road led to a large bridge that spanned a gorge he could not see the bottom of. Guard towers protected either side of the bridge. He could make out the misted breath of sentries stationed atop the squat towers. That was the only road he could see.

"I know what you're thinking and I wouldn't advise it," said Olsen. "Every escape attempt has failed. The Company makes each attempt very public and revels in telling the stories of the failure. They never clean the blood of those that attempt to storm the towers. And for those that freeze to death trying to go overland through the Talons? They excavate the bodies and display them as frozen statues in the Hall of Failure."

Kavi turned back to Olsen and nodded. "I was captured with three friends. We were all on some list. Will they end up here too?"

Olsen shook his head. "No. If they were on the list and they're not here, they got drafted by a different Company. You're better off forgetting your old life."

"And it was that easy for you?"

Olsen's eyes flashed in anger and Kavi thought the healer might pull his supporting arm away. A jolt of satisfaction passed through Kavi at getting a rise out of the placid healer. He wanted to yell at the man. *Get up. Fight. Do something!*

Then the man deflated. "I was captured with the woman who was to be my wife. That's why I volunteer for these trips...for any bit of news. It's been five years now and nothing."

"I'm sorry," said Kavi.

"The world is a cruel place."

As if his statement were clairvoyant, one of the Candidates un-loading from one of the less protected wagons took her chance and ran down the road towards the bridge. The two guards caught her easily and tackled her into a snowbank. They beat her until she fell unconscious. Kavi watched the fire drain from many of the other Candidates as they loaded her on a stretcher.

Kavi took a calming breath and looked at the building they limped towards. It was painted black and green, inside and out. The pattern matched the guard's uniforms and the light leather armor Olsen wore. A small crest of a raven perched upon a squat crenelated tower atop two dice adorned the left breast of each uniform. Even the men unloading boxes from the carts wore the colors. Olsen saw Kavi looking at the image which was also stamped on the doors.

"Welcome to Company Sugoroku, young lion," he said.

"Her shadow," said Kavi softly.

"What's that?" asked Olsen.

"That's what I was running from. Please, just call me Kavi."

Olsen looked at him for a long moment then nodded. "Right. I won't mention your family again."

"Thank you."

It was hard not to think about one of his last conversations with Carlin. Kavi wanted desperate. Now that he got it, he would have given anything to be walking up the hill to the keep in Stonecrest instead of this squat, ugly structure.

* * *

The inside of the building was a large, open space. There were boxes of supplies stacked against every wall but the back one. There were two rooms near the back. Olsen led Kavi to the first. As one of the doors to the small room opened, Kavi saw healers standing around a table where a dizzying array of steel implements had been set out. Kavi recognized the tools from surgeries he had seen the physicians from Loam conduct in the operating room in Stonecrest.

He took a deep breath and slowed his pace. Everything in him wanted to run the other way. Olsen tightened his grip on Kavi's shoulder and kept him moving forward.

"Just get it over with. Once the Company gets you here, they try to keep you alive. You're an investment they want to see pay out."

Kavi nodded but continued to stall. "Do they call it the Nest because it's high in the mountains? I expected something more from what I overheard in the box."

Olsen chuckled as he pulled Kavi along. "This is only the intake building. We drop supplies here and get rookies ready for classification. I hope you're not afraid of heights." He pushed Kavi towards the open door. "Quit your stalling. I promise, they'll knock you out first."

The three physicians standing around the table wore dark green jackets trimmed with black in the Sugoroku colors. The closest took Kavi's hand and helped him on the table. She cut off his clothing as the other two poked and prodded the purple and yellow bruises around his broken leg and torn shoulder. "Barbarians," muttered the man probing at his shoulder. "What they do to them should be criminal."

The woman physician raised her head. "Enough Gibbons," she snapped.

"What? He's not going to remember once we give him the anesthetic," said Gibbons.

"Maybe, but you don't know who's listening. The Company has ears everywhere." The woman shook her head.

Kavi watched Gibbons roll his eyes and decided he liked the man. The woman stuck his arm with a small needle. She pumped fluid into his arm from a small glass bulb she held above his head. Kavi's anxiety eased immediately. He was fascinated by the contrast when she took his pale hand in her cocoa-hued one. The last thing he remembered was her whisper, "now count to five with me."

* * *

He stretched his entire body when he woke. The sensation felt so good he completely forgot his surroundings for a moment. Then it struck him. Nothing hurt. He sat bolt upright in bed and looked around. He was in a recovery room with seven others who appeared to be sleeping.

He blinked twice, the room was like nothing he had ever seen.

Gibbons was standing in front of two large rectangular, metal tubs. A tube arced from behind the tubs looking like a utilitarian version of a metal swan Kavi had seen in one of the fountains in Krom. Out of it's mouth spewed water that Gibbons was using to wash his hands. Plumbing. Kavi had heard about the Bricker technology but had never seen it except in the newest fountains in the Capital.

After a moment, Gibbons turned a crank behind the two tubs and the water stopped. The fountain in Krom was rumored to cost several thousand gold and this healer was using the same technology like it were an every day thing. Where the hell was he?

The memories came flooding back. The intake building wasn't anything out of the ordinary, but he supposed that made sense. That was where Team Sugoroku interacted with the outside world.

Kavi was in the inner sanctum now.

He looked back at Gibbons who had moved to one of the prone patients. He lifted up the sheet which covered the woman's leg, exposing a long, narrow open wound. He put clockwork lenses over his eyes and a small mask over his mouth and nose then leaned over the cut so his face was only centimeters away. He examined it for several moments, reaching up to turn a dial on the clockwork that covered his eyes. After a moment he stood back up and took the mask off. He leaned down again and took a big sniff of the wound then nodded.

He placed the mask on a small metal table that stood next to the woman's bed. He grabbed another device that was shaped like a divining rod or a small narrow slingshot. It too was made of metal. He positioned it over the open wound and slowly pushed a sliding lever on the rod with his thumb. A liquid, spider web like material welled from the insides of the two prongs of the tool and tented over the woman's leg wound. After a moment it settled to completely obscure the wound from view. When it set, it looked almost like skin.

"What kind of healing magic is that?" asked Kavi with a croak.

Gibbons leaned over the newly formed artificial skin for a moment longer, examining his handiwork. Then he turned to face Kavi. "No magic at all. It's a combination of Loamian knowledge and Bricker ingenuity. We call it nature tech. That material," he nodded his head to the woman's patched leg, "is a natural mixture of a bunch of things, but the primary ingredient is bark from the white fig."

Kavi couldn't wrap his head around what he was seeing. "What is this place?"

Before Gibbons could answer, they were interrupted by a deep voice rapidly growing in volume outside of the room. The owner of that voice was being fended off by the female physician who spoke in his ear in the operating room.

"Categorization starts today, Clarissa, you know that," boomed the voice.

Gibbons winked at him then returned to the sink to wash his hands all over again.

"How many times are we going to have this argument Coach? Even with our skills, the body and brain need time to accept the healing. You rush them into training and they're going to be back here in two days. I told you they would be ready today. I didn't say it'd be first thing in the morning. Don't you dare raise that hand at me if you or the other coaches ever want to be healed again," said the physician.

"Unacceptable. You need to figure out how to speed their healing!" yelled the Coach.

"I've got an idea, how about you don't beat them within an inch of their lives. Then they won't need extensive healing. We had to re-break and heal twelve broken bones Coach. Twelve! Do you remember when you broke your leg? How long were you out?" Clarissa yelled right back.

That earned a moment's pause before the voice returned to a natural volume. Everyone in the room was now wide awake and straining to hear. "Two o'clock Clarissa. Have them ready." The Coach stomped away.

The physician turned to face the room of patients. "Clehold, you can leave now. Doctor Gibbons was able to reattach the three fingers with a little help from Healer Brand. Go ahead and get back to your squad."

The unassuming Bricker in the bed next to Kavi grabbed his glasses and took off the gown he wore. He replaced it with black and green overalls. He tightened his boots and pulled on a black leather duster littered with pockets. He stood and bowed to the physician. "Thank you Doctor Cleary," he said. He stared forlornly down the passage the Coach just exited down. "I don't know what would happen if you weren't around. Knowing you're fighting for us is the only thing keeping half us going."

A small, sad smile moved over her face. "Lean on each other Clehold. Don't let the competition tear you apart. Now get out of here you big ox. I don't want to see you back for at least three months."

She watched him fondly as he left then turned back to her remaining patients. "You all have been through serious trauma. That leaves permanent marks on body and soul. When you break a leg," she motioned to Kavi, "your brain expects that leg to hurt for months. When we heal that leg, the brain can't process immediate recovery. It manufactures the pain signals it expects to receive. The only way through these phantom pains is by training the brain to accept the healing. We do that by identifying those pains and proving to your brain that the injury is no more. Don't try to be tough. Acknowledge the phantom pain. Let us help you work through it. Until one of us reaches you, start feeling the pain your mind expects."

She checked in on two other patients before reaching Kavi. He spent the last ten minutes trying to relive the pain he experienced since the auction. His brain was happy to comply. The pain in his leg came roaring back and the only thing that seemed to distract him from it was the pain in his shoulder.

"Tell me, which phantom injury hurts worse?" asked Doctor Cleary.

Kavi winced. "The one I focus on."

She grinned. "Exactly. You know how stubborn we are when we cling to a belief. Your mind is doing the same thing, it believes that leg of yours should hurt like hell."

"I don't get it. Clehold lost three fingers and you rushed him out of here like it was just a scratch."

"With experience the brain accepts the healing more quickly. In this place, you get a lot of experience," she said. The smile left her face. "So tell me, how do you get rid of a stubborn mindset or opinion?"

"You leave yourself open to new evidence or other ideas," said Kavi.

"Which means accepting what?"

Kavi thought for a moment. "That you might be wrong."

"Exactly," she said again. "The people who take the longest to heal phantom pain can't accept they're wrong about anything. Take the coach, he is so set in his convictions, he had to rehab for almost three weeks."

"I've been wrong before," said Kavi. He looked hard at his leg. "I don't get it, I can see it's healed but it still hurts."

"And what if I do this," said Doctor Cleary. She slapped the healed leg hard enough that the smack resonated throughout the room.

Kavi took a huge intake of breath and quickly pulled his leg out of the way when she raised her hand again. Then he realized the pain was minimal. More, he moved the leg he had been favoring since he arrived without any pain at all. He released the breath and looked at her in amazement.

"That's only the first step," she said. "You're going to have to learn to trust it again. Anything we can do now before the coaches take you will give you a real chance to survive."

The next several hours were spent with the other patients. They squatted, caught and threw a medicine ball and even pivoted with all of their weight on recently healed limbs. The weight bearing torque, more than anything, convinced Kavi's brain his injuries were gone. He had a hard time believing the pain would return. He found camaraderie without speaking with the other convalescents in their newfound healing.

Two o'clock arrived with a piercing whistle. The large man removed the shrieking instrument from his lips. He took up the entire doorway to the room as he walked through it. He reviewed the activities in the room with a level of disgust Kavi had only seen on the face of slavers.

"I'm glad you all had fun with Doctor Cleary. You have three minutes to put on the uniforms issued to you. Playtime is over. Now you're mine."

18

The Categorization

Kavi pulled the uniform on and marveled at how well it fit. The thick material stretched with his motions. Even without stretching it was tailored to his tall, broad-shouldered frame. He pulled shoes made of a similar stretchy material over thick socks. He ran a hand over the hard sole on the bottom and marveled at the tactile grip. It felt like one of his father's creations, sticky or smooth based on the direction he ran his hand.

The front of each of their uniforms had a large A embroidered in the center. Kavi's shirt had the number eleven sewed into the back with a smaller eleven on the breast. Each candidate in the room had a different number.

The whistle shrieked again and the candidates turned towards the coach. The man came only to Kavi's shoulder but he was solid, with a torso like a small oak. His hair was short and his face bent in a permanent sneer.

"Line up and follow me," he said. The man expected immediate compliance. Kavi guessed he served in one of the Garden City militaries. He wasted no time on extra words.

When they left the recovery room the temperature dropped dramatically. Kavi was thankful for the thick uniform. The hallway was hewn from the rock without any attention paid to smoothing hard edges. It was such a stark difference from the welcoming and otherworldly experience of the recovery room that Kavi knew it had to be intentional. But why?

As the Coach started to jog, Kavi kept pace. He expected the weeks in captivity to destroy his conditioning, but it seemed to have the opposite effect. He felt stronger than he ever had. His recently injured leg felt brand new, better than brand new, it was like his muscles had been replaced with that of a horse.

Not everybody had the same experience. The Vonderian at the rear sucked big lungfuls of air after only moments of light running.

"The air is thinner here," said a woman between breaths. She wore the number seventeen on her back and her eyes flashed with an amber glow. "You'll get used to it in a couple of days."

"I hope so," said number Twenty-two, a large Krommian directly behind the coach. The scars on the back of his neck glistened with sweat. "Because this suuucks."

They reached the first stairway. This too was cut directly out of the stone but the stairs had been worn smooth by the passage of many feet. The stairway, much like the hallway they just left, was lit by mage light. The light emitted a faint green hue that reminded him of reflected sunlight ricocheting through the Draydale on a summer afternoon. Kavi found it soothing.

The run was anything but. The hallway may have been easy but running up the stairs was torture. They were endless, no landings, no pauses, just up and up and more up. The Vonderian and the short Harpstran woman with the tattoo of a snake wrapping around her neck had fallen far behind. Kavi could no longer see them when he looked back.

After eons of climbing the light began to shift. A lighter blue washed out the green and Kavi had to shield his eyes at the brightness. The temperature dropped again and he realized they had *finally* come to a landing. The landing had an opening in the rock wall to the outside. Two men in uniforms similar to theirs but with AA embroidered on the front shoveled snow that had drifted on to the landing. The Coach paused on the landing and shooed away the shovelers. The man wasn't even out of breath. "Go ahead and take a look," he said to the three candidates who had made it up to join him.

Kavi peered out the rough hewn opening which started at waist level but loomed far above his head. The ground lay hundreds of meters below him. The sight made him dizzy. He knew he hadn't climbed that far so somebody must have hauled his unconscious body up to the recovery room. He winced at the thought of putting another slave through that experience.

"Why don't they put a window in there?" asked Twenty-two.

"And miss out on a training tool?" said Coach. "You better get your asses moving!" he yelled down the stairs in common. Now that Kavi thought about it, every word spoken since he got to the Nest was in the trade dialect, formality and proper punctuation replaced with idioms and coarseness. It made sense, if all the races from the different Garden Cities were to communicate. "If you're late to Categorization, you're going to be living on these stairs. Now, move!"

The Harpstran woman collapsed on the landing a moment later but the Vonderian had just come into view, huffing and puffing his way up the stairs.

"Krom help me Twenty-six, if you're not up here in three...two... one."

This brought the Vonderian up in a sprint, his eyes and skin had turned a dark scarlet. "If they didn't lock our powers, I would have been the first one up Coach," wheezed the doughy man. "What good is physical conditioning when I can use a first year cantrip?"

"What good?" asked the Coach in a dangerously low voice. He walked to the man and got into his face. "What happens when you run out of ether, or you don't have access to those powers, like right now!" He pulled a small rod out of his back pocket that telescoped into an arm's length baton and struck him twice in the stomach.

Twenty-six wheezed, doubled over and stumbled three steps back down the stairs.

"Damned rookies," muttered the Coach. With a flip of his wrist the baton retracted back to rod size. "The Categorization room is down this hall, you have three minutes to get in there and line up by number."

Kavi had the opportunity to catch his breath by now but the tall Vonderian whimpered. Kavi chased after Twenty-two as he sprinted down the hall. The man pulled up abruptly as the passageway opened into an enormous cavern. Kavi couldn't help but join the man and stare.

Giant stalactites loomed overhead so he assumed the hall was a natural formation. It was large enough that Kavi had to squint to see the other end. Even with its size, the cavern was well lit. A trio of massive spherical lights hung suspended from the three largest stalactites jutting from the ceiling. Each of these had a yellow glow that emulated sunlight. Green mage lights lit the perimeter of the room and the combination made for a training area that lived in permanent daylight. A mossy lichen covered the floor of the cavern and Kavi enjoyed the springiness that pushed against his feet as he walked on it.

Kavi's eye was drawn the far side of the room. He watched in wonder as stalagmites pushed through sandy ground in spiny exhalation. They grew at least a meter a second until they formed a series of mini-peaks and obstacles. Moments later it began to snow atop those peaks to create a perfect simulation of mountainous terrain. His instructors at the Bastion would have drooled over the possibilities.

There were at least a dozen groups of men and women spread around the different biomes. They ran through exercises and mock combat. Many of the combatants used projectile weapons Kavi had never seen before. They fired much more rapidly than any flintlock. Kavi smiled as he imagined his father's reaction to this place: a kid in a curio shop.

Three minutes, have to focus.

Counting coaches and servants there had to be two hundred people in the cavernous room. He shoved down his awe and curiosity and looked out at the field to get an idea for how the groups broke out. He started to notice some patterns.

"Where do we go?" asked Twenty-two. He looked to Kavi.

The others had caught up by now, even the Vonderian. They also turned to Kavi. He ignored their attention, sharp eyes watching as Coach slipped in behind the Vonderian. Coach made his way over to a group milling around as other coaches yelled at them. "Over there," said Kavi, pointing. "Look for jerseys with a single A on front."

They trotted over to the group, arriving a couple of steps ahead of Coach. One of the other coaches had already lined up the group who didn't spend time in the recovery room. With a glance, Kavi saw they were lined up from left to right in numerical order. The farthest number to the left was twelve. It was worn by the Vonderian who stood with him when he fought the Ach'Su.

Kavi ran over and took his place in line. He could hear the others behind him doing the same. "The name's Kavi. I never got to thank you for saving my ass with the Ach'Su," whispered Kavi out of the side of his mouth as they both looked forward. He relished in calling it the name the League loathed.

The defiance brought a smile from the Vonderian. He stifled it as the three coaches huddled several paces away broke up and walked towards them. "I'm Pip and I hear the ass saving was mutual," he whispered.

Kavi jutted his chin out. "You ever see anything like this place?"

"Not even in Vonderia," said Pip, "not even at the Acade—"

"Silence," yelled the largest of the three coaches. Scars crisscrossed his wide face. One of the scars exposed a serious underbite making him look like a misshapen warthog. Most of his scars looked like they were received in battle, not the carefully curated ones of a typical Krommian warrior. The other coaches, including the one that harried Kavi and the others up the stairs, flanked the hideous man.

All whispering ceased.

"My name is Coach K, and flanking me are Coaches L and M. Our job is to get you sorry lot ready to be fodder for our professional team. The season starts in one month so we don't have a lot of time. Most of you are not going to make it through the season. Hiding these facts from you will only get in the way of your training. So here they are: last year's class had twelve survivors from the original twenty five. Three years ago only four made it through the season. If you do somehow survive your first season most of you will be given minor roles for Team Sugoroku. These are jobs like training dummies for the pro team, guard duty for our supply caravans and even servants. We need servants to keep this whole operation running. For those few who excel throughout the season, you will have the opportunity to try out for our triple A team. Spend a year or two in their company and you'll get a chance to try out for the professional team."

The man started walking down the line but his loud voice carried. "For those of you that piss us off or somehow survive without bringing value to the team - you will also spend next season as fodder." He turned towards the coach that escorted Kavi and his group. "Coach L, how many candidates have ever survived two seasons on the fodder team?" he asked.

Coach L made a big show of ticking off numbers on his fingers before closing his fist. "That would be zero, Coach K."

Coach K turned back to the line. "That is correct, Coach L. Zero. No one has ever survived two seasons. So, what's the moral of the story? Do the work, improve every day, and you might, I repeat, you *might* make it through this."

"Great pep talk," Kavi whispered to Pip. Coach's words had shaken Kavi but he was tired of being bullied. Looking for a brother in arms in Pip, he was able to release some of that anxiety.

Coach K's head whipped towards Kavi. "Did you have something to add eleven?"

"No, sir," said Kavi.

Coach K materialized in front of Kavi, warthog face up in his own. "Let's get one thing straight. I am not a sir. This is not the military. So break that habit right now. You are now part of the Sugoroku Company where the highest rank is Coach. You will refer to me as such or there will be pain. Is that understood?"

"Yes, Coach," Kavi said quickly and loudly. Kavi hated this crap. He thought he left these games behind him at the Bastion, but he knew his way around them. Follow the rules and don't stick your head too far out of line.

Coach K stepped back and addressed the line. "That goes for all of you. Those that have served in the military are the hardest to break of the habit. Coach L and Coach M will help you." Both men pulled out identical rods and flipped them to baton mode. "Those lessons will not be pleasant."

Coach K scanned the line and his eyes rested on a woman with a tear streaked face. "I don't care who you are or who your parents are. You were on the list. There was no mistake."

The woman dropped her eyes.

"Some of you may remember when the daughter of the Harpstran

Prime Minister disappeared five years ago. She was on the list. The power you had in your former lives is nothing now."

His glare fell over the line like a ray of hopelessness. More eyes fell to the ground.

"To understand what your day-to-day existence will look like at Team Sugoroku, you must first be Categorized. This will test your usefulness to the team. Over the next two days, you will be tested in three ways. Martial ability - how you fight against others. Trap identification and disarmament - eliminating traps without getting yourself or others killed. And battle against beast and non-human combatants." He turned back to his two coaches. "Did I miss anything?"

Coach M held up his baton. Coach K nodded. "Thank you, Coach M. Our batons create a power submission field. For those of you who have been whining about not having access to your power, this is why. Think of it like the opposite of sulimite, call it an anti-suli field. And please, clear any fantasies about trying to steal one of these to use it in a daring escape. Each baton is linked by blood and aura. It will only function for its owner. For those of you wondering, the answer is yes. The submission fields will be off for the Categorization process."

Seventeen raised her hand.

Coach K gave a feral grin as he looked back to the other coaches. "You believe the balls on this one?" he asked.

"Since when does courage require having dangly bits in you pants?" asked Seventeen. "Are questions permitted or not?"

The smile never left Coach K's face but everyone on the line tensed as Coach M and Coach L circled around behind the line. "Generally, not. They are only permitted when one of the coaches explicitly asks if there are any questions. In this case I'll allow it."

"Will we have access to suli in our training?"

Coach K laughed. "You think we would waste suli on you? With the long shot exception of tinkerers building devices that help the team. No, you will never have access to suli until you make the professional team."

Coach L stood behind Seventeen. With a lightning strike he hit the back of her thigh with his baton and she dropped to her knees. As she fell, she took a long look at the baton as if trying to make out its secrets.

Kavi couldn't tell if Seventeen was a hothead or if she provoked the coaches intentionally.

Coach K stood over her. "Get this straight. I could care less about gender, race or skill set. The expectations are the same. Drop the attitude or risk pissing me off." He held her eye for a moment longer then yelled, "Healer!"

Healer Brand jogged over and laid a hand on her injured leg. Her grimace of pain evaporated and she took his hand as he helped her back to her feet. She lined back up.

Coach K moved back to take in the whole line. "Categorization will start with martial ability. We will *not* be pitting Krommians against each other. Nor will we have Astrans fighting Krommians as they have been warring for centuries. You will be paired against fighting styles you haven't seen before. We need to understand how you improvise, how you adapt. When you get sent out in the field, there aren't any rules of engagement. Improvisation will be your ticket to survival."

Coach K pointed. "Five circles have been set up, with standard dueling rules. All weapons, tinkering devices and props will be blunted. Deal a mortal wound or knock someone out of the circle and you gain a point. Two points wins the duel. Everyone fights four duels."

"Coaches, set em up!"

* * *

The other groups training in the large facility moved to watch. Even the professional players wanted to see what the newcomers could do. The first fights were called out. Adrenaline flowed through Kavi as his number was called. He would fight number Twenty- six, the Vonderian who struggled so mightily to climb the stairs.

Kavi chose a long staff. He had trained with every weapon on the rack. He thought the reach the staff gave would afford him the best chance against the ranged power of the Vonderian. He looked across the circle and the man who had been whining earlier was now sneering. His upturned nose and narrow eyes lay below an aristocratic bowl cut. The sneer looked natural on his narrow features. Kavi looked forward to wiping it off his face.

Coach M stood in the middle of the ring between the two combatants. He held up a hand between them then brought it down signaling the start of the duel. Kavi charged as the Vonderian muttered under his breath. The mage's eyes turned a misty white and his skin matched the hue. He knew enough about Vonderians to guess the man was preparing a wind attack. Kavi had to beat him to it. With an underhand swing of his staff Kavi caught Twenty-six in the chin hard enough to lift him off the ground. The man's back hit the edge of the circle hard and air exploded out of his lungs. Kavi was almost certain he knocked the Vonderian out. The crowd around his circle grew. So did the volume of the excited whispers. He stood straighter.

Kavi stepped back and moved to his side of the circle. Healer Brand ran over and checked the man's pulse. He muttered something and the Vonderian woke. The healer, Olsen, found Kavi's eyes and gave him an inscrutable look. It wasn't judgmental or even sad, more searching and realizing he hadn't found what he hoped to find.

The look hit him hard and his adrenaline vanished. *What the hell am I doing? Why am I playing their game?* He knew his back was against the wall and the Coaches would show zero clemency to any defiance but it felt so much like one of his mother's ultimatums. My way or leave. Fight or die. He hated it.

The Vonderian moved unsteadily to the center of the ring. When he looked at Kavi the arrogance was replaced with fear. Coach M walked over from another ring he had been monitoring and once more stepped between the two. When the hand went down, Kavi felt a malaise engulf him. He couldn't seem to care what happened next. His opponent's eyes and skin tinted blue and he launched a cone of freezing water. Kavi couldn't summon the energy to dodge it. It swept him into the air and out of the ring. He was able to find his feet but the point was lost.

The sneer was back as they faced off for the third and final time. This time, the man pointed his own staff, his eyes paled and Kavi knew another burst of air was coming. If Twenty-six hadn't announced the strike so blatantly, Kavi would have let him have the match. The training he received from his mother and the Bastion kicked in and Kavi dodged. The Vonderian's strike missed and instinct took over. Even moving through apathetic air, Kavi was able to grapple and throw the man from the ring.

Between bouts, he took the opportunity to watch other fights. Most were one sided. One of the combatants, would have combat experience and they were set against a combatant that had none. These fights ended quickly accompanied by sympathetic groans from the crowd.

None of the three Brickers were appointed first round fights. The coaches gave them time to tinker defenses and weapons. Kavi looked over at the awestruck group of tinkerers. They chatted as they marveled at the tools and materials available. That awe quickly turned into diligence as they worked away on their contraptions.

His number was called again. He would be fighting number Seventeen next and he glumly stepped into the ring. Coach M announced their undefeated records. All Kavi knew was she beat her previous opponent. He had no idea how.

As he lined up to face her, the adrenaline refused to come. He couldn't stomach the idea of being a pet monkey for these shadowy bastards. He knew it was stupid but he needed a reason to fight. His tolerance for being bullied into battle disappeared when he finally stood up to the Lioness.

When Coach M's hand dropped, he didn't react when she jumped backwards. Her lithe form arched like the skinny barn cat back home when she stalked a mouse. Seventeen looked him in the eyes and frowned at the apathy there. He held his stance, waiting for her to attack first without realizing she already had. When she charged, he tried to step aside and found his feet bound to the springy turf. Small tendrils snaked around his shoes. Damn. He knew some Loamians could commune with nature but thought it took a lot of time. Since he couldn't step aside to dodge the kick, he ducked and put a hand down to avoid her. This trapped the hand too. The green tendrils were thin but strong as steel wire. Kavi couldn't free himself. With three of his limbs trapped, the woman pushed him forward and let nature pull him down. She held a dull knife to his throat until Coach M called the point.

He tried to stay on his toes for the second fight but the point ended in much the same way. He figured that if he struck quickly, constantly charging, the tendrils would not be able to gain purchase. But he didn't have anything against number Seventeen, she hadn't wronged him. He didn't want to hurt her and he didn't want to fight like a puppet on a string.

This time when she held him down to the turf, she hissed in his ear. "You don't think I'm worthy of an effort? Is that it?" she whispered.

Her breath was warm and smelled like the earth.

"You're not my enemy. If I fight, they win," he said, his voice muffled and barely audible with his mouth pressed into the ground.

She pushed his head down when Coach M called the point and Seventeen's victory. Coach M gave Kavi a suspicious look. When the tendrils receded Seventeen glared at him, those amber eyes flashing. "You're not better than me," she said and stomped off.

His next opponent was a Bricker. The young man was spindly and much shorter than Kavi, coming only to his shoulder. He looked nervous as they lined up. Kavi could see the outlines of the augments he had on each leg through the uniform he wore. The Bricker had crafted a harness which was slung over each shoulder and attached to a device on his back. He kept angling away from Kavi so the larger man didn't have the chance to inspect it. Kavi raised an eyebrow when he heard the man's record. He had won his first and only fight, starting after the others to tinker his gear. When the hand came down Kavi took a defensive stance. Coach K came over to watch the fight.

This made Kavi care even less about the outcome, if only to spite the man.

The small Bricker reached for the device strapped behind him and pulled two cylinders that hung from the sides so they rested in each hand. Kavi started to move. He knew enough about technology from his dad to fear it. Projectiles began flying towards him. Even the Bricker looked surprised by the speed and frequency of the blunted pellets flying Kavi's way. Kavi had never seen anything like it. He did he best to dodge but one struck him in the temple and he dropped, dazed. Coach M called the point and Coach K stared hard at Kavi.

Kavi stared right back, adrenaline returning with the defiance.

They lined up again. The small Bricker smiled and Kavi saw something dark there. The fake smile smoothed the skin on his face making him look serpentine. "I hope that hurt," he said.

153

"Why?" asked Kavi. Sparring always raised the blood but it was rare to see anyone take joy from hurting someone. Unless they were a psychopath like Roanik.

"It's time Krommians are taken down a notch," said the small man as the hand dropped.

"And if I told you I'm half Bricker?" said Kavi, circling. The adrenaline sharpened his senses and he was able to dodge the first round of projectiles easily.

The Bricker snorted. "Not a chance. Even the coaches can see the dust bunnies swirling between your ears."

Kavi continued to circle until Coach K yelled. "You better make a move Eleven. This isn't a dance circle!"

That enraged Kavi but not enough to bully him into fighting smart. He dropped his defenses and ran at the small Bricker with arms held wide in the dumbest move possible - a bear hug. The Bricker's smile widened as he pulled a small rod still attached to the device on his back. As Kavi neared, he could hear the same buzz of energy that came from the coaches' batons. The man brought the rod to Kavi's neck.

The power of lightning coursed through him. The Bricker kept the rod at Kavi's neck as he writhed in pain. Kavi thought he could hear the man giggling. Coach M called the point but the Bricker held the rod there. His angry face smiled as the smell of burnt flesh began to waft from Kavi's wounds.

"Enough Nineteen," said Coach M. "He's done."

"Not quite yet Coach," said the Bricker. Kavi convulsed as the Bricker twisted the rod to find more exposed skin.

Coach M expanded his baton and hit the rod so the current pulsing through it ceased. He struck Nineteen in the chest six times in rapid succession until he lay broken and bleeding. "That was not a recommendation, when I say enough, I mean enough. Healer!"

Nineteen glared at the Coach.

Olsen held his hands over Kavi's wound and the pain eased immediately. "What are you doing, Kavi?" asked Olsen in a barely audible voice. "If I can tell you're throwing your fights, you damn well better know the coaches can too."

"I'm not trying to hide it," said Kavi. Even as he spoke the words, he realized how stupid he'd been. Intentionally sticking his head into the lion's mouth while in the lion's den was no way to be defiant.

"Then you're dumber than I thought," hissed Olsen. "And it's going to get you killed. Defiance without purpose is meaningless. Play the long game and turn it in to something," he hissed.

Kavi nodded and accepted the hand he offered as he stood up. "I need to know this isn't all there is," whispered Kavi, eyes pleading.

Olsen looked at him and sighed. "I can't offer you that," he said sadly. "Gather information, look for opportunities and use the defiance when you're not in the middle of the viper's nest, you idiot."

That brought a rueful smile and Kavi dusted himself off. He knew Olsen was right. He came to that conclusion himself, moments before the man said anything. He also realized that thoughts of his mother made him act like an idiotic child. He needed to be very wary of childish defiance in this place. The defiance felt good. It was the only power he could exert. But if it got him killed, he wasn't helping anybody. The bouts continued around him. The power dynamic of the fodder squad slowly began to be established. Those with martial ability inevitably looked down on those without.

They called the final round fights and this time Kavi would be paired against Pip.

* * *

Pip raised his eyebrows when he heard Kavi's record as they lined up. Pip was undefeated having just beaten Seventeen. "So, are you throwing fights or are you just bad?" Pip asked.

Kavi grinned at the man's bluntness. "I'm struggling with fighting for our captors' enjoyment."

"Then don't. I'm fighting for myself until I can figure a way out of here," said Pip.

"Well, you're smarter than me."

"I would have thought that obvious." He gave Kavi a cocky grin which highlighted handsome features that looked almost feminine in their perfection. "So, how about we spar and see how good you really are?"

That was something he could do. When he charged, Kavi and Pip shared the same smile. This time when he struck, the malaise was gone.

19

So, This Is Home Now

"Tomorrow, Categorization will continue," said Coach K. "The Coaches will show you to your quarters. Tonight is the only night you do not have additional duties. I highly recommend you take advantage and get some rest. Traps in the morning, monsters in the afternoon." The man walked out of the cavern and left them in the care of Coaches L and M.

The coaches led them to the far side of the huge cavern stopping in front of a wide hallway. A series of passageways led off the main drag. Of course, there were more stairs - some going up, some going down. The passageways looked almost random in their construction. With so many people moving from place to place the area resembled a giant rabbit warren.

"This is the main hall for Sugoroku Company. This floor is where the Coaches and most of the professional team live. There is the primary dining hall and around that corner you will find specialty training rooms. You'll see more of those tomorrow afternoon. The triple A team quarters are a short climb above the main hallway. The double As live above that. Can anyone guess where you will be staying?"

Kavi sighed. When no one volunteered, Coach L continued. "That's right, you live all the way at the top, like princesses in a magic tower. Now, who's excited for more stairs?"

Kavi found himself standing next to number Twenty-six. The man sobbed softly at the words.

"Each floor has its own mess and facilities. Your room is one large dormitory. You won't have a chance at a single room unless you make the triple A squad so get comfortable with group living. Be happy we provide you with beds and a blanket."

Coach L tromped forward and led the group to a wide, steep staircase. Green mage lights lined the stairs and even with the lighting Kavi couldn't see the top. From here, the stairs could have gone on forever.

Coach M cleared his throat and the group turned to the taller man. His face was gaunt but his eyes burned with the same intensity of the other coaches. "All resources provided are first come first serve. We will not be monitoring how you manage those resources so don't waste our time with complaints. Wake up tomorrow is when Coach L?"

"Dawn. Don't worry, you'll know when that is," said Coach L.

Coach L looked at the small Bricker who had beaten and zapped Kavi. The small man still wore the contraption he built. "I don't care if you carry your practice weapons but I wouldn't recommend using them on the other squads. They will crush you. Some of you think you are good. Wait until you train with us for six months."

Coach L examined the squad standing before him. "Make no mistake, you've landed in hell. If you pay attention, we'll turn you into the demons you need to be to survive it."

He moved out of the way of the stairs. "Go ahead, stake your claim."

* * *

Any sense of competition faded after ten minutes on the stairs. Kavi passed the overeager who charged out in a sprint. He took a measured pace. As he forced tired legs to move, he wondered if Grim and Nettie were going through some similar torture. He wondered if Carlin ever made it back to Stonecrest and if the Lioness was mounting a rescue operation. His snort sounded more like a wheeze. Not a chance. She made it very clear that her first duty was to her people, not to any individual family member.

After five minutes he had passed all but Pip, number Twenty-two and number Seventeen. Twenty-two seemed to be made entirely of leg muscle but he huffed and puffed as he climbed. More muscle, more weight to drag.

When the four of them finally crested the top of the stairs they loosed a collective groan. It was only a landing. They dragged tired legs to the next set of stairs. Thankfully, the top was visible. They reached the top to find the air even thinner this high up. Deep breaths were hard to find.

The hallway at the top of the stairs was rough cut and no amenities had been made for comfort. None of the clockwork or nature tech displayed so prominently below made it to *these* quarters. Kavi understood it now. They were supposed to live rough, to suffer. Luxuries were for those that earned it.

Twenty-two had to avoid several sections of ceiling lest he whack his head on a low hanging cut of rock. They moved slowly down the hall, exploring this high point of the warren. The first room they passed generated wonderful smells of cooking meat and root vegetables that made Kavi's mouth water.

The aroma proved too much for number Twenty-two. He left their spontaneous foursome to investigate the source.

A moment later, they heard a deep voice yell, "No, not ready yet! The bell will ring when it is time to eat." The shout was punctuated by the hollow sound of a pan striking something.

Twenty-two walked back out a moment later, rubbing his shoulder. "Careful, cook's got a wicked skillet arm."

A little further down, on the other side of the hall, lay the privies. Kavi stuck his head in the room and staggered at the stench. They smelled and looked like they hadn't been cleaned in years. A trickle of mountain water ran into one of the stalls and he wondered if the icy water would be their only opportunity to bathe.

At the end of the hall was the dormitory room. As soon as they walked in, the idea of a pecking order became obvious. On the near side of the hall was a large fire. Kavi could see through the fire to the dining hall beyond. The fire provided heat for the dormitory while simultaneously being used as a cook fire; several cooks monitored meat on spits on the dining side of the flames.

The beds were lined up in rows. Calling them beds was generous; they were little more than straw pallets topped with thin blankets. At the far end of the hall was a giant opening that led out into the void. There was maybe twenty paces between the opening and the last bed. Sleeping on the cold side of the room would not be easy. On closer inspection, the opening was hewn at an angle, like a crude dormer. The snow would have a hard time swirling into the room but the cold would find little obstacle.

Kavi ran his hands along three words that had been carved directly into the rock above the large opening. *Only way out.* In the cold, darkening room the words felt foreboding and prophetic. Kavi rested his head against the stone and refused the burgeoning despair.

The biggest discovery they made in the dormitory were three others wearing the numbers eight, nine and ten. The two women and one man didn't make eye contact with the newcomers. They sat on their pallets lost in thought. They must have been candidates from the previous season who angered the coaches.

The three claimed pallets in the middle of the room. They weren't too close to the fire or to the gaping maw that led out to the mountain air. Their silence was unnerving to any that walked into the room, so everyone gave them a wide berth.

Kavi claimed a pallet near the fire between Pip and number Seventeen. Twenty-two paced in front of the fire, often stopping to crouch and look through at the spits. He looked like a gorilla in captivity.

"It's got to be almost ready," he said for the third time. "Don't you think, Eleven?"

"Kavi," he said.

Twenty-two stopped in front of Kavi and stuck out his hand. "Jansen," he said. "I'm tired of the number crap too. Why do you think they do that?"

"Control," said number Seventeen. Jansen looked at her but she didn't elaborate.

Pip nodded. "She's right. It's easier for them and it's dehumanizing. I'm Pip." He jutted out his own hand.

"You move like a warrior," said Jansen. "I've never met a Vonderian who wasn't a waste of a space when they weren't doing all that magicky stuff." He wiggled his fingers dramatically. "Watching you and Kavi spar was like watching the Suli Elites teach at the Bastion. You almost had him a couple of times. How'd you get so good with the staff?"

"I came into my magic very late. Living in Vonderia without magic is like living in another city without use of your arms. Everyone calls on ether to do even the simplest tasks. I couldn't call the ether. I got bullied a lot until I learned how to fight." Pip shrugged. "When my magic finally manifested, I had already learned the value of discipline and physical activity."

Kavi turned to Jansen. "Where'd you serve?"

Jansen pulled his uniform tight against his right arm to show off a scar in the shape of a shield. "Fourteenth shield regiment. We slung mud along The Whisper Sea for eight months in the last Astran campaign. I dug a mountain of trenches but saw no action except when those crazy, unarmed fundamentalists charged our position."

"I heard about those attacks, even up north," said Kavi. "They called it a mass suicide. Sure sounded like standard Krommian bloodthirsty propaganda to me."

Jansen stopped pacing and his face turned red. "Oh yeah, where did you serve?"

"The Eagles."

"Well, excuse me, milord," said Jansen with a theatrical bow. "I wondered why you had nothing but baby scars on your face, but I was there. Those crazy bastards kept throwing wave after wave of people armed with nothing but faith. They hit our shield walls and not one of us drew a weapon. S'honest truth. I swear it. They kept coming and coming. It wasn't just men. Women and children were in the mob too. They pushed and pushed until their faces squished against the wall, pushed by those behind them. They never stopped, like mindless, hairless drones. Not even when the front lines got trampled. Not even when...when...their children's bodies were crushed against our shields."

"What did they want?" asked Pip.

"Don't know. None of us did. We weren't occupying any holy sites. But you know what the worst part was?"

All three leaned forward, waiting and dreading for him to answer his own question.

"The singing. The mindless, horrible, beautiful drone of Astran hymns as they trampled their own believers into...sausage meat against our shields. We could do nothing except hold the line." He shuddered at the memory. "That was my last campaign."

"I heard the Fourteenth also fought off some sort of monkey monsters," Kavi said. "Top brass didn't believe it and told us to shut the rumors down because it hurt morale."

Jansen's face darkened and he shook his head. "They were no rumor. We called them Banglors. After the massacre, the regiment got orders to resupply in Krom and give us grunts some rest. Most of my squad was pretty shook up. As we're crossing the Elindil, we start to hear drums. We forded quick, not wanting to get caught with our pants down in a river crossing. Once we crossed, the drums stopped. We thought we were safe. They didn't attack until we traveled into the Draydale."

"When they attacked, it was from the trees. We were tired and unprepared and had no idea where to set a shield wall. They looked like apes. Their long hairy arms hit the defensive positions we set up at the same beat they hit their drums. A constant Bang, Bang that dented metal shields and shattered wooden ones."

"Banglors," said Pip. "Got it."

Jansen nodded. "They attacked eight times the first night. Same pattern - strike, drumming, fade back into the trees. Each time they disappeared so did some of our platoon. By the third day, only half the men that held the line at Whisper Ridge were still with us. We almost made it out of Draydale where we could set up a defense and take a little payback from their hairy hides. The last two attacks from the night before we came out ahead. Then they staged one last attack before we left the woods. I got knocked out in the fighting and woke up in a cage with three others on my way to the Northern Market. I don't even know what happened to my unit."

"I know what that feels like," said Pip.

Kavi nodded.

"You sure they had monkey faces?" asked Seventeen. She moved hair out of her eyes and Kavi could see a light streak of white hair that stood out from the raven black on the rest of her head. She had a very small nose and broad cheeks. She looked far more catlike than the Lioness of Valun.

Jansen looked at her, incredulous. "Hell yeah. Three days of fighting up close. Those gorilla mugs are seared into my dreams."

Seventeen held his gaze for an uncomfortable moment then nodded.

"Why? What did you see Seventeen?" asked Kavi.

"Call me Tess," she said. "In the jungles outside Loam, there were several sightings of what the younger rangers called Irborra. I, like the others, thought it was nonsense. Until I saw one. Irborra is the legendary panther god of the Kal'Ka Loam, the aboriginal Loamians from our Garden City. He's the trickster god who once fooled Uthriel into betting the moon on a single throw of Irborra's weighted dice. When Uthriel lost the toss, he was forced to give a portion of the moon to Irborra each month which the great cat slowly eats away at until Uthriel starts the long process of rebuilding it anew."

"Panther god. Really?" asked Jansen.

"What? I didn't create the legend," said Tess.

"And?" prompted Kavi.

"I was scouting the far reaches of the jungle, east of the Rhune, almost to the edge of the Wastes when I saw it. The thing came out of the early morning mists and attacked a family of monkeys. It moved faster than a dark thought. One minute it was two trees away, the next it had killed two of the monkeys and was toying with one of the young ones."

"How do you know it wasn't just a panther?" asked Jansen.

"After it ripped apart the young monkey, another Irborra arrived. When they faced each other across the family of dead monkeys, they shimmered. Their snouts shrunk into their faces, their ears retracted and their paws turned into something like hands."

"Oh come on," said Pip.

"Says the guy who fought an Ach'Su," said Tess.

"Fair point, continue," said Pip.

"Then they started to speak. It was a sibilant, throaty rumble but they were words. I tried to edge a little closer to see if I could make out what they were saying. When I did, I disturbed the leaves of the banyan I perched in. I know, I know, not what you'd expect from a Ranger but there was a certain amount of shock involved. The moment I made that tiny noise, the throaty sounds stopped. Both heads turned my way and they transformed back to their original forms.

I took off and they chased me for what seemed like hours. I ran top speed, using all my senses to detect the movement of these two creatures. I was moving so fast I ran directly into a slaver's camp where I found myself entrapped by a simple, pathetic snare. I was tired and hungry, but that was no excuse. My Ranger Captain, Findaeleus, would never-"

A huge crash interrupted her story as one of the pallets shattered against the wall on the far side of the room. The slower members of the fodder team had made it up the stairs. When they got to the dormitory, they quickly realized the remaining beds were going to lead to a terrible, frozen night's sleep. Those who could fight began to challenge the weaker candidates for their pallets.

The pallet shattered when number Nineteen used his augmented arm to pull it from beneath a young Harpstran woman who refused to move. This one had brightly colored tattoos in the form of scales that decorated her neck almost to her chin. She fell when he raised the pallet above his head. He threw it against the wall to make his point. He looked at her companion with his beady eyes until she moved off her bed. The two moved to open bunks closer to the large window.

"It's amazing such a small man can be such a huge asshole," said

Pip.

Kavi stood to help the two Harpstran women when the dinner bell began to chime. Jansen jumped and ran to the chow door. No one had eaten all day so he was not the only one hustling to get in line. Kavi made sure the two Harpstrans moved toward the dining hall before his own hunger forced him to follow Jansen.

* * *

Hunger is the best sauce and that sauce was a necessity. The bread was brown, the meat was charred and the soup was burnt. In spite of all that, it tasted amazing. Kavi realized it was the first time he had eaten anything but thin gruel or crusts of bread since his capture.

As he took his last bite, he looked to the line. There would not be enough for seconds. Those in the back of the line would barely eat enough to make it through tomorrow's trials. Since everyone was still hungry, tempers ran high and the inevitable contests began.

Twenty-six made the mistake of swiping the last piece of bread from Ten, the woman from the previous season's fodder class. She was quicksilver as she dodged his wind strike and hit him with his own plate. She took the last of his bread before spitting on him and making her way back to her seat.

The bully in the small body used his augmented arm to wrest the full tray from the Harpstran woman he terrorized earlier. When the other Harpstran ran towards him to retaliate, he stopped her with a padded bullet to the chest. She whooshed as the air ejected from her lungs.

Kavi had enough. He stood and moved to confront Nineteen.

"Here we go. Every Eagle thinks he's a peacekeeper," said Jansen from his seat at the table.

Whatever. He'd deal with that comment later.

Nineteen saw him coming and slowly started eating the food off the Harpstran's plate. "Hey there, hero, looking to get your ass kicked again?"

The urge to wipe the sinister smile off the man's face became overpowering. "I'm not sure you learned the correct lesson earlier," said Kavi.

Nineteen set his tray down. He shot another padded bullet at the Harpstran already hunched over rubbing her chest.

She yelped when this one struck her leg.

"Got to be thorough," Nineteen said. He took another bite. He took aim at the other Harpstran and Kavi charged. Nineteen's eyes widened and he shifted his aim to Kavi.

Time once again began to slow. Kavi felt like he had an entire afternoon as he languidly closed on Nineteen. He could see the man's fingers flicking to launch projectiles. They moved far too slowly to make a difference. Kavi reached the man and made his way behind him. He started pulling hoses and metal pieces off the collection of tinkered devices strapped to the man's back. Almost immediately, he found the power source and pulled. Everything on the pack went dark. The weight of the dormant gear pulled the small man on his back like an upended turtle. Even his augmented legs and arm couldn't help flip him back over.

Time snapped back to its regular flow. Kavi made sure to give Nineteen a quick kick to the ribs as he walked past the bully. He looked at the two Harpstrans. "He's all yours."

The two women grabbed their food first then his. They stuffed some in their mouths, then started to kick the small Bricker until he began to howl then cry. As the first kick landed, the Bricker stared hatred at Kavi.

"Good thinking, Eleven," said Tess. "Now you're going to have to sleep with one eye open."

"I'm not sure how you move that fast but none of us needs more enemies in this place," said Jansen.

Kavi spat, angry now. Before his liberation, comments like these would have bothered him enough to rethink his actions. Not anymore. "You cowards can keep on surviving. That's not good enough for me. There's got to be something more or who cares if you survive?"

Then he stormed out of the dining hall.

20

Traps and Monsters

I f there were more battles for beds that night, Kavi didn't see them. He was exhausted from the healing and the Categorization. And from the travel to the Nest, and the auction, and the slave carriage....How long *had* it been since he left Stonecrest? At least two weeks, maybe three. He didn't dwell on it. The sensation of lying in a bed, that wasn't in a hospital, for the first time in however long pulled him into a deep sleep the moment he lay down.

The light which woke him bathed the dormitory in yellow fire. He couldn't even look out the window, the sun's rays were so brilliant. Now they knew which way East was. Kavi closed his eyes for a moment and reveled in the warmth of the dawn sun. The fire turned to embers in the early morning hours. It was being stoked by two kitchen workers. The others chopped mushrooms to add to a hearty gruel.

Kavi stood and stretched. The rest of the room began to awaken from the sun and the sounds and smells of cooking from the next room.

After a hurried meal, Coach L harried them down the stairs.

When they lined up for Day two of Categorization, Kavi expected to see the three newcomers. Oldcomers? When he didn't, he realized they were likely given other duties as they had been categorized the previous season.

Coach K moved the group from the main training hall down the central passageway. They passed the living quarters of the coaches then took a left and stopped in a vaulted antechamber. It was a smaller room that led to another cavernous room with a new collection of passageways worming away in different directions.

Coach K turned to face them. "Let's get this over with. Yes, Quests are real. Yes, you will be running Quests as the first line of defense for our professional team. And yes, this is how most of you will die."

He violently brought his hand down as several hands rose to ask questions. "No, I will not be taking questions. The primary cause of injury and death in Quests are traps. We have no idea who creates them. It could be an agent of the Ancients or maybe the Sages create them with their minds. What we do know is the traps are getting more complicated and more difficult to detect and disarm. Our master trapsmiths innovate and build simulations to show you what traps we have encountered in the past. They also make modifications of their own to keep our professionals sharp."

Coach K signaled to Coach M who grabbed something out of the large duffel he carried. Coach M set the device on the ground. He retracted the spiked blades from their closed position into an open one. With the careful placement of a metal lever, he hooked it to the central plate. This kept the trap open.

"The standard trap has three parts: the trigger, the release and the killing device," said Coach M. He pointed at the plate, the spring and the teeth on the trap he set down. "Your job will be to trigger or disarm the traps in a way that does not make the Quest impossible to solve."

Coach M used his long arms to push the baton on the metal plate. With enough pressure, the trap slammed shut around the baton with a huge amount of force. The baton was wrenched from Coach M's grip to stand vertically, trapped within the jaws of the foothold. Coach M stepped on two small levers on either side of the trap and the jaws fell open.

"This is the most basic trap. What you encounter will be anything but basic. Triggers link to pressure plates like this one. We have also seen them linked to puzzles that need to be solved, heat sensors, and more recently ether sensors to take out our magickers. They could have any other possible trigger you can think of. We're going to do our best to train you to identify these traps to trigger them in a way that does not kill you. Once triggered they are easier to disarm. In some cases, they can be disarmed before they're triggered at all," said Coach M.

Coach K stepped forward again. "Each time you successfully trigger a trap that does not kill you, it gives you the opportunity to trigger another trap. At some point, your luck will run out. We will try to provide you with enough skill to extend that luck for as long as possible...who knows, maybe you'll even make it through the season."

* * *

Coach K led them into the larger room. Different challenges ran in different directions from the main room. Some sloped up, others had stairs that led down.

"There are five passages and twenty-five of you," said Coach K. "Number Eleven will start in the far left passage, number Twelve will go through the next one, and so on. After five minutes, the cycle repeats. If you get caught in the killing mechanism it will hurt but will not be fatal. You will be categorized based on how many traps you are able to trigger on your run."

Coach K signaled to his assistants who lined them up by number via the passages they would explore. Once they were lined up to his satisfaction, he nodded. "There is one cardinal rule. If you identify a trap, you *must* trigger it. Our professional team has earned the right to avoid these traps. You have not. In the field, if a single A finds a trap and doesn't trigger it, our pros are given standing orders to eliminate that team member."

"This is stupid," said Thirteen. She stood several feet from Kavi. She was a small Bricker with bright yellow hair that stood upright in spikes. Piercings ran the length of each ear, one of the earrings looked like it was connected to an augment set within the ear, probably to enhance hearing. "What happens if we say no?"

Kavi winced at her words. He didn't recognize the woman, either from last night or from Categorization yesterday.

Coach K's scowl was hard to determine from his resting warthog face but the surprised chuckle did not bode well for the young Bricker. "You must not have made it out of the hospital ward yesterday, Thirteen."

He snapped his fingers and Coach M reached his skeletal arms out to snap a metal collar around her neck. It was made of the same material as the batons the coaches carried.

"Since you missed yesterday's demonstration, this is what I call a motivational collar. The first thing you probably noticed is that your body is moving much slower. Our Vonderian example yesterday found he could no longer reach his magic. Any special skills you have are also suppressed. But what I find really fun," he nodded to Coach M who flicked something on his baton, "is the shockingly powerful motivation of the collar itself."

Number Thirteen began to shake. Her hands clenched and her body stiffened as her face distorted in a rictus of pain.

Coach K put his face inches from hers and said. "I would highly recommend not saying no." He nodded to Coach M and the shocking power ceased.

The young Bricker sagged, spikey hair now frizzy, a symbol of defiance conquered.

"Any other stupid questions before we start?" asked Coach K. His eyes never left Thirteen. She shook her head and Coach M removed the collar. "Excellent, let's begin."

Kavi cursed his low number which forced him to go first. He took a deep breath and followed his mother's advice. 'If you wait until you're ready, you'll be waiting forever.' When she wasn't giving ultimatums she sometimes made sense.

Kavi approached the passage tentatively. The cavern was lit with the same green mage light of the central passageways. The intensity of light in the trapped passages was much weaker. This increased the shadows and added to the overall creepiness of the experience.

It reminded him of the last time he explored underground. He winced at his naivete as he remembered how poorly their exploration of the Royce's Barrow went. A stark reminder of how dangerous Quests were. If those traps hadn't been triggered already he, Nettie and Grim would have died. His mind wandered again to how Grim and Nettie were doing. He tried to imagine how they would approach a trapped tunnel. Nettie's keen eye and agile fingers would make her a natural, but Grim? Kavi grinned and imagined Grim lowering his head and running as fast as he could down the hall.

The thought distracted him enough that he almost stepped on the first, very obvious, pressure plate. It held a trap almost identical to the one Coach M had demonstrated. The teeth around the mechanism had been blunted but if the contraption closed on him, it would hurt like hell.

Kavi regretted not grabbing a staff off the rack to use as a triggering mechanism. He hadn't thought a weapon would help him past a trap. He looked around for another way to trigger the plate but could only see small rocks and smaller pebbles. He threw some on the pressure plate but they were not heavy enough to trigger the trap.

Inspired, he looked to the lights mounted on the wall. They were removable so they could be replaced when they ran out of power. Kavi reached for the handle and carefully removed it. When he pulled the light out of the sconce he heard a clicking noise and froze. The large gate hidden in the wall had nubs instead of spikes on the front of it. It swung across the width of the cavern and swept Kavi along with enormous force. It slammed then pinned him against the wall.

"Ow," was all he could get out through his bruised face.

His thoughts flashed back to the barrow and he realized how lucky he got. He, Grim and Nettie were idiots to have thought they could tackle a Quest on their own. *Krom, I hope they're ok.*

Minutes later, Sixteen walked down the same passage. She was a tall Loamian who walked with a forest's worth of confidence. Her greenish brown hair rippled against her back like vines swaying in the wind. She looked at Kavi, squished against the wall and muttered, "Pathetic." She poked Kavi with her staff hard enough to make him grunt.

The Loamian used her staff to trigger the pressure plate and moved the spring trap to the side. The woman continued to walk forward at a measured pace and Kavi's eyes tracked her as far as he could. When she was nearly out of view, he saw her disappear as the floor beneath her vanished. He couldn't help a smile when she began moaning and cursing in pain from the bottom of the pit.

When the next three passed, only Twenty-six grinned at his plight. Each of them were caught by traps not too much farther from the Loamian. When he heard number Thirty-one scream as she triggered the last trap, he winced.

We are so screwed.

* * *

It took several hours for the coaches to release and extract the fodder team from the traps. In discussions over lunch, nobody was surprised the technically-minded Brickers and the artistic Harpstrans fared the best. Kavi was surprised to learn nobody made it anywhere near the end of the trapped passages.

After lunch, Coach K stood in front of the group again, this time in another specialty room barely large enough to fit the entire squad. Behind him sat four pools of water with steam misting off their surfaces. The thought of a hot bath had each of them shivering in anticipation. The trepidation Kavi felt came from the silver glow of the pools.

"Behind me is the latest and greatest in Vonderian neuromance magitech," said Coach K.

Pip sucked in a quick breath. Kavi looked over but Pip didn't acknowledge him.

"These pools simulate an environment of our choosing in the comfort of your own brain," continued Coach K. "I can see the nervous faces of the Vonderians in the room. It warms my heart you have so little faith in your countrymen. Don't worry about it. These pools are in their third revision. This is not just any neurotechnology, this is League certified and has been tested on ten seasons of single A subjects before you. Our professional team sometimes uses it to train."

"Lest you think I care about your comfort level, I *only* mention this so you do not fight the effects. Focus instead on the environment you will encounter. What you fight within your own brains is a simulation but the creatures you find there are based on the real world." Coach K drew his baton and tapped it against his leg.

"The hard fact we've had to face is: monsters are real. Something happened to Grendar in the last forty years. What used to be myth is now reality. These monsters used to be only seen on a Quest but that's no longer true. One of the functions of the League is keeping that reality from the masses. We protect as many people as possible from these manifestations."

"Yeah, the League's a bunch of real heroes," said a voice from the back followed by the whacking of a baton against legs.

Kavi agreed with the man's sarcasm and knew he was not alone.

"You may not believe it, being slaves and all," said Coach K. He didn't acknowledge the interruption. "But we protect a lot of people from things that go bump in the night. What you are about to experience in the neuro pools are things from nightmares. You will learn to fight them and become used to them here so you don't freeze when you encounter them on a Quest."

They were told to disrobe. Kavi did so without hesitation. Any modesty he and the others once had had long disappeared in captivity. Kavi waded into the pool and found it warm, even relaxing. He waded through it and found a seat on the far side of the first pool.

The seats were cut to fit a body and had armrests under the liquid. When he placed his arms and legs in the appropriate places he felt fabric straps wrap and clamp around his limbs, holding him in place. By the shocked looks of the others, they were also restrained.

With everyone secure, Coach K and his assistants moved to a smaller room with a viewing window. They shut the door and those in the pools could see them fiddling with a control mechanism.

A loud whirring sound filled the room and a large ball of light began to drop from the ceiling. When the ball descended to head level, the light became very intense. With a heartbeat, the world disappeared.

* * *

Kavi found himself in a forest. He breathed in and smelled hints of juniper and wet leaves. If this was a simulation, it was amazing. He looked around but could not see other team members. He sighed. He was going to have to face whatever it was, alone.

He breathed deep and found his mantra. *Move like wind, strike like fire, defend like earth, parry like water.* When the drums began, he hoped he knew what to expect.

The first banglor dropped in front of him. With a thought he reached to his back to grab the twin swords he carried while with the Eagles. He wasn't surprised to find them there. He imagined himself wearing the armor of an Eagle and that appeared too. He breathed deep to get comfortable with the steel around his body.

Time didn't slow, but he didn't need it to. After he avoided the strikes of the two banglors that dropped, they moved awkwardly towards him. Their climbing advantage afforded by long arms disappeared on the ground. He ducked under the swipe of claws from the closer one and with a roll over his swords, he was next to, then behind the creature. As he came out of his roll, his right sword swept backwards and removed the head from the gorilla beast.

The decapitation caused the other one to scream. Then, it charged. Kavi stood still until it leapt into the air to attack with a two arm overhead strike. While flying through the air, it lost its advantage. *Never leave the ground in combat.* The words had been drilled into him at the Bastion. It made you predictable. Kavi sidestepped the overhead strike and plunged both blades into the creature's back.

Kavi fought for hours. Corpses piled up around him. This was the third time he moved locations to gain enough space to use his blades. He took two deep lungfuls of air before the drums began again. Each time the drums started he had to fight another round of banglors. Each time they showed up with more companions. In his previous battle, there were five of them. Kavi used the mantra to convince himself he was in a simulation, leaving him slightly refreshed. This time he couldn't trick his mind into it.

Only two of them dropped out of the trees this time. The larger one wore a feathered headdress and a knucklebone necklace.

"You fight well for an unfurred," said the large banglor. The words came out in a series of hoots punctuated with chest beating but Kavi could understand it.

His eyes widened. He did not expect speech. When the green light sprang up around the shaman's hands he knew he made a grave error in underestimating this one. To treat them as little better than beasts was going to get him killed.

Reminiscent of his battle against Tess, tendrils of vines reached from below his feet and from the branches above to hold him in place. Rooted, Kavi could only watch as the shaman's companion lumbered closer.

"See you next time, little unfurred," said the shaman.

The pain was intense as the banglor's claws opened his stomach. He made sure Kavi watched as he started to pull organs from his belly. It began to eat them in front of him.

Kavi screamed from the pain until his vision began to fray at the edges and finally darken.

"-cking banglors!" he yelled in common as he awoke in the viscous liquid. He gasped and stared at his ruined stomach only to find the skin smooth and unmarked.

Pip gave him a weak smile. "I think Jansen might have undersold how terrifying banglors are."

They both looked to the big Krommian but the man stared down at the thick liquid, lost in thought or nightmare.

21

Training

Dying is humbling, more so when it happens in your own head. There was no jockeying for position that night. Even Nineteen was subdued. He sat quietly on his bed rebuilding the rig Kavi damaged the day before.

"You good?" Kavi asked Jansen. The man lay on his side facing Kavi and the flames of the cookfires. His broad, stubbled face looked a lot younger even crisscrossed in scars as he gazed into the flames.

The big man flipped over to face the other way.

Kavi had asked for the companionship to work through his own nightmare. It was harder on Jansen. With every banglor he faced, he had to relive the trauma of losing his old unit on the edge of the Draydale. Kavi was certain Jansen accounted for a score of the beasts in the simulation before they took him down. Or, the man panicked and froze. Either way, he died in the end.

They all did.

Kavi's attempts to get Pip or Tess to open up ran into similar walls. He wished Grim was around for the hundredth time. His friend was as stoic as they came but he always listened when Kavi needed to vent, even if he didn't offer anything of his own.

Grim would struggle in this environment, or whichever one he ended up in. He would be forced to hurt people. He would withdraw again. He would turn back into that husk. They always kept each other sane at the Bastion but the big man was so intimidating others would be afraid of him. He would have no one to talk to. Kavi cursed at himself. He never should have gotten Grim involved in any of this. What happened to Grim was all his fault.

Kavi turned and stared at the fire. The images conjured in the flames were of ape men gnawing through intestines. Finally, he stood. He turned and stretched, surveying the room.

One of the Harpstrans Kavi assisted last night drew on the wall above her pallet with chalk. He walked over to watch.

"It's beautiful," he said. "What is it?"

She continued drawing, caught up in the work. With a step, she stood on the pallet so she could reach higher. She reached into a small pouch around her belt to grab other pieces of chalk. She added a color here, a different thickness there. The figure she drew was a symbol, ominous yet strangely hopeful. Her agile fingers drew delicate lines where necessary, then deep thick accents to punctuate a feeling.

Kavi was mesmerized by her creation, enamored with how confidently she put down new lines. He found himself fearful each new stroke of chalk would ruin what was already there. It never did. Her skill blended calligraphy with art and a symbol unfolded in a tapestry of emotion.

At some point she stopped drawing and got off the bed. Kavi continued to stare at her creation, not noticing when she stopped. It made him feel stronger.

"It's a Harpstran death rune," she said in a surprisingly deep voice.

Kavi jumped, having completely forgotten about her, lost in her work. He ripped his eyes from the symbol to her. The glow from the fire stippled chaotic light across her making the tattooed scales on her neck glisten. The firelight made her hair glow with a reddish hue making her look angelic and demonic at the same time. She had a small cleft on her chin. With her hair pulled back in a ponytail, he could tell her ears were slightly too large for her thin face. Chalk dust covered her hands and much of her uniform.

"Who died?" Kavi asked after a moment.

"Me," she said.

Kavi nodded. "Thank you." He looked back to the symbol. "It captures how crappy I'm feeling right now but also makes me feel a lot better about it."

"The masters were supposedly able to infuse power into their creations. With that power, runes could elicit emotion but also heal, or increase confidence and even strength. DesGahn's masterpiece in the Musee de Rean was said to bring hardened soldiers to tears before it built them back up again."

"Looking at this, I can believe it."

"I am no DesGahn," she said. "But we have a saying in Harpstra - only art can heal the deepest wounds. I'm not sure I understood what that meant until today."

"I don't know who Day Gone is but this is the first time I've felt something other than pain and disgust since walking out of that pool. There's power here. Even if I don't understand it."

Kavi felt drawn to the symbol as if it called to him. Staring at the symbol, Kavi realized that ever since waking up from his fight with the Ach'Su, he had felt stronger, his senses sharpened. The realization came like a slap to the face: fighting the Ach'Su changed him - old scars healed, his body upgraded.

The sensation from the rune felt similar, like a new, internal sense, deep inside, calling to him. He wanted to touch the symbol but feared damaging the drawing. Instead, he placed his palm beneath the symbol and gasped at the warmth that ran up his arm. Confidence and life filled him. The idea he might make it out of this alive entered his mind for the first time. When he moved his hand from the wall, the feeling faded.

"Put your hand right here," he said, keeping his hand on the spot.

"Thank you but I'm not looking for any-"

"No, I'll move my hand." He looked at her as he removed his hand. "Do it. Please."

She placed her own hand in the same place. Her eyes widened and her cheeks flushed as the sensation filled her. "The legends spoke of true power imbued in art but I've never..." She breathed deeply, looking more alive by the second. "Some masters claim pain or trauma can create something with real power. Others say sulimite is the only thing that can add power to art. Skill of the artist and materials used are contributing factors but it's all theory. I've never experienced it."

"I've heard dying can be quite traumatic," said Kavi with a hint of a smile.

She laughed. The sound ricocheted through the somber room like an unwelcome house guest. She covered her mouth to muffle the laugh but he removed the hand.

"No, we need laughter," he said, letting go of her hand. He looked around the room. "We've got more than enough sadness and pain."

She looked around the room and nodded, but the laughter, and the moment, faded.

"Thank you," he said again then looked at her number, "Thirty-three."

"Clara," she said.

"Kavi."

"I know," she said. She turned from him, reached for a piece of chalk and began work on another drawing.

* * *

Defiance was replaced with sad acceptance as the fodder squad for Company Sugoroku lined up. They would have bristled at the term surrender but, deep in their hearts, they knew it wasn't far off.

Coach K smiled broadly, like a tabby who cornered a mouse. "Nothing like dying for complying, eh coaches."

Coaches L and M nodded their heads and smiled, playing their roles.

He ran a hand across his nose then wiped it on his pants. "Categorization allows us to focus your training. While most of you will die during the season, some *will* survive. This training extends your usefulness to the team while you're part of the fodder squad."

Coach K held up a hand, fingers splayed wide. "There are four roles in each Squad: Striker, Guard, Disarmament and Fortifications." A finger collapsed each time he listed a role. "I haven't put my thumb down because there is a fifth team the wounded or generally useless end up on. We call it Logistics and Support. Coaches, give em a breakdown."

Coach L stepped up. "I'll work with the offensive teams, Strikers and Dancers. That's what the pros call the disarm teams because they dance with death as they float over trapped earth. The Strikers take down whatever monsters the Sages cook up to let our Dancers get rid of traps." He looked to Coach M.

Coach M stood from a crouch to his full height, looking like a pill bug unrolling. "I'll work with the defensive groups. When we take ground, we never give it back. When Strikers get wounded, they need to fall back without losing progress. Guards are shields and front line defense. Fortifications build static defenses like trenches and walls and man those defenses with ranged support."

In spite of his distaste for the Coaches, Kavi was riveted. The League had turned Quest solving into an enterprise, something they had been improving upon for decades.

"Thank you, coaches," said Coach K. "This is how the pro and triple A teams operate. Most of you will die to random traps and monsters before you establish a cadence. Since we have four weeks of training, we're going to use all of it to increase your chances. You will train from morning until an hour after noon meal. Then, you will work. That work will continue until eighth bell when you will take supper. Who sleeps where, who eats what, is up to you. This is your life now. The sooner you accept it, the better your chances of making in through the season."

Coach K pulled out a sheet of paper and looked down at it. "I will call out your number and categorization. No one is on the L&S crew this early in training."

"Eleven - Striker. Twelve - Striker. Thirteen - Dancer. Fourteen - Guard. Fifteen - Fort...."

Kavi made his way to stand behind Coach L as Coach K continued to read off the names. He offered a fist to Pip which the Vonderian bumped as they grouped up. Seventeen, Nineteen, Twenty and Twenty Six were added to the Striker group. Jansen went into the Guard group. Clara became a Fort while her Harpstran companion became a Dancer.

The biggest group was the Dancers and the smallest the Forts. Kavi wasn't sure if that was because the Dancers were the most expendable or for some other reason. Either way, he was happy he wasn't in that group.

Coach K took the Dancers back to the trap caverns. Coach M had Eight and Ten take the Forts to a far corner of the primary training hall. The ground there was already torn up from previous construction projects.

This left Coach L with the Strikers and Coach M with the Guards.

Coach L wasted no time lining them up in front of the spar circles. "You will spend your time sparring with each other and sparring against the Guards. You will learn how to identify traps so you don't get blown up before you reach the monsters. Mostly, you will be fighting in the glow pools."

The Strikers released a collective groan at the last.

Coach L held up a hand. "No bitching. If you want to improve there's no better motivator than trying not to die. You have a week until we put you back in the Pool. Use it to get stronger."

The hangover from dying made everyone sloppy. Kavi could never find calm as he squared off against Pip. Pip actually dropped his staff twice while warming up. After an hour of uninspired sparring Coach L had enough.

"If you're not going to fight, you're going to run," he shouted. "Five laps around the Rim."

The Rim was the track that circled the big room. It was a little over two kilometers in circumference and completely flat. Compared to running the Rock at the Bastion it was an easy stroll.

Kavi set a slow pace for those that didn't have the benefit of running twenty kilometers a day for four years. Pip and Tess had no problem keeping up. Neither did the rest of the Strikers save for Twenty-six and Nineteen. Both of them relied too heavily on magic or augments and trinkets. They were breathing hard after one lap.

The slow pace gave Kavi the chance to observe. He didn't see any of the double As training but the pros and the triple As had each taken over a part of the big cavern. The triple As appeared to be playing a game of capture the flag. Their actions were coordinated and executed with incredible speed.

Kavi watched a Krommian Striker charge a Guardian shield wall. When he was almost to the wall, he leapt and landed on a cushion of air provided by his Vonderian teammate. This allowed him to attempt a flip over the wall. The Guards defending were ready, two in the front row elevated to meet the Krommian flying through the air. Kavi couldn't tell how they moved vertically until he realized they were tethered to a spindly platform operated by a Bricker in the back. The Krommian struck the shield wall and ricocheted backwards. The man wore a smile as he landed.

His attack was a feint. While the two men launched upwards to block, a small Harper woman slipped undetected beneath them. A shimmer surrounded her so she blended in to her surroundings. She grabbed the flag and split into three mirror images, each running in different directions. Tendrils from the ground pierced the fake images but were unable to snare the real one.

Kavi slowed his pace even more to see how the encounter would resolve. The large defending Guard on the far end reached the flag bearing Harpstran but instead of pulling her down, he turned to block the rest of his team from attacking her.

"Cheap trick!" yelled one of the Guards as the Krommian laughed.

One of their coaches blew her whistle. The big Guard defending the Harper threw down his shield in disgust. He pointed at a slim Vonderian woman standing in the back of the Striker line. "Stay the hell out of my head Yan!" he yelled.

The Krommian did a small dance. "Cheap trick, but we won. You knew Yantzy was going to neuro-control. You need to learn how to defend it."

Another Harper materialized behind Yantzy, dagger in hand. He had lined up a strike to take out the willowy Vonderian mage. "Three more seconds!" the man yelled. "Coach, you blew the whistle too fast."

Kavi had nearly stopped as he and his team of Strikers watched in fascination. The triple A Striker Coach noticed them watching and blew her whistle again. "Keep moving Ghosts or I'll tack on another five laps!"

Kavi picked up the pace, shocked at what he'd seen. The entire triple A squad had to be training with suli. The speed at which they moved and the...the powers they had. They used them flippantly, as if the miracles of motion were everyday occurrences.

There were legends from every Garden City culture of hidden powers the old heroes supposedly had; some intrinsic, others unlocked by sulimite. Sure, Krommians today claimed to berserk in battle while Loam-touched could manipulate nature and Vonderians had access to magick, but that was everyday stuff.

What he just saw was new.

It was going to take a while to get his head around Harpers disappearing and Brickers tinkering on the fly. If the triple As were this good, imagine what the professional team was capable of.

As he picked up the pace he realized what surprised him most. They might have been training hard, but the triple A team looked like they were having fun.

The concept was so foreign, not only in this place but to him. He hadn't had fun since...well, since before Brink didn't return from his first mission. He threw himself into being what Stonecrest and his mother needed. There was some satisfaction in a job well done, but nothing like joy.

Kavi shook his head and kept running. Rumination wasn't going to help with his current situation. That life was gone. Now he had nothing but his own abilities. Cultivating those might just keep him and the others around him alive.

* * *

He reported to work detail with a new perspective. His situation hadn't improved but there was a lot he could learn from the League.

For work detail, Coach L told the Strikers to meet in the intake area. They would be directed from there. After a quick argument about which direction the stairs were to get down to the squat building, the group set off.

The squat building looked a lot different with no people. The crates stacked against the walls were mostly empty now. Servants or team members had lugged their contents somewhere within the Nest. Two double As sat at desks near the double doors leading outside.

"Striker A team reporting for work detail," said Kavi as he approached the two men.

"Right," said the man on the left. He adjusted his spectacles and looked down at the schedule on his desk. The man looked comfortable behind the desk, a natural bureaucrat. Kavi wondered how he survived the trials during his time on the fodder squad. It gave him hope.

"You have not been issued mountain gear. Is that correct?" He continued to skim the paperwork in front of him never looking up at Kavi or the Strikers.

"That's correct," Kavi said.

The man pointed to several crates on the far wall. "Go through those until you find heavy coats, gloves and thermal headgear that fits." He pointed to a small closet to the right of the double doors. "Once you're outfitted, grab a shovel and get started."

"Get started on what?"

"The road to the bridge," said the bureaucrat. "We get a lot of snow up here. Two of my teammates will join you when they finish their training." The man looked back up. "Go!"

The Striker team began pulling heavy coats out of the crate. The first one out of the crate fit Kavi perfectly so he began rummaging through the next, looking for gloves.

"These are all too big," said Nineteen as he discarded coat after coat.

"Go through the ladies bin," said Tess. She stared down his angry look. "Stop acting like a child and grab a coat," she said.

He swore but did as she directed. He looked slightly mollified as the one that fit him looked exactly the same as the coats in the men's bin.

The gloves were thick and comfortable and the thermal headgear was a simple wool hat.

As they grabbed their shovels, two more double As joined them in front of the doors. They carried their own shovels and were already garbed in their winter gear.

"Now I'm hot," whined Twenty-six.

"Hang on to that feeling, it's not going to last," said one of the newcomers. He opened the door and a gust of freezing air swept in. It rustled the papers on the two desks, earning him a dirty look from the bureaucrat. The newcomer gave a rakish grin and headed outside.

"It was downright balmy when you all showed up earlier this week," said the man on the left. His features were shadowed by the hood he wore but they could still make out the hilts of the crossed dagger tattoos that crested at his chin. "My name is Stix and I'll be your work detail guide with my buddy Stonez over here. He's the strong, silent type so I'll be doing most of the talking. We're Guards by trade but haven't been on a Quest in four years. Thank Harp's shiny globes for that. Our job today is to clear the snow from here to the bridge. Last night's drop was only ankle deep, so this should go quick. You all know how to use a shovel I hope."

He looked at them as if somebody might say no. "Only rule to work detail is no powers and no tech. It's assigned to help tone your bodies to increase survival for your first Quests. That rule will change later in the season but for now, consider yourselves suppressed. I recommend you take advantage and work your butts off. The lazy ones in my class died quick."

He pointed at the road. "Let's get started."

Kavi started scooping snow next to Stix. "You been here four years?"

"Yup."

"Is it that hard to make the triple As?"

Stix barked a laugh. "You got to be crazier than a Harper on a bender to try out for a team. You know triple As sometimes get deployed, right?" He looked at Kavi. "Of course you don't, you just got here. A piece of advice, keep your head down, do your job and don't stick out."

Kavi looked over at Pip shoveling next to Stonez. When Pip tried to strike up a conversation, Stonez turned to him and said, "Do your work and don't talk to me ghost."

"Ghost. One of the triple A coaches called us that earlier," said Kavi to Stix. "What is that?"

"More than half of your class is going to die. It happens every year. So, you're just ghosts until you make it through your first season."

"A little harsh to keep reminding us of that isn't it?"

"The sooner you accept your own death, the better your chance at surviving," said Stix. He sent another scoop over the bank along the side of the road.

"Coach K said something like that too. Please don't tell me *he* has our best interest in mind," said Kavi.

"Hell no. That guy is as rotten as they come. He takes joy in your pain, but don't judge the rest of us quite so harshly. Calling you ghost is as much for us as it is for you. We learn quick not to make friends with the fodder team, too painful with how many die. You'll earn a name if you make it through your first couple Quests."

Kavi nodded and went back to shoveling. He had a lot to think about and physical labor was exactly what he needed to free his mind.

22

Back in the Pool

"Fear?" asked Kavi. "That doesn't seem right, I've been afraid many times, terrified in fact. I've never been able to do anything like that."

"I didn't say fear," said Stix. "I said *mortal* fear, being afraid you are going to die."

They had fallen into a pattern over the last week and a half. They trained relentlessly every morning into the early afternoon. The fodder team slowly expanded their knowledge of traps, mostly by getting caught in them. Olsen and the other healers worked overtime to mend broken bones and reattach severed digits. The deeper the teams progressed down the halls of the Gauntlet, the nastier the traps.

Some of the Dancers became almost proficient at disarming. Thirteen, the young woman who 'greatly prefers it if you just call her Sliver, thank you very much,' had a knack for finding the weakness of a trap. She disarmed many before they were triggered.

The last time Kavi did a Gauntlet run with Sliver she made it clear who should be walking point. "No matter how much I enjoy looking at that perfect ass of yours Kavi, if you walk in front of me one more time I'm going to ram this Allen wrench so far up it you'll be shitting hexagons for weeks."

"Yes, Ma'am," was all Kavi could think to say, chastised but slightly flattered, as the group laughed at him.

The sparring evolved into team drills. They were still a disorganized mess so the teams ended up running the Rim more often than not. The professional team reserved the Pool for all of the past week. The pros trained against new monsters that a competing Company spotted to the northwest. The pro squad's last day in the Pool was today.

Coach K already reserved it for the fodder team tomorrow.

The only task Kavi and the rest of the Strikers looked forward to was work detail with Stix and Stonez. Stix was a fount of knowledge as long as you asked the correct questions. Kavi made sure to pair with him as often as possible. This afternoon was an unseasonably warm day, the snow in liquid retreat after two days of sun. Their daily shoveling exposed dark cobbles underneath which accelerated the melting such that most of the snow was gone from here to the bridge. He took a deep breath of air that smelled like spring days of playing in the mud. With so much less snow, Kavi thought they might have a less physical work detail.

He was wrong.

Instead of shoveling, they would replace cobbles. Many had cracked and broken after long winter seasons of contracting and expanding under dual forces of snow and sun.

"We have to wedge that broken cobble out before we replace it," said Stonez. "Nineteen, get the crowbar inside the crack and lever the bigger piece out."

Kavi waited until Stonez finished giving directions. "What's different about mortal fear?" asked Kavi.

The other Strikers kept working but they all listened. "Think about it," said Stix. "What's the first thing most of us do after brushing shoulders with death?"

The ex-Guard opened his jacket in the relative heat exposing the tattoos of the two daggers that ran up either side of his neck, ending with the hilts just under his chin. Kavi hadn't met many Harpers before coming to the Nest. He now understood they expressed themselves and told their personal histories through a series of tattoos instead of the scars he was familiar with.

Kavi grabbed a cobble and handed it to Twenty-six who helped Nineteen place it as he pondered the question.

"We try to forget about it," said Pip as he pushed down on a crowbar of his own. The broken cobble popped out with a crack, splitting an adjacent cobble as it did.

"And how do we do that?" asked Stix.

"By doing something stupid," said Tess.

Stix laughed. "True. We normally try to forget about mortal terror by doing something that proves we're still alive. We spit in the eye of death to show it doesn't have control over us. Seventeen's right, most of the time that's something stupid."

"Or we hide," said Nineteen. This was the first time the angry Bricker had contributed to a discussion. The team was so surprised they stopped and looked at him. He sat back on augmented haunches and raised narrow eyebrows in challenge.

"Or we hide," repeated Stix. He nodded to the Bricker. "We do everything we can not to think about it until we've built walls around any thought that reminds us that, someday, we're going to die. You know the old biddies who talk about death in hushed tones like mentioning it will somehow summon it."

Pip nodded. "I knew twin brothers like that at the Academy. They were brilliant, way ahead of the rest of the class. Until they tried to do an elemental merge in our second year. Their working tripped something in the Academy defenses. The Academy drained their lab of breathable air and they suffocated. Professor Acker was able to release the defenses and pump air into their lungs but they were never the same after. They were so afraid of dying they stopped living. Last I heard they became researchers who never leave the library."

"You talking about the Alvey twins?" asked twenty six. "I wondered what happened to them. I was in their younger sister's class, who was gorgeous by the way, but she wouldn't talk about it. Every weekend she was in the stacks trying to get them to leave until fourth year, she finally gave up. Pathetic family," he said.

"No! You have to lay down new sand *and* lime before you put down the cobble. I just showed you how to do it, dipshit," yelled Stonez.

Nineteen picked the cobble back up.

Everyone looked over at the commotion for a second before getting back to their own work and the more interesting conversation.

Stix passed the bucket of lime powder to Stonez. "Think about what happens when you know you could die. What happens in that moment?"

Kavi shook his head. He took the broken pieces of cobble back from Twenty-six and dumped them on the small sledge.

"Let me rephrase. What isn't happening in that moment when you think you're going to die?" asked Stix.

"You're not thinking about anything but surviving," said Kavi.

"Exactly!" said Stix. "Terror brings absolute focus. With absolute focus comes freedom to do things you've never imagined possible."

"Is that why the coaches keep telling us to accept we're going to die?" asked Tess.

"Yep," said Stix. "They try to help in their own way. Unfortunately, they can't get passed being total suckwads while doing it."

"I don't get that," said Kavi. "If we accept we are going to die, doesn't the terror go away?"

"Good question," said Stix. "We might make a philosopher out of you yet. Seventeen, spell it out for him?"

Tess grabbed one of the broken cobble pieces and brought her hammer down on it, reducing it to gravel. "Think about big cats for a minute."

"I don't know anything about big cats," said Kavi.

"Fine, think about a dog. Have you ever seen a dog feel sorry for itself? Even one that loses a leg, they don't waste time feeling bad. They live entirely in the present."

Stonez grunted. "Not bad Ghost, but you Loamian tree pumpers always get it first. All that nature communing crap, I guess."

"How colorful," said Tess.

Stonez shrugged.

"That's one of the first things our tree pumping instructors teach us," said Tess. "Nature doesn't care about the future. No matter what happens, everything in nature adapts. With adaptation comes struggle. Those that accept the struggle adapt and survive. Those that don't, die." She grabbed another cobble and lined it up.

"Living entirely in the present might work for dogs but when has that ever worked for us?" said Kavi. "Without our ability to think to the future, we would never take on large projects. We wouldn't create art or community."

"True, but that's not the point. If we accept the struggle, like everything *else* in nature does, acceptance allows us to tap into something primal, something....instinctual. The moment you accept death is inevitable, you stop worrying about being a special little flower and realize you play a tiny role in the constant struggle of nature."

* * *

That night, tension hovered over the dormitory like a buzzard circling a wounded animal. They were back in the Pool tomorrow. They all dealt with their impending, simulated death in different ways. Nineteen went back to tormenting the less martial oriented candidates.

Sliver took him aside and spoke with him for about thirty seconds. His face dropped and he ran to the bathroom. No one had seen him since.

That was an hour ago.

"What did you say to shut him up?" asked Pip, catching her as she made her way back to her bunk.

Sliver winked. "A girl needs her secrets, even in a place like this."

Kavi paced in front of the fire. He couldn't let it go, especially since they were getting back in the Pool. As he explained the conversation the Striker team had earlier to Jansen, Clara wandered over with several other higher numbers.

She cleared her throat. "It's like art and pain."

They stared at Clara until Tess nodded encouragingly.

"If you embrace the pain to try to understand it, you can express it, you can harness it. Maybe this is the same thing? If you embrace the fear, the fear loses some of it's power over you. It lets you take that power back."

Tess nodded and gave Clara a calculating look.

"Can't we just forget about it?" asked Jansen. "Booze does the trick."

Pip slapped him on the back. "If you get your hands on some booze, you let me know first."

Tess stood. "You two are idiots. Thirty-three is the only one here with a little sense."

Clara stood over the sitting Jansen and looked at him with soft eyes. "Booze and drugs don't work. Believe me, we have plenty of those in Harpstra. Not for pain, anyway. It just delays it." She turned to Tess.

"Clara, not Thirty-three, Clara."

Tess nodded. "Clara then. Can you show me the rune you were working on the other day?"

* * *

The door to the Pool was open. Coach K stood before it. He had been babbling on for a while. Kavi caught snippets here and there. It sounded like they would be linked this session so they could face the beasts as a team. He couldn't focus on the man's words.

"Strikers and Dancers in the left pool," said Coach K. "Guards and Forts in the center. We'll switch it up tomorrow."

"We're coming back tomorrow?" asked Jansen. His face drained of blood.

"Did I say I was taking questions Twenty-two?" asked Coach K. He looked at Jansen's pale face and smiled. "I'll allow it. Yes, we have the Pool for the rest of the week." He smacked the large man on the back. "How lucky do you feel right now? Now, get undressed and get in the damn Pool!"

Jansen sagged but took off his uniform.

Kavi waded through the heavy liquid and took his seat. It was warm, but felt anything but welcoming. To calm himself, he took a deep breath and tapped into his other senses. The water smelled of sea air, redolent of patrols near the Whisper Sea as an Eagle. He held on to the memory and waited for the restraints to strap him in.

Something about Clara's statement last night stuck with him. He wasn't looking forward to the impending fight for his neuromanced life, but he wasn't dreading it as much either. Anticipation battled with fear, like learning a new fighting style. A lot of pain at first, but eventually the work paid off.

Coach K and his assistants readied themselves in the viewing booth. He spoke to the group through lamped receivers that hung over the Pools. "Today, we start slow. This will be the first time in the simulation as a group. Get your bearings quickly, use the skills we've taught you and survive as long as you can."

The intense simulation lights descended from the ceiling. When the brightness grew unbearable the Pool disappeared.

Kavi blinked to reorient in space. He was in a small room. An old man with papery skin sat at a desk writing something with an ancient quill. Kavi tried to look over his shoulder and the man turned. His milky gaze pinned Kavi in place. Kavi flinched. The man's raggedy beard was wine stained and hosted a battalion of crumbs. He smelled of rot and madness.

"Hello and welcome to the great game. Your challenge today is to live as long as you can. Perhaps my words can help. Alligator okra in a serpent stew. Three dashes of nightshade but it only needs two."

Kavi cocked his head. "Is that a hint to a Quest? Is that what we're doing?"

"No, that's what I had for dinner last night. I had the sense you were wondering. Is there some left in my beard?"

The man rooted through the hairy recesses and pulled out a small chunk of rancid looking meat. He popped it in his mouth and chewed then made a slight moue of pleasure.

Kavi looked away in disgust.

The man finished chewing, grabbed the piece of paper in front of him and handed it to Kavi. "Memorize this, it might help in the hours ahead, but it probably won't." He laughed.

This must be a Sage, or at least a simulation of one, Kavi thought.

The Sage daubed at cataract shaded eyes with that disgusting beard.

"The Ancients did me no favor when they called my number. Messages come then messages stop. Each missive stretches and pulls at my mind like that taffy they sell in the Whisper Sea marina. Have you tried it?"

Kavi shook his head then realized the man couldn't see him. "No."

"You should." He pointed at the scroll in Kavi's hands. "Read that. Now! Before you're out of time."

Kavi looked at the piece of paper. The words were written in a clean, tight hand that didn't fit the man in front of him.

I reach to the sky but clutch to the ground
Sometimes I leave but am always around
Solace I offer in the spikes of my crown
To those who pose no threat to my gown

Near the bottom of the page was scrawled a single line in a shaky hand.

Heed the Rose, her thorns offer the one true way

Kavi looked at the man and frowned. The world turned a blinding white yet again.

He blinked and found himself in greenery so lush it could only be a simulation of the storied Jungle of Kar'Toon. He brushed himself off and saw his team doing the same. The exception was Tess. She knelt with one hand submerged in the loamy earth.

"I'm not sensing anything nearby, but the plants are muted, like they're not connected to the earth. I think the natural network is too big a stretch for the simulation," said Tess.

"Everybody meet with the disgusting old guy in the tiny room?" asked Kavi.

"Pretty sure that was a Sage," said Sliver. "That riddle make any sense to you?"

"No. I'm terrible at riddles, but why does it matter? It's not like we're solving a Quest. We're in the Pool, we fight until we die," said Kavi

"Maybe it's a hint to survival," said Pip.

"It's a tree," said Nineteen. "I reach to the sky but clutch the ground, sometimes I leave but am always around."

Nineteen sneered at Kavi's incomprehension. "sometimes I *leave*," he raised his eyebrows. "Too bad you're brain's not as fast as your body. It's a tree."

Kavi swallowed the impulse to punch the small Bricker. "That sounds right. The riddle talked about solace, maybe we use a tree in our defense?"

Kavi and Nineteen looked around and their eyes fixed on the same target, an enormous tree with a broad trunk with vines hanging around it like a verdant robe. It could serve to protect their backs.

Kavi turned to Sliver. "What's the best use of your squad in a combat situation?"

The Bricker turned from her group of Dancers to face Kavi. "If we're in combat we're already kinda screwed. Most of us don't have much in the way of military training. We can give some ranged support but that's about it." She smiled wickedly. "But if we've learned anything since we got here, it's that we know as much about setting traps as we do disarming them. We can put together a perimeter quick."

She screwed her eyes shut, touched the augment in her ear, then reached into the backpack that appeared at her feet. She rummaged through the pack and her smile widened at how much she was able to summon. "Oh yeah, we'll be able to put together a perimeter real quick."

She started issuing orders and backpacks appeared at the feet of the other Dancers as they called on the powers of the Pool.

"Dig in here," Kavi said to the Strikers. "Our strongest fighters will form a semi-circle around the trunk. Nineteen and Twenty-six, you provide range support and-"

"Kavi, I don't think-"

"One second, Tess. Pip, Twenty and I will join you and Tess to hold the outer line of the semi-circle. We can keep the Dancers protected in the middle."

"Kavi!" shouted Tess.

"What?!" he shouted back.

"They live in the trees," she said. With eyebrows raised over amber eyes, she growled like a furious lynx. She pointed to the biggest lizard he'd ever seen crawling along the limb of the giant tree. "Thought you might have picked up on that from the banglors."

"Well, shit," said Kavi.

They heard a couple of explosions but a lot more screams from the Dancers setting the perimeter. Sliver came running out of the jungle with a giant black cat chasing her. Its massive paw swept down and severed her spine. She lay twitching on the ground as the cat stopped to stare at the Strikers. It stood over the remains of its kill protectively.

"Back-to-back!" yelled Kavi. "Nineteen and Twenty-six, start blasting."

Kavi drew his twin swords and tried to find his mantra but the calm wouldn't come. Thirty-five, Clara's Harpstran friend with the snake tattoo, came crawling out of the undergrowth. Parts of her face were badly burned from a trap that went off prematurely. One of the lizards bit into her back leg and she screamed. Twenty-six shot a column of flame from his staff at the lizard who started to chew the flesh it pulled from her leg.

"Yes!" he shouted, eyes flashing scarlet as he called his ether. The lizard burned. The tail of another creature wrapped around Twenty-six's neck and pulled him off the ground and into the tree meant to serve as their defense.

Nineteen launched projectiles into the tree but the strike happened too quickly. Twenty-six was gone, pulled into the canopy. Moments later another tail dropped and pulled Nineteen away.

Kavi managed to draw blood with his swords when one of the large lizards got close. He was powerless to stop the big cat from tackling Pip to the ground. Tess fell moments after Twenty went down screaming and Kavi was alone. He continued to track the lizard he injured but he was badly exposed. He barely felt it when the claws cut through his armor and into his spine. The last thing he saw was the face of the lizard as it bit down.

He gasped as he woke back in the Pool. There was soft whimpering all around him as the fodder team again faced their new, grim mortality.

Nineteen stared at him. "Wonderful plan, moron," he said.

"Can we get out of here now? I need to get out of here," said Thirty-five. Her voice rose to a fevered pitch. An image of her being eaten by a lizard flashed through his mind.

As the sobs continued around him, he looked at the completely demoralized team. That's when the wonderful, terrible idea struck.

23

Once More Into the Breach

"Again," said Kavi. "We've got to do it again."

"I think that's enough for me for one day," said Pip.

"Are you out of your fucking mind?" screeched Thirty-five. "I can't go back in there. I'm not going back in there."

"Look, I don't like dying any more than you," said Kavi. "But when we die in there, at least we come back."

"He's right," said Sliver with a sigh. "If you listen to the rest of these assholes who keep calling us ghosts, the main reason they made it through their first season was luck. But, if you watch the pros and triple As fight? Those people are good. Fighting in the Pool could give us a chance to load the dice."

"No, no, no, no..." muttered Thirty-five.

"I'm with crazy lady on this one," said Twenty-six.

"Hypothetical then," said Kavi. "Tess, if we were to go back in, how would we fight those things in the jungle and win?"

"We wouldn't," she said. "Creatures will always use their natural habitat better than us. In a jungle, their advantage is too big."

"But why the riddle?" asked Kavi. "It's leading us to take solace in the trees, no? Pip, you have the best memory, think you can repeat it verbatim."

Pip took a shaky breath. "Best memory when I haven't just been torn apart by giant cat."

"This is important," said Kavi. "Can you remember it or not?"

Pip glared at him. "You're so irritating when you're focused." He closed his eyes and recited.

I reach to the sky but clutch to the ground
Sometimes I leave but am always around
Solace I offer in the spikes of my crown
To those who pose no threat to my gown

"That sounds right," said Tess. She gave Pip a grin. "Not bad, beanpole."

"What about the last part, with the rose?" asked Kavi.

"That was all of it, Kavi. I didn't read anything about a rose."

"At the very end, the Sage wrote something like Heed the rose, it's a way out. Nobody else saw that?"

The other Strikers and Dancers shook their heads. *Why would there be a message specifically for him?* He'd have to puzzle it out later.

"Sage messages always have a twist," said Kavi. "What are we missing?"

"What if the solace it offers is not for us but for the enemy," said Nineteen. "To those who pose no threat to my gown, the gown has got to be that dress of vines. It's a perfect place for an ambush from those lizard things."

Twenty-six looked to Tess. "So we burn it down?"

Tess nodded.

Sliver smiled. It was shaky, but it was a real effort. "We can make that happen."

The Forts and Guards were starting to come to. They lasted longer than the Strikers and Dancers but that was to be expected. They were defensive in nature. When Twenty-two finally woke up he did it with a scream and a splash.

When the lights retracted back to the ceiling, Coach K walked into the room.

Kavi yelled. "Send us in again!"

"I'm not sure I heard you," he said to Kavi.

"Yeah, you did," said Kavi. "We need to go back in."

"It doesn't work that way," said Coach L. "We have to reset the simulator."

"Then put us back in the same simulation," said Kavi. "Either way, we go again!"

Thirty-five let out a soft whimper and the Guards and Forts from the other Pool looked at Kavi like he was crazy. Coach K shook his head at Coach M when he pulled out his baton. The tall man tucked it back in his belt. Coach K stared at Kavi for a long moment. Finally, he nodded. "Ok, you go again."

* * *

Kavi nodded to Twenty-six. The man directed his fire at the tree. Everything in the jungle was so wet that the fire caused a crackling hiss which made it sound like the tree was screaming. Nineteen stood behind Twenty-six, holding his cannons upwards until the hissing of water turned to popping then cracking noises.

Sliver directed the Dancers to summon exploding traps. They set the charge for contact and spread a perimeter around them. When the traps went off, geysers of earth appeared in a circular symphony of destruction with the team in the middle. Kavi watched Thirty-five throw trap after trap, the fear on her face replaced with a rictus of hate.

Thirty-five's last trap caught the very same lizard who turned her into a meal last time. When it's face exploded she yelled. "How do you like it, slimy suck face?!"

"That's it Thirty-five," said Sliver. She continued to direct her Dancers in concerted destruction.

The tree finally caught fire. Nineteen fired a burst at one of the lizards with the long tails as it released a wad of acidic spit towards Twenty-six. "Move," yelled Nineteen, but he wasn't quick enough.

Twenty-six juked but the spit struck him in the left shoulder. The acid ate through his robes and he began to scream, his red eyes and skin faded to its original color as pain consumed him. The fire he directed disappeared but the damage to the tree had been done. The canopy was clear and most of their opponents had fled to safer perches. The tree still stood but as a charred husk, blackened branches reached towards the sky like a claw.

"Twenty, can you do field healing on Twenty-six?" asked Kavi.

Twenty nodded his bald head and began to pray. The angry bubbles on Twenty-six's sizzling shoulder began to ease and shouts of pain fizzled to soft whimpers.

One of the lizards Nineteen injured leapt towards them. The lizard spread its legs wide to reveal webbing that allowed it to glide. "You've got to be kidding me," whispered Nineteen. He fired at the lizard as it banked and turned. It readied itself for another spit of acid.

A trap exploded on its snout and Thirty-five yelled. "A lot more where that came from, you cock jugglers!" The explosion hit the acid sac inside the lizard and there was a secondary explosion which knocked Nineteen to the ground. He looked at the diminutive Thirty-five, who he had bullied only hours ago and nodded in thanks.

She ignored him, looking for more targets.

A moment later, the smoke cleared. The fodder team stood in a burnt out crater they shared with one very charred and lifeless tree. The tree shimmered then disappeared. In its place sat an oaken chest with shiny brass bands running along its length. The top of the chest was slightly open. It looked like something out of a kid's fairy tale book.

Kavi nodded to Thirty-five who was closest to the chest.

The small Harper walked to the chest and opened it. When it opened a river of gold motes flowed out of it then slowly disappeared. "What the fuck was that?" she asked.

"I think we made it past the first round," said Kavi. "Anyone besides twenty six injured?"

Twenty walked around the group healing minor wounds.

"I can't imagine the simulation is going to allow the peace to last," said Sliver.

"You trying to jinx us Thirteen?" asked Nineteen. "We finally win one..."

She was right. Large black cats congregated on the far side of the burnt out circle. Lizards gathered on the closer side. One of the cats shimmered and took humanoid form, moving from all fours to stand upright on its back legs in an effortless motion.

"Not good," whispered Tess.

"Irborra?" asked Kavi.

"I thought so in the first battle but we didn't last long enough."

"How do we fight them?" asked Kavi.

Tess shrugged. "I ran the last time I saw them."

The closest Irborra cocked its head as if listening to their conversation. *Damn thing probably is listening.* The pointed teeth in its half feline, half human face were horrifying. Two of the cats flanking it shimmered and shifted. They put furry hands on the closest Irborra's shoulder and it began to draw power.

"Pip!" yelled Kavi.

"I got this." Pip moved in front to face the cats.

"We're all gonna die at some point, we gotta accept it before these cock gurgling cat pumpers pull one over on us," said Thirty-five to no one in particular.

"Thirty-five is freaking me out man," said Twenty-six. He rolled his shoulder experimentally.

"We each deal with it in our own way Twenty-six. Find yours!" Kavi barked in his best drill sergeant voice. "Now, are you good to blast some of those damned lizards?"

"I think so," he said. He and Nineteen faced the other way.

The Irborra finished gathering its dark energy and pushed a sphere of dense night towards their line. It didn't move fast but it keyed on Pip like iron to a lodestone. When the dark ball hit Pip, Kavi expected it to evaporate as magic did around the tall Vonderian. Instead, Pip caught it and spun, his eyes turning the color of the night sky as his skin darkened. The ball flew towards the line of lizards at twice the speed the Irborra sent it at Pip. When it struck the lead lizard, it exploded in a wave of dark energy. All the lizards facing them shriveled as water was sucked out of their bodies.

"What the hell was that?" asked Kavi.

He smiled fiercely and shouted, "Embrace the shittiness!"

Thirty-five laughed at that. "Embrace it!" she shouted. Then she pointed at the Irborrans and yelled, "My turn to take it to these fuck frogs." Then, she disappeared.

"What the-," said Sliver when the Harper vanished.

Nineteen and Twenty-six turned back to face the cats after Pip devastated the line of lizards. Flames joined the projectiles that shot out at the Irborrans. With a flick of its wrist, the lead Irborra threw up a shield which neatly stopped their attacks. It glared at them with contempt.

Contempt turned to pain and fear when twin daggers sprouted out of either side of its neck. "Time to die, little pussy," whispered Thirty-five in its ear. The Irborra to the left of the leader shifted back to cat form and swiped at Thirty-five, ripping her throat out. She died with a smile on her face a heartbeat after the lead Irborra fell to the ground.

"No!" shouted Kavi, hearing his yell echoed by the rest of the team. They charged as one.

* * *

"Again," said Thirty-five as they woke up in the Pool. "I said AGAIN you dunderfucks!"

Coach L couldn't let that one slide. The baton struck her hard in her exposed arm.

She bared her teeth and stared at him. "Put. Us. Back. In. You. Turd. Herder."

Coach L lifted his baton again but she didn't flinch.

Coach K had come out of the booth too. He faced the group, a smile teasing the edges of his porcine mouth. "While I appreciate your enthusiasm, we're not approved to run a team through more than twice a day. The neuromancers who built the magitech made it clear that too many times in the Pool runs the risk of losing the ability to tell fantasy from reality. Once that link is broken, you're useless to us. You might as well be dead," said Coach K.

"But Coach, haven't you heard? We're the Ghost Squadron, we're already dead!" yelled Kavi.

Thirty-five laughed, the sound high pitched and broken. "Again!" she yelled.

The rest of the team in Kavi's pool began to join in. "Again! Again!"

The team in the adjacent pool were as stunned as the coaches.

Coach K held a hand up. "Fine. I will get approval today. When I do, there is no backing out, understand?"

"Again!" yelled the team. It was the only answer necessary.

Coach K shook his head. "In the meantime, you won the right to pick whatever meal you want tonight thanks to finding your very first Quest Chest."

Everyone in the Pool cheered except for Thirty-five and Pip. They both looked green.

Kavi was about to say something when Thirty-five began to convulse. She vomited black and red goop as she shook. The stench was of rotten meat and, oddly, baked carrots.

The coaches stared at her.

"I've heard about it," said Coach L. "But I've never seen it before. What do we do?"

"Healer!" yelled Coach K.

Then Pip started to convulse and the stench started all over again.

* * *

When they returned to the dorm that night, the mood was neatly segregated. Half the team, Kavi's squad in the pool, was celebratory. They had what felt like their first victory since being captured. Sure, they died in the end but because of overwhelming numbers.

"No, I feel great, better than I have in years," said Pip. "Though I did have some really strange dreams. In one of the dreams, one of my professors at the Academy kept telling me I was a new species. He said something about a switch flipping in my brain and a bunch of other nonsense I couldn't understand. Doctor Cleary said the League called it an evo and seemed to think it was a good thing."

"You remember when I woke up in the cart after our fight with the Ach'Su?" asked Kavi. "Remember that gunk I was covered in and the stench?"

Pip nodded.

"When I woke, I felt stronger too. These things have to be linked. Somehow."

The discussion was interrupted by a curse from Jansen. On the other side of the room, Jansen's team looked at Kavi's group like they'd lost their minds. They had no desire to do more than one run a day in the Pool and were angry the other team forced them into the situation tomorrow.

The two groups had been trading angry words since dinner.

The exceptions were the three stoics from the previous season. Eight, Nine and Ten sat alone on their beds wrapped in their own thoughts. Even after several weeks, they never initiated conversation with anyone in the squad. They did their work, they fought their battles and they went to bed.

Kavi grew tired of trying to convince Jansen that facing death was the only way any of them were going to survive. He grabbed a stool and moved over to Eight's bed. The woman was writing what looked like a letter.

He hadn't once considered contacting his parents in the three weeks since he got here. There didn't seem to be any point. He knew it would never be sent.

It was easy to imagine his parents waiting for news of him. He was sure his dad was worried sick. Kavi had always been good with correspondence. On every tour with the Eagles, he wrote at least once a week. That desire to please never knew when to quit.

His mother though, he could imagine her sitting in her council and getting the news from Carlin. She would say something like, "Every family is asked to make sacrifices." Fuck her and her stoicism. The anger infused him. It felt good, indulgent. It made him warm inside. It helped him forget that world, that life. He raged for a minute or two more into the silence until he realized Eight was looking at him.

"So, what's your deal anyway?" he asked. "You all just gave up?" She ignored him and went back to writing.

"We made serious progress today. Two of our group even went through some type of transformation," he said. "If your experience could help us survive when it gets real, we need you to share it."

Eight sighed. "Yes, the pros call them skills. My cohort had wins too," she said. "Then people started to die. For real. Waking up in the Pool is one thing, even if you feel like you just got ripped to pieces. But watching someone actually get ripped to pieces..." She shuddered. "Don't get close to anyone in here, Eleven. It never ends well."

When he tried to speak again, Eight held up a hand and shook her head. "No, that's it for the elder wisdom today. I'm going to get some sleep."

"Have it your way." Kavi stood and walked over to Clara and Thirty-five who sat on the bed having a conversation.

"No, I'm not going to call you Trixie," said Clara. "You're name is Tricia and you were always the best of us, the kindest of us. Why are you turning into this...crazy thing?"

"Kind will get me killed here Clar," said Trixie. "And I'm going with a whore's name because that's what we are. Our bodies were sold to the League, not for sex, but to be fucking blown up! The only way we get out of this shithole alive, with tits attached anyway, is by accepting that and owning it."

"Tits, shithole?! That's what I mean Trish, I've never heard you swear. Not once! All of a sudden you're a foul mouthed whore? I can't get my head around it."

"You need to. That's the epiphany I had today." Trixie rubbed at her neck where the snake tattoo used to be before her stint in the Pool today. "What you have mistakenly called kindness is actually just being nice. Yes, I was polite. Yes, I was the sunny one that brought smiles. That's not kindness. Kindness is more than empathy, it is doing something tangible. Kindness is taking your own personal pain and turning it into inspiration for others." She pointed at the death rune that Clara had put up the other day. She saw Kavi and nodded to him. "Kindness is stepping in and preventing two people from being bullied without asking for anything in return."

She pointed at Nineteen and shouted. "I still haven't fucking forgiven you for that, One Nine."

He turned to look at her. "I'm sorry," he said. "I didn't realize you were such a badass."

She stood up, raven hair mussed, crazy look painted on her face. "He still doesn't get it. Now, I've got to go explain it to him." She stomped over to Nineteen.

"She inspired a lot of people today," said Kavi softly.

"I heard," said Clara.

"She was able to go invisible, just like the triple As."

"I heard that too. She calls it poofing." Clara grabbed her bag of chalks and sighed. "Because of course she does. She's always been a free spirit Kavi. I don't like what the training is doing to her and not just because of those horrible seizures she had in the Pool. When that happened, she lost her tattoos. She looks so strange without them, like she did when she was a kid. But it's not the physical stuff that worries me."

"I don't like what the training's doing to any of us. Try to remember that none of this is her fault," said Kavi. "Or yours. It's the bastards that caught us and brought us here. Some day, we'll bring them to justice."

"I hope you're right," she said, sounding resigned. She didn't believe it either. She grabbed an orange piece of chalk and stood on her bed.

"Any inspiration from the Pool today?" he asked.

"When I died today, I remember feeling...incredibly cold. I knew, deep in my bones, that I would never, ever be warm again. Let's see if art can change that."

She began to draw. She switched chalks several times but did it so quickly, often mid-stroke, that the creation took on a magical quality. It looked like it was being grown instead of drawn. While the lines of the death rune were solid and solemn, this rune was whimsical. She would scratch out a line, then scratch over it with another. The foundation was chaotic. The rune itself took on several different shapes throughout the process. With two final strokes, she stood back and observed the creation.

"Unbelievable," said Kavi. "Have you always been able to create this fast."

She shook her head. "No. Dying changed me too."

Kavi stood up. "May I?" he asked.

She nodded.

Kavi pressed his hand on the stone underneath the rune and the drawing appeared to flicker for a second but when he stared directly at it, he could see nothing in the drawing change. Then a wave of heat swept through him and he heard Clara gasp next to him.

"Did you feel that?" he asked.

She nodded.

"Why does it only activate when I put a hand under it? Do you think there's a way we can make the effect permanent?"

"I have no idea," said Clara. "But maybe it has to do with materials. Chalk is flakey, impermanent. I bet sulimite could power it."

"That's not an option anytime soon," said Kavi. "What if we were to get you some paint? I might be able to get some from the double As on my work detail."

"Yes! Can you imagine it? If we could make this permanent, this side of the room would be as warm as the side with the fire."

"What about an engraving?" asked Trixie.

Kavi looked over to see if Nineteen was still in one piece. Nineteen was healthy but pensive as he reclined on his pallet.

"You mean chisel out the rock?" asked Clara.

"Why not? Couldn't I grab a chisel and cut out the first rune you made?"

Clara looked at the rune and lightly tapped her index finger on her chin, thinking. It left an orange smudge on the cleft of her chin that Kavi found enchanting. "Maybe," said Clara. "But I think it would lose power in the translation of medium. I have no experience with this, but I think I add the power when I add the emotion in the original creation. I bet you're right Trish."

Clara looked at her friend who gave her a dead stare. "Sorry, Trix! I'll try to remember. If only I could engrave or sculpt with the skill I draw."

They continued to look at the drawings above Clara and Trixie's beds. Trixie kept putting her hands underneath the two runes then groaned with pleasure in a mock seductive way as the heat and confidence poured into her.

"You're disgusting," said Clara.

Kavi laughed. The temperature on this side of the room had raised considerably.

"I wonder if it depends on the rune itself," Clara said. "The death rune is permanent. I bet an etching or a carving would be perfect for that one. Doesn't it seem like the fire rune has to be transient to be effective? I bet if you were to etch that one, it would lose its power."

"Oooh, I bet you could test all this in the Pool tomorrow. We can summon anything we need while we're down there," said Trixie. "Are we paired up tomorrow? No, damnit, the Dancers are with the Guards tomorrow. Ooh, but the Forts are with the Strikers. Kavi, make sure she tries this ok?"

At the mention of the Pool, Clara folded inward, like a flower withdrawing sensitive petals at the first touch of night. Kavi found himself hoping the excitement generated by her fire rune would bloom again under the bright lights of the Pool simulator.

24

The Dune

He tracked the path of a small scorpion skittering between the bunks and didn't raise his feet. It was hard to find fear in the ordinary. Besides, a venomous sting might offer him a couple of days rest to get his thoughts together. The small creature avoided his foot and disappeared into a tiny hole between the adobe bricks of the wall.

He leaned over, elbows on knees, and massaged his temples. Sometimes that helped with the headaches. The large man thought back on the past several weeks and did what he could to fill the gaps in his memory.

Every time he woke to a new day, it took several minutes for him to remember where he was. Once he remembered the Dune and the Ghosts he shared a room with, the Coaches would come in and throw them into some new trial. After facing it, he was rendered unconscious. Except for his first night in the Dune, he couldn't remember going to sleep. Only waking up. The Coaches had a tool to knock him senseless that he had no defense against.

The only clear day in memory was when he first woke in a recovery room in the Dune, surrounded by the most advanced clockwork and magical equipment he'd ever seen. A friend of his would be mightily impressed by the tools used by Senet's medical team.

No, not the friend, his friend's dad. That's who would be fascinated with all the magical clockwork.

When he lined up the first day, the Coaches of Team Senet eyed him hungrily, like lions drooling over a plump antelope. They told him he would play the role of fodder for Senet's professional team. If he made it through the first season, his status would change. In the meantime, he was a dead man, a Ghost, as the rest of Company Senet called him.

If only he could remember how he got here! A flash of pain accompanied a memory of facing bandits outside of a tunnel leading underground. More pain as he remembered brief snippets of fighting on a stage in front of a crowd. He cringed as he remembered breaking an opponent's neck. *Why did they keep making him fight?* The minute he saw red, he lost control.

He couldn't remember the details of the past several weeks but was plagued with images of hurting people whenever he closed his eyes. He couldn't piece the images together. It felt like reading a book with missing pages. His story was broken. Something inside of him was broken. He rubbed his temples harder and fought to remember.

The training facilities in the Dune would have made the drill sergeants at his military school cream their pants. The thought struck with a dagger of pain to his temple. That's right, he was a soldier. Whatever magic or clockwork the League had access to, it was far beyond anything he'd seen before. He should have seen these types of weapons because he was a special kind of soldier (another spike of pain), one who field tested the latest weaponry his military built or bought. His special unit didn't have anything nearing this level of sophistication.

Out of the corner of his eye he saw a Ghost edging towards him.

The other Ghosts were terrified of him. He had no memory as to why, but he heard the whispers in the early morning hours as he pieced himself together. He wounded or killed at least two of his fellow Ghosts. By the fear which threaded the whispers, it was probably the latter. What a grim situation. Grim situation. Something brushed at the thin foundation of his sanity.

"Pssst, Eleven," whispered the Ghost.

He ignored the man as he clung to the thought. Friend's dad. Kavi was that friend. Grim situation. The cobwebs began to clear.

"Pssst, Eleven," repeated the small man. He knelt just out of arm's reach. The man was covered in an array of tattoos common to Harpstrans.

He looked at the Ghost with the number Twenty-eight embroidered on his left breast. The numbers perched over a blue eye sitting atop a squat, inverted conical structure, the symbol for Team Senet.

"The name's Grim," he said in a raspy voice he hadn't used in weeks.

The man scampered backwards, eyes wide with fear. With a big breath, the man gathered his courage and crawled slowly back to Grim. "Nice to meet you Grim, my name is Albin."

Grim looked up from the man. All talking ceased. Everyone in the dormitory stared. *Why? Why did he always become the center of attention?* Did that sound right? It had to be, because he was tired of it. Grim nodded once to Albin, unwilling to trust his voice.

Albin looked back at the Ghosts staring at him and pulled strength from their curiosity. He turned to Grim, face pale and shivery. "I was wondering....well, I guess, *we* were wondering if there was any way you could go easier on us when the group is sparring? Maybe just a little?"

Grim rubbed his temples again, looking for memories. He didn't want to ask the question. He didn't want to know the answer. "What did I do?"

"You don't remember?"

Grim shook his head.

Albin cocked his head, trying to decide if Grim was telling the truth. "Well, in those early days, during Categorization, you killed two Ghosts and one of the Coaches before they zapped you with their batons. The other Coach you hurt so badly we haven't seen her since that first day."

Grim felt a sob boil in his throat. He let out a small piece of the heart rending cry which fought to get out.

Albin jumped back. "No, please! You start that cry when you start killing! I'm not blaming you for any of this; they've done something to you. We all know it."

Grim stabbed his index fingers into his temples until the pain his fingers caused was greater than the pain revealed by memory. He took a raggedy breath and choked back the sob. It wasn't the first time he heard that. That's why he was kicked out of his army squad. A stab of pain. The Suli Elites. That's what he was, an Elite. The best killer of the bunch. It didn't matter if it was friend or foe. Krom, he needed a drink.

Grim shook his head. "No. They haven't done anything to me. It's me. I'm an abomination."

A woman with the precise sicari scars of a decorated, Krommian shield warden came to stand next to Albin. She wore the number Fifteen on her breast. "You're a berserker, aren't you?"

Grim nodded. "I think so."

She took a step closer and examined his scars. "You were a Suli Elite. How could they put you on a squad like that? Didn't they know?"

Grim shook his head. "Not until my third mission. The evil only comes when something inside thinks there's no other choice. Usually it's a no win situation or I'm pretty sure I'm going to die."

Albin snorted. "Really, a berserker? You're in the biggest no win situation ever. You're a Ghost. You're going to kill all of us!"

"Not helping, Albin," said the woman with a fierce look directed at the man. "I heard tell of only one other berserker in my two tours with the Second Tower."

Grim nodded. "Tower Two, you turned the day at Valun."

She shrugged. "Before my time."

"Wasn't that the Lioness' regiment?" asked Albin.

"Quiet," snapped the woman with another fierce look. She turned back to Grim. "He has a point. If you keep killing and maiming Ghosts, you're going to be the only one left as fodder on this first Quest. You have to rein it in."

Quest. The word brought another searing memory. Nettie and Kavi. That's what they were doing before they got captured by that bastard Roanik. The cobwebs cleared more. He nodded and rubbed his temples.

Fifteen looked down on the sitting Grim. "Many men in my squad claimed they berserked in battle, but Quirrel Toms was the only true berserker I ever saw. When he went to war, all reason fled until he was knocked unconscious. He was an incredible warrior, so knocking him out became harder and harder. Finally, they tossed him at the front of the vanguard and gave him a wide berth. The only difference I see between you and Quirrel is that he never hurt anyone while training."

"You have to stop killing us!" said Albin.

Grim stood. He towered over the two of them. Albin squeaked and jumped back. Fifteen held her ground but Grim could see her hands tremble. "I never used to hurt anyone in training. Krom, I fought in six battles before this thing inside of me woke up."

A searing pain hit him as he remembered the fight with Roanik and the thugs on the bridge. Did that count as a battle? It didn't matter. All that mattered was he kept it together in his first fight after leaving the Elites. So he *could* do it. He just didn't know how.

"This is the first time you've talked to any of us since we got here," said Fifteen. "I wonder if that's the problem. Whatever the Coaches are doing when they zap you unconscious is keeping you in that no win situation."

Grim stroked the raggedy beard which formed over the last four weeks. "What happened last time they knocked me out? My head feels clearer this morning than any time since I got here."

"One of the pros whacked you in the back of the head with a blunted mace. You went down before you got zapped by Coach's baton," said Albin.

"So the baton scrambles my memory. I need to keep my temper in check with the Coaches before they use it. I can explain the baton is what's causing me to berserk."

Albin snorted. "They don't give a shit about us. You're the prize; the top draft pick. They'd see all of us dead if it meant they could get you on one of their Quest teams."

"So I need to keep my cool before they use the baton. Think you can help me with that?"

Fifteen looked up at him. "How?"

"Maybe humor will work, know any good jokes?" asked Grim.

"What's the difference between a lentil and a chickpea?" said Albin.

Grim thought about it for a second then shook his head.

"I'm not going to pay four coppers to have a lentil on my forehead," said Albin.

It took Grim a second to remember Harpers called their young, beautiful women chicks. His booming laugh ricocheted off the sandstone of the dorm.

* * *

Grim assembled with the Strikers and Forts in a squat outdoor arena. He felt like a feast-day goose roasting in the blazing sun of the Margon Desert.

This arena was the smallest of the four outdoor training zones. The other arenas had misters, chilled by Vonderians on each squad, to keep warriors from passing out from the heat. Dead men weren't afforded such niceties.

He watched as the ground of the arena rippled and formed into small hills. Grim sighed. Sparring on uneven terrain, his favorite.

Coach Torin approached the group and Grim clenched his fists. His pulse thickened. This man had done terrible things to him, even if he couldn't remember the details.

"What do you call a person who never farts in public?" whispered Fifteen.

"What?" growled Grim, eyes never leaving the coach.

"A private tutor."

His heart rate fell from the sky. "That's terrible."

"Did it work?" asked Fifteen.

"I think so."

Coach Torin strutted in front of their line like a Vonderian peacock. "Today, Strikers will form up behind whatever your Forts can build. See what you can do to stop Eleven."

Grim raised his hand.

Coach Torin's eyebrows raised but he nodded to him.

"Wouldn't it make sense to fight as a team Coach? Most of our training sessions are me against everyone."

Coach Torin moved in front of Grim, annoyed he had to stare up at the Ghost. His hand dropped to rest on his baton. "The monster speaks! I didn't know you had a vocabulary outside of grunts and sobs."

Torin looked at Fifteen. "Fifteen, please explain to Eleven why we don't fight as a team?"

Fifteen nodded. "Because he killed two of us during Categorization Coach."

Torin nodded. "I don't think the squad feels comfortable fighting next to you, Eleven. I know I wouldn't."

"And if I can control the rage? We'd be more effective as a team."

"Anybody willing to take that risk?" asked the Coach. He looked down the line.

Fifteen and Twenty-three raised their hands.

Coach Torin nodded. "Very well, you three can attempt to take the hill together."

As the rest of the Strikers and Forts set up, Grim huddled with Fifteen and Twenty-three. "Let me take the lead with a frontal assault. They'll focus on me while you two flank them."

"Can you take their hits without going berserk?" asked Fifteen.

"I think so. This is the first time I've stood on these sands without feeling desperate."

Coach Torin blew his whistle and Grim charged the hill. He dodged the first arrow but a blunted crossbow bolt hit him in the shoulder. He grunted at the pain and felt a sob building. *Chickpea. Chickpea. Chickpea.* The chant brought a smile to his face. He could do this. He reached the first half wall and kicked with all his strength. The wall splintered and Grim raised his arms and roared.

The defenders cowered. They'd seen this man toss people around like a toddler throwing dolls during a temper tantrum. More than half threw their weapons to the ground.

Fifteen and Twenty-three rushed the back side of the hill, swords drawn. They placed their weapons at the necks of the two remaining defenders.

Coach Torin pranced up the hill with baton in hand. "Well, if that wasn't the most pathetic defense I've ever seen."

Torin walked by number Thirty-two and lightly touched her neck with the baton. She seized until the baton was pulled from her skin.

Grim clenched his fists. *Chickpea. Chickpea.*

Torin knelt next to Thirty-two. "Never, *ever* drop your weapon during battle. That's suicide. The creatures you're fighting will not show mercy."

Grim hated the man but it was good advice.

Torin pointed the baton at Grim. "Apparently, Eleven figured out how to spar without send you all to the healers. I'm not sure I like it. He was a valuable coaching tool I could use to impart the gravity of the dangers you'll face when on a Quest. If he's not going to lose control, I'll have to figure something else out. For now, we do it again. We do it all morning until Eleven loses his cool or you put up a real defense."

They charged the hill nine more times that morning and won every time. On the final two assaults, the melee Strikers held their ground long enough for Grim to need Fifteen and Twenty-three to win the assault.

After the fighting, Grim sized up the defenders. He pointed at Twenty-four, a young Krommian woman who was as stout as Fifteen was tall. "Your form is good but you rely too heavily on the reverse grip. It gives advantage when in close but it's inefficient against a large opponent. If you're fighting me, or anyone that outweighs you, use a standard grip."

Coach Torin brushed Grim's back with his baton. The pain coursed through him and his heart raced. The other Ghosts backed away from him.

Chickpea! thought Grim desperately. His vision reddened. Right before he lost control, the pain stopped. The big warrior stared hatred at Torin.

"What are you doing, Eleven?" Torin asked. "You're not their friend, you're not their leader and you're certainly not their coach. You're the nightmare that will keep them sharp. Nod your head if you understand."

Grim just stared. When the baton struck again, he refused to convulse. He refused to show pain. He held Torin's eyes until the Coach pulled the baton away and smacked the device in his palm twice.

"It's working," said Grim, his voice a slice of winter.

Coach Torin's eyes widened and he whistled twice. This brought the other coaches and two of the triple As that stood guard over the Ghosts after Grim killed the coach.

The Guards and Dancers followed the other coach to where the Strikers and Forts trained. Coach Torin took two steps up the hill and turned. "Since Eleven has decided to play nice, we no longer have an easy way to scare you into working hard. You know what that means?"

Torin nodded gravely. "That's right, we're going back in the Pool tomorrow."

He pointed at Grim. "You, come with me."

25

Coach Torin

The triple As bound Grim's hands behind his back. Coach Torin led them towards the Dune's primary structure. It was an ancient desert palace built around an oasis forgotten by time. That's what it looked like from the outside, anyway.

Double As patrolled the wide adobe walls that surrounded the palace. It was a work duty they all shared. Like all League bases, the fortress was surrounded by harsh conditions which made escape nearly impossible. This was drilled into the Ghosts from the moment they arrived.

The western gate to the palace compound opened at Coach Torin's approach. They passed through wide marble halls, boots clicking against the polished tile. They descended three flights of stairs to an area of the palace Grim had seen only once before, when he fought the banglors in the Pool. Grim shuddered at the memory. *Would have been nice to forget* that *memory.*

"Get undressed. If the baton doesn't work, we have new ways to get you to comply."

"Who said anything about not complying?" said Grim. "I did everything you asked of me today, without killing anyone. Isn't that a good thing?"

"You're a better monster than man," said Torin. "I intend to get you back in that state. You can carry the entire fodder team on your back but only if you don't go soft."

Grim waded through the waters of the Pool and found a seat. He looked at the observation booth to see if anyone else knew about his solo trip down here.

Were Torin's actions sanctioned by the Company? Probably. The idea of dying, even in his own head, terrified him. That was probably a good thing. It meant he still wanted to keep on living.

That wasn't always true back when he lived in a bottle.

The straps thwacked around his arms and pulled tight. Head on a swivel, he looked for witnesses. Would anyone care if he died here? The triple As were outside the door and only Torin and a tech sat in the observation booth.

The sphere of light descended.

Torin's voice echoed over his head. "Let's see if we can't find the berserker I've grown to love."

The world went white.

Grim woke in a dark cell. His only companions were two scorpions fighting over a dead beetle. Their claws did most of the work. Their tails hung over the battle like deadly question marks, sometimes dropping down to look for a gap in their opponent's armor. The larger one pushed its opponent back to a crack in the cell then derisively turned its back on its enemy to finish its meal. That's when the smaller one struck, quickly and efficiently. It clipped off a piece of the larger scorpion's back leg then wedged it's venomous stinger through the crack. The larger scorpion slowly folded in on itself until it stopped moving.

All life is a battle for survival, Grim thought. These creatures are just a little more honest about it than we are.

He felt a pinch on his left calf then another on the pinky toe of his right foot. While he watched the fight, three other scorpions decided he looked tasty. Who was he to deny them a meal? Two more pinches and Grim's legs went numb.

It hurt but it wasn't the gruesome death to the banglor shamans during his first time in the Pool. This death didn't make him angry. The opposite. Right before he died he felt slightly drunk and entirely peaceful. Loneliness and pain were old companions to Grim, something a man like Torin wouldn't understand.

He opened his eyes with a smile on his face.

"Not afraid of the creepy crawlies?" asked Torin through the speaker.

Grim ignored him.

"Let's try something more personal."

The sphere of light descended.

This time when he opened his eyes, it was to something familiar. He looked about the small cottage with fondness.

The Freison Farm had fallen on hard times since he'd left. Small pencil drawings of Goodman and Goodwoman Freison hung above the fireplace in a spot reserved to remember the dead. Grim wondered what happened. If only he and Kavi had stayed. Maybe they could have made a difference.

When he heard the cry, he reached for the hand-axe that appeared on his belt. It took him a moment to realize it was a cry of pleasure, not pain. It was definitely Fallon who made it. He looked to the closed bedroom door and every horrible scenario raced through his head.

A man's grunts joined in, accompanied by a headboard striking the wall. After several moments the noises faded into satisfied sighs. Then, a giggle. Grim turned from the door in pain and shame, wondering why he hadn't already fled.

When he heard the voice, the pain turned to rage. "You are such an unusual slice of beauty in this dark place," said Kavi.

Kavi had always been better with women. He had that uncaring, relaxed calm of the naturally talented. This was the one woman Grim had pined after since childhood. How could Kavi do this to him?

Grim took a breath. He knew it was a simulation and he was letting Torin get the better of him. Kavi would've never done something like this to Grim. Would he?

The screws turned. "I know you're still grieving Kavi," said Fallon. "But Grim, just like Brink, was too big, too powerful, for this world. They were asked to hurt too many people and it broke them. I hope they're in a better place."

Grim shook his head. They thought he was dead? At least they waited until they thought he was dead.

"How long have you been afraid of Grim?" Kavi asked.

"The first time I saw him wrestling Alan Bolson when we were kids. He didn't mean to hurt the smaller boy. I know it was in jest and I know he had a gentle heart, but he still snapped Alan's arm like a piece of kindling. I've been terrified of him ever since."

Grim groaned in pain.

"Did you hear that?" asked Kavi.

Grim heard the rustle of clothing and the clinking of weapons. His first thought was to escape through the door but he knew it was pointless. Kavi would see him. He next looked for a place to hide but there was nothing in the small cabin that could conceal his bulk. He took a deep breath and faced the door.

Kavi was in his small clothes when the door opened. He blinked his eyes twice. "Grim? Is that you? How?"

Kavi rushed over and gave the big man a hug. "You died. You died because I dragged you into that damned fool's errand. Thank Krom you're alive!"

Grim couldn't bring himself to wrap his arms around Kavi. The pain was too fresh. He peeked through the open door to see Fallon covering herself and waving shyly to him.

"And how long after my death did you wait before courting Fallon?" Said Grim. "One week? Or was it two?"

"Grim, you disappeared over three years ago."

Grim shook his head and stared down at the man he once called brother. What was this new trickery? "No, it's been two, maybe three weeks since we saw each other."

Kavi opened his mouth to answer when the large, eastern window exploded into shards that covered them both. A terrifying beast crawled through the broken window. It had the torso of a lion that looked to be crawling out of the enormous body of a vulture.

The front talons of the beast passed cleanly through Kavi's chest. The creature gave a shriek of victory and it turned its eyes to Grim.

Blood burbled out of Kavi's mouth. Kavi looked at Grim sadly. "Why now? We finally got the chance to see each other again."

The creature wrenched the two talons apart and ripped Grim's friend in half. It speared Kavi's liver with a talon and brought the organ to its mouth. Its eyes never left Grim's.

Grim screamed and threw his hand-axe at the beast. The head of the axe bounced off the beast's heavy hide. He summoned his two handed battle axe and readied himself to charge.

"What's happening out there Kavi? Grim?" yelled Fallon from inside the bedroom.

The creature's head whipped in her direction. It didn't bother with the door. It broke through the flimsy wall and with a single bite, tore Fallon's head from her shoulders.

Grim screamed and charged. "Die!" A sob burst from his throat and the rage returned.

He swung twice with the battle axe and chopped the front talon off before the creature impaled him with the other. He swung at the creature's face and chest until it bit into his neck.

Grim welcomed death when it came.

He sobbed as he woke in the Pool.

"There's my monster," said Torin.

* * *

The rest of the Ghosts tiptoed around him when he returned to the dorm that night. No different than any other night, he supposed, except he was conscious. He had nothing against them. They had a right to be afraid; of him and of their time in the Pool tomorrow.

Torin understood Grim's weakness and would do everything he could to exploit it. Just like Grim's father. Why did the authority figures in his life want to turn him into a weapon, a killer? The coach would push and pull and prod and hurt others until he complied.

It was page one of the bully playbook.

Why did bullies believe *not* wanting to hurt others was a weakness? He chewed on it for a second. That was the source of strength, hurting others. No, it was more than that. The *fear* of those they preyed on was the source of their strength. The fear they inspired made them feel powerful. It filled a hole in them that should have been filled with friendship or love but got distorted at some point in their past. It didn't matter if it was a parent, like Grim's father, an enemy or someone they trusted. It broke something in them. They used the fear of others to hide their own.

As bullies aged, they repressed their own insecurities by picking a select few, those they saw as worthy, to follow in their footsteps. The smarter bullies normalized cruelty; built a society, a hierarchy, filled with bullies and the cowed, with them sitting on top. They tried to turn Grim into a perfect killing machine they could control. He became a proxy for their need to make others fear them.

Grim nodded in the dark. That felt right, but so what? He couldn't do anything about it. Torin held all the power and he wasn't afraid to use it to get what he wanted. Plus, he had an entire organization behind him dedicated to turning Grim into his 'monster'. Grim's weeks-long campaign of defiance had gotten him nowhere except an early bedtime and persistent memory loss.

He needed another way. His defiance so far was anger and indignation, neither of which worked against cruelty. Team Senet wanted him angry and he was playing into their hands. He needed another tool.

Kindness and camaraderie were not going to work in this place either. Kindness in the Dune was a teardrop in the desert, a waste of moisture and sentiment. All Grim had to do was watch how the Ghosts treated each other. The strongest Ghosts had their bunks camped around the small spring that ran through the far corner of the room. The spring brought fresh water and cool air. The strongest were the first to eat, drink and bathe. The scrawnier Ghosts often went without meals and no one cared. Team Senet built a system where the strongest and cruelest thrived.

They wanted bullies.

Grim overheard one of the stronger Ghosts say he came from a noble house. Grim was sure the man wasn't the only one. He couldn't imagine how the League got away with this. Why had these nobles not been rescued?

As he pondered the bullying nature of the pecking order Senet set up, he formed a theory. They kidnapped these powerful descendants and encouraged them to be cruel. They were being groomed by the League for something. Team Senet claimed no one ever left the Company, but that rang untrue. They were sending these young nobles through this fiery crucible for a reason.

The League had to be gaining influence. Whether they were holding them as hostages or it was some sadistic initiation ceremony, children of the powerful were specifically targeted. Maybe they were being brainwashed to represent the League later? Far-fetched, but that's what he thought about Nettie's theory about a secret cabal of Quest solvers. So far, she was proven right and he was proven an idiot.

How would Nettie think about his current problem? He only knew her for a couple of days before they got captured but she had a clarity of thought he deeply admired. She spun a problem around to look at it from all sides; she looked under it, then tore it apart and looked at it from the inside.

How would Nettie defy the League in his place? She was fond of the phrase: 'You're not asking the right question.' So, what was the right question? It probably started with: what did Grim want from defying the League? Freedom? Revenge? Those goals were too lofty. What he really wanted was to shift the power dynamic, even a little.

He might already be on the right track. Albin and Fifteen had given him a valuable tool and he wasn't using it in all the ways he could.

Tomorrow would be interesting.

26

Bloody Grim

They assembled outside the room to the Pool. Coach Torin turned to face them before leading them in. He wore a smug look any time his eyes met Grim's. He came out on top in their last interaction.

"The Strikers will pair with the Dancers and the Guards will fight with the Forts," said Torin. He smiled at their shock. "Yes, we can link you together in the Pool."

Assistant Coach Krill organized them in to the two groups. Team Senet still hadn't replaced the Coach Grim had killed during Categorization.

Torin looked back at Grim's group and that sadistic smile crept back on his face. "You are in for a treat! New monsters, new traps, and the best part is, you get to fight until you die. Even better, Eleven will be there to watch your backs, like your very own pet ogre."

Torin barked the short, wicked laugh he loved to share when he was about to send them into some new torment.

Grim laughed uproariously into the silence following Torin's laugh. The sound was so loud and unexpected that most of the Ghosts flinched. Grim kept laughing until the satisfied smirk on Torin's face disappeared, then turned to a scowl. Grim looked to the other Ghosts and pointed at Torin. "This guy, the Coach. Has he always been this funny? Or am I just learning to appreciate his subtle sense of humor?"

"What are you doing Eleven?" whispered Fifteen. "Do *not* taunt him, he'll take it out on *us.*"

Grim ignored her and continued to laugh. He started to fan himself with a hand as he bellowed. "So good to see you've kept your sense of humor, Coach. Most small men struggle with humor, especially when they start losing their hair."

Torin's scowl deepened. Bullies could never laugh at themselves. That was the tool. If he could get Torin to go over the edge and lose control, he could gain some power over the small man. The man spun the baton in his right hand but Grim knew he was reluctant to use it. He wanted Grim in the Pool.

"Go ahead Coach, zap me. I'm due a nap," said Grim. He wiped a tear of laughter from his eye.

Torin shook his head, trying to understand the big man's game. "Rumor has it, that was your signature skill when you were in the Elites wasn't it Eleven? Napping, or should I say, getting black out drunk?"

Grim laughed all over again. "You got me Coach. I was known as the whizzer, for my tendency to piss myself when I drank. I couldn't tell you how many pairs of pants I went through in those first couple of weeks with the Elites. Hey, that reminds me, how many times did I piss myself when you hit me with the zapper? Are these uniforms hard to wash?"

Torin's face rippled through a variety of reds and purples. Grim knew what the man was feeling. His father told him more times than Grim could count. To have a man as large and powerful as Grim admit something that should have embarrassed him, was so foreign to a bully like Torin, he couldn't process it. Just like his father. Grim had the strength and presence a man like Torin would kill for, and he had to watch this lowly Ghost squander that power. Grim knew it was infuriating. That's what made it so delicious.

The other Ghosts watched the stand-off in horror, knowing things were about to get worse.

Torin re-hung the baton on his belt, showing admirable restraint. He gave Grim a smile. "Don't worry Eleven, we'll work on your attitude in our next private session in the Pool. For now, I wouldn't want the rest of your Strikers and Dancers to miss out on your presence in the sim."

Torin jerked his head towards the glowing water. "Get your asses in the Pool."

The Ghosts waded into the viscous liquid and found their seats. Once they were strapped, Torin and Krill stepped into the observation booth.

Torin's voice came through the speakers above their heads, sounding tinny. "Thanks to Eleven's outburst, we will not be sharing the Sage's hints at the start of this simulation. Please be sure to thank him when you arrive on site. Don't worry, there's plenty of fun still to be had, even if you don't get hints. Enjoy yourselves in there!"

The sphere descended and the world went white.

* * *

Grim shaded his eyes from the brightness of the golden sand. It was exactly what he imagined he'd see if he walked a kilometer in any direction from the Dune. Desert. The flaxen, rolling hills of the Margon were shaped into sharp ridges by a steady, abrasive wind that pulled all moisture from the air.

"Would it kill em to give us a different place to die?" asked Albin. "If it has to be sand, why not a beach? Something with scantily clad, beautiful women splashing about in the water. Doesn't matter if they turn into demons, just give us a break from the desert."

Grim smiled at the Harpstran Dancer.

"Any ideas?" asked Fifteen. "If this is anything like the banglors, we don't have much time before we're attacked."

"Summon weapons and armor," said Twenty-three. "Dancers, if you can summon defensive traps, do it now. Set them on the backside of this dune."

"Where do you want me?" asked Grim.

"No offense Eleven, but we'll have a better chance if you move a dune over. Torin's a prick, but he wasn't wrong. I liked fighting with you yesterday, but we're going to die in the sim, so it's only a matter of time before you go berserk. It'll be too hard to fight whatever they throw at us while fighting you too."

Grim nodded. "No offense taken. I'll go now."

"Can you do it loudly?" asked Fifteen.

"Like a decoy?"

She nodded.

"I'll do my best," said Grim. He summoned a set of plate armor with a full helm. The armor was made from the latest suli-alloys, so it was a fraction of the weight of traditional plate. He took off for the adjacent dune at a clatter that was noisier than three chefs in the same kitchen.

When he crested the dune a flight of arrows fell around him. The decoy plan worked. The missiles bounced harmlessly off his armor, making even more of a racket.

Grim looked across the ridge to his attackers. Two squads of Bedouin warriors sat atop dusty horses and camels. Their faces were impossible to make out with the light scarves used to protect them from sun and sand. Their hand signals were unmistakable though. They were coordinating their attack, one squad for Grim and the other for the rest of the Ghosts. Grim wished his comrades luck and started summoning weapons.

After a moment, he had an arsenal of hand-axes lying at his feet and the heavy weight of a two-handed ax strapped to his back.

The squad targeting him charged down the valley between the dunes at a sliding canter. Once they were in range, Grim started throwing hand-axes. His throws were devastating in their strength and accuracy. The leading warrior caught the first ax in the face and the force of contact launched him off his horse and into the rider behind him. Three more died in succession as Grim's axes plowed through them. Of the ten desert warriors who charged, only one lived to make it to the top of the dune.

Grim pulled the battle ax off his back and swept low, severing the legs of the man's mount. The horse screamed and the final warrior flew over the other side of the dune. Grim yelled in triumph as the first wave of warriors lay dead and dying below him. The victory cry was half exultation of being alive and half celebration of not letting the blood lust consume him.

Grim looked to the nearest dune where his fellow Ghosts won their battle. They must have watched him summon hand axes because each Ghost had a pile of ranged weapons and ammo at their feet. The squad who targeted them were dead or dying with only one Ghost down. Number Thirty-two lay prone with a spear in her chest.

Albin yelled something. Grim took off his helmet to hear. "What?!" he yelled back.

"It doesn't look like you're trying very hard!" the man yelled, parroting one of Torin's favorite phrases.

Grim chuckled, grateful for the man's humor. The laugh died on his lips as he saw their next opponents crest a rise, four dunes to the west.

There were four squads of desert warriors this time, but that wasn't what chilled his blood. Each squad was accompanied by a sand mantis. Grim had never seen one, but he heard the legend from other members of Company Senet. The mantises dwarfed even the camels. They had six legs, their front legs had serrated chitinous barbs. Their eyes floated above their bodies, tethered by reedy eye stalks. It was the intelligence in those eyes that gave him pause. These were not mindless insects.

Grim summoned another pile of hand axes. It wouldn't be so easy this time. The enemy warriors carried small shields and looked as if they knew how to use them. Even his strongest throw would struggle to crack the carapaces of those beasts.

The enemy squads spread out and closed on their position. They moved at a careful pace, looking for traps and ambushes, a discipline Grim found concerning. When they reached the next dune, the enemy had evenly split their forces. Grim gave a nod to the other dune and grabbed two hand axes.

The enemy stopped a dune away and one of the Bedouin warriors raised his fingers to his lips and gave a high pitched whistle. At the signal, the mantises burrowed into the sand.

How the hell was he supposed to defend against a creature who could appear anywhere below his feet?

Grim summoned a tower shield, placed it strap-side down on the sand and set his feet on it. The other Ghosts followed his example and, within a moment, the dune under them had a metal shell.

The same warrior gave a secondary whistle and the enemy squads converged on the dune which held the larger group of Ghosts. They came at the dune from every direction but from where Grim stood.

This had to be Torin's doing! The scenario was forcing Grim to engage in close proximity to the rest of his squad.

The enemy squads continued their measured pace towards the larger hill when the sand at the top of that dune exploded. Ghosts went flying as sand mantises erupted from below. With shields at their feet, no one died in the breaching attack but the Ghosts tumbled to the ground and became easy prey.

Twenty and Twenty-seven were impaled on both sides as the beasts paired to kill a Ghost at a time. Their front claws moved in sickening synchrony as they extracted in different directions to rip the Ghosts in half. Each mantis speared a body part and dropped it into open maws as they ate on the job.

The Ghosts retreated towards Grim's dune when the arrows from the four squads of warriors rained around them. The missiles bounced harmlessly off the mantises, but two Ghosts fell when arrowheads found unarmored necks.

A large part of Grim embraced the challenge of fighting the beasts. His blood rose in anticipation of a worthy foe. He knew he would die on this dune, just like his companions. It was a matter of how. Did he jump in to rescue the other Ghosts and run the risk of killing them as the blood lust took over? Or, did he wait and watch as the Ghosts died one by one. Neither approach would win him trust or respect.

Albin made the decision for him. He limped towards Grim, an arrow sticking out of the back of his left knee. "I think we could all use a little lunacy right now, don't you?"

Another arrow struck Albin, this time in the back and the man fell to a knee. Grim stifled a sob from surfacing at the image of another dead companion. As Albin fell he whispered just loud enough for Grim to hear, "Chickpea, best four coppers I ever spent."

Grim's sob turned into a body laugh. He marveled at the poise of the small Harper in the midst of all that pain. Sim or not, the man wanted to bring a smile to Grim's face as he died. Grim's vision narrowed and his pulse throbbed.

He was losing control.

He laughed as he swung his ax into the hardened plate of the first sand beast's head. He laughed harder as the greenish goo of the creature's brain painted his face and arms. Grim surrendered control to the beast inside, but this time was different. He didn't black out when the killing started. He was allowed to look on as an observer.

Grim spun, continuing to laugh as he faced another sand mantis. The creature scored a glancing blow off his left pauldron that Grim didn't feel. He didn't feel anything except power and...joy? He spun, bringing his axe over his head and converting all that torque into a decapitating blow of the second mantis. He howled with laughter as the final two beasts dug back into the earth.

Grim turned to face the human warriors who summited the dune. He laughed in their surprised faces at seeing Grim standing over the bodies of two dead mantises.

The men yelled and charged.

Grim yelled back at a volume he didn't know he was capable of. In the face of that titanic roar, the charging horses reared and threw their riders. Grim embraced the hilarity of it and his scream reverted back to laughter. He waded through the warriors, ax stilling them before they found their feet.

In one of his back swings, he struck a warrior who moved to his flank. The bloody beast who took over his body laughed with joy. When he spun for another attack, Grim noticed the warrior he struck was Fifteen. She lay bleeding. Grim frowned at the wound he inflicted on a companion but his bloody doppelganger gave it no thought as he wreaked havoc on the desert warriors. He tried to wrest back control from Bloody Grim, but his body was not his to control.

Bloody Grim's ax mutilated every warrior who came near. Battle lust entwined with rage in a body consuming laugh.

Bloody Grim engaged with three desert warriors when the two remaining sand mantises boiled out of the earth under his feet. He laughed through blood burbling in his throat as the sand beasts punched through his armor and into his torso.

His final breath was a giggle.

* * *

When he woke in the Pool the first thing he noticed was the stench. The glowing liquid had turned brackish and tacky. He wrinkled his nose at the smell and realized the blackish, red goo oozed from him. The Ghosts who shared the Pool stared at him in fear. When the straps released, they rushed to the stairs to exit the Pool.

Grim convulsed, reminded of the first time he experienced the power of the baton. This sensation was similar, except there was no pain. He convulsed again, twisting his body into an unnatural angle that threatened to break his spine.

The world went dark.

27

What's in a Rune

Their first time that morning was painful. They went in with a ton of confidence; the defenses the Forts put up looked strong enough to hold off anything. They might have been if the enemy hadn't burrowed through the floor and ceiling. Giant millipedes with crystalline mandibles evaded defenses by creating their own path.

Another painful lesson learned.

"Again!" yelled Kavi as his team of Strikers and Forts awoke in the Pool. He looked over at Clara, trying to catch her eye. Her gaze was vacant as she processed being eaten by a bug.

This was their first simulation in an underground environment. Kavi berated himself for such a stupid first attempt. They needed to let go of the old rules.

The light descended from the ceiling.

The room hadn't changed in the half hour since his last visit. This staging room was more extravagant than the last which housed the dirty, blind Sage. The man standing with his back to him now had a warrior's build. The muscles in his arm flexed as he leaned over a large war table with topographical maps built into its surface.

Kavi cleared his throat and the man turned.

His hair was cropped as short as possible without being shaved. His mouth was framed by a fiery red goatee. The man looked Kavi up and down. "What can I do for you this time, young warrior?"

Kavi couldn't believe this man was a Sage. He didn't fit the profile, too young and hale. Could he be an assistant to a Sage? He didn't look crazy, but the story he shared last time made no sense. A different approach was needed. Could Kavi rile the man into giving something away?

Kavi threw the dice. "Hopefully more than last time. The riddles you and the other lunatics give do nothing for us. Why waste our time with this nonsense?"

The man clenched his fists until the color of his face matched the color of his beard. The Sage took two deep breaths until some of his normal color returned. When he spoke, the words quivered with barely suppressed rage. "Nonsense? Sage Arlo taught you to look with a different perspective, even if you're too dense to absorb the wisdom. Not all riddles have you at the center, boy. I would heed the lesson."

Kavi rolled his eyes in an effort to get the man to react. He wouldn't act this way outside a sim, but he committed to the new approach and would see it through. "The lesson didn't come from the riddle. We learned it the hard way, by dying. Besides, the League has Quest Crackers to solve these riddles so we don't have to."

The man scowled, his face again shifting through a gradient of scarlet. "The Ancients would be furious if they knew about these Quest Crackers. Those that don't risk it all, in mind and body, have no business in this business."

Kavi snorted. "Don't act like you don't know it's happening. You're a glorified pet of the League."

The man grabbed a wooden chair near the war table. He held it over his head and slammed it into the map table, crushing the carefully crafted topographical hills. He slammed the chair down again and again until the maps were destroyed and there was nothing left of the chair but splinters and the small top rail. He threw this piece of wood on the table and turned to face Kavi.

"Apologies," he said in a calm voice. "Sometimes my anger gets the better of me."

That was more than anger. This man was as mad as Sage Arlo, he just hid it better. Kavi nodded in respect anyway.

"On good days I remember my compliance is irrelevant to our... benefactors."

Kavi was convinced the man was about to say captors before he caught himself.

"By benefactors do you mean the League or the Ancients?"

"The League." The man pulled hard at his goatee, as if he wanted to rip it off. "They have our best interest in mind and help stave of the madness," he said through clenched teeth. "The Ancients could care less about us, they are a force of nature and we are their conduits, whether we want it or not."

"So you don't want to be here either."

The Sage's grimace turned to a wink. "Those are the breaks, my boy. You're a slave, I'm a Sage. All we can do is the best with what we got. Now can I recite the clue again?"

"Sure," said Kavi. It couldn't hurt.

The Sage began to speak in a sing song tone:

A man draws a circle on a clean white marble tile. This is no ordinary man and no ordinary tile. The man breathes life into the circle but that circle is trapped forever on that tile. It can move around it, but can never leave. The circle can't see the world above or the ground below, it's entire universe and view is the surface of the tile.

Many years later, the non-ordinary man breathed life into a bouncy ball. He gave the ball to a boy. The boy bounced this ball off every surface he could find. One day, the ball is bounced on the very same tile the circle lived. The circle rejoiced and called, "I'm not alone, you're a circle just like me!"

The ball replied, "No, I'm so much more," then bounced out of the circle's life forever. The circle still misses that crazy circle who visited him that autumn day."

The Sage eyed Kavi up and down as if seeing him for the very first time. "So, tell me, why did the circle think the ball was crazy?"

Kavi shook his head. If only Nettie were here. She would be able to piece together this crackpot nonsense. "I still have no idea."

Kavi squinted as the world turned a blinding white.

Kavi opened his eyes and did a quick count of the Striker and Forts. They were all here which meant the clock was ticking.

Nineteen pulled a couple of torches and lit them. Twenty-six's eyes flashed burgundy as he summoned a flame which danced above his head.

Kavi looked to them and nodded. "Find us some stone," he said. Nineteen took the downward passage while Twenty-six started up.

"Tess, you feel anything in the earth? I know I saw greenery down here in that first attack."

She closed her eyes. "Bits and pieces yes," she said. "But nothing communicates like in the real world. I'm sorry my skills suck in the Pool. It's so frustrating!"

"As long as they work when we need em in the real world," said Pip.

Tess growled at him. Her frustration made kind words sound patronizing.

Kavi nodded. "Pip's just trying to help. Clara, when you and the Forts retreated upwards, do you remember traveling over rock?"

"No, but I was running for my life."

"Anybody remember rock?" asked Kavi.

"No, there was nothing solid up that way," said Eight. "They kept appearing out of walls and floors. I stabbed one of those disgusting crab looking beetles right through the eye and another popped up behind it."

"Ok, we follow Nineteen then," said Kavi.

"I'll lead," said Pip. "What do you army people call it? Point. I'll take point."

"You do that," said Kavi. "Yell back if you see movement."

After nervously walking for a minute or two, they came across one of Nineteen's torches. It was wedged into the wall where the unstable dirt passage, dug by who knows what, had transformed into a natural cavern.

"Look at this," said Tess. She rubbed her hands along several grooves of the short stone passage into the cavern. "It looks like they *can* burrow through rock. We have to hope it takes them a lot longer."

The cavern held several clear advantages over their disastrous fight in the passageway. First, even if Tess was right, the stone which made up the cavern should offer some protection from getting overwhelmed from all directions. Even if the creatures could dig through stone they might get forewarning. Second, the ceiling of the cavern was much higher so the Strikers would have room to maneuver. Finally, the scattered rocks within the large cave would provide a base for defensive fortifications.

Kavi turned to Eight to share these observations but the Fort was already issuing orders.

"Two small palisades, there and there." Eight pointed to the hallway they just came out of and another passage that was illuminated by what must have been Nineteen's other torch on the far side of the cavern. "In front of those, set tar sheets and all the caltrops you can summon. I don't know they'll do much against bugs but the noise they make when rolled over should give us time to prepare for each wave."

Kavi grabbed one of the four pronged metal spikes that Ten scattered in front of the passage they came from. The caltrop was built such that no matter how you threw it, at least one of the spikes landed up. The Forts tossed at least fifty in front of each wall. Hopefully, the nasty spikes would cause damage or even slow the insect horde.

Pip investigated the far passage. It was a natural entrance that wasn't created by a disgusting worm creature. Jagged rocks lined the passage. Pip concentrated and summoned a torch so he could see once he traveled far enough from Nineteen's second torch. Just outside the corona of light from the mounted torch Pip saw something that brought him up short.

"Kavi, check this out!"

Kavi ran over and stared at the rock wall. Inscribed upon it, written in big black letters was: *Freedom lies outside the doorway of rebellion.* Below it was stamped the image of a black rose. The rose itself was intricate and looked like one of Clara's runes.

"Didn't you say something about a black rose in that last scenario?" asked Pip.

In these scenarios, Kavi defaulted to his discipline and training. He could hear his mother's words: *Prioritize the threat and give me a plan of action.* The black rose held no threat, it was a distraction to staying alive. Military training would have him dismiss it.

He felt in his bones that this was important, that new sense since his fight with the Ach'Su which told him not to dismiss this. He needed a different style of thinking, his father's. *Understand the problem, break it down into core principles.* The black rose messages seemed directed at him, personally. But why? He thought of the Sage's emphasis on perspective, the circle and the ball. The circle couldn't understand a three dimensional perspective having only ever experienced two dimensions. Was this similar?

He understood it within the context of bugs burrowing through three dimensions of earth but felt there was something broader too. Were the Sage's trying to tell him something? Were they reaching out in a dimension outside of the sim? Maybe the symbol held answers. "Clara, can you check this out?"

Clara got the nod from Eight, who led the Forts, and jogged in their direction. "What is it?"

Pip and Kavi pointed to the statement on the wall.

"What is it?" she repeated

They looked back at the wall but the inscription was gone. "What in the hell," said Pip. "Kavi, you saw it, right?"

Kavi nodded.

"I've still got loads of defenses to put up. Let me get back to doing something useful," she said.

No, something else was happening here, Kavi wasn't ready to dismiss it yet. "Wait, I don't know what we saw, but maybe the rose was a sign to try something on this spot. Clara, can you summon paint and put one of those fire runes here?"

She looked at him and frowned.

"Please. I'll clear it with Eight."

"Fine." Clara concentrated then reached into her pack and pulled out brushes, paint and a palette. She started mixing as Kavi moved to clear the experiment with Eight.

Ten shook her head as Kavi explained their idea, but Eight agreed.

"This is the place to experiment."

The two veterans went back to work lashing spears at a forty five degree angle from the base of their small palisade. The speed at which they erected each structure was stunning. They summoned, placed and lashed each piece in seconds. The newer Forts didn't work as quickly but, with the experience of Eight and Ten, both entrances into the cave were quickly and effectively fortified.

If Clara was fast with chalk she was lightning with paint. She mixed, made broad strokes of the brush then mixed some more. She switched to a smaller brush and repeated the process. In less than a minute the basic structure of the rune was complete. Then she started to add detail. In the flickering torchlight Pip provided, the painted fire rune took on a life of its own.

Pip leaned back as the heat from the rune got uncomfortable.

The heat didn't bother Clara. She continued to paint and the rune began to glow. With a final stroke, she completed it. It gave off light and enough heat to be uncomfortable while standing in front of it.

Kavi walked over to them. "What do you think would happen if you activated it?" he asked Clara.

"Don't know. Only one way to find out I guess. Why don't you two back up a little."

Clara waited for them to clear then put her hand under the rune. A stream of fire shot from the rune and engulfed her.

"No!" shouted Pip and Kavi together.

Clara removed her hand and stood, smiling and unharmed. "I don't think a rune I create can hurt me. All I feel when I activate it is the anger and pain I used to create it." Clara blocked Kavi's arm as he moved it towards the rune. "I'm almost certain the same will not be true of you. If you activate it, you're going to burn."

"Damn," said Kavi. "So how do we use it? We can't just have you stand here with your hand on the wall. Those things will rip through you."

"I wish I could access the library in the Academy," said Pip. "If anybody has anything on runes, it would be them. Maybe we put in a request?"

"Pip, how much time do we have left?" asked Kavi.

"I would say three minutes. They gave us nearly a half hour last time before the attack began."

"How do you know?" asked Clara.

"It's one of the first things they teach us at the Academy. Tracking time is critical to launching more involved magickal workings. Vonderians with bad timing don't live long. If I'm right, it's time to head back to the fortifications."

"I would have expected to see Twenty-six and Nineteen by now," said Kavi. "I'm not sure how accurate the Bricker's clockwork is, but I know my father's clocks we're always spot on."

As if on cue, they heard yelling from both tunnels. The yells from the lower tunnel were punctuated with howls of pain. Nineteen was in trouble.

Those in the upper palisade could see Twenty-six running their way. "Watch out for the caltrops and tar!" yelled Eight as Twenty-six barreled towards them. When he came into the light from Nineteen's first torch he wore a victorious smile on his face. That's when the right wall of the tunnel exploded. The massive millipede who terrorized them last time caught him in its pincers.

"Mother—" started twenty six. He didn't finish the curse. Instead, he shifted to mumbling out a magickal working.

Pip and Tess were assigned to protect the upper fortifications while Kavi and Twenty protected the lower ones. Pip watched Twenty-six's hands move as he continued to mumble his spell. The millipede began to scissor through his torso with sharp mandibles.

"Oh, you idiot," said Pip. "Everybody down!" he yelled. The upper group ducked behind the wall of the palisade.

Twenty-six turned into a giant fireball. The explosion vaporized the top half of the millipede before sending waves of flame down both sides of the tunnel. The insectoid chittering increased in frequency then stopped. The chittering was replaced with the crackling of chitinous husks.

They carefully peeked their heads over the palisade wall. The caltrops had been turned to slag, the tar was gently burning and half the spike traps had turned to ash but the walls still stood. The acrid scent of burning chitin and bug guts assaulted them.

"I wonder if there's anything left of him," said Tess softly.

The tunnel collapsed.

"That's what happens when you screw up the timing and that moron did it on purpose," said Pip. They heard the sound of battle come from the other side of the room. "Oh no, Kavi!"

"Let's go," said Tess.

Eight nodded. "Go. We'll rebuild and reinforce what we can before the next wave."

Nineteen limped up the lower corridor with a host of creepy crawlies closing fast. The group behind the walls of the lower palisade cheered him to move faster. He was almost to the rune when a barb shot from an overgrown scorpion struck him in the back of his left knee. His leg locked up from whatever poison the mutated beast had shot and he tripped and fell. He reached down to pull the barb out and screamed at the pain. Blood squirted out of the wound to cover his hands.

The bugs closed in.

"Can you heal that if I make a big enough distraction?" asked Kavi. He leapt in front of the palisade and started yelling to try to draw the attention of the bugs.

To his credit, Twenty jumped down and stood next to him. Then he shook his head. "I don't think so. It looks like arterial blood, look how fast it's spilling out."

Kavi yelled in frustration. That's when a terrible, brilliant idea came to him. "Nineteen, use the rune above you! Put your hand under it like we did in the dorm."

The bugs were less than a meter away from Nineteen now. It would be his only chance. Kavi hoped that lying on the ground might keep him out of the way of the flames.

Nineteen reached up and slapped his bloody palm under the rune. The hallway lit up so brightly Kavi had to close his eyes. When he opened them, the wall of flame still stood. He shaded his eyes and could just make out Nineteen's smoldering bones. All the bugs, who moments before were about to shred Nineteen into bite sized morsels, were now smoking husks.

Kavi walked back to the palisade. He knew Nineteen was going to be one angry Bricker when they woke up in the Pool. He looked back at the smoldering, angry pile of bones. The wall of flame continued to burn and the bones turned to ash.

"It's the blood!" yelled Clara. She didn't seem bothered by how Nineteen discovered how to permanently charge a rune. They never got along that well.

"How long will it last?" asked Kavi as he moved behind the wall.

Clara laughed. "Like I would know? We're going to have to find out the hard way." She jumped off the wall with an oomph. Then she pulled the paints and pallet back out and faced the wall. This time she chose black and began to paint.

* * *

When they woke up in the Pool, Clara joined the other voices in yelling

"Again!"

"I've never felt that good about dying," said Kavi. Clara met his eyes when he looked at her. When she activated the death rune they were filled with power and purpose that let them fight wave after wave of bugs. What finally killed them was the rocks that fell from the roof of the cavern when the really large bugs showed up.

"You're still a dick," said Nineteen looking at Kavi.

"Would you rather have been eaten?" asked Clara sweetly.

Nineteen shuddered but shut his mouth.

Kavi looked into the observation booth and saw the Coaches were not alone. At least two other coaches stood in the booth along with a tall hooded figure. "Looks like we've got fans," said Kavi. He jutted his chin towards the booth then looked back at Clara.

She was too busy convulsing to respond.

* * *

"Do they always start with the yelling when they wake back up?" asked the thin, hooded figure, his voice silky darkness.

Coach K had never seen the man's face. He wasn't ashamed to admit the thin man scared him. "Only recently," he said. "Once they started unlocking skills."

"And how many skills have they unlocked?"

Coach K shrugged off the hooded man's intensity. He had been reporting up the chain since the first day. "Twelve of the twenty five have unlocked at least one." He looked out at the Pool to see Thirty-Three convulsing. "Make that thirteen."

One of the other coaches in the room whistled. "I don't have thirteen double As who have unlocked skills on my whole roster."

The thin man turned towards this new speaker. His hooded eyes bored into him until he began to wilt. Finally, the hooded figure turned back to Coach K. "Has the mental strain caused any of them to fracture?"

"Not any more than usual sir," said Coach K.

"The results you have produced are admirable. However, if they break and run during the season, they are worthless to us. I want our in-house neuros to conduct psych screening three times a week on each candidate. If more than one of them cracks, you will suspend the Pool program for three days until I get a chance to look at the data."

"Sir, can I move my double As into the Pool cycle? It may be a chance for us to accelerate the feeder program," said the Coach the hooded man had recently cowed. It took courage to ask the question and he trembled as he waited for the response.

The hooded man stared him down again. Finally, he spoke. "Not yet. We continue to gather data on the fodder. As long as they perform during the regular season, I don't care what happens to them. If the data looks good, we can increase the usage of the Pool."

"Should I take the screening time away from their work detail or training sir?" asked Coach K.

The hooded man shook his head. "And I thought the League didn't want to be micro-managed. Don't bother me with trivialities. Just get it done. Oh, and Coach?"

"Yes sir," said Coach K.

"Congratulations, I want you read in to Stage Four."

Coach K trembled. "And once I'm read in...you'll...you'll release her?"

The hooded figure nodded again. "Once you gain the understanding of Stage Four, you will no longer need outside incentive."

The thin hooded figure swelled then vanished.

"I hate it when he does that," said Coach L.

"I'm not afraid of much," said Coach M. "But that man melts my spine."

28

Skills

"Today, we shift our training regimen again," said Coach K, standing in front of the door that led to the Pool. "Thanks to my brilliant idea of multiple Pool encounters a day, your progress has surprised and emboldened the leadership team to push for more."

Coach K backed through the doors to the Pool chamber. "For those who have unlocked a skill, you will advance to the introductory triple A training program. The theory is basic enough for the uninitiated, but should help with the upcoming Quest. The rest will continue to work in the group Pool until you unlock a skill."

Coach K pointed to a fourth Pool at the back of the chamber. None of the Ghosts had been in this Pool before. Kavi assumed it was because three Pools was more than enough to host their entire squad so they never needed it. As he waded naked through the viscous water, he realized the Pool was slightly different. The large bright spheres hanging above the other Pools were replaced with small headrests behind each seat. Below the headrests floated miniature versions of the big spheres.

Kavi listened for the schwick of restraining straps as he leaned his head against the comfortable headrest.

Coach K waited while those who qualified strapped in. "I'm sure you noticed the headrests. These are not for your comfort. The first time you went solo in the Pool, you ran the same banglor simulation. This Pool allows our neuro mages and their Bricker techs to load customized simulations for each of you. The goal is to train and evolve the skills you've already unlocked."

Kavi looked to the Ghosts who shared the Pool with him. Most looked excited. Trixie shared an exaggerated smile and Kavi had to smile back.

"You will learn what you need inside the simulation," said Coach K. The coach pointed at Kavi and nodded to the observation booth. Kavi frowned. He wondered why the coach hadn't taken cover in the booth when the world went white.

Kavi closed his eyes and took a breath to regulate the adrenaline which pumped through him when a simulation began. When he opened his eyes, the white nothingness persisted. Floating through the vertiginous void brought him to the edge of vomiting so he screwed his eyes shut.

"You can open your eyes now, young warrior," said a soft, commanding voice.

The wide trunks of ancient trees surrounded him. In front of him stood a man he'd seen several times while walking the main floors of the Nest. He had whitish, grey hair and a serenity that had set up camp in his eyes. He had an ageless face common to Loamians but Kavi wasn't certain the man hailed from any of the Garden Cities. The calmness he exuded pulsed through the simulation, making the forest feel peaceful.

"I'm head coach of Team Sugoroku, most call me Coach Sug."

Kavi nodded. That's where he'd seen him, working with the professional team. He wasn't sure how interactive this simulation was, so he decided to relax and listen.

"This is triple A training. The basics. If you're here, you've unlocked what the League calls a skill. Skills are recent discoveries. We don't fully understand how they work, but in this session, I'll share what knowledge we have."

"Let's start with the different cultures of Grendar and how they impact the skill discovery process." The six Garden Cities flashed behind Coach Sug, the broken, transparent domes surrounding the cities visible as negative space. Nothing grew around the domes and clouds parted far above where they reached into the sky. The rotation of the cities stopped and Kavi found himself standing on an Astran dock jutting into the Whisper Sea.

Coach Sug turned to look at the city and he and Kavi floated upwards. They drifted from the docks towards one of the massive temples within the walls of the inner city. "Being raised in a certain culture creates evolutionary proclivities. Astrans, for example, are raised in a deeply religious culture. They worship the god Astra, deity of purity and health. Through worship, they learn about their bodies at an early age within the context of purging impurities. Because of this, their minds have built pathways of knowledge focused on understanding the body. More often than not, Astrans will evolve skills which advance healing and protection."

Coach Sug blinked and now they floated over the Harpstran art district. Kavi's stomach did a back flip at the jarring transition. He took a deep breath and stabilized enough to look down. People milled about, laughing and enjoying street performers juggling or orating in front of colorful murals. "Harpstrans come from a culture of music, art and grandiose storytellers. Based on their early upbringing, we often see Harpers evolve skills from their stories – the mythical song smith, the rune scriber and the back alley assassin."

The scene shifted again and this time they floated above the

Krommian colosseum. Kavi squeezed his eyes shut and when he reopened them he was able to focus on the warriors battling below. "Krommians are raised in a martial society where we find archetypes like berserkers, defenders and dervishes."

The cityscapes below continued to flash, from the natural beauty of Loam, to the gaudy towers of Vonderia, to the industrious factories of Brickolage. "Each culture has its stories of heroes and demons. At the root of those stories lie seeds of truth. Anytime a League warrior evolves to unlock a skill, we learn as much about that skill from cultural legend as we do from observation and analysis. Look back for the inspiration to move forward. So it has ever been."

A moment later, they stood back in the peaceful forest. "Hybrids are interesting. If you've survived this long, there's a chance your mind has been molded by two cultures. It's said that being the product of two cultures is like having two souls. Take Sucellia, the Greenginer. We don't know if all the stories about her were true. She died over four hundred years ago, but most know the legend. She created the Hanging Gardens of Lo'estra, a symphony of nature and clockwork working together. Every plant, flower and tree is pruned, watered and maintained through an extensive miracle of engineering integrated with nature. It still functions today. Both cultures laid claim to her genius yet no one has been able to recreate even a fraction of what she grew and built.

We believe the creation is a result of skills Sucellia unlocked when surviving desperate conditions while living alone in the slopelands of Lo'estra. What's interesting about her case, and others the League has seen, is that respect for both cultures trumps any inherent paradox between the cultures to create something new."

"Can I ask a question?" said Kavi.

Coach Sug didn't even pause. "What's most interesting about our research is that cultural upbringing is not a guarantee of skill set.

We've competed against Loamian troubadors and we've cultivated Bricker assassins."

"Guess not," said Kavi as Coach Sug talked over him. The simulation must have been an early version the neuro magitechs hadn't converted to be fully immersive.

"Surprising right?" said Coach Sug. "We don't understand why but we believe inner character plays as big a role as cultural upbringing."

"If you've watched the professional team practice," said Coach Sug and the environment shifted to the cavernous training room, making Kavi queasy again.

Behind Coach Sug, a group of warriors faced off. Kavi didn't recognize any of them so it must have been years ago. "You've probably seen that once a skill is unlocked, the chances of unlocking more increases exponentially. Once the mind is shown what was heretofore impossible has become probable, the knowledge becomes a catalyst to opening new pathways. This leads to unlocking new skills."

"With me so far?" asked Coach Sug.

"What if I say no?" said Kavi.

"Good," said Coach Sug. "Let's talk about skills. The skill makeup of each warrior falls into the same categories as the roles of a League squad. At least for basic skills. Let's discuss the movement based Dancer skills."

Behind Coach Sug, a Dancer vanished only to appear behind one of her team members ten meters away. "A common assassin Dancer Skill is Wraith step. You just watched Penumbra vanish from one place and appear in another. Dancer skills are usually unlocked first. Do you know why?"

Kavi shrugged, assuming his answer would be irrelevant.

"That's right," said Coach Sug, proving Kavi's assumption. "Because we're always moving, so our minds have many open pathways to accept new forms of movement."

A large Krommian sprinted towards Penumbra. He held a dagger in one hand and a short sword in the other. When he closed he began to spin, whirling so fast that the steel from the weapons became metallic streaks, like a deadly version of a child's top. Penumbra vanished again in an effort to avoid the attack. "Varsted is using his Striker Skill, Whirlwind. Pay attention as Penumbra's teammate, Trivalent, activates her Guard skill, Gargoyle."

Kavi was riveted by the battle, reminded of the first time he saw triple As practicing. These warriors were far superior in movement and coordination. Trivalent stepped into Varsted's path, swelled in size then turned the greyish color of stone. When Varsted's blades hit the statuesque Trivalent, the result was the muted sound of metal striking rock. Varsted's whirlwind vanished and the Krommian launched himself at the top half of the statue in an effort to topple it.

"Fortification skills are rare but when unlocked they can singlehandedly change the momentum of a battle. Watch as Trip successfully defends his position against five charging warriors."

Kavi braced for the transition and this time felt none of the dizziness as he watched four men and a woman run up a small hill to attack a tall, thin Bricker standing at the top. The man looked unbothered by the charge, paying very close attention to the path each warrior took as they closed on him.

"Notice the impeccable timing as Trip actives his Fort skill, Harvest of Spears." The charging warriors screeched to a halt as stakes grew out of the ground in a semi-circle in front of Trip. "Fortification skills differ from Guard skills by number of opponents countered and the permanence of the defense left behind."

"Finally, we have Logistics and Support skills which are a wide variety of talents which resist any categorization at all, save for not being particularly useful in a battlefield setting. We will not be spending time on those today in this section of basic training."

Coach Sug flickered for a moment then turned to Kavi. "Hello young lion, I look forward to seeing what you can do."

"Can I ask questions now?"

"Of course. We saw no need to re-simulate the basics, but this point forward is immersive."

"Okay then, why me? Why was I on the list to be captured?"

"That's above my pay grade young man, but I assume it's because the League looks for specific qualities in its Candidates - courage, restlessness with the status quo, not fitting in. Believe it or not, the coaches don't have much more information than you do. Our job is to give you a fighting chance when you're thrown in a Quest. That's where we need to focus, okay?"

Kavi growled but nodded.

"You've unlocked a Dancer skill we've never seen before. Your speed is a tremendous advantage but it could become a liability if untrained. I worked with the neuro-magitechs to put together a series of exercises to explore and stretch your limits. Let's begin."

The first time Kavi died, Coach had him running through a forest, dodging trees, fallen logs, jumping over streams and running from predators. What ended his simulated life was when the forest he sped through started a gentle decline which quickly led to a steep downward hill. At the speed he traveled, he didn't realize he had left the ground until he was thirty meters in the air. He was still screaming when he woke up in the Pool. That one hurt. He lay for several agonizing minutes at the base of the hill with every bone in his body broken before he expired.

That pain turned to anger, anger at the coaches, anger at himself for not anticipating the result of an incline. He spun his finger in a circle above his head and was thrown back in the sim.

He died fourteen times before lunch.

Coach Sug had him running through mountains, marshes, deserts, cities, every terrain imaginable. Then the weather started. Speed while running through icy streets caused by an endless deluge of sleet and snow ended in disaster four times before he got the hang of it.

Then Coach asked him to dodge the rain. When time slowed he could make out each specific raindrop and he found ways to twist his body to avoid most of them. It wasn't the rain that killed him, but the lightning. Kavi discovered the hard way that lightning comes from the ground and the sky at the same time. At least it killed quickly. On his third time through the lightning sequence he learned to smell the ionization of the air splitting before the strike, teaching him to trust all of his senses, not just eyes and ears.

He collapsed into his bunk that night, completely spent.

29

Eve of Quest Day

"So tomorrow we start dying for real," said Jansen. "Good thing we've had all that practice."

The man had become increasingly bitter over the last several weeks. Each time he died in the Pool, his rage and hatred grew. Instead of focusing that rage on the League and their situation, he turned it on Kavi and anyone who supported they go 'again'. The situation hit its nadir when he beat Trixie within an inch of her life two nights ago.

Kavi couldn't erase the image from his mind. He remembered waking to the sounds of violence. He looked over to see Jansen, fists bloody, standing over the small woman with number Thirty-five stamped on her back. He continued to beat her yelling. "You want to go again! I'll give it to you again...and again, as many times as you want." Each word was punctuated with a punch or knee to her small form.

Kavi jumped out of bed and tackled Jansen.

The big man rolled and put Kavi in a headlock. "But we all know you're the real problem, don't we, hero boy?" he hissed as his massive bicep began to squeeze.

Grappling was not Kavi's strength. He relied on speed and movement. While he knew how to throw that was only when he had leverage. He had none here and his vision tunneled.

Surprisingly, it was Nineteen who joined Tess and Pip in pulling Jansen off him. As Jansen started down the bully path, Nineteen found a little perspective on how unattractive the look was. Especially when it was turned on him during a late night meal. It was Trixie who vanished to appear behind Jansen to deliver three well timed kidney punches that brought the big man low. No one believed Trixie had done it *for* nineteen. Since her evolution, she made it clear she would not take bullying from anyone.

Jansen formed a group of ten team members of Guards, Forts and even one Dancer who were violently opposed to going in the Pool. After the first required trip into the Pool, they would slit their own throats the moment their groups entered the simulation. The coaches didn't know what to do about it. It didn't violate League rules so any runs with the Guards and half the Forts inevitably ended up short handed.

Coach K put it in their hands after one frustrating simulation. Only three Forts were left to fight when the Guards and Forts were teamed together. "If you idiots don't want to learn what the Pool has to teach, you'll die first. Your choice!"

The concept of choice invigorated Jansen and his 'no-neuro' group. They didn't seem to care that their choice of dying early imperiled the rest of the team. It wasn't their fault. They never agreed to go 'again'. The only skill they unlocked was playing the victim.

Over the past week, the Coaches started splitting them into squads of eleven like the professional teams. Coach was very clear on why. Kavi had to smile at the memory.

"As you know, I could give two shits about you idiots. Since some of you have unlocked skills, it makes sense to treat you like a team.

Most fodder get thrown into their first Quest by random number draw because after a month you're more useless than tits on a boar." He laughed at his own joke which brought smiles from the fodder team. When Coach laughed he looked even more like the boar he mocked.

Outside of the Pool, they learned basic team strategy. These consisted of offensive and defensive tactics pulled from a playbook used by triple A and pro squads for years. They were mostly employed against other teams but could be effective when used against beasts and monsters too. The advantage of a pre-planned strategy was the eleven person squad knew exactly what their team members were doing at all times. In theory. Real battle never went according to plan, but that's what made these strategies effective. Each play took less than fifteen seconds to execute. In an actual fight, when things went off the rails, strategy could be changed by making a different call.

Inside the Pool, they started to rehash old scenarios. Since they knew what beasts were coming, they had an opportunity to use strategies in real time against know foes. They were getting better. The Dancers gave them even odds of clearing an approach of traps before they encountered resistance. Those were the odds for new scenarios. For old scenarios, the Dancers treated each trap like insults to their intelligence. They turned it into a game of how fast they could eliminate the trap. Sliver was currently twelve points ahead of Trixie on the Dancer leader board she put up in the dormitory.

Kavi looked around the dormitory, fondly now. It might be the last time he saw it for a while if he was selected for the Quest. The team had made it their own. Clara chalked several fire runes up on the window side and charged them with her own blood. Since they were done in chalk, they didn't shoot flame but they eliminated the chill from the open scar facing east. Thanks to her, there wasn't a bad bed in the room anymore.

The Strikers still gravitated around the fire pit but welcomed all who wanted to talk tactics. The 'no-neuros' stayed together. They set their beds up just outside of the fire pit, more to aggravate the Strikers than for the heat. They made sure to complain loudly enough so the Strikers could hear it.

It reminded Kavi of his time in the Bastion. Soldiers loved to complain. Even during his time as an Eagle, he knew you only really had to worry when your men stopped bitching. In this case, the complaining was targeted at the Strikers and Dancers to get a rise out of them. More often than not, it worked.

"Are you planning on doing us a favor and slitting your own throat before we start tomorrow Twenty-two?" asked Pip. He no longer used Jansen's name.

Sliver caught the ball and ran with it. "At least then the Forts can use your body to hide behind." Some of the Dancers laughed. "If you're not going to fight with us tomorrow big man, we'll have you run in front and see how many traps you can set off before you blow yourself up."

Trixie made a big show of adding the number Twenty-two to the Dancer leader board. She then put a zero next to his number and quickly turned that zero into a skull and cross bones. This got an even bigger laugh out of the Dancers.

Jansen pointed a finger at Trixie and drew a line across his throat.

She smiled. Trixie had so embraced death that nothing intimidated the small Dancer anymore. "Clever," said Trixie. "You should join a Harpstran acting troupe. I wouldn't recommend any speaking parts but you could be part of the scenery."

Jansen grunted, emphasizing her point. This set the Dancers laughing again.

The laughter only seemed to strengthen the group of 'no-neuros'.

"Ignore them. Sheep use base humor to avoid what is right in front of their eyes. We know the Pool is brainwashing us to become willing slaves of the League," said Twenty-four. The man was a sour Astran Fort with a crooked nose. He was the first to join Jansen in slitting his own throat.

"Who are you calling willing?!" shouted Tess.

"Forget it Tess," said Kavi. "What argument can you make that will convince someone who will slit their own throat before trying to learn something? Don't waste your breath."

"There's a reason the no-neuros haven't unlocked a single skill," said Pip. "They made that bed. We'll see who sleeps in it forever tomorrow, won't we?"

As if his words were prophetic, everyone in the room turned their heads to the door. The approaching footsteps could only be the coaches. They said they wouldn't be monitoring the dorms and they kept that vow. Tonight they would share the roster for tomorrow. Instead of posting it, they would share the first roster in person.

"How are my bodies doing tonight?" asked Coach K as he walked in. The other coaches flanked Coach K.

He looked around the room he hadn't visited in weeks. His eyes lingered on the runes. "I like what you've done with the place."

"Before I post the list of who's traveling tomorrow, let me share how we picked the team. In a normal season, we do a random draw from the entire fodder pool for the first Quest. For most ghosts, role is meaningless this early in the season. You've done better than your predecessors with your work in the Pool."

Kavi was surprised to find that Coach K's words filled him with pride. He still loathed the man. He still loathed the League, but he couldn't deny the respect he had gained for his team of Ghosts. Most of them anyway.

"We are sending a team of three Strikers, three Dancers, three Forts and two Guards like we would near the end of the season," continued Coach K. "Those picks are random but from within your groups: Strikers were picked from the Striker pool, Dancers from the Dancer pool, etcetera. If you get picked and you survive this Quest, you automatically get the next Quest off. So if you don't get called this time, expect to get called for the following Quest. Understood?"

He didn't wait for a response. He pulled the list from a pocket and began to read. "Here's the roster for Quest One. Strikers - Eleven, Seventeen, Nineteen. Dancers - Thirteen, Twenty-three, Thirty-five. Forts - Eight, Ten, Thirty-three. Guards - Nine, Twenty-two."

"Random my ass," snorted Eight from her bed.

Coach K gave her a malevolent smile. "Coaches, I'll leave you to any pep talks if you want. For the rest of you, good luck out there. The better you do in these Quests, the better I look to my bosses. So, go get em!" He stuck the list to the wall by the dormitory door and walked out.

Coach L faced the room. "There's not a whole lot we can do to make you feel better about tomorrow. For those of you going, it's going to suck. Coach M and I were able to save a recording from the Pool. You might not know it but the neuro-tech the League contracted allows us to capture your immersive experiences so we can review them later to see what the team could do better in their next encounter. The pros use this technology to sharpen their techniques."

"Coach M and I believe that sharing a review of one of your most successful runs in the Pool would be more motivational than any words we might share," said Coach L. He held up a small sphere that looked like a tiny version of the giant spheres used to start a scenario in the Pool. "Rub the top of it and it will project the recording on to the wall. It's not immersive, but you can learn from it."

Coach L put the sphere on the small table that lay below the posted roster list. The Ghosts had grown so used to the new wonders of technology the League introduced to them that the recording crystal didn't surprise anyone.

Coach M looked to the team in front of him and nodded. "Regardless of what Coach K says, we don't want you to die. Some of you will and that sucks. Remember what you learned here and do everything you can to survive." With that, both coaches left the room and the team listened until their footsteps faded down the hall.

Kavi caught Tess' eye and nodded. They would be going in together with Nineteen. That was a relief. The only other Striker he would have liked with them was Pip.

"What do you think? Should we start the show?" asked Trixie. She stood over the small sphere and looked back at the room. "I wouldn't mind seeing some of our best."

"Ah yes, revel in the power the League has over you. No thank you," said Twenty-four.

"Welp, you no-nos can find yourself somewhere else to sit. Maybe in the shitter? I'm going to start it."

Twenty-four stood up and walked out of the dormitory. Most of the 'no-neuros' followed him. Surprisingly, Jansen did not. He was going to have to face the real thing tomorrow. It might be the only thing that would change the man's mind. Kavi hoped so. If he didn't hold his own tomorrow, people were going to die.

Trixie rubbed the top of the orb.

The image appeared on the wall and Kavi put his legs up, leaned back and relived the experience.

The image centered on Kavi as he discussed orders with his team that day. They were going to be assaulting the Argent Temple on the edge of the Awakened Plains. It was a real place but the neuromanced scenario replaced crumbling ruin with an active temple inhabited by snake looking creatures the team called nagas. This was based on one of the old Bricker myths. Their ancestors had successfully crossbred snakes with people. These crossbreeds immediately turned on their creators and became evil. Because...snakes.

Kavi dismissed one of Nineteen's ideas as they were contemplating their approach to the temple. He then issued some orders and the team started to move.

"So bossy," said Sliver as the group watched the scenario played out. "But still...that ass."

"Two words," said Trixie. "Bun...Tastic." She waggled her eyebrows suggestively at Clara.

Clara whacked her on the shoulder.

Nineteen moved over to the orb. "Does this thing have sound?" he asked Trixie. "As much as the rest of us love hearing you slobber over Kavi, I wouldn't mind hearing this next part."

"Awww, he called you Kavi," said Tess. She put a hand on Kavi's arm. "First step on the way to becoming besties."

Nineteen fiddled with the side of the orb and sound started blaring out of it. "Shh. I want to see how this went down. I still don't understand it."

Focus on the recording turned intense. Everyone wanted to understand how a skill was unlocked. Kavi strongly suspected even the League didn't fully understand it. By now, they knew accepting death was a part of it but clearly wasn't all of it.

The Coaches chose the recording well and the Ghosts watched with rapt attention.

They cheered when Nineteen saved Kavi's life after unlocking the skill, Upgrade. Nineteen turned Kavi's leather armor into plate mail with a thought, preventing a surprise attack from one the naga's barbed tails from ending Kavi's life. The cheers grew louder when Tess unlocked her Striker skill, Death Fungus. She did it in style, by destroying a cobra the size of a small temple. The roars of the Dancers were the loudest when Sliver unlocked her Golem skill. The giant metal man, who Sliver named Herman, turned the tide of the battle at the doors of the Argent Temple.

As Kavi watched as he and his teammates ripped through hordes of giant snakes, he started to feel something new. Hope. Hope that they might actually make it through this Quest.

30

The Trip

Nobody slept well that night. When Clara reactivated her death rune in the wee hours of morning, some of the anxiety fled but not all. When the first rays of sun began to brighten the room Kavi finally gave up. He sat up and looked around. Most of those drafted for the Quest were up and doing what they could to prepare.

Nineteen had his gear laid out on his bed. He cleaned and oiled each component in a methodic, meditative trance. Sliver sat across from him, on her own bed, doing the same with golem parts.

Eight, Nine and Ten sat facing each other, heads bowed in discussion. Kavi overheard Eight say, "The fortifications will be there Pete, you just cover me when it gets hairy."

Clara sat next to Trixie, knees touching. "Don't do anything crazy Trix. This isn't a simulation and we need to walk out of this one alive."

Trixie nodded and put a hand on Clara's leg. "Use the runes C, we're going to get through this."

Jansen sat on his bed, head in his hands, no-neuros nowhere to be seen.

Kavi stood up and stretched. He checked his armor and weapons but knew it would all be there. The Coaches gave them plenty of time last night to pull from the armory. He wouldn't be able to summon gear when out of the Pool. He had a month to get comfortable with the equipment they trained with outside of the Pool. His dual swords were shorter than average but let Kavi move through katas he couldn't with full longswords. They fit the style he worked out with his mother years ago. The leather cuirass around chest and back was stiff enough to block most blows without restricting movement.

Pip watched Kavi and Tess prepare their gear awkwardly. "You two better come back," he said finally. "You're the only thing that makes this place bearable."

Kavi nodded. "Keep the rest of the team running the Pool when you can," said Kavi. "If we do make it, our chances have to get better as we go."

Coach K showed up as the brightness of the sun overtook the room. "A Squad, grab your gear." He was all business. He didn't offer his regular insults. "You'll get chow on the ship. It's time to move."

Tess looked at Kavi with a raised eyebrow and mouthed the word *ship?* She grabbed her gear with everyone else.

They lugged their gear down the long stairs and waited outside the armory. Eight, Nine, Ten, Jansen and a few of the others grabbed their gear from the armory. They had stopped lugging the heavy stuff up the stairs long ago.

From the armory, Coach led them to a new stairwell with a sign in block letters that read: MISSION DOCK. These stairs were wider and better lit than the stairs to the dormitory but no less imposing.

"Strap that gear tight, A Squad," bellowed Coach K. "Now comes the fun part."

"I hate this climb," said Nine.

Eight nodded. "Let's get it over with."

The Fodder Team had been running stairs for over a month now.

Kavi felt he could scale any mountain in the Talons without breaking a sweat. He had grown used to counting the stairs up to their dormitory as they climbed each evening. At first, it was to see which step he tired on. As the weeks passed, the goal became beating the rest of the team to the icy trickle shower before dinner. That gave him enough time to dry by the main fire before chow was served. If he was moving full speed when he reached the thousandth step he could have the shower to himself for a full minute before Pip or Sliver showed.

They passed stair fifteen hundred ages ago and continued to climb. The Guards and Forts dropped behind, armor and shields weighing them down. Kavi admitted he was impressed that Coach K managed the climb without slowing pace. Those tree trunk legs must have been climbing stairs for many years.

They finally reached the top of the winding stairs. Kavi grabbed a breath and passed through large double doors into a brilliant sunny day. The platform was larger than their indoor training field. It bustled with activity as nearly a hundred people loaded crates filled with weapons and armaments on to an airship docked to the far end of the natural ledge.

The ascender of the airship looked like a whale impatiently poised above a large wooden vessel. The vessel had multiple decks on to which people loaded supplies. Kavi heard airship prototypes talked about in his father's lab. The Brickers in the lab discounted the reality of the technology due to the massive scale needed for an ascender to take even a small gondola off the ground. Scale was the correct word. If the entire fodder team stood one on top of the other's shoulders, they *might* match the ascender's height. It would take the entire population of Team Sugoroku to match it's length.

Kavi had to wonder how people hadn't seen these behemoths floating through the sky. They would have been a source of endless gossip across the Garden Cities.

Before he had the chance to ask the question, Sliver piped up. "You have got to be kidding me."

Kavi turned to where she was looking. It was a small outbuilding halfway to the dock where the double As pulled the equipment from. Kavi looked at her in confusion.

She pointed. "Look at the capstan on the other side of the building. What do you think happens when those four men start pushing on those crossbars?"

He shrugged.

"I thought you said your dad was a Bricker. That's a hoist. It moves a whole lot of stuff up and a whole lot of stuff down in a big ol lift. But no, we had to carry our own gear up those damn stairs."

A sweating, wheezing Jansen crested the last step. He dropped his tower shield, took the huge pack of armor off his back and lay on the ground. "I don't care if I make it back if I don't ever have to climb those stairs again."

Nine spat on the ground near his head. "Don't even joke like that Twenty-two."

Jansen was too tired to respond. He turned his head away from the spittle and his eyes widened as he noticed the enormous airship for the first time. "What in the hell is that thing?"

"Our transport," said Eight.

"The League has been operating for at least twenty years," said Kavi. "Why hasn't anyone seen one of these humongous ships?"

"Oh, it's got to be a lot longer than that," said Sliver. "Look at this place." She did a half circle to take in the dock. "You don't hollow out a mountain in two decades and build something like....this...in a couple years."

"Tess, what do you think?" asked Kavi.

Tess had been staring at the mountains since they walked on to the dock. "What? Oh, about the ship? I figured they had to be using some

Bricker sulimite mumbo jumbo to hide it from everybody. If Trixie can disappear, why can't they do something similar to a whole ship?"

"They call it an obfuscator," said Nine. "I have no idea how it works but we heard the captain talk about it."

Jansen pushed himself up to a sitting position as he caught his breath. "Do you mean they hide the entire ship? So, we'll be floating through the air with nothing around us?" The man's face turned deathly white.

"No, you idiot," said Eight. "How could they fly the ship if it was invisible? It only hides the ship from those that aren't on it."

Kavi had to admit he thought the same thing as Jansen. He let out a breath he didn't realize he was holding. He wasn't a fan of heights after his dad's experiments.

"We did it with small objects at the University," said Nineteen. "It's about how you bend light. I don't know how it's possible with something this big."

"Not to mention the shadow," said Sliver.

Nineteen nodded.

"What shadow?" asked Jansen.

"Something this big is the size of a cloud. It's gonna leave a huge shadow. How do you hide that?" asked Sliver.

"Focus!" snapped Coach K. "You'll be loading up once the pro team is settled. Stay out of their way where you can, do your jobs and make it back alive. I've got a lot riding on this team, don't screw it up."

"You don't travel with us?" asked Trixie.

"Nope," said Coach K. "Our coaching happens before you leave. Once you're on the ship, you're on your own. You'll be taking orders from the pro Tactician. She knows the Quest. She's built a strategy with the Crackers and the professional Coaches. They then built a series of tactics for as many scenarios the pro team could brainstorm. You do what she says, when she says it. Got it?"

As the Coach finished, the professional team walked on to the dock. They didn't look the slightest bit winded from the climb. Kavi noticed none of *them* carried any gear. Seniority had its privileges.

"They don't look different than any other scared shitless ghosts to me," said a huge Krommian Guard as he walked by with his team.

"Shut it, White," said a diminutive Bricker woman. She stopped to stretch her calf after the climb. "If they can clear a path before Risk's ghosts, we might actually have a winning season this year."

The large man didn't lose his smile but he shut his mouth.

The small Bricker walked towards them. Her eyes flashed with anger that she quickly stifled as her eyes fell on the coach. "Thanks, Coach K. I look forward to seeing what your development team can do. We've heard good things."

"Bring some of em back alive. A couple more weeks in the Pool and we'll have a team ready to rival the Triple As."

One of the Vonderians snorted. "What a load of crap, my team would wipe the floor with them."

Kavi recognized the woman, the neuro-mage from the triple A team they watched practice weeks ago, Yantsy something or other.

The small Bricker ignored the woman's comment and turned to White. "If the alternate opens her mouth again, I want you to put your fist in it."

White smiled and cracked his knuckles.

Yantsy paled.

"No promises," said the Bricker. "Quests aren't getting less dangerous. I won't waste lives but I'm not in the business of saving them either. We'll do what it takes to meet our objectives faster than the other team."

"I'd expect nothing less," said Coach K. "Kick the crap out of Risk and bring glory to Team Sugoroku." He turned to Kavi and the rest of the ghosts. "That holds for you too A Squad."

"If it's all the same to you Coach, we prefer Ghost Squad," said Kavi.

"I'll allow it. Only because some of you ain't coming back," said Coach K. "Good luck Ghost Squad." He turned and walked back down the stairs.

* * *

The small Bricker issued orders and the pro team and alternates loaded on to the ship. Once her team started moving, she turned her attention back to the Ghosts.

"Ghost Squad. I like it," she said. "Rumor has it, you're the first team to fully embrace we're on borrowed time."

"Not all of us," said Trixie. She shot a dark look at Jansen.

"I didn't give you permission to speak," said the Bricker. "Keep your mouth shut unless spoken to, understood?"

Trixie snapped her teeth together with an audible click.

The Bricker smiled. "Good. When we're on a Quest, there's no time for discussion, you follow orders, or somebody dies. As you've probably guessed, I'm the tactician for Team Sugoroku. You call me Tack. You might hear others call me Promo. That's because they earned that right. You haven't."

Tack's words were abrasive but instilled confidence. This woman knew what she was doing. Since they were forced to go on a Quest, it was much better to go with someone who had an idea of how to survive. Jansen stood up with the others and they formed a line. Tack watched impassively but allowed the reorganization.

"I've heard some of you have manifested skills. Coach K told me we have an upgrader and a golem specialist among us."

She looked to each of them until Nineteen and Sliver nodded when she met their eyes.

"That's incredible news." She stopped in front of Nineteen. "Find me on the ship before we land, I've got pointers for you."

"Yes ma'am...Tack" said Nineteen.

"We also have at least one assassin." She found Trixie's eyes. "I knew I liked you." She looked down at the roster book for a moment. "A rune scriber." Her eyebrows went up and she loosed a low whistle. "Holy crap, that's rare. I heard Mehen had a rune scriber but it's just a rumor. They don't have you dancing, do they?"

"No Tack, I'm a Fort," said Clara.

"Good, and we also have a ranger."

Tess met her eyes.

"Lean into it. It's much more effective outside the Pool."

"Yes, Tack."

"And then, whatever the hell you are." Tack looked at Kavi.

"What do you mean?" asked Kavi.

"I mean nobody has ever manifested skills like yours. Nobody in Team Sugoroku, nobody in the League."

Kavi shrugged. "Great, I'm one of a kind. So much for keeping my head down and surviving." He had figured his speed was out of the ordinary with the amount of attention he and his squad had been garnering, but it was never good to be the *only* one. That's how somebody got diseases named after them.

Tack smiled. "Sounds like something Stix would say, he heading up your work detail?"

Kavi nodded.

"He's a good man. Anyway, the pro team watched the recording and we heard about the auction. You're something new. Do something good with it."

"Like what?"

"For starters, keep yourself and your team alive. We'll build on it from there," said Tack. "That brings us to you three."

Eight, Nine and Ten withered under her glare.

"What the hell were you thinking, Pete? I told you they have eyes everywhere. Not only do you try to escape, you try to do it on a Quest? Are you out of your damn mind? Team leadership will make sure you're dead one way or another before this season is over."

"You tried to escape?" blurted Trixie.

Tack pointed at Trixie. "I won't tell you again. Next warning comes with a beating." She looked back at Eight, Nine and Ten. "You try anything like that on this Quest...know that we have a standing order to take you out ourselves. Are we clear?"

"How do you do it?" asked Kavi quietly. "How do you willingly execute orders like that for these League bastards, knowing they're still kidnapping people?"

Tack got up in his face which was impressive considering that he towered over her. She pointed a finger a millimeter from his left eye. "Don't for a second think you know me. Or any of my team. You get your jobs done and we all might live to get another chance. Now get your asses on the ship."

* * *

The crew of the airship scampered about unloosening ties from their moorings. The rumble in the ship grew as the captain primed the suli rotors.

Clara gripped the sides of her small hammock with white knuckles as the ship pulled away from the dock. Her eyes rimmed with fear as she looked out one of the small portholes in the tiny cabin they gave the eleven members of Ghost Squadron.

"Think of it this way, you've been floating several kilometers above the ground ever since you got on the ship," said Trixie. "So nothing's really changed."

"Not helping," said Clara through clenched teeth.

Trixie shrugged then looked at Eight, Nine and Ten. "Ok, spill. You guys tried to escape and screwed it up? Come on *Pete*, this may be the last time we get to hear this story."

"Fine," said Pete, previously known as Nine. "Yes, we tried to escape on one of our last Quests. We saw so many of our teammates die throughout the season. The three of us decided that death by monster didn't seem a whole lot different than death by slaver if we got caught." He shrugged. "Why not try?"

"What happened?" asked Kavi. "Did Tack sell you out?"

"No. There's a lot of real bastards on the pro team but Tack is one of the good ones. One of the pro team members overheard us plotting and Tack took us aside and shared some things that almost talked us out of it."

"Like what?" asked Trixie.

"Her secrets aren't mine to share," said Pete. He did his best to settle his massive frame into the tiny hammock. "I'll never get used to these things. Anyway, we cleared the area and the pro team had been sent in to finish the hard parts. It was a town scenario. We had to go in, get some information from townspeople, then find the nest of horrible things that would try to kill us. The nest for this Quest was a cellar under a warehouse in an unpopulated part of the town. We lost four people clearing traps and killing the scrubby demon things that waited for us. We had the chance to lounge outside until either we won or...who were we competing against Mar?"

"Wari," said Eight.

"Right. Until Wari took the prize or we did. Most of our fortifications were in the warehouse itself so we waited outside. There was a festival going on in town and we could hear people partying from where we holed up. While we were in there dying, people were drinking less than half a click away. So, we made up a lame excuse that we would get more water for the team. I gathered these two and we melted into the crowd. We traded in our gear for traveling clothes and made our way to Loam. The town was only thirty K from the Garden City so we thought we were in the clear."

"What happened?" asked Trixie breathlessly.

"Don't know. I was unconscious for most of it."

"We camped in the woods that night," said Mar, previously known as Eight, picking up the story. "Pete's Loamian. He doesn't have the same skills as Tess but he knows how to hide a trail. We didn't risk a fire. We didn't talk or make any noises I can remember. I was on watch. One second, we were free, and the next a hand covered my mouth. I felt a sharp prick in my neck and then darkness."

"We woke up in the Nest to a lot of angry coaches," said Pete. "Coach M can be one scary son of a bitch. He smiled when he told us we would be Ghosts for the rest of our very short lives."

"So, we're going to be *randomly* selected for each mission this season until something gets us," said Mar.

"Don't try to escape. Got it."

"Shut up Jansen," said Trixie and Clara together.

Kavi looked over to Tess who was uncharacteristically quiet throughout the story. She had always been the most vocal of the Strikers about finding an escape plan. Yet, when the story of Ghosts actually trying to escape was told, she seemed disinterested.

"You ok?" Kavi asked her.

"Me? Yeah, why?" she asked still looking out the small window.

"You seem distracted."

"Maybe because I find myself forced against my will to participate in a Quest."

"Ok, but that's different from anything that's happened this last month, how?"

"Now we can die for real," said Tess.

Kavi didn't get the chance to reply because White slammed open the door and pushed his giant frame into the Ghost Squad's quarters.

Trixie was closest to the door and she accidentally brushed against the sword strapped to White's belt in the tight quarters. She pulled her hand back with a yowl.

"What the hell were you thinking? Nobody touches Bianca," White snapped at Trixie.

"I didn't touch it, you bumped against me!" said Trixie. "Besides, who names their sword? Only creepers name their weapons."

White gave her a big smile. "I didn't name her, she named herself." He pulled the sword to show the Ghosts, a gladius with a maroon tint to the hilt and edge of the blade.

"I found Bianca on our second Quest last season," said White. "We were up against Team Wari. Their Ghosts cleared the traps before we did, but a rampaging minotaur wiped out half their Ghosts and two of their pros. Rake wraith stepped behind the beast and shoved his pig stickers into its back, but that only pissed it off. Next thing I knew, eight hundred kilos of angry bull charged my way. I was able to toss down a shield wall and hold it off while the rest of the team snuck around it to claim the Quest chest. Bianca was nestled inside, waiting for me to claim her."

"You didn't have to fight Wari for the chest?" asked Tess.

White shook his head. "I forget how little they tell Ghosts. Once you reach the Quest prize, it's over. The other team can't touch it."

"But couldn't they break the rules?" asked Kavi. "Why didn't they just attack you and take it from you, or kill you while you were fighting the minotaur?"

White shook his head again. "No, the other team literally can't touch the chest once it's been claimed. It becomes insubstantial to everyone but the winning team, Sage magick transports the prize into a pocket dimension which only the victors can access. It keeps the competition between teams civil. It's frowned upon to kill the members of the other team. It happens of course, but we do our best to avoid it and keep our focus on killing monsters. When team's clash it's more like the capture the flag battles you might have seen in the Nest. It's all about position and getting to the prize first."

"What about Ghosts, is it frowned upon to kill Ghosts?" asked Kavi.

White gave him a flat stare that told Kavi everything he needed to know.

"She's beautiful," said Jansen, oblivious to Kavi's questions. He was still staring at White's sword. "That blood red tint makes her look menacing, almost like *she* has powers."

"No almost about it," said White. "Bianca is a siphon, a life stealer. When she damages an enemy, that damage is converted into healing me."

"I'm surprised the League let you keep the blade," said Kavi.

"It wouldn't fight for anybody else. Once I claimed her, she's mine until I die or she gets destroyed. That's what your little friend was feeling when she touched the hilt, Bianca will suck the life from anyone but me."

White waved down any more questions. "Briefing in five, main deck. Don't be late."

He left, slamming the door just as loudly as he opened it.

* * *

There wasn't as much room on the main deck as Kavi thought when they first boarded the airship. Tack stood in front of her team on the starboard side. The Ghosts had to cram into a small corner between the pro team and crates of ship parts. The corner allowed them to face Tack and stay out of the way of busy sailors hustling to execute orders the captain yelled from the helm. Several Guards on the pro team spread their bodies out even further as the Ghosts tried to squeeze in.

"Damnit Ham, quit wasting my time!" shouted Tack at the Guard blocking Clara from squeezing into the small space.

"What?" replied the Guard in a mock wounded voice.

Tack glared at him.

"Fine." Ham grabbed Clara by the waist and lifted her on top of one of the crates so she could see.

"Ok," shouted Tack. Her voice carried over the wind whipping past them and the steady thrum of the rotors. "Based on the location identified by our Crackers, this is going to be an abandoned village scenario. We agreed to approach through the North entrance. Risk will approach from the South."

"Any evidence of a third entrance?" asked White.

"Not on any of the official maps," said Tack. "The village was called Angorn. It's about a hundred and forty clicks south of Brickolage and it's been abandoned for years. If they manufactured a third entrance it will most likely be from the West as the East borders the Wastes. Our Rooks haven't seen evidence of a new entrance, but we know that means shit all."

Tack looked at the confused looks on the Ghost's faces and took pity on them. "I'll explain this once, since it's the first Quest of the season. Bring this information back to the rest of your Squad so I don't have to explain next time."

"If you make it back," interjected White.

"If you make it back," said Tack. "The Sages can See the future, or part of the future. Hell, I don't understand the theory but I suspect even the League's Quest Crackers don't fully get it or they'd be a lot more helpful. When the Sages divine a Quest, they *also* See the groups that will attempt to complete it. For the last century, the League has had a monopoly on pet Sages, so they always divine two entrances to the Quest. This gives rise to competition between two League teams, just as the League wants it."

She opened a hand to White. "Lately, as of the last three seasons, there's been a new player. A non-League sanctioned player is getting wind of the Quests. When they do, the Sages divine a third entry point. As you can imagine, that royally screws up the competition and turns it into a general melee."

"We lost two team members last time those pricks showed up," said Ham. "I look forward to them showing up next time." He squeezed his hands around an invisible neck.

"Easy Ham," said Tack. "If there is a third player, we have orders to band together with Risk. We eliminate the third player before continuing the Quest. For you Ghosts, Risk's uniforms are red and blue with an insignia of a rearing horse with four stars over its head. The third party doesn't wear uniforms."

"Rearing horse, how majestic," whispered Trixie to Kavi.

White backhanded her hard enough to send her reeling into the rail.

"I warned you," said Tack as Trixie wiped blood from her mouth. "The objective is the fort on the hill. We're supposed to find something in there. Ghosts, your role is to clear the way to the fort and open the North entrance. We'll take it from there. Any questions?"

Kavi raised his hand.

Tack nodded to him.

"Can you share the details of the Quest with us? Exactly what the Sage said, I mean," said Kavi.

"No."

"Please," said Kavi. "We're going in first and any advantage that can keep us alive, even a little longer, will also keep the monsters off of you that much longer."

Tack looked at him, considering. "I can't share the Sage's words because I don't have them. The Sage's words usually only tell us where to go and our Crackers were a hundred percent sure they had the right location. Our only job is to show up and beat Risk to the prize."

Her callous disregard for the Sage's words troubled Kavi but he knew he had to be careful not to show it. If she didn't have the Sage's text for this Quest, antagonizing her would accomplish nothing. "Apologies Tack, but if we learned anything in the Pool, it's that the Sage's words often have more than one meaning that you can't figure out until you're in the middle of the Quest. Did the Crackers warn you of anything else to keep an eye on?"

"Three weeks in the Pool and he thinks he knows more about Questing than Tack," said Ham with a laugh.

Tack nodded. "We've got this, Eleven. Do your job of getting rid of traps and the fodder monsters and we'll make it through."

Kavi nodded doubtfully but raised his hand again.

"What now?" said Tack.

"Did you say a hundred and forty clicks south of Brickolage?"

"Your point?"

"That's around where Pip and I fought the Ach'Su."

That got everyone's attention. They fired questions at him to explain what it looked like and how to fight it. Kavi filled in what he could.

"Enough!" yelled Tack to regain control over the group. "We'll keep one eye open for a giant lion vulture that smells like burnt butter. It shouldn't be a threat once inside the fort but it's my team's top priority if it shows up outside."

Kavi nodded.

Tack looked over the group. "We land in six hours. Get some rack time. The assault starts as soon as we land."

31

The Quest

"Why can't we use the ship to scout?" said Sliver. "That's ridiculous. You have an asset, you use the asset."

"I love watching Ghosts try to think," said a tall, skinny Harpstran. The man had an intricate pattern of metallic looking scales inked in a deep sapphire blue that covered the entirety of his neck. They continued over his face to stop under his eyes and nose. Where Clara's tattoos, before disappearing in the transformation, were playful and aquatic, this man's design was hard and serpentine. "It's like watching a cat try to do math."

"Screw you skinny," said Sliver.

"Enough," said Tack. "We don't have time for this. You're not going to want to hear this Thirteen, but it's against the rules."

Sliver tugged at one of the yellow locks of her hair in frustration. "Have you thought about putting those rules together into a little book." She held up a finger as if about to present a great idea. "I know, we could call it a rule book!"

"Can I smack this one?" asked the serpentine Harpstran. The man was rail thin and moved like a predator.

"Yes, we do have a rule book," said Tack.

"And you didn't think that might be worth sharing with the team about to clear the way for you?"

"Honestly? No," said Tack. "Ghosts don't live long enough. In a regular season, it would be a waste of time. Until I see if this team is as good as the coaches think you are, we don't have that time to waste. Now get your asses in position."

Sliver took a wistful look at the sky. The giant airship vanished a moment later.

"Line up," said Kavi. "Sliver, release your spiders and we'll do ten meter outs on alternating sides. Eight and ten, set up fortifications at each intersection facing east and west. Leave the center open until we hit resistance. Strikers, follow close behind our Dancers."

The pro team stood behind Kavi as he issued orders. At the last, the Harpstran began to clap excitedly. "Aww, he thinks he's people."

"Enough Rake," said Tack. "Mission started, quit the bullshit."

"Strikers, we're following the Dancers as they do their sweep. Do *not* move in front of the spiders. Tess, you...Tess, get your damn head in the game!" said Kavi.

Tess looked north towards the canyons. She held up a hand as he called her name. "Wait," she said. Then she turned to face the Ghosts. "Ok. We are facing lizard creatures I've never seen in the Pool. They have red and blue hues to their scales and they walk upright."

"Where are you getting this information?" asked Kavi.

"I'll explain later." She put a hand on his wrist and found his eyes. "Please, trust me."

"Kobolds, really?" asked White.

"I would also like to know where you're getting your intel Seventeen, but I'll wait," said Tack. "If they're kobolds, this could be a cakewalk. Fire doesn't do much to them, but other than that they're one-shot kills. They do set plenty of traps. Dancers be on your toes."

Tess shook her head. "No. There's something tainted about these."

She sniffed the air. "It's like they've been broken and reassembled. Nothing about them smells right."

"Let me guess," said Kavi. "Burnt butter?"

"Not quite, more like animal fat left on a fire overnight."

"Hmm, similar to the Ach'Su, but different enough."

"Good intel," said Tack. "No matter where you got it. But it's time to move or Risk is going to get too big of a head start."

The afternoon sun hung tired and low in the winter sky. The cottages they passed were broken down, offering endless ambush opportunities. With the low light and tall shadows, it was a nightmare scenario. After their training in the Pool, this no longer deterred Ghost Squadron. They had a job to do. The sooner they got it done, the sooner they could get back on the ship.

Sliver's clockwork spiders skittered ahead of them down the street. They were small but dense, heavy enough to trigger pressure-based traps.

They reached the first intersection without incident. Sliver directed the spiders east and west as the forts set up barricades to give the team time in the event of a flanking attack. Clara skipped the fire runes and helped Eight and Ten set down stakes and tar paper. Tess hung back with the Forts as the Dancers and Strikers advanced behind Sliver's spiders.

The traps they found were simple to disarm before they were triggered. Sliver helped Trixie with an obvious net trap placed along the east facing wall of a crumbling house.

"Something's off," said Trixie. "They're lulling us in to dropping our guard."

Kavi nodded. "Stay sharp." He followed close behind Sliver as she made her way towards the second intersection.

On the far corner was one of the better preserved buildings they'd seen. The sign hanging out front dangled from a single chain, but the crudely painted flagon hadn't completely faded. This used to be a tavern that doubled as an inn.

Sliver's spiders crossed the intersection when Tess came running up behind them.

"Fortifications in place?" asked Kavi without looking at her.

"Yes."

"Have them advance to meet us."

"Already did. Two scouts incoming from the west. One wounded," said Tess.

"Think the Risk team wounded them?"

"Don't know, also don't know if the wounded one is playing at being hurt."

Kavi turned to address the advancing Guards and Forts. "Set up a strong side wedge angled west. Forts, drop half palisades on a forty five facing east *and* west."

"In the intersection?"

"Before it."

"That's going to piss Tack off," said Eight.

"We'll deal with her later," said Kavi. "We need to know what we're dealing with right now. How much time until the scouts see us?"

"Two minutes."

"That give us time for a rune on one of the half walls?"

"If you quit asking questions and let me work," said Clara.

Kavi smiled. "Seventeen and Nineteen, cover the Forts and open fire on those scouts the second you have a shot. Guards in front. Don't switch to the strong side wedge until those barriers are up."

"You want me to summon my golem?" asked Sliver.

"You mean Herman?" asked Kavi.

Sliver smiled. "Aw, you remembered his name."

"Not yet. I have a feeling we're gonna need him when we get closer to the keep."

Eight put up a full wall instead of a half on the east side facing the inn and Kavi agreed with her strategy. It would limit their visibility but the cover might prove crucial. When Clara made a small cut on her arm to activate the rune, Kavi felt strength and confidence fill his body and mind. They could handle whatever the Sages sent their way.

Jansen and Pete linked shields when the two scouts rounded the corner. Tess loosed three arrows and Nineteen unloaded a burst of steaming metal at the same time. They tore the wounded kobold apart. It's blood spattered the wall with blackish green ichor. Tess's last arrow found a gap in the scales on the second kobold's shoulder and it made a high pitched squeal. It turned tail and ran.

Jansen and Pete moved forward, pinching their shields westerly in the defined wedge.

"Wait," said Tess. "Something's still off."

"What?" asked Kavi.

"Don't know, no plants in this intersection. I can't feel anything until halfway down the street."

"Trix, can you do your disappearing act? Cross the intersection and see where the wounded one is headed."

"Don't worry, my spiders already scanned the area Thirty-five," said Sliver.

Trixie disappeared. The team couldn't see her progress but the moment her feet crossed the intersection the world went to hell.

Three scaled hounds exploded out of the earth, looking for the heartbeat passing over their hiding spot. In the same moment, kobolds stood from the second story windows of the inn and fired short bows.

If Trixie hadn't been invisible, she would have been dead. If they hadn't gone through the underground scenario in the Pool ten times, they all would have been dead. Trixie moved fast, making her way back to the cover of the high walled palisade.

"Bone loving fucknuggets!" she hissed through clenched teeth. She pulled up her pant leg to show the claw marks that ripped through her light leather pants. The claw marks bisected a recently inked tattoo of the Irborra's face she killed before she transformed.

Ten ran to her side. With a quick prayer to Astra, the ragged edges of the wound faded.

Jansen and Pete took the worst of the fire from the inn. They quickly shifted east to manage the barrage. Their shields looked like porcupines as they filled with the quills of many arrows. Several arrows made it through and both men earned dents on their heavy armor while they re-positioned. Jansen had an arrow sticking from the joint of his left shoulder.

"How bad is it?" asked Ten.

"Leave it in," grunted Jansen as the dogs advanced. "Until we get rid of these things."

"Tess, Nineteen, cover me. I'm on the dogs," yelled Kavi. "But I can't be dodging arrows!" He darted around the far side of Jansen and Pete, finding his mantra as he moved.

It was an odd sensation. His adrenaline was through the roof but the mantra and Clara's rune brought a sense of calm that made everything slower. His team was in trouble. If he didn't take care of it, friends were going to die. He had to make sure that didn't happen.

Tess and Nineteen unloaded into the upper windows until Nineteen yelled, "Reload!"

Kavi slid through time. He dodged the bite of the largest of the three dogs but did not expect the scaly tail which whipped at him. He winced in pain as the tail scored a strike to his leather cuirass. He didn't think it broke skin but it knocked the wind out of him. It took everything he had to stay in the moment. The hounds were faster than anything he'd ever fought, almost matching him in speed.

Training with Coach Sug to get comfortable with his speed was the only thing that kept him alive. He had grown too used to having an unfair advantage and it almost got him killed. He took a deep breath and analyzed the threat as his mother taught him. Kavi had three things the hounds lacked. He used the first, a head for strategy, to feint a strike at the left leg of the largest hound. He used the second, his twin swords, to cut deep into the right flank of the same hound with devastating accuracy.

The hound squealed and bit at the air around it as it dropped to the ground.

He fought to keep the attention of the other two hounds. He danced and dodged lightning strikes of tooth and claw until he could use his third advantage, his team.

Jansen and Pete issued angry overhand blows to unprotected hindquarters. Pete's blow drew blood but Jansen's glanced off the dark, glimmering scales. With his wounded shoulder, Jansen couldn't strike with force. Both hounds turned to face this new threat. Both guards raised shields.

They needn't have bothered. The moment the hounds turned their backs to Kavi, he struck. Kavi's sword severed the spinal column of the dog facing Jansen and the beast sunk soundlessly to the ravaged earth. He attempted the same strike on the mongrel facing Pete, but the dog was too fast. It rotated and juked so Kavi's blow skittered off the scaled hide.

The dog's movement gave Pete the opening he was waiting for. This time his thick gladius sunk deep into it's side and found a lung.

The dog gave a wet whine.

Kavi moved forward to finish the creature and caught movement out of the corner of his vision. He pivoted and sliced through the shaft of an arrow which would have taken Jansen through the eye. It clattered harmlessly against the big man's breastplate.

Jansen stared at Kavi in disbelief but Kavi was already moving towards the inn.

Pete finished the dying devil dog with a squelching thrust to the back of it's brain. He held up his sword and roared in triumph.

Kavi looked towards Nineteen and Tess, angry they let one of the kobolds get off a shot but the two continued to lay down cover fire in a series of alternating ranged volleys. Kavi glanced towards the windows of the inn and could see the devastating effect their barrage caused. Two kobolds hunched over the sill of the easternmost window, arrows pincushioning lizard bodies splattered with black and green blood.

The other window was a smoking ruin. The relentless volleys fired from Nineteen's hand cannons obliterated any cover the window once offered.

Who fired the arrow?

Kavi saw the glowing eyes of the two kobolds as they drew back bows from hidden perches on the roof of the inn. They must have moved there in the chaos of the fight with the hounds. The other Strikers hadn't seen them yet.

"Roof!" shouted Kavi.

Tess loosed and struck the first before he could get his arrow off. She would be too late for the second as the kobold aimed at Ten's unsuspecting back. *Damnit, they were going to lose their healer and Kavi couldn't do a thing about it!*

Before the kobold could loose the arrow, it shuddered. A small bump appeared at the front of it's throat which turned into the point of a stiletto. The edge of the blade carved a wicked smile through the soft scales below it's chin.

Kavi breathed a sigh of relief as Trixie appeared behind the creature. She moved in front of the kobold and watched with unsettling glee as the life left its eyes. Then she began to kick its corpse over and over again.

"Enough Trix, we're not done yet, get back down here!" yelled Kavi to the small Dancer.

Trixie spit on both corpses, then scaled down the front of the inn.

* * *

Tack had to admit she was impressed and a little frightened. The Ghost Squadron comported themselves like a real team. They were not the fodder they'd grown to expect from the newbies the League normally saddled them with. The first encounter last season had killed three quarters of the ghost 'team' they sent in with them. Tack knew this was a big factor in their dismal record last season. The pro team had to join the fray earlier and earlier as the season progressed. They lost Isaac and Jackson before the midway point, two damn good Dancers who had been on the pro team for over three years.

Her fear came from the ferocity of the kobolds and the dogs that popped out of the ground. If this was the caliber of monster they sent at the fodder team, what awaited the pros inside the fort? Her team would have handled the overpowered kobolds easily enough, but they would have struggled with those hounds.

"Did he just slice an arrow in half with his sword?"

White's voice interrupted her grim thoughts. She walked over and put a hand on the big Guard's shoulder. If Tack was the brains of the operation, White was the rock they leaned on when things got nasty. "I believe he did," said Tack.

"This season's gonna suck isn't it, Three?" said White.

Tack smiled at his usage of her Ghost number. She and White had been fighting together a long time.

"Something's changed," she said.

"What?"

"I wish I knew."

* * *

The Ghost Squad patched their wounds. Eight and Clara built fortifications east and west of the site. Ten did her rounds among the
wounded.

"The arrow went into the muscle Twenty-two," said the Astran
healer. "You're going to be fine."

"I still think I should sit out this next round just in case."

"This isn't the Pool, Twenty-two," said Trixie. "Do us all a
favor and kill yourself for real or pick up your damn shield and quit
bitching."

Jansen looked for support but found nothing but stony faces. None
of them *wanted* to be here. They'd be damned if they'd let him freeload
in the back when his shield could keep them alive.

Sliver uncovered a nasty spike trap that required two spiders
walking down different sides of the street to trigger. It was a trap
meant to take out groups of people at a time. It destroyed half her
spiders. Not only were the spikes freshly sharpened but there was a
layer of caustic liquid at the bottom of the pit that melted the spiders'
protective casing. Sliver was down to four of the dense little scouts.

The final intersection before they started the ascent to the keep
looked clear. Only one squat building sat on the northeast corner.
That building had two standing walls. There were enough gaps that it
would provide no cover for friend or foe.

Sliver offered to walk through the intersection first but it was
Twenty-three who held her back. "My turn," said the Loamian Dancer

with big ears and giant feet. "I don't always sense the fauna around us but I can feel the dormant roots under the street. I have the best chance of getting us through this one."

Sliver nodded to the man and he walked forward. He smiled as he walked across the street to the other side. The team let out a collective sigh of relief.

Then, as he was walking back, in the middle of the intersection Twenty-three began to shake as the earth below him shuddered. "No, no, I know what you are!" he yelled.

"Get out of there Twenty-three!" yelled Tess.

Two gnarled roots came out of the ground and anchored the man in place. He stared at his team in horror as a sickly green and black weed grew right in front of him. What first looked like disease was revealed to be scales on the plant itself. The weed grew to chest level and as it formed a point, Nineteen opened fire.

The metal shards destroyed the first weed but three more grew next to it. Nineteen couldn't keep up.

The third weed was almost entirely black with shimmering scales. Twenty-three closed his eyes to feel the earth around him. If there was a moment to embrace and accept mortality, it was now. The team cheered when the man caught the sharpened tendril that shot towards him. Then, the wicked point at the end of the weed slid relentlessly through bloody hands as he resisted. It continued through his leather armor and into his heart.

Twenty-three gave a surprised gasp and slowly sank to the ground.

With a grotesque slurping sound, the plant began to drink. Twenty-three's shocked face crinkled and fell in on itself as the moisture left his body. Within seconds, all that was left was the cartilage of those large ears and the boney protrusions of those giant feet.

Clara let out a soft sob.

"How do we fight an underground lizard plant?" squeaked Jansen as he formed up with Pete.

"A Vonderian would be pretty nice right now," said Sliver. The party backed away from the flailing weeds popping up closer to their position.

"It may be time for some fire runes C," said Trixie.

"I'm going to need a minute!" Clara took several stakes from the small cart the forts trundled behind them. She reached for a brush and began to paint.

"We're going to need to dig the wall several feet down so that plant doesn't immediately burrow under," said Eight.

"I don't think it's going to matter," said Kavi. He jumped back to avoid a weed sprouting in his direction. He looked to Tess. "Can you do anything to slow it down?"

She knelt and closed her eyes. Her brow furrowed in concentration and beads of sweat formed on her forehead. She stuck her hands into the earth and muttered.

Kavi stood in front of Tess as the black green weeds sprouted in front of her. His blades passed easily through the smaller sprouts that emerged but it was like fighting the rain. New sprouts replaced old and Kavi didn't believe his strikes were doing anything to damage the overall organism.

"So much rage," whispered Tess. "A plant shouldn't be capable of rage." She began to hum. The soft lullaby was so completely at odds with the chaos surrounding Ghost Squad that some of the team stopped and looked at Tess.

The plant was also affected. The tendrils of scaled greenery around Tess and Kavi had stopped its aggressive growth. The shoots flowed sinuously back and forth in sync with the soft melody.

Clara began to hum in concert with Tess as she painted. The tendrils around the Guards and Forts wavered. The effect was so obvious that the rest of the team took up the melody.

Eight and Ten took the painted sections of the fortifications and added them to the defenses. Clara had managed *two* fire runes in that short period of time. The long weeks of practice under extreme pressure had made her elegant strokes precise and fast. She reached for the small knife to cut her palm to activate the runes when she had an idea.

"What are you doing?" asked Eight. "Activate the damn things."

"Not yet," said Clara. "Tess, do I have time to try an idea?"

"If you hurry," said Tess. The strain in her voice made it sound like she carried Kavi on her shoulders.

Tess stopped humming when she spoke. Even the brief pause caused the plant to flail wildly. While the humming of the rest of the team helped soothe the plant, their accompaniment was meaningless without the communication Tess pumped into the earth.

Clara began to paint. This creation took a different form than anything she painted before. She hummed the soothing song in harmony with Tess as her strokes found rough wood. It was born of fear, like everything powerful she created, but the feeling she injected into the painting came from the tranquility of the song. She thought of all the times Tess had accomplished the impossible in commune with nature in order to protect those around her. Those memories turned into strokes that made up the roots and trunk of this new rune. She embraced the fear and pain of Twenty-three when the man realized he was going to die, yet resisted to the end. She painted life struggling against all odds to find a way. When she finished, what she saw in front of her held peace and strength. Just looking at the symbol made her feel part of the world around her, something which had alluded her from a young age. It made her feel like she belonged.

"Put it up," said Clara to Eight and Ten.

The two women were entranced by her new creation.

"Now!"

Her yell was enough to break the rune's spell. The two Forts pounded the stakes into the ground in the center of their formation. The new rune would provide the baseline for their defense.

"Tess, I'm going to need you to activate this one. Once the forts have it in place, add a trickle of your blood underneath the rune."

Tess found Clara's eyes. The burden of holding the plant had become too strong. She would lose control in seconds, not minutes.

With a glance, Clara read her exhaustion. "Kavi, help her over to the rune. She's not gonna make it!"

Kavi put his arm under the ranger's shoulder but even with his assistance she wasn't going to make it to the wall. He picked her up and ran to the Forts as Tess hummed. Her body was taut but she didn't resist. He set her in front of the new wall with Clara's freshly painted rune. He sighed with relief as he looked at the calming image in front of him.

He realized Tess had stopped humming. His calm vanished in shock and pain as one of the weeds wrapped around his calf and stabbed into the meaty flesh of his leg.

Kavi's scream woke Tess from her exhaustion. She grabbed the dagger from the sheath at her waist and sliced the pad of her thumb deep enough to cover her hand in blood. She slammed her hand beneath Clara's rune and collapsed.

A wave of energy emanated from the rune passing over Kavi, Tess and the angry plant. Kavi collapsed with Tess. The plant slowly withdrew it's angry tendrils back into the earth.

The gates to the keep opened.

32

Loss and Pain

The runes appeared to be holding. Sliver had no idea for how long. With Kavi and Tess unconscious, it was her show. She wasted no time in piecing Herman together. The large golem stood between Nine and Twenty-two, inert until she added his power cell. Sliver cursed for the umpteenth time as she thought about how much more effective the massive golem could be. If the League would just give her a little sulimite so she could give him a proper suli core instead of the poor organic substitute she was forced to use.

The Forts and Guards continued to dig in. Everything north of their position had been heavily fortified and trapped. Clara created two more Tranquil runes, her name for the new creation. The plant hadn't bothered them since. She looked to Ten who still worked on Kavi's leg. Ten nodded at Sliver and walked towards them.

"Mmmm, thanks. How long was I out?" asked Kavi. He tenderly stretched his healed calf and stood.

"Thank the tinkerer's shiny brass ba-"

"Good to see you too Sliver," interrupted Kavi before she could get started. "You mind telling me who those guys are?"

"No idea. Seconds after you and Tess passed out, the door opened and these mounted kobolds trotted out of the keep."

"Why haven't they attacked?"

"No idea," she said again. She plucked a stray hair that dropped into her view from her straw colored spikes and winced at the pain. "But it doesn't take a genius to know they're waiting for something."

Horns sounded from the south and one of the large kobolds stood in the stirrups of the scaled dog he sat on. It issued orders in a tongue Kavi did not recognize and the mounted kobolds began to spread out in a line.

"Nineteen, can you upgrade weapons into spears?" asked Kavi.

Nineteen looked to the hill then back at Kavi. The man read enough military history to know the best way to stop a cavalry charge was with long spears braced against the ground. "It doesn't work that way," said Nineteen. "But I think I can do us one better."

The small Bricker walked over to the Forts. The Forts already planted two rows of wooden spikes in front of their walls but they would be static. They wouldn't be as effective in stopping large dogs as they would in stopping horses. Holding spears would be their best defense in the event of a charge.

When Nineteen ran a hand over a wooden spike, it elongated and became thinner. He grunted in satisfaction when the wood turned to steel.

Sliver whistled. "Damn Nineteen, you're going to have to teach me that trick."

Nineteen continued upgrading and passed the spears out to the team.

Once everyone had a spear, Kavi moved to the front of their group and turned to face them.

"What we doing boss?" asked Sliver.

"Pinch and pound. We already have the formations in place. Those mounted troops should only be able to get at us down the center of the street. We need to make it obvious that any other approach is a death trap. Nineteen, any chance you can upgrade the wooden stake along those fortifications to metal?"

"Don't think so Eleven. Finishing those spears gave me a massive headache. I'm tapped."

Kavi nodded. "How many pre-sharpened stakes do we have left in the cart?"

"That's most of them," said eight. "We could pull some of the fortifications we laid a couple of streets back."

Kavi wished they had access to the unlimited defenses of the Pool. "Let's pull the stakes right in front of our Guards and add them to the angled defenses to the east and west. That should guarantee they come right at us. Clara, where did the fire runes end up?"

"They're still there. One on each side. They just haven't been activated."

"How do you feel about activating them during the charge?"

"Risky. Maybe Trixie can do it if she poofs," said Clara.

"Can we put a gap an arm's width on either side of each rune? Then you don't have to be on the other side to activate it," said Pete.

Eight nodded. "It weakens the fortification a bit but the flames should prevent them from exploiting it."

"Why are we worrying about fire at all?" asked Jansen. "I thought these things were immune."

"I don't think they're immune," said Kavi. "Just protected. Worst case scenario, it adds a distraction that throws off the charge."

"Don't know how those two things are any different," muttered Jansen.

Kavi ignored him. "Sliver, we need Herman anchoring our line. How much time do we have with him?"

"Thirty minutes....forty? It depends on how heavy the fighting is."

"Expect it to be heavy. Don't put the power source in until we're damn sure they're going to charge. If we don't stop that charge, we're done. Forts, can you join Seventeen and Nineteen with flanking fire?"

"You want me firing or healing?" asked Ten.

"Firing in the initial assault and healing after."

* * *

The pro team moved into the town. They double checked weapons and gear and readied themselves for their part of the Quest. The fodder team was several blocks up but Tack and White found an elevated position where they could watch the Ghosts prepare.

"He's got a head for it," said White.

Tack nodded and surveyed the field. "They've done better than I expected, especially with the crazy difficulty." She stared up at the keep for a long moment. "I can't shake this feeling. Line up our suli application stations now."

"Before we make it to the keep?"

"Something feels off. I'd rather be ready than dead."

White nodded. He didn't like seeing Tack rattled. They had been through a mountain's worth of shit together. He'd never seen her look this nervous. He issued orders and the team pulled out their sulimite gear. Yantzy and Flan would apply tattoos while the Harpstrans loaded up their hookahs.

Each Garden City had their preferred method of taking the powerful substance. In a pinch, anyone could swallow or snort sulimite powder but only novices or the very desperate took it that way. The powder severely dampened its impact and caused massive withdrawal after the effect wore off.

The refined application allowed the effect to last for hours instead of minutes. Even so, they hadn't breached the keep yet. If the effect wore off before they finished the Quest, White knew they were going to be in trouble. He trusted the voice in the back of Tack's head though. Anytime they hadn't listened, they lost team members.

When Tack gave the order, the team began to take their suli. Nobody grumbled or complained. After years of questing the team had built good instincts of their own. Tack wasn't alone in her unease.

* * *

"What are they waiting for?" asked Jansen.

Even the line of mounted kobolds standing in front of the keep looked bored.

"Are they waiting for us to attack them?" mused Pete.

"But they have walls," said eight. "If they were waiting for us they'd be behind them. It doesn't make sense."

"Intimidation," said Sliver.

"It's working," said Clara in a soft voice.

"They're waiting for the other battle to finish," said Tess.

"What other battle?" asked Pete.

Kavi looked sharply at Tess. He was annoyed he didn't know where her information came from. She had been acting cagey since they got on the ship, very unlike her.

The horns to the south sounded again. The large kobold grabbed a horn from his saddle and responded with three sharp blows of his own. The thirty mounted kobolds moved forward at a walk.

"Here we go. Sliver, get Herman moving," said Kavi.

The Bricker inserted the power core into the large golem and it whirred to life.

"Kavi there are at least sixty coming from the south. They're going to try to flank us by riding around," said Tess. Her voice was calm but her eyes were wide.

"Sixty!?" squealed Jansen.

"The pro team is back there. Trix, make sure they know what's coming."

Trixie nodded and ran towards Tack and her team.

"Spears ready. Only worry about what's in front of us," said Kavi. His voice was calm and commanding but his pulse quickened. He knew he had to show confidence for his team. "We got this. We faced way worse odds in the Pool."

The large kobold raised the horn to his lips and blew. The scaled cavalry charged.

Tess and Nineteen fired as soon as the kobolds were in range. With a brilliant shot, Tess put an arrow into the eye of the leader and the kobold fell twitching to the earth. His mount continued to charge without its rider.

Nineteen was even more effective. He aimed for their mounts. The first dog he dropped fell in the path of another rider and got tangled in its legs. Kobolds and mounts fell in a bouncing, tangled heap. Nineteen raked them with his hand cannons. Blood and scales exploded like fireworks.

Through the haze, the kobolds continued to charge.

"Spears!" shouted Kavi.

The line of charging kobolds hit the line of spears with an ear-splitting crash. The scaled mongrels yelped in pain as momentum caused metal points to push through scaled hides. Their sharp teeth snapped at the defenders. Once the spears had done their work, the defenders dropped back and pulled their own weapons.

Trixie made it back in time to activate the rune on her side as Clara activated the one on hers. The kobolds shrieked alongside their mounts as flames engulfed the back line of charging attackers. Scales offered protection but tender ears burned and eyes melted under the waves of fire.

Herman wreaked massive havoc as his big fists connected with kobold and mount alike. A pile of corpses lay at the golem's blocky feet.

Several of the kobolds catapulted over the line in the initial impact but the back line was ready. Sliver and Trixie stabbed deep into unprotected backs as Kavi cut through the survivors in a whirlwind of steel.

The line of cavalry had broken and all that remained was to put the survivors out of their misery.

"More coming," shouted Tess as she knocked another arrow.

The gates had opened again and organized rows of heavily armored kobolds began to march down the hill. Archers followed.

"Kobolds with organized infantry? Really?" asked Jansen in disbelief.

The Forts repaired their defenses. The Strikers joined the Dancers in finishing the wounded and pulling corpses aside. They wouldn't have more than a minute of rest before the next wave arrived.

Kavi gratefully took the canteen Sliver handed him and gulped at the water. "Who's hurt?" he asked.

"No serious wounds," said Ten. The woman wrapped a cut on Eight's left side. "I healed the wound, but those ribs are going to be sore for awhile."

The defenders were forced to take cover as the archers walked into range. Their projectiles flew over the heads of their own infantry to fall around the Ghosts.

"Damnit!" yelled Nineteen when an arrow struck his backpack. "That took out my left hand cannon."

"We can't shoot under this barrage anyway," said Tess as arrows continued to fall.

Once the infantry was ten meters out, the arrows stopped. Clara and Eight had each taken arrows in their shoulders. Ten frantically tended to them.

Tess and Nineteen stood to fire when the infantry charged. Tess did a better job of finding gaps in armor and she felled three of the charging kobolds. Nineteen sprayed the line but with only half the firepower. He still managed to force the left side of the charge to slow as they brought up their shields.

When the infantry hit their line, the defenders were hard pressed. Herman swung his large metal fists. With each swipe a kobold flew back into the infantry behind it. Jansen and Pete held firm on either side of the large golem. They stabbed out behind tower shields at any kobold that came close.

The press of bodies took its toll on their fortifications. The small barricades began to fall and the eastern fire rune dropped followed by the western one.

Nineteen was fully exposed. He fired burst after burst into the kobolds swarming through the felled barricades. When it looked like he was about to be overcome, Trixie and Eight stepped in to stem the tide. All three took slashing wounds as their defense turned into a wild melee.

On the other side, Tess and Sliver found their own rhythm. Tess alternated between shooting arrows and summoning fungal decay on any open wound she saw. Sliver tossed throwing knives at any kobold that got near Tess. Each of her shots found eyes or mouths and the lizardmen fell. Clara did her best to repair the fortifications on that side. The speed at which Tess and Sliver worked allowed her to shore up some of the basic defenses.

Kavi was everywhere. His unnatural speed allowed him to plug holes at the rate of three men. Twice, he spitted kobolds who made their way around their front line to get behind Ten. The healer stopped to heal Trixie and Eight. Twice more, he stopped a surge that would have ended the valiant defense Nineteen led on their western front.

So many kobolds died. So many more continued to attack.

"Kavi!" yelled Tess. "To the north!"

"Oh, come on," Kavi muttered.

The barricades from the previous street had been dismantled. The kobold cavalry riding from the south flanked them and began to charge.

* * *

"If we don't go now, they're all going to die," muttered White so only Tack could hear.

Tack nodded and gave the signal.

With a yell, Team Sugoroku charged.

* * *

Kavi faced the line of cavalry by himself. He smiled when he saw Tack's team charge but knew his own team would take the brunt of the attack. There were too many of them and his team had no defense in place for an attack from the north.

The infantry attacking their southern fortifications had thinned but there was still at least thirty of the scaled bastards engaged with their crumbling defenses. Herman did massive damage to any kobold who came close. At least the center of their line held.

This gave Jansen a chance to look back when he heard hissing growls from behind them. When he saw Kavi facing the cavalry charge on his own, something clicked.

Survival without humanity was not enough. "Nine, can you hold with Herman? I'd like to try something to cover our backs."

Pete risked a look back and paled. "I'll try," he grunted.

Jansen turned to face the new threat and sprinted in Kavi's direction. He finally accepted he might die today. No, he accepted he *was* going to die today and he had his first completely unselfish thought in as long as he could remember. He took all the shame he had been nursing since deserting his company after the fight with the banglors. He tossed in the rage at facing that shame and mixed it with purpose - a chance to protect, a chance at salvation.

He stood next to Kavi as the kobolds riding their demon dogs bared down on them. When the beasts were five meters away Jansen yelled, "Not today!" He slammed his shield to the ground. Replicas of his shield rippled outwards to either side until at least twenty copies stood firmly planted in the ground.

The kobolds struck the impressive barrier at full speed. One or two of the mounts had the presence of mind to leap over it. The rest slammed into the shields and their riders went flying. The summoned shields lasted for several seconds before disappearing back into the ether. They had done their job.

Kavi gave Jansen a nod of respect.

The riders and stunned dogs began to rise.

On the southern front, it was Eight who fell first. Her small buckler broke in half earlier in the melee. She hadn't noticed or simply forgot. When she raised it to block a strike the kobold's blade found her neck. She died instantly in a spray of arterial blood.

Trixie screamed and disappeared to appear a moment later behind the kobold. She planted her own daggers deep into the beast's neck.

Nineteen fired as he retreated to one of the nearby buildings. He ran out of real estate as the stunned cavalry began to recover. Calling on all the power of the clockwork augmentations in his legs, he jumped to the crumbling roof where he continued firing. An arrow loosed from one of the trailing kobold archers took him in the thigh and he slid to a kneeling position. He never stopped firing.

Ten fell next. She left her back exposed as she desperately tried to revive Eight. She kept yelling, "No Mari, no!" as she prayed over the fallen Fort. The thrown javelin took her in the back hard enough to pass through her entire body and plant itself in the ground in front of her.

Kavi moved faster than ever before. He killed three kobolds that closed on Trixie before the woman even saw them. He hamstrung two of the dogs closing in on the small Harper. She smiled at him through bloodstained teeth and vanished. He took a fraction of a second to analyze the battlefield. When time slowed like this, Kavi was at very little risk and it was worth understanding where he could be most effective.

Team Sugoroku's Strikers neared Nineteen and Trixie's position. Kavi sighed in relief. They would be safe soon. The majority of the revived cavalry that charged from behind moved towards Tess and Sliver's position. Clara had managed to put a series of spikes facing the new threat in front of them but it wouldn't be enough. Jansen did his best to slow them down but he was one man moving at regular speed. There was still at least thirty kobolds and fifteen dogs closing on their position. They were in trouble.

Kavi moved.

He screamed when the first dog leapt for Tess. He wasn't going to get there in time.

A giant cat leapt from the roof of a nearby building and intercepted the dog in mid-air. It's claws rent scaly flesh and it's teeth ripped the mongrel's throat out. It landed in front of Tess and hissed at the dogs and kobolds advancing on their position. They paused at its ferocity, if only for a moment.

The moment was enough for Kavi to whirlwind into the back of the group with blades spinning and cutting. Many fell but many more remained. Even in his time delayed state, Kavi could tell they were going to lose this fight. He made peace with it. If he were to fall, he would do so protecting his friends.

The first wound Kavi took was a bite to his left leg. The hounds were too damned fast. The bite drove him to one knee. He was able to kill that hound but two more stepped over it. The giant cat swatted one of these and the two animals bounced away in a yowling tumble.

The kobold that replaced the dog had spiraled horns on its head. It was a full head taller than the other kobolds. It gave Kavi a malevolent smile filled with angry intelligence as it slashed it's serrated blade towards him. Kavi blocked but it was Clara that slammed a cavalry spear into the beast's shoulder. It screamed in pain. Most the kobolds on the field joined in the scream which turned into a howl of rage.

The beast grew taller and its muscles swelled. "Now is the time for humans to die!" it roared in common tongue. The shout caused the kobolds around it to renew their attack with ferocious vigor.

Kavi made his way back to his feet and his back found Jansen's. He found his mantra as the giant kobold attacked. The beast was fast and strong but it telegraphed it's movements. He only needed to block twice when Kavi saw the gap. He moved quickly. He slashed first at the giant's knee which caused it to drop its head. Then Kavi used both swords to slice upwards, opening the giant kobold's neck. Kavi was showered in blood. The black green liquid covered his ears, eyes and even inside his mouth as the giant kobold toppled. The remainder of the beasts went into an insane rage and Kavi braced himself.

He took a fraction of a second and looked to see Rake and Flan cutting a swath through the kobolds. They made their way to Trixie and Pete who, along with Herman, held the line alone against what was left of the infantry. He watched Rake pick up one of the kobold's javelins. He knew the man was going to throw the javelin at the back of the kobold sneaking behind Trixie. Rake had clearly seen the threat. He raised the javelin to throw but instead of throwing it at the kobold he threw it at Pete's back.

The kobold sneaking behind Trixie found its mark and the young Harpstran fell to a dirty sword pushed into her back. Trixie died before a final curse could reach her lips.

Pete died without a sound as the force of Rake's blow punched through the back of the man's breastplate and into his heart.

"No!" Kavi screamed as he lost two teammates in the blink of an eye because of one man's betrayal. He lashed out at the raging kobolds closing in but there were too many. They were all going to die here today. Lightheaded, he fell to one knee.

He, Jansen, Sliver, Clara and Tess stood or knelt in a pentagon of exhaustion. When the kobolds charged he heard Tess mutter and a wall of brambles surrounded the five of them.

Kavi passed out in pain and misery, falling on the already unconscious Tess who lay beside him.

33

Repercussions

The large bunker had none of the tasteful elegance the owners were accustomed to. They were deep below the Garden City of Krom in a room hewn from stone. The rough edges fit the mood in the room.

The Majordomo waited until the owners found their seats. She sat patiently, until the restlessness in the room settled. "We all know why we're here. Senet, since you called this emergency meeting, I will pass the floor to you."

The man was impeccably groomed as always. His three piece suit was cream colored rather than his trademark brilliant white. It was a sign of trouble for those that knew him, he only wore off-white when truly furious. "I would like to lodge a formal complaint with the Collective on behalf of Company Senet and, with the agreement of my fellow owners, the rest of the League." Remarkably, none of his anger reached his voice.

"And what would be the nature of that complaint?" asked the Majordomo, voice just as steely.

"A stunning lack of information, regarding this new breed of Marked, going into the season. We pay hefty dues to the Collective in return for information. When that information is withheld it brings into question the nature of our agreement."

"And if the information was withheld because it was incomplete or theoretical?"

"The fact that it was withheld at all should have been disclosed per our agreement."

Majordomo considered pushing him to identify where in the agreement such a disclosure was required. That tactic might work to slow someone like Ch'es but Senet was too sharp. If he brought this up, he knew the exact clause and provision. So, she opted for intimidation. "I'll have the thin man reach out to you personally to offer his regrets."

The man's nostrils flared but Majordomo couldn't tell if the reaction was rage or fear. "Regrets are meaningless, even when delivered by the boogey man himself. What I want is restitution." His tempo and intonation didn't change at all.

Rage then, thought Majordomo, *to provoke or mollify?* "In that same agreement, it clearly states the League takes on *all* risk associated with accepting Quests. You know how this works. The better prepared your Companies are, the more difficult the Quests become. I didn't think I'd have to explain the nature of precognition to this group. With the potential of great reward comes the possibility of great loss. Past success in mitigating team losses is no guarantee of future success. These results only confirm the League has stopped evolving, stopped innovating. Until that trend shifts, expect heavy losses."

"The losses we took weren't heavy they were cata-fucking-strophic!" blurted Mehen, reverting to common, her face blotchy with rage.

Senet took a breath, removed his glasses and cleaned them with a handkerchief. He put them back on and turned to the fiery owner. "Thank you Mehen. We agreed to let me handle this, did we not?"

Mehen nodded curtly, her angry focus never leaving the Majordomo.

"While Mehen does not speak for the group, her complaint reaches to the heart of the matter. Charles, if you would?"

Senet's assistant read from a report. "Four Quests were attempted, only one Quest successfully completed. Losses: Risk – eight A team members, five professional team members. Sugoroku – five A team members, one professional team member. Quest completed by Sugoroku. Go – six A team members, four professional team members. Mehen – nine A team members, five professional team members. Quest failed. Senet – seven A team members, three professional team members. Ur – five A team members, four professional team members. Quest failed. Wari – *all eleven* A team members, two professional team members. Though we believe that five of the A Team members left with the Liberators who showed up at the Quest site." The young man coughed as he realized his mistake. "Excuse me, who left with the Agitators that showed up at the site. And finally, Ch'es – nine A team members, three professional team members. Quest failed."

Senet looked back at Majordomo. "If we continue to sustain this level of loss, we will not be able to finish the season. This disaster caused a series of uncompleted Quests which will eventually make their way out into the world. That will result in a loss of control over the entire Questing process. I can't imagine that is a desirable outcome for the Collective."

"That is the first thing you've said that I absolutely agree with," said Majordomo. "None of this is a desirable outcome for the Collective. Let's start with the losses. Why is it that your Company had the fewest losses Sugoroku?"

"I believe it has something to do with our Ghost Squadron's success unlocking skills in the Pool," said the small woman in the flowing black robe. "This forced us to reevaluate our training methodologies.

Now, even our triple A and professional teams have benefited from it."

"Sugoroku and her teams evolved using Risk's latest technologies. Yet, none of the rest of you have done the same."

"You know damn well what happened when we tried to use the last version of that brain mangler," said Ch'Es, his jowls wiggling in anger. "Half our fodder squad and a handful of double As turned into head cases. One of the double As *killed* our tactician a half hour after she left the Pool. You'd have to be an idiot to send even the greenest recruit into those death traps."

"And yet...Sugoroku did it," said Majordomo. "The Collective shared the reports. You all had access to the information and you did...nothing."

"To get back to the matter at hand, I'm more interested in the information you did not share," said Senet. "Why have the Marked shown up during every Quest this season? Why doesn't the most powerful organization on Grendar know how the Marked are being created? And why the huge power differential within the Marked? An evolved kobold is something our teams have a chance to defeat but something like the Ach'Su? Don't give me that look Domo, if you insist every evolved monster is called Marked, then the Collective needs a better way to identify specific Marked. If we don't know more about the Marked, how can we possibly defeat them?" His normally level voice gained in volume with each question.

The other owners looked taken aback, never having heard Senet raise his voice.

Majordomo smiled inwardly. A rattled Senet would help her negotiations. Before she had the chance to utilize the information she felt a bony hand on her shoulder.

"I'll field this one M," said the thin, hooded figure that stepped out of the shadows behind Majordomo's chair.

The owners in the room visibly paled. Even Senet dropped his stoic mask for a moment to show, if not fear, certainly surprise.

"The Collective has provided you and your Companies with information and resources for nearly a hundred years. In that time, you became more powerful than any other merchant warlords in history. The moment you come upon a Sage challenge that stymies you, what do you do? You blame the Collective for a lack of information. The problem is not a lack of information. The problem is you've become soft. Your predecessors faced these type of losses every Quest until they improved."

"Asking for shared information we already agreed to in order to b—" Senet cut off abruptly, his mouth no longer able to create sound even as his lips continued to form words.

"I did not give you leave to speak," said the thin man. As his voice grew in volume, his body grew in size until he and his tattered black cloak took up half the room.

No one said a word.

"Evolution is formed through challenge. That is the goal of the Quests. Since we have captured the Sages, things have been too easy on the League. How do I know this?" He directed his question towards the Majordomo.

"Because the Companies have not unlocked any new skills since we have captured those sages," said the Majordomo.

The thin man patted her shoulder softly. "Exactly. We have stopped evolving because we have stopped being challenged."

Senet raised a hand. The thin man nodded, impressed the man had the courage to ask a question after his demonstration of power.

"I did read the report about the new skills Sugoroku has developed. What if the opposite is true? What if when we develop new skills, the challenges get more difficult? Isn't that a disincentive to evolve?" asked Senet. He once again used his measured tone.

"A fair question that relies upon a faulty assumption."

Senet tilted his head showing he was ready to learn from the thin man.

"Quest rewards are a secondary objective for the Collective. They provide us with the resources necessary to continue funding the League and our research but they are not the primary desired outcome. The primary outcome is progress through evolution and advancement - something this current group of owners has done a poor job of over the past decade."

His hood encompassed the entire room in a shroud of dissatisfaction. He shrank in size and turned back to Senet. "That said, I do appreciate critical thinking." He nodded at the particular man in the off-white suit. "So, I will share my theory on your second question. I believe progress and challenge are inextricably linked. When we advance, so will our opponents. The road to greatness is built upon the evolution of conflict."

"Regardless of the number of bodies that lie on the side of that road?" asked Go. The old man didn't look angry, just thoughtful.

Instead of anger, the thin man nodded. "*Because* of the number of bodies...which is why I believe the volunteer campaign you've proposed will fail. The stakes aren't high enough for volunteers. All hope must be lost before acceptance can mold our candidates into vessels capable of evolution."

Senet raised his hand again.

The thin man nodded to him. "I understand your theory about idealism and choice, though I don't agree with it, even if the data from Sugoroku's time in the Pool supports it. Thus far that data's anecdotal. However, I will not forbid you from trying something different if these early losses haven't changed your minds. Evolution requires new pathways, new ideas."

"Thank you," said Senet. "Do we have any idea as to why the

Marked have become so big part of the Quest landscape this season?"

"We don't have anything but theories," said the thin man. "And weak ones at that. The more Marked beasts we capture or kill, the more we can learn."

"Would you mind sharing the prevailing theory? It may gave us something to work with when we encounter them in the field."

The thin man stared at Senet for a moment, his hood gathering darkness around it but then he relented and nodded. "We believe the Marked are mutations created by a new substance, similar to sulimite. Where sulimite effects are temporary, the effects of this new substance seem to be permanent. The theory has not been proven nor have we found any of this new substance ourselves. Do NOT rely on this information. However, if you find any data confirming or refuting the theory, please share it with us."

It was Senet's turn to nod. "Do you mind if we return to the business at hand?"

The thin man nodded and faded back into the shadows. They could feel his presence but could no longer see him.

"Since we have sustained such high losses, I propose we implement the volunteer campaign on an accelerated schedule," said Senet.

"Before we get into rebranding, can we discuss the Agitators? I lost nearly as many Ghosts to the Black Rose as I did to the Marked," said Wari. "Have we made any progress tracking down the fifth Sage?"

Wari looked around the table but the owners shook their heads. They knew Wari's confirmation with them was pretense. His question was directed at the Collective.

When the thin man did not reappear, Majordomo took the question. "The fifth Sage continues to elude the Collective. However, we are working on a plan in concert with the other four Sages to trap her. Each Sage only know parts of the plan in an effort to try to throw off the fifth Sage's precognition. It's a bold plan with a low probability of success."

"Anything the League can do to raise that probability?" asked Wari.

"Capture the Agitators. While most don't know anything about the fifth Sage's plans, they may have other information. Keep an ear out for things like safe house locations, armaments and Agitator skill advancements."

"Don't they work in small cells?"

"Typically yes, their cells are no more than four or five people. The exception is when they hijack a Quest. That is when they are most exposed. They will often bring four or five cells together to complete or prevent a League team from completing a Quest," said the Majordomo.

"Do we have any proof the Agitators are completing Quests given by the fifth Sage herself?" asked Wari.

"No direct proof," said Majordomo. "But they have a surfeit of resources that has to be coming from somewhere. It stands to reason."

"Which is a good segue back to the volunteer campaign. The Agitators are doing a far better job of marketing themselves than we are," broke in Senet.

"How so?" asked Wari.

"Charity," said Senet. "The Black Rose has become synonymous with hope. They spend at least some of that surfeit of resources on the people. The name Liberators is viewed in a positive light across most of Grendar. If we're going to move to destroy their name and elevate ours it has to happen soon. What progress have we made with the leadership of the Garden Cities?"

"The leaders of Vonderia and Harpstra are bought and paid for," said Ch'Es with a sloppy smile on his fat face.

"Stuff the grin Ch'Es, anyone can bribe children with sweets," said Mehen.

"I take it the High Priest of Astra hasn't flipped yet?" asked Senet.

"Pious bastard's a stickler," said Mehen.

"Are you using the right bait?" asked Wari.

Mehen shot him a puzzled look. "If gold and suli aren't enough, not sure what else we got."

"Followers," said Wari. "Guarantee him followers and show him how gold and suli build that path. A couple of quick conversions and he'll be eating out of your hand in no time...even if you have to buy the converted."

"Buying the converted. That *is* an interesting thought. We pair that with a conversion campaign...," Mehen said. She gave Wari an impressed nod. "I think you're on to something. I'll put it into effect the moment we leave the room."

"Lord Go, Ur?" asked Senet.

"Krom was difficult. *Donating* a large cache of weapons and armor to the Bastion and the Krommian Regulars seemed to do the trick. They'll give us a platform when we want it," said the old man. His perfectly groomed goatee looked sparser than a month ago.

"Brickolage was a similar challenge. They bristled at bribes but donate a university building and sulimite to be used only for research? They'll do what we need," said Ur.

"Which brings us to Loam," said Senet. "Risk, I don't know if you or Sugoroku have made any inroads with them."

"I've come up empty," said Risk. "I can't find any levers to pull. They pride themselves on subsisting in harmony with the land. They have carefully cultivated their sulimite and use it in ingenious ways. I've offered donations to plant trees and shepherd the land. While they're happy to take them, they will not do so in exchange for favors."

"Similar, disappointing results," said Sugoroku. "My team and I have tried water and mineral rights. We offered help with regulations on merchants that pollute the Rhune but to no avail. Sure, they're happy to take our money and our suli but don't offer a platform in return."

"Water rights is a fascinating idea," said Wari.

Sugoroku nodded enthusiastically. "I was sure that would do it. I even thought it would surprise them into compliance but it felt like they were expecting the offer. I wonder if the Agitators are conducting a counter campaign."

"You may be giving them too *much* respect," said Ch'Es.

"And you may be giving them too little," snapped Sugoroku. "If history teaches us anything, it is that women Sages are *not* to be trifled with."

"Assume and plan for the worst," said Senet. "We need to launch the volunteer campaign before the next Quest competition. That gives us a little over two weeks. Our campaign would be more successful if we had the backing of every Garden City but let's assume that Loam is a lost cause and focus our efforts on the other five."

"What about a counter campaign?" asked Sugoroku.

"We need to craft multiple messages. We've all destroyed competitors. None of us is afraid to sling a little dirt. Assume the audience is hostile and sweep the legs from their campaign before it begins. Every message that lauds the League will have a corresponding message that blames the Agitators for everything from red fever to the Marked. When we link the Marked and the Agitators we should use their language. Let us make Ach'Su synonymous with Liberators. Force them to own the monster under the bed."

"Then what?" asked Wari.

"Then, we welcome the volunteers to the glorious facilities of the League. That will provide us with as many ghosts as we need to execute our next step of evolution," said Senet.

He smiled at the dark shadows in the corner of the room.

34

Holden & Amelie

When Kavi opened his eyes, the bramble shield was gone. He was alone. It was dark but for the flickering of candlelight. He sat up and looked around.

The cave was much as he remembered it last time. Waking here felt like a homecoming of sorts. In the back of his mind, he knew this was a dream but it didn't diminish the terror he felt as he looked for Holden.

The man sat on the cave floor below him. He wasn't alone. Kavi watched in astonishment as the man threw dice with the Ach'Su. When it caught sight of Kavi, the giant beast reared up on its hind legs and rammed it's leonine head into the ceiling of the cave. The violent motion caused rocks and dirt to rain down on Holden and the dice. Holden shushed it and the beast calmed.

Kavi stood and walked gingerly towards the pair.

Holden threw the dice again. He held up an eye to look at the pips then cursed. "Midnight again? What are you doing to these damn dice?"

Kavi mustered up the courage to ask a question. "Do you know why I keep dreaming of this place?"

The Ach'Su reared up again and more dirt and rocks fell.

"Cut it out Lenny, that's annoying," said Holden.

The Ach'Su squenched its lion face into something that looked like contrition. It grabbed the dice and threw.

"Lenny?"

Holden shrugged. "It's your head kid, don't ask me." Holden held up an eye to scrutinize Kavi's face. "I see you still haven't taken my advice."

"Yeah, I'm not pulling out my eyes. I'm more interested in what else you said about trauma and violence. The other Ghosts who evolved... they had dreams too. We're putting together the pieces."

Holden laughed. "That *is* a good one. Puzzles and pieces, like chickens and geeses. You think you're close but Lenny's got a better chance of geesing his way to knowing. 'Sides you know you can't be blabbing what you learn here, not until you can see."

If it was all in his head, why would he warn himself not to discuss these dreams. To protect himself from other's opinions? He didn't care about that anymore, did he? And why all the bird references. The Ach'Su was here – lion and bird. Young cub and Sugoroku raven. This had to be deeper than his subconscious. He was being set up for something. There were too many coincidences to think otherwise.

"Who are you?" Kavi asked.

Holden stood and walked over to him. He poked a finger into Kavi's forehead. Kavi winced as he felt the finger bore into his skull, but there was no pain. "I'm the third eye in the storm, the catalyst of the reaction."

Holden's finger moved and Kavi felt the calmness of time slowing. Holden nodded, "This here's the temporal, it holds more power than a kettle of hawks. Learn to control it young lion before the clock ticks nil."

Holden moved his finger around as if stirring a pot and Kavi heard a roaring in his ears. In his other hand, Holden held an eye millimeters from Kavi's and hissed. "You think you've embraced it, yet you refuse to sacrifice. That's the only way to see."

Kavi pulled back in dread. He heard the welt squelch of finger leaving forehead. "I'm not giving up my eyes."

The man smiled with far too many teeth. "Then you're never going to be able to see." He walked back to hold his eyes over Lenny's throw. "See, midnight again!"

It was the Ach'Su's turn to grunt in disappointment.

"Take a throw," said Holden.

Kavi grabbed the dice and from their smooth feel he knew they were made of bone. He threw. Double sixes. Midnight.

"See, just a single dose of tru and the world changes. The second snake slithers from its hole. True night seeps from the earth and all luck is bad. End times kiddo. Not a great time to be alive."

The Ach'Su grunted again.

"Oh yeah, Lenny's wondering why you didn't ante."

"I didn't know this was a betting game."

"Yeah, you did."

Kavi searched himself for anything of value, but he had nothing. "I don't have an ante."

"Well, then you're going to have to give up them peepers," said Holden. The flames behind his eye sockets flared in anticipation, his shark grin took up his entire face.

The Ach'Su reached it's talons towards Kavi's face and he screamed.

* * *

When he opened his eyes he looked upon the aftermath of another battle. This one was fought over a river crossing. Even the current couldn't wipe away the stench of blood and shit that only the dead and dying can make. Most of the dead creatures had skin of a greenish hue. Their most prominent features were sharpened tusks with a massive under bite. Kavi couldn't help but think of a caricature of Coach K painted green with bulging muscles and pauper's clothing. He wrinkled his nose. They smelled no different than any other dead thing. Several of those hanging on to life squealed softly in pain as they prayed or cried.

A large man carrying a long spear walked the battlefield with a small woman in a flowing black robe. She stopped at each of the wounded, human and green-skinned humanoid, and offered a short benediction. The act brought a cry of relief from those in the most pain, the prayer easing suffering. The large man with the spear trailed her. He offered an end to suffering via a thrust to the head with his wickedly pointed spear.

The woman winced each time he struck but carried on. These fallen were past salvation. With the uncomfortable duty complete she walked with her protector to the small group huddled on the near shore.

She knelt at the river and rinsed her hands of blood and grime then turned to the group. The hem of her black robe was wet and caked with mud. This added to a presence that jumped between divine and very human from one moment to the next.

She looked at the five ghosts dressed in blue and yellow and a tear tracked its way down her dusty face. "What was done to you was barbaric. No living creature should be forced to face the horrors you've faced these last couple of months."

Kavi struggled to recognize the woman's face but her voice was burned into his memory. She was the same woman who helped keep him sane on his first trip to the Nest.

"We'd like to offer you an alternative to constant pain and blood-shed," she said.

Some of the ghosts looked up at her words as if seeing the woman for the first time. Kavi could swear he recognized one of the smaller Brickers but those parts of her that weren't covered in armor were covered in filth so he couldn't be sure.

"Why can't we just go home?" asked the small Bricker.

Kavi's heart leapt as he recognized the voice.

"What's your name my dear?" asked the woman with almond eyes.

"Twenty-nine," said the small Bricker.

"Your real name."

"Amelie Nettie Patching. My friends call me Nettie."

"Nettie it is then. You can't go home because that's the first place the League will look. Until we give you the tools and the time for the League to forget about you, going home will endanger your family."

Nettie sobbed and Kavie knew she was thinking about her family and her lost brother.

"I know," said the woman. "I wish it were a different world. If you come with me, you will never be forced to kill or fight again."

This caused Nettie to cry harder. Some of the others joined her.

"My name is Rose and my group is known as the Liberators. After you recover, I will ask you to help us in whatever way you can for a period of one year. After that year, you can choose to go back to your old lives if that is your wish. Or, you can help me free as many as we can from the grips of tyranny."

She walked among the five ghosts she rescued. She offered kind words and touches of sympathy. When she was done, each felt they were the most important person in the world, if only for a moment.

Rose faced the group. "I know it's not much of a choice. Stay with me or try to make it on your own but I can promise your chance of survival goes up if you join us. What do you say?"

The five ghosts clamored over each other to accept her offer. The woman in black smiled graciously then looked over her shoulder to where Kavi hovered, invisibly watching the exchange. She met his eyes and he felt guilty for eavesdropping, even if it was a dream. Her smile broadened in a way to let him know she approved of his trespass. "You are but the first to be freed this season. Know that the Black Rose is coming for all Ghosts. We will expose the League for who they are. Be ready when we come."

She waved to him and Kavi felt his grip on the dream world loosen but not before catching a scent of the otherworldly priestess. Roses. He sank back into the darkness.

35

Empty Bunks

The next time he woke it was in the medical pavilion in the Nest. He cracked an eye and saw Healer Brand sleeping in a chair next to his bed. "Hiya Olsen," croaked Kavi.

Olsen sat up. "You're up! From what the team told us, you've been out for days. Except for a couple scratches, I couldn't find any wounds."

The experience from the Quest flooded back. His wounds were on the inside. "How many did we lose?"

"Too many. Eight, Nine, Ten, Twenty-three and Thirty-five. And we lost one of the professional Dancers."

"Damnit Olsen, use their names!"

The healer looked at him with sad eyes. "I'm sorry Kavi, I never learned them. It's too hard."

"What about that traitorous scum, Rake. Did he at least suffer serious injury?"

Olsen frowned at him, perplexed.

He was saved from explaining when Doctor Cleary walked in. "Enough of that talk unless you want to end up on a slab next to your friend Pete."

Kavi was so angry he couldn't speak for a moment. "I'm just supposed to accept that a *professional* murdered one of my team and got another killed?"

"Don't turn that anger on me young man. And yes, that's exactly what you're supposed to do." She held up a hand to forestall another angry outburst. "You have no power in this place. Make it through the season and earn a place with the triple As or the pros. Then, challenge that psychopath for a spot. Accidents happen in challenges all the time."

Kavi took a breath and reminded himself Doctor Cleary was one of the good ones. "And what if I bring a complaint to the coaches or to Tack? She seemed alright."

"Think it through, Eleven. What's more likely? That crazy bastard randomly killed team members who might help keep him alive? Or he was following orders from somebody in the organization? You've been here long enough to see how this place works. Eight, Nine and Ten were on the shit list. Don't add your own name to it."

Kavi was so frustrated he wanted to scream but he complied as Doctor Cleary started an exam on him.

"Interesting," she said. She felt the nodes in his neck arms and near his groin. "You're healthy but the limbic system driving your awareness and spiritual chakras are working overtime. Have you been having any weird dreams?"

Kavi choked back a laugh. "Only since I got to this damn place."

She looked at him sternly. "Pay attention to them. There's power in dreams." The doctor finished her examination and had him dress. "I've run out of reasons to keep you here Kavi. From what I hear about this last Quest, the Lioness would have been proud of how many of your squad you kept alive."

Kavi shot an angry look towards Olsen.

The healer's eyes widened in surprise and he stared at Doctor Cleary.

Doctor Cleary rolled her eyes at Kavi. "Healer Brand didn't break you confidence boy. I served with your mother in the war. The resemblance is uncanny. You've been right not to try to contact her. The League is too big for even the Lioness to tackle. Gather power and station and make changes from within."

He pulled his uniform back on. "Thank you doctor, you've given me a lot to think about."

She smiled at him sadly. "Embrace the pain and the sadness of your losses. Feel it. Share it. It might not seem like it, but it will make you stronger."

* * *

All eyes turned to him as he walked into the dormitory that evening. The room was somber. Some of the no-neuros spoke in hushed conversation on the far side of the large room. Kavi noted Jansen hadn't joined the no-neuros. Other than that, the room was silent.

The empty bunks of fallen teammates lay like gaps in a perfect set of teeth, dead roses in a beautiful bouquet. Kavi ignored the eyes and walked to the first set of gaps where Eight, Nine and Ten once slept. He rubbed a hand over the coarse fabric that covered each pallet. He moved to Twenty-three's bed and did the same.

Clara sat next to Trixie's bunk and stared motionless out the large window. The chill no longer reached inside the room since she drew the fire runes on either side of the window. She didn't register his presence until he reached down to touch the fabric that made up the dead Harpstran's bunk.

"Don't," she said sharply. The word rang through the quiet room like a mournful gong.

He stopped trying to hold in the tears. This expression of emotion in the Bastion would have seen him scorned for weeks, but he no longer cared how others viewed him. He let the tears flow down a face long frozen to emotion. The room watched his display. Even the no-neuros stopped their conversation.

"I'm sorry," he said, voice breaking. "I wasn't fast enough to save her."

Clara refused to look at him.

The tears continued. He stood for a long moment thinking of the young Harper - the first of them to unlock a skill. So full of life even while she was embracing death. The complete lack of fear of authority, of anything. "I'm sorry," he repeated.

Several of the Ghost Squadron looked away awkwardly, not knowing how to handle the emotion he wore so openly. They too had been schooled to hide it, afraid to show weakness. Vulnerability was so foreign in this new world, most couldn't process it.

It was Nineteen who broke the awkwardness. He walked over, put a hand on Kavi's shoulder, his own face wet with tears. "None of us were fast enough. We're all worse off for having lost Thirty-five."

Nineteen took a deep breath, sniffed then stood to his full height and faced Kavi. When he spoke it was loud enough the entire room could hear it. "You know what? Fuck that. She's not a number. I was a complete ass to her when she was *number* Thirty-five. A number isn't human. She was an obstacle to a warm night's sleep and a full belly. I admired Trixie. I admired how she could curse in a way that made no sense except to express very admirable levels of rage. I admired how she gave it her all every damn day in the Pool. No more numbers."

Kavi turned to the small Bricker as if seeing him for the first time. "You're right," said Kavi. He looked to the other empty beds. "I miss Pete and Mari too, and I think Ten's name was Prudence. Does anyone know what Twenty-three's name was?"

One of the Loamians stood and said, "Topher. He was a good man."

Kavi turned to the Bricker. "Maybe we try this again. I'm Kavi, nice to meet you."

Nineteen grinned. "I'm not giving you my real name because I hate it. You can call me by my Ghost Squadron name. It fits me better." He took Kavi's hand. "Nice to meet you Kavi, I'm Boost."

Kavi nodded. "It suits you, nice to meet you Boost." He turned somber again. Clara hadn't moved from her silent vigil. "Let's figure out how to stop this from happening again."

The words were a balm for a room desperately searching for hope.

Kavi felt the weight of the hopeful looks. He needed a plan that gave his broken team something positive to work on. It was the only way to rebuild shattered morale. "We debrief over dinner, all are welcome to join," said Kavi. "Tess, Pip, Boost, Sliver - you got a second?"

* * *

They reorganized the tables in the mess in a giant U shape to fit everyone. Clara still hadn't left her place of mourning. Some of the no-neuros steadfastly refused to participate in any cooperative effort, unless they were protesting the Pool. Everyone else attended. Out of the twenty-three survivors of the Ghost Squadron, eighteen sat in the debrief.

They decided Sliver would tell the tale. She had the most animated delivery. The only person who might have been better was Trixie, Kavi thought. Tess and Boost joined Kavi in adding color. Even Jansen jumped in a couple of times with self-aggrandizing comments. He told and retold the experience of unlocking his skill until Sliver told him to shut up.

Kavi made sure everyone understood how Pete and Trixie died. The Ghosts needed to know the professional team members were not allies. He realized he might have overdone it when he looked to the team once the story had been told. A lot of faces, especially those that didn't go on this last Quest, wore expressions bordering on panic. They were in the fire next.

"So we're pretty much screwed. Is that what you're saying?" asked Twenty-six.

"No," said Kavi. "But we have to start with truth. We need to understand what we're up against before we-"

"Yeah but isn't that the point of the Quest? We don't know what we're up against until we get there."

Kavi had to concede with a nod. "True, but the tactics we pick up in th—"

"The fact is, no plan we make here will hold up for a minute once we get into the Quest," said Twenty-six, continuing to interrupt Kavi.

"Vonn help me Twenty-six, you interrupt him again I am going to put you in a headlock," said Pip.

Kavi took a deep breath. "Everything Twenty-six said is true. The big advantage we have is the Pool. We can't plan for every scenario but we can use everything we learn in the Pool."

"Time in the Pool is priceless. I didn't believe it until I caught the look on the faces of Team Sugoroku. There was real respect there," said Sliver.

"And we still lost five people," said Pip.

"It should have been three," growled Tess. Her pupils turned oval and her amber eyes flashed in the firelight.

"Three, five, it's still too many," said Kavi. "That's why we train. We train until we drop. If we're not training in the Pool, I want us challenging the triple A team. Hell, let's challenge the pros. I wouldn't mind a shot at Rake."

"What about work duty?" asked Twenty-six.

"There's no getting around it," said Kavi. "I want us practicing skills at all times, even during work duty. Pump the double As for information on their Quests. Every little bit helps."

He looked around the group and could see resolve in return. He needed to give them more to do. "That's only a start. If you unlock a skill, whether in the Pool or outside of it, you share it with the group. What were you feeling when the skill unlocked? What specifically do you need to do to use it? Tack was able to give Boost pointers because she has a similar skill set. We need to do the same."

"Let's take it a step further," added Pip. "We compile this data and share it until we're the strongest Ghost Squadron the League has ever seen."

"I'm in," said Tess.

"Me too," added Sliver. "We meet here every night after chow and go over anything new we picked up."

"Look," said Twenty-six. "I don't want to be Negative Ned here and kill the enthusiasm in the room-"

"but...," said Boost.

"-but one of the things we haven't addressed is what happens when you're not on the Quest with us. We all saw the recording. Without your speed, do we have a chance?"

All eyes fell on Kavi. Twenty-six was annoying but he made a strong argument. If they were being honest about being truthful this had to be addressed.

"I don't know yet, but we'll figure it out," said Kavi. He had no idea what he'd be able to do about that particular problem. Hopefully, someone else, anyone else, would manifest a similar powered skill in the next two weeks.

"How can you know that?" asked Twenty-six.

"Because we have to."

36

We Need a Plan

On day three of their new training regimen, Jansen left the Pool with the rest of Ghost Squadron. He managed to unlock a second skill, what he called shield circle. Shield wall let him defend a large area on either side of him, while shield circle surrounded him and anyone near him in a cylinder of translucent tower shields that protected vertically to a height of three meters. He was celebrating the unlock on the way to grab a bite before work duty when Twenty-four stopped him.

"You've gone all in haven't you?" asked the dour faced Astran that had become the de facto leader of the no-neuros. "Nothing you said before changed. The Pool is still a tool of the dark one."

Pip stepped forward but Jansen held up a hand.

"Everything has changed Rance! You haven't been on a Quest. On a Quest all of it counts. I was wrong, but I want to live. To live in the real world means training and dying in the Pool. Use the time we have left to get better. All of you."

Jansen turned away from what was left of the no-neuros. There was only four of them now. At this point, they weren't much more than a nuisance. Jansen faced Kavi. "I'm sorry. I was an asshole because I was scared."

"I get it Jansen, we're all go—" started Kavi.

"No, I need to say this. I lost too many friends in that battle with the banglors. Because of that, I dropped my shield and deserted the Fourteenth Regiment." Jansen's face paled as the confession spilled out. "I'm a worthless piece of shit and I deserve everything coming to me. Then, I used that fear to stop other people from learning what they could. Tell me what I can do to fix it....Please!"

The silence held for an uncomfortable minute as Jansen looked to Kavi for atonement.

If he was being honest, Kavi was still angry with the big Krommian for stunting Ghost Squad's growth. His one selfless move during the Quest was a good step towards redemption but was it enough? The team needed him. Especially after Pete died. There weren't many strong Guards on the team.

"Jansen, I'm not a priest that can offer absolution," said Kavi hesitantly.

"But admitting you screwed up and owning it is a good first step," said Pip, jumping in.

Tess lay a hand on the big Krommian's shoulder. "Everybody screws up. Dropping your ego to admit you were wrong is real strength."

Jansen nodded but his eyes remained on Kavi. Kavi could tell that the soldier in him expected punishment. No, it wanted punishment. He *needed* to atone. Only a superior officer could give that to him.

"We need Guards, Twenty-two," said Kavi channeling some of his anger. "You're the only one of that group that has unlocked a skill. That is unacceptable. I need you working twice as hard as the rest of the Guards and Forts-"

"That I can do," said Jansen.

"I'm not finished. I need you to turn the Guard and Fort squads into a real force. That means they need to start unlocking skills. You need to get them there."

Jansen's face paled. That was a tall order for anyone. They hadn't figured out exactly *how* to unlock skills. "I'm not a leader Kavi. I'm a grunt. Besides, I lost their respect weeks ago in the Pool."

"Then get it back," snapped Kavi.

Jansen gave him a pained look but Kavi didn't relent. "I'm not asking your opinion soldier. I'm giving you an order."

Jansen bowed his head then offered a crisp Krommian salute. "Yes, sir. I'll get it done."

"One more thing," said Kavi. "Your scars disappeared in the change, just like mine, except for these baby marks. You need to come up with a new scar for Ghost Squad for anyone who wants it. Make it mean something. Ask Clara for forgiveness and maybe she'll help you."

Jansen held the salute.

"Get it done. Dismissed Ghost."

Jansen marched past the rest of the Ghosts. Kavi watched as Jansen grabbed a mobile ration from the public mess hall then gathered the Guards and Forts for a conversation.

"Sure you weren't a little harsh?" said Tess.

"If absolution is easy, it's meaningless," said Kavi.

Tess cocked an eyebrow at him. "Who are you trying to absolve?"

Kavi started to answer then snapped his mouth shut. It was a fair question. Some of the anger he felt for Jansen was directed at the parts of Jansen that he saw in himself. The old Kavi didn't take responsibility for dragging Grim into the League. The old Kavi would have been able to rationalize that it wasn't his fault that he wasn't fast enough to save Trixie. He decided he didn't like the old Kavi very much. So, who was he trying to punish? He finally mumbled, "Not sure yet."

They continued walking to the mess but came up short when the pro team walked in. Team Sugoroku walked to the front of the line as they always did. They pushed Ghosts and double As out of the way where necessary.

Kavi's fists clenched when Rake pushed number Twenty-six out of the way. He moved without thinking. He was surprised to feel Tess keeping pace as he moved forward.

Tack saw them advancing and stepped in their path. "Whatcha doing Ghosts?" she asked cheerily. "You weren't trying to start trouble, were you?"

Tess laughed in her face. "Us trying to start trouble...good one. I didn't quite catch your sense of humor when we first met. And we would do that how? By getting pushed around by psychopath over there?"

Tack shook her head. "You've been pushed around since you got here. You go out on one Quest and all of a sudden you expect to be treated with respect? You know it doesn't work that way. Get over yourselves, it was just a push."

"Right, just a push," said Kavi, voice brimming with icicles. "Right up until that push becomes a kobold javelin in the back of one of my teammates."

Pain flashed across her face but she masked it. "There is no proof of that disgusting allegation. We earned our spots on this team. I will not accept disrespect from you or any of your Ghost...Squadron," said Tack. Her voice matched Kavi's intensity.

Kavi didn't back down. Her presence no longer held the same level of intimidation. Not after watching Rake kill Pete. Not after Trixie died. "I saw it with my own eyes. But you know what? Go ahead and keep lying to yourself." He spat on the ground at her feet. "As for respect? You're not worthy of it."

"You want me to take care of this gnat?" Rake asked in his high pitched voice. His hand brushed against a new dagger sheathed at his belt. It had a bright blue hilt that matched the bright blue, scaled tattoos which covered most of his exposed skin.

That son of a bitch must have won the dagger in the last Quest. Kavi's rage grew. Not only was Rake responsible for the death of Pete and Trixie, he was rewarded for it!

"Shut it Rake. Not helping," said Tack. She stopped a charge from White with a finger to his chest.

A circle had formed around Tack and Kavi. The Ghosts stood behind Kavi doing their best to look intimidating. Team Sugoroku stood behind Tack, not having to try.

"Be careful, Eleven," said Tack. "You don't want to land on the list."

Kavi snorted but it was Pip who answered. "He won't. Have you noticed the amount of attention Ghost Squadron gets? They're changing training protocols because of what *we've* accomplished. Think about what the Company would say if you harmed such an interesting investment."

White and Rake glowered at the Vonderian. Pip smiled back sweetly.

Tack sighed. "It doesn't have to be this way."

"It does. Until you stop treating us as expendable," said Kavi, looking down at the short tactician.

Tack shrugged. "That's the job, *we* all did it," she said.

"Not anymore," said Kavi. "I don't care if you weren't smart enough to embrace the Pool properly. We will do what it takes to protect our own, even if that means creating our own list. Right now, there's just one name on it. Let's not add more."

"You're playing a dangerous game," said Tack.

"The game has always been dangerous. All I'm doing is changing the rules."

Tack smiled. "Have it your way. But remember Eleven, we're always being watched. Threaten *my* team and you're going to lose any allies you might have already made."

Kavi shook his head. "You've never been allies Tack. Besides, accidents happen all the time on Quests." He pointed at Rake. "Watch your back out there Flake."

Rake flipped him off but Kavi focused on his face, not his hands. He liked what he saw there – a twinkle of fear.

* * *

"So. Much. Vonn. Damned. Snow," said Pip, each word punctuated with a shovelful over his shoulder.

"Can't you use that void thingy to send it somewhere else?" asked Tess. "Could save us a lot of work."

Pip put down the shovel for a second and eyed her through a spread index finger and thumb as if measuring her. "Sure, I could send about two Tess's worth of snow through the void gate but then you'll have to do the rest. I'll be passed out in the corner nursing an ether headache when I wake up."

Snow fell every day over the past week. Snow removal had become their latest waking nightmare. The Strikers were on the road with the Dancers. The snow fell so heavily Kavi could barely see the guard towers near the bridge.

Earlier in the week, Sliver crafted a couple bladed plows she attached to either side of Herman's knees. With the amount of snow, the Company finally eased the restrictions on powers during work detail. The golem trundled down the center of the road moving the heaviest snow to either side. The rest of the Dancers followed behind removing what the plows couldn't reach. The Dancers had cleared most of the road before the Strikers cleared half the courtyard leading to the intake building.

"I wish we had four of those," said Stix. Their double A work detail mentor materialized out of the snow so quietly that Kavi, Pip and Tess all jumped.

"You scared the crap outta me," yelped Kavi. "I can't believe you were a Guard. They should have made you a Dancer."

Stix smiled, teeth camouflaged by the snow in his new beard. "My da taught me how to hunt when I was young. After a while, moving quietly became habit. You Ghosts are making a stink all over the Nest. I heard about the tussle you had with Tack today."

Stonez shouted a string of curses at the Dancers.

Stix looked his way before turning back to Kavi and his companions. "Go easy on Tack, she's one of the good ones. She pulled my bacon out of the fire more than once. She always did her best to do the right thing in a bad situation."

"You were Ghosts together?" asked Tess.

Stix nodded. "I know how bad this place sucks, especially when you're the one in the fire. Not everybody in here is your enemy though." His gaze lingered on Kavi. "Now let's finish this damn courtyard so we can grab a cup of tea."

Kavi wiped his forehead with a snowy glove to get rid of the sweat which gathered there. All it did was add more moisture to his face. He struggled to get used to the idea of being hot and cold at the same time. It had gotten easier. He couldn't have imagined clearing the entire road and courtyard of a meter's worth of snow in just a couple of hours when he first arrived at the Nest.

"What are you thinking Kav?" asked Tess. She and Pip worked on either side of him as they usually did. The companionship not only helped get the job done, his friends helped wrestle the darkest thoughts. He would have gone insane otherwise.

"Ghost Squadron and keeping everyone alive," he said.

"How's the plan coming?" asked Pip.

"I've got an idea," said Kavi. "But I need your help figuring out a couple of things. You have to promise me you'll keep it to yourselves until we get more information."

All three of them paused their shoveling. They looked around. The rest of the Strikers were working the other side of the courtyard with Stix offering comments here and there.

"I think we're good. Even the Company would struggle to pick up a conversation with the snow coming down this hard," said Pip.

Kavi nodded. "I've been avoiding it but it's time we talked about some of these crazy dreams I've been having." He described the dreams in the cave with Holden and the Ach'Su.

Pip leaned against his shovel. "I thought I was the only one. Mine have been coming in the form of an old friend, Krayla. She's an incredibly talented magicker that was my only real friend at the Academy. In the dream, she's angry and keeps yelling at me to push my limits, totally out of character for her."

Tess nodded. "My tormentor is my old Ranger Captain. He was always a hard ass though, so I haven't paid it much mind."

"My dreams are most vivid after we fight one of the Marked," said Kavi. "The first time was when we fought the Ach'Su. The second happened after fighting that horned kobold."

They continued to shovel in silence for a while. The courtyard was close to being cleared.

Pip finally broke the silence. "Your dreams sound prophetic, like something the Sages would say. Could the Sages and these evolved monsters, the Marked, be linked somehow?"

"Maybe, but I was thinking more about what each one of these dreams seems to be saying. Evolve," said Kavi. "Transform, find a new state of being. What's another way people have been using for years to upgrade their capabilities?"

"Sulimite," said Tess.

"Exactly," said Kavi. "Some of us have evolved without any sulimite by embracing death and some other mix of characteristics we haven't figure out yet. What if we got our hands on some suli? Could that push the others over the edge?"

"So, that's the plan?" asked Pip.

Kavi nodded.

"Try to steal some sulimite?"

Kavi nodded again.

"You realize the Sugoroku hoard, where they keep suli, is more secure than the Krommian treasury, right?"

Kavi smiled.

"You're nuts," said Pip. "I'm in, where do we start?"

"Tess?"

She sighed and slowly blinked those disconcerting cat eyes. "Fine, I'm in."

37

The Big Idea

They spent the next three days trying to identify where the sulimite reserves were stored. It was even worse than they assumed. The vault was located below the coaches quarters in the executive wing of the Nest. Only the coaches had the keys to open the lock to that wing.

"Oh, it's worse than that," said Olsen when Kavi pressed him. "Only the head coaches of the triple A squad and the professional team have the key to get down there. Why do you want to know all this anyway?" Olsen's eyes widened. "Oh, you can't really be that stupid, can you?"

Kavi shrugged. "No, to whatever you are thinking. I'm just trying to learn more about this place."

Olsen huffed, not buying what Kavi was selling. "Don't even try Kavi. If they find out, Sugoroku pet project or not, you're star status isn't going to save you from being tortured and killed. Do not mess with these people. Whatever you're planning, find a different way!"

They came together that night in the corridor outside the communal privy. Tess set up a nightly cleaning schedule weeks ago which was shared between the four groups. While the privies would never be a nice place, the Ghost Squadron made them as clean as they could with the tools they had. They could hear the Forts in there now as they scrubbed down the facilities.

"There's only three days until we get sent into the grinder of the next Quest, Kavi. You know damn well my number's getting called this time," said Pip in a fierce whisper.

Tess put a hand on the Vonderian's back.

Pip shrugged it off. "All the trash you threw at Team Sugoroku is going to be taken out on us. You know that right?" He no longer whispered.

Tess shushed him. "We're doing everything we can to give you the best chance possible. We've even started two-a-days in the Pool."

Kavi understood his desperation. He felt it before. Krom knew, he felt it every time he went into the Pool. The Pool. Something tickled his mind until the connection was made. "Can we summon sulimite in the Pool?"

"What the hell does that have to do with anything?" asked Pip, fear taking over his mouth. His brain finally caught up. "Sulimite in the...oh. Oh. Somebody had to have tried that before right?"

Tess shook her head. "Nobody from Ghost Squadron."

"Do you remember the rules Coach explained after each failure in the Pool?" asked Kavi.

Pip closed his eyes. When he opened them he nodded. "First rule: you learned this one the hard way. When you die in the Pool, you return here unharmed. The experience and memories you gained are yours to keep," said Pip in perfect imitation of Coach K's voice.

Tess and Kavi stared at him. "What was that?" asked Tess.

"I...uh...have a good memory," said Pip.

"You sure that's not a skill?" asked Kavi. "Sounds like something void mages might have. Pulling memories from the void with perfect replication. Keep going."

"What about the nightmares?" asked Pip in a perfect facsimile of

Jansen's voice. "Those are yours to keep too," he responded in Coach K's voice.

"That's creepy," said Tess.

This brought the first smile to Pip's face either had seen in days. "Maybe it is a skill."

"Ok, but that's not the rule I was talking about," said Kavi.

Pip shut his eyes and continued. "Second rule: conservation of energy. While in the Pool, you have access to all knowledge and skills you've ever learned. However, your brain can only accept what it already knows. If using those skills would make you tired in the real world, using them in the Pool will also make you tired. Even if the experience is only happening in your head. That's why fitness is critical to training inside and outside the Pool."

"I forgot about that one," said Tess.

"Me too," said Kavi.

"Third rule: your brain can summon any weapon or tool you've ever worked with. That includes everything in Team Sugoroku's armory. That's why it's critical to train with every weapon, tool, armor or armament outside the Pool. The training you use outside of the Pool can be mirrored here," Pip said in Coach K's clipped voice.

"That's the one," said Kavi. "We got stuck on the armory part."

Pip nodded. "But he actually said, any weapon or tool that you've ever worked with. We've all worked with sulimite. We should be able to summon it."

"Do you think it will work in the Pool?" asked Tess. "Sulimite is a chemical that impacts the brain. Simulated sulimite may not work at all."

"True," said Kavi. "But we have to try. We still have two days before the Quest. We have to unlock as many skills as possible."

* * *

They explained the plan to Ghost Squadron the night before. A sea of determined faces stared back as they lined up for the Pool. All the Ghosts had worked with suli at least once in their lives, so they would all get the chance to see if simulated sulimite did anything.

After their losses from the first Quest, Ghost Squadron had enough to field slightly more than two full Quest teams of eleven. Kavi and the survivors from the first Quest would be in one Pool. Pip would take those who had not experienced a Quest yet.

Kavi caught Jansen's eye as they slid into the Pool. Jansen held up three fingers and Kavi nodded. The large Krommian had helped three Guards or Forts unlock skills. The man had taken his role very seriously. Kavi rarely heard him talk about himself anymore, only about the accomplishments of his charges.

Jansen had new angry scabs on each side of his face. The new scars took the Harpstran rune for death and wrapped them in the Krommian symbol for life. With Clara's help this new symbol of life embracing death looked almost like the Loamian symbol for strength. Jansen had cut them into either cheek, the place traditionally reserved for marriage scars. Jansen was effectively stating he was married to the Squad.

The Guards and Forts were the smallest teams, especially after losing Eight, Nine and Ten. Marigold, Pete and Prudence, Kavi reminded himself. Because they were the smallest teams, they became tight knit. Jansen's leadership in relentlessly driving them made them even tighter. Every one of the Guards and half the Forts had scarred their faces to match Jansen's, even the Astrans and the Loamians.

Kavi planned to scar his own face when they were done tonight.

Only Twenty-four continued the no-neuro nonsense. Until yester-day. Kavi remembered the exchange vividly. He hadn't seen Jansen that angry since he beat Trixie.

They had just woken up from the Pool where Twenty-four had sliced his own throat again. Jansen stared daggers at the man.

"Just because the rest of you sheep follow the dark path to false immortality, doesn't mean I have to," said the Astran with a scowl.

"You're going to get people killed out there. I can't have that Rance," said Jansen. "If you don't do your part tomorrow in the Pool, you're less than useless to us. You're a liability. You'll get none of our food and when you get chosen for a Quest, you're riding point until you're dead. That way, no one dies because of your incompetence."

Rance looked to Kavi.

Kavi nodded in agreement with the big Guard. The stakes were too high. "Jansen has my support," said Kavi. "Did everyone hear that?" Kavi spoke loud enough to address everyone in the Pool. "Twenty-four doesn't eat tonight. We're not wasting food on a liability."

As they entered the Pool this morning, Twenty-four looked hungry and surly. Jansen refused to look at the man.

Kavi asked the Coaches if they would do a reset halfway through so they could switch up Pool partners.

Coach K laughed. "You think I'm going to use that many resources on you idiots?"

It was worth a try.

Kavi nodded to Pip, sitting in the next Pool over. The coaches had allowed them to pick their teams and Pip chose all of the Ghosts who hadn't yet been on a Quest. They needed as much time working together as possible.

The lights descended.

* * *

Pip opened his eyes and took stock of his surroundings. There were tents everywhere and a lot of people rushing back and forth. A battlefield scenario - something they could work with. They would get time to prepare.

He turned to his team, comfortable in the tactician role. He and Kavi were the Ghost's primary tacticians. "Gear up and get your suli tools ready. Once we get our orders, we take the sulimite."

He looked for the officer that would be running their way to give those orders. He grinned when he saw him. The man had a red plume attached to the top of his helmet that bounced up and down as he ran. Pip looked at the insignia on his chest and choked back a laugh. It was a silver eagle. He couldn't wait to make fun of Kavi.

The Krommian fop stopped to catch his breath then addressed to the group. "I am Lieutenant Fallon. It's my understanding your squad missed the briefing due to your recent arrival from Fort Stumpry."

Pip stifled a laugh at the man's formality but played his role. "That's right. What are our orders?"

"Your squad has been added to my platoon. We are to harry the enemy's western flank. Strike and retreat. Your secondary objective is to ensure they do not have an avenue to flank our primary advance force from the west. You will be working with three other squads. They have been briefed and are already on the move. You will need to be ready to spell them within fifteen minutes. Will your squad be ready sergeant?"

"We'll be ready," said Pip. "Is there a fallback point in the event we get overrun?"

"We have a numerical advantage. That should not be a problem."

"Nonetheless," said Pip, assuming a similar stuffy tone to the officer. "It would be beneficial to understand where to meet our allies in the case something goes sideways."

The officer gave him a hard look. "Put these armbands on so our squads do not mistake you for the enemy. The fallback position is that ridge."

Pip looked where he pointed and could see why it would make a solid rallying position. One could see all sides of the battle to come. The serious downside was they would almost certainly have to retreat uphill. A daunting proposition in the best of times.

"These are the platoon colors?" asked Pip. He looked at the black and green uniform the officer was wearing.

The officer nodded and Pip looked to his squad. "Surprise, surprise. Black and green today team, put on your colors."

With a breath, the Ghosts made the shift.

"That's a neat trick!" said the officer. "You're going to have to show me how you did that."

Pip nodded. "If we survive. Now let me prepare my troops. I'll see you on the field, Lieutenant."

When the lieutenant ran off towards his horse Pip turned to his Ghosts. "We're going to be running a contain left defense with a harry offense. Apply the suli now. I have no doubt we'll see action the minute we get on the field."

The suli tools came out and they were as varied as the team itself. The Astrans pulled out a bushy plant form of the substance that looked a lot like sage. They lit the plant and started waving it around as the three of them hummed and swayed in rhythm. The Harpstran loaded a small hookah, lit the bud of an almost identical plant, and smoked it. Pip grinned at how similar the Astran and Harpstran methods were considering how much the societies loathed each other.

The most interesting methods, by far, were the Loamians. Their one Loamian Guard, number Thirty, a man by the name of Grundle was one of their early hard cases. Over the past six weeks he had converted his significant obesity into something resembling muscle. Now he looked a bit like a bear. He pulled out a brightly colored frog and licked it. Their Loamian Dancer, Sixteen, pulled out an enormous, struggling bee with orange and yellow colorings. She began to convulse when it stung her.

Pip started on a tattoo using suli ink. He looked over at Twenty-six who was doing his best to tattoo a flame on his left forearm. Neither of them were artists. He wondered what Clara might be able to do with a tattoo. He hoped their neophyte artwork would have the desired effect.

"You feeling anything?" asked Twenty-six. The man's real name was Raztan but he tried to get everyone to call him Pyre. So far it wouldn't stick. His arrogance made it hard to let him come up with his own nickname. Pip and the others still thought of him as Twenty-six.

"Not yet," said Pip.

The others looked disappointed. The accelerant should have had some impact by now. A wave of depression flooded through Pip. This might be their last chance to learn life saving skills before getting tossed into the grinder for real. Without Kavi...no. Pip wouldn't let his head go there.

"Well, that's disappointing," said Pip. "But, we still have a job to do. Let's mount up and make it to that ridge. There is plenty of opportunity to embrace the shittiness once we get into the action."

The party summoned their horses and mounted. As they rode down the valley to the ridge, horns began to blare. The central attack had begun.

"There it is!" yelled Twenty-six as they rode. "You have to embrace it. Start thinking about the terrible ways you're going to die. Do it now!"

Pip followed the advice and felt the flush of suli hit like a charging buffalo. His senses honed, he felt stronger and faster. His teeth ached in anticipation. For Vonn's sake, there better be something to fight over that ridge!

When they crested the hill, it was obvious the intelligence their fop of a Lieutenant gave was worthless. The enemy's vanguard ascended the ridge fifteen meters away. The enemy had moved their entire force west to take the allied army by surprise.

And all Pip could think was: it's about damn time we get someone to fight! "Charge!" he yelled and the squad charged into the teeth of the massive army.

The first arrow took Pip in the eye and he woke up in the Pool a moment later.

"Charge. Really?" asked Twenty-six.

"Shut up Raztan," said Pip. "I forgot how aggressive suli makes you."

"But it worked!" said Twenty. The Astran striker, a dour man by the name of Rice, had a smile on his face, maybe the first one Pip had ever seen there. "We ready to go back in?"

Pip lifted a finger, pointed towards the booth and swirled it once around his head.

"Again!" the team yelled.

* * *

Pip kept an eye on Twenty-four. The man must have been really hungry because he didn't immediately slit his own throat. Instead, he joined the other Astrans in their suli ceremony.

This time Pip managed to push down the aggressiveness caused by the suli. He had his team sweep far to the west. The passage up the ridge was steeper but it put them in a reasonable position to harry the enemy army.

"Ranged, loose on the squad struggling to get up the ridge!" yelled Pip.

Twenty-six let out a yell and released a massive burst of flame. The flame morphed into the shape of a charging bull which engulfed the entire squad struggling up the last few meters to the ridge.

The team's shock was mirrored on Twenty-six's crimson face. They stopped and looked at the destruction the arrogant Vonderian created.

"Pyre it is," said Pip, impressed in spite of himself. "Ranged, keep attacking. We don't move until a larger force comes in our direction. Forts drop basic stakes and a half wall to slow them down."

This snapped everyone but Twenty-four out of their reverie. The man stared at the destruction he just witnessed.

"That means you Twenty-four, hop to it!" yelled Pip. Pip reached deep and opened a void gate in front of another squad scrambling up the hill. His gates were normally man sized. His suli powered void gate was ten times larger and the entire enemy squad scrambled through it before realizing what they were doing.

The enemy squad screamed as they exited the gate twenty meters above a brigade of pikemen at the base of the hill. The fall killed most of them. The spikes on top of the pikes did for the rest. The falling bodies doubled as dangerous projectiles. Many of the pikemen they landed on did not get up to resume their march.

"That got their attention!" yelled Rice. "Do we stand or mount up and move?"

Pip saw Rice had the right of it. The enemy moved an entire company in their direction. Pip's squad was good but they weren't good enough to take on a hundred armored infantry.

"Mount up!" yelled Pip. He led his squad down the enemy side of the ridge while circling to the west. If they could split the enormous force, even a little, their allies might have a chance. Two more gargantuan, flaming bulls summoned by Pyre charged the lines causing more of the enemy to shift direction and march towards them.

They got their third surprise of the fight when Eighteen, their small Bricker Fort, threw a glass flask at the enemy squad closest to them. The bottle exploded with a titanic boom and men went flying.

Finally, a group of cavalry wheeled off and charged. The Ghost Squad's horses would have no chance of outrunning this threat. Pip frantically looked around. They were on a small hill with several large boulders nearby. This was a great place to make a stand. "Dismount and fortify!" he yelled. "Focus on spears. You got more of those Flask?"

The young Bricker smiled and nodded. Just like that, another Ghost Squadron handle was born.

They placed the stakes quickly. Twenty-nine was able to erect a palisade on the side of one of the boulders which would split the charge into something manageable.

The barrier turned out to be unnecessary as Eighteen and Twenty-six broke the charge. A charging bull of flame and the explosion of two more flasks sent screaming men and horses burning and flying through the air.

They didn't have time to celebrate. Following closely on the hooves of the cavalry marched a band of pikemen.

"I need a breather," said Pyre.

"I only have one flask left," said Eighteen.

"Good job, both of you. It's time we practiced traditional tactics anyway. You ready to hold the line Ghosts?"

The Guards and Forts moved up front, executing the defense call. Twenty-nine joined Twenty-four in putting up barriers. They now had a respectable defensible position. Pip turned a critical eye to the mass of pikemen charging them. All things being equal, he felt pretty good about their chances.

"Summoned suli was one hell of an idea, Kavi," Pip said. He wished he could tell him in person.

"Pip? Is that you? We're in different Pools, how are you talking to me right now?" asked Kavi.

Pip whipped his head around but Kavi was nowhere to be seen. "I don't know," he answered back through the void. "But that was one hell of an idea." Pip's mind whirled at the possibilities. The power to communicate at a distance would be a game changer. They would have to test it to see if it worked outside the Pool. He cleared his head as the pikemen closed. One problem at a time.

The Ghosts were outnumbered by at least ten to one but they had the high ground and the sulimite advantage. Pip knew the biggest challenge would be reigning in the urge to dive headfirst into the fray when the two sides closed. "I don't care if you feel invincible," yelled Pip. "You hold the line with whatever you got. We have a better chance if we work as a team!"

The Guards slammed their weapons against their shields twice as the Forts pulled out long pikes of their own and closed the line. Grundle joined Sixteen, their Loamian dancer, in finding concert with the earth. Vines and roots grew out of the ground to snag the legs of pikemen who moved from a double time march to a full charge.

This was enough of a disruption that when the pikemen struck the line, it was a disorganized mess of individual efforts. The Guards rebuffed the early attacks easily.

To no one's surprise, Twenty-four fell first to a pike in the throat. The man had missed too much training.

Rice filled the gap in the line. Pip worried when the tall Astran Striker lost his staff in the scuffle. The center of the line was about to buckle. Then, Rice began to move. He was not as fast as Kavi, but his suli enhanced speed closed the gap. The man was almost unbeatable in unarmed combat before taking suli. Now, his arms and legs turned into a blur. It wasn't until his fists began to glow that Pip knew they were looking at something new. Twenty punched through armor and weapons. When he punched through a man's steel helm into the brain it protected, the pikemen around him looked for easier prey.

Sixteen made her way on top of the boulder which allowed her to rain arrows down on the pikemen. It also made her a target. One of the pikemen threw his pike and Sixteen fell.

"Leesta!" yelled Grundle. He moved to pull her injured form back and one of the pikes stabbed into his meaty arm. With a mighty roar, he threw Leesta behind a palisade where she could be healed. Then he began to grow. His massive bulk doubled, then tripled as his already hairy body became covered in fur. The pike popped out of his shoulder as his hands became paws. That's when the grizzly Grundle took out his rage on the puny pikemen in front of him.

"Who the hell are these people!" yelled one of the pikemen. He threw down his pike and ran. The rest of the regiment followed.

The Ghosts cheered. Then three regiments of pikemen headed their way. They were accompanied by a full squad of Vonderian mages.

"That can't be good," said Pyre, standing next to Pip.

Pip grinned. "I never expected to make it this far. Let's give them hell!"

* * *

When they woke in the Pool, it was a jubilant atmosphere. Everyone but Twenty-four discovered at least one new skill thanks to the usage of the sulimite.

Kavi looked to the happy group, hiding his concern. He seemed to be the only one who noticed that none of them had vomited any of the syrupy grossness that signaled an evolution. "Tomorrow, we do it without suli."

38

Roster Changes

The optimism didn't last. The next day, not one of the suli enhanced Ghosts was able to replicate their skills in the Pool without the assistance of the powerful drug. Knowing salvation was just out of reach made it all the more painful.

"They're announcing the lineup for Q two tonight Kavi. We're not ready," said Pip.

Kavi felt for Pip. His number was almost guaranteed to be called and most of the strongest Ghosts had been called in the first Quest and so would not be called for this one.

The two walked from the Pool to get a bite to eat before work detail. As they passed one of the windows facing out from the Nest, Kavi saw a flock of geese fly by in a perfect V formation. He counted the number of birds in the flock, fourteen. Something about that number seemed important.

"If we only had a couple more days," said Kavi. "Now that they know how to tap into those skills, I know at least three of them would make the jump."

"We barely have a couple more hours," said Pip, desperation coming back hard.

"We'll think of something," said Kavi.

"We might be out of miracles."

They turned to watch the pro team stroll in to the mess. Team Sugoroku's full roster was only fifteen. It reminded him of the geese. They had eleven regulars and four alternates. They never swapped people out unless they lost somebody in a Quest. Kavi wondered why that was. Team cohesion was critical but people got injured. Sometimes they burned out. Why not keep a roster of double the number and send different groups on Quests like what the Ghosts were forced to do?

Something didn't add up.

Team Sugoroku made their way to the front of the line but didn't push anyone out of the way. They waited until others made room for them, a change Kavi noted with some satisfaction.

Kavi stared daggers into Rake's back. The Striker did everything he could not to look over at the Ghosts. Tack caught Kavi's eye and nodded once. Kavi did not return the gesture. All he could think of was Trixie's cold, dead eyes. Fuck Tack and her entire team.

"That's what I'm talking about. Your bad blood with her is going to get me and my team killed," said Pip.

Kavi sighed, Pip had a point. "Hopefully she's not that petty."

"I think she's exactly as petty as you. You're two alphas circling each other, looking for weakness."

"A bit of an exaggeration. She's *the* Tack for Team Sugoroku and I'm just a Ghost."

"Oh please. You're the golden boy and every one of the pros knows it. You're the biggest threat to her in the whole Nest. Maybe not this season, but I wouldn't be surprised if they pushed you past triple A and moved you directly to the pro team once the season wraps up."

"Fine. I'll make amends before tomorrow," said Kavi.

"No time like the present," said Pip. He angled his eyebrows to where Tack and White just sat down.

"You're right. Grab my lunch? I'll work this out."

Pip nodded and moved forward in line.

Kavi walked towards the pro team not looking forward to the taste of crow. He would happily face any monster for Pip and the other Ghosts, he wouldn't be intimidated by something so simple as apologizing. He took a deep breath and got on with it.

Tack spotted him then crossed her arms and leaned back in her chair. When he closed the distance to the table, she kept eye contact until he stopped moving. "To what do we owe the pleasure of the golden investment gracing our table? Here to issue more threats? A lecture perhaps on how to fight in the Pool?"

Kavi's smile didn't reach his eyes. "Neither, I'm here with an apology and a request. I let my emotions get the better of my yesterday. I'm sorry."

Her eyebrows raised. "And the request?"

"Please don't take out any of the animosity you and I have on the Ghosts who go with you tomorrow."

"You give yourself too much credit, ghost," she said. "I'm going to treat the squad that goes tomorrow the same as I treated your squad. The same I treated every squad before you. As fodder. You're meaningless. A ghost's job is to clear the way of traps and monsters before we get there. If you die, so what? Who mourns the loss of a bug?"

Rake laughed his hyena laugh which made those disturbing blue, scaled tattoos ripple on the side of his neck like some exotic lizard. The rest of Team Sugoroku joined in.

Kavi shook his head ruefully. "Stix got you all wrong. He seems to think there's still a human in there. I think he'll be sad to find out that person died long ago. All that's left is a shell. It would be horrifying if it weren't so depressing."

Kavi could see the Stix comment struck a chord but she didn't rise to the bait. "You haven't been desperate for long enough. You're facing real pain for the first time and all of a sudden you think you have all the answers. But you're just a snot-nosed kid. Someday, you'll learn all that matters is the group around you that you *can* protect. Getting attached to anyone outside that group is weakness."

Kavi nodded and walked away. Her words were eerily similar to those Carlin spoke all those weeks ago.

He realized something else too. Those that suffered often believed no one else suffered as much as they did. No one else could ever experience as much pain as they did. It became this weird race to the bottom where a pit of victims wallowed in despair.

Those that grew from the pain never compared suffering. They were too busy living.

Tack did have a point with the small group. A tight knit crew could be managed. Kavi never had more than four or five friends he considered family. After that was the slightly larger circle of really close friends he would drop anything for if they asked. Interesting. That group was about the same number as the professional team. Bigger than that, it was too hard to keep track. Maybe that was the secret? The Ghost Squadron couldn't find it's true potential until it was the same size as the pro team.

That caused a ripple of dark thoughts. Why not two teams? One core team and one back up team that was good enough to survive? Just like the pro and triple A teams. The problem was Pip's team wasn't ready. If they went out tomorrow there was a good chance most weren't coming back. They found cohesion in the Pool in the last couple of days but it wouldn't be enough.

Kavi knew what he had to do.

* * *

The Coaches' footsteps echoed down the hall like the picks of grave robbers desecrating a tomb. All who hadn't yet been on a Quest waited with baited breath. They lost five team members last time. Five! And that was with their greatest asset, Kavi, watching their backs. What chance would Pip's team have?

Coach K walked into the room flanked by his two assistants. He held the list in his hand.

"Before we begin, I've had some complaints you ghosts are butting heads with the pro team." Coach K looked at Kavi. "Don't do that. Team Sugoroku is some of the best trained fighters in all of Grendar. They've faced unimaginable horrors for years. This group is going to be pulling your asses out of the fire in each Quest. What were you thinking?"

"Permission to speak?" asked Kavi.

"The question was rhetorical but I'll allow it."

"Team Sugoroku can fight. Nobody doubts that. But they care as little about us as you do."

"Oh, come now," said Coach K with an expansive smile. "You are like children to me."

Kavi rolled his eyes. "We have a job to do and they have a job to do. To be honest, they need us more than we need them. If we do our job well, their job is easy. If we die in the first couple minutes, there's a lot more danger they have to face."

"True, but I'd rather have allies at my back than enemies."

"Me too, but the minute we think about the pro team as allies, we're screwed."

Coach K raised an eyebrow.

"The reason the pros are successful is because they aren't fighting for us or the League. They fight for each other," said Kavi. "While some of the pros could care less whether we live or die, Tack is different."

"Then why are you feuding with her?" asked Coach K.

"Not different in the way I'd hoped. Her reasons are self-serving which is how you know they're honest. For her team to make it through the season, they need to use us like the diminishing resource we are. They're not going to take any more of us out unless the personal bounty is big enough, but we can't *ever* forget Rake killed Pete. That happened *before* my feud with Tack. They'll never be allies."

"Blah blah blah, great speech," said Coach K. "I have things to do. Anyway, here's the lineup. All numbers have been pulled from the list of ghosts who haven't yet been on a Quest. The three of us picked names out of a hat from each of the four groups." Coach K held the list up and squinted to read it. "Strikers - twelve, twenty, twenty six. Dancers - sixteen, twenty five, thirty one. Guards - twenty one, thirty. Forts - eighteen, twenty four and twenty nine. I'll post the list on the wall."

"I volunteer in place of Twenty-four," said Kavi.

Coach K looked at Kavi, shocked. "I don't think you can...I mean, no one has ever. Coaches?"

Coach M pulled a small book out of his back pocket and began to read. After a moment he looked up. "Nothing against it Coach."

"But you're a Striker," said Twenty-six. "Why him? Not only is he a Fort, he's a waste a space."

"That's exactly why him," said Pip. "You don't have to do this Kavi."

"Yeah I do," said Kavi. "We have to start acting like the pro team. Nobody else is going to take care of us."

"Then I'm going too," said Sliver.

"Me too," said Tess.

Kavi held up a hand and stood. "While I deeply appreciate it," said Kavi. "We're going to need two full teams. The rest of our teammates need the experience too."

"Don't do this Kavi," said Clara, she grabbed his arm and spun him to face her. She hadn't spoken more than ten words to him since Trixie died but now her eyes were wide and desperate. "I can't lose more people I care about."

The words were a balm. It was too soon to offer a hug. The coaches wouldn't allow it anyway so Kavi nodded to her. "I can't either. That's why I'm doing this. I've got the best chance of stopping it. Even if it's a small chance, I have to take it."

Clara sniffed then turned away and walked, dejected, back to her bunk.

Coach K rolled his eyes. "Oh, for Krom's sake! Enough of the hero melodrama. If you want to risk your neck and the rules say nothing against it, I have no orders to stop it from happening. Just keep the hero worship to a minimum while I'm in the room."

Coach L cornered Coach K before he left and all three of the coaches had a short huddled discussion. Kavi inched towards them to hear. Coach L was really animated but Coach K finally pushed away and said, loud enough for Kavi to hear, "...they're the one's going on and on about choice. Well, the kid's made one. Feel free to take it up with the thin man yourself if you want."

Coach K walked away and his assistants followed closely behind like two worried hens.

"Coach!" yelled Kavi to their retreating backs. "You didn't post the list."

Coach K handed the list to Coach L who ran back. Coach L looked at Kavi once and handed him the list. "You've really stirred up the hornet's nest haven't you Eleven?"

"I sure hope so," Kavi said.

"Be careful out there. There's a lot of careers riding on your survival," said Coach L.

Kavi spat at his feet. The coaches weren't allies and he could care less about this man's *career*.

Coach L chuckled then turned and jogged to catch up with the other two.

When he walked back into the dormitory, Kavi posted the list and turned to meet Tess and Sliver. Unlike Clara, they didn't look worried or scared. They looked angry.

"What the hell were you thinking?" asked Sliver.

"If you're serious about the team thing, you're an idiot not to take your best players," said Tess without a hint of modesty.

Kavi nodded. "I am serious about the team thing and I'm just as serious that we need two strong teams if we're going to make it through the season. Believe it or not, I have a plan."

"Well? I'm all ears," said Tess.

"I only want to do this once. Let's get everyone together and I'll explain what I can."

39

A Short Flight

They met in the mess connected to the dormitory. The tension in the room was palpable.

"You can't keep putting yourself at risk Kav," said Jansen in a last minute plea to get him to reconsider. "Ghost Squad, all of us, will break if you fall."

"That's less true every day," said Kavi. "In large part because of you! And because of everyone working their asses off to get better so we can survive out there. Keep pushing the training regimens. I know we can tap into those skills without suli, you have to figure out how to do it while I'm gone."

Kavi turned to face the larger group. "We're out of time though. That's why I have to go."

"Let's hear this plan of yours," said Pip.

"First, Pip is still tack for this squad. That's not going to change. He's got a better head for strategy. Sliver, Tess and Boost made me look smart in our last engagement."

"That's true," said Sliver.

"Quit stroking us and tell us the plan," said Boost, he clenched his hand several times causing the clockwork augmentation in his arm to whir rapidly.

Kavi explained. When he got into the details it became obvious why it had to be him. He talked for what felt like hours. Ghost Squadron hung on every word. They threw questions and objections at him. Each one honed the plan. The fire burned to embers as they explored every way the plan could fail and how they might deal with it.

"You're right, this might work," said Clara after doing her best to throw cold water on the idea. "But if it's going to, you all need to get some sleep before hopping on that ship tomorrow."

There were nods all around. Resolve flooded the room. With Kavi's plan, they had a chance of walking away from this one.

* * *

The morning arrived reluctantly. The sun a stubborn mule refusing to pull through the slate grey clouds that owned the snowy peaks. This far north, daylight was a scarce commodity in the winter months. The cloudy day dropped temperature and mood.

Jansen ordered the Forts and Guards who weren't going on the Quest to carry the gear to the loading dock for those that were. "Quit your bitching," he shouted for the third time. "We could use the workout and team two needs to be fresh."

"Who you calling team two?" asked Pip with a smile.

"One of these days, you all might catch up," said Boost. He helped the Strikers load their gear. "But until then, remember, second place is just first of the losers."

Jansen smiled and flexed.

"I liked you better when you were the surly Bricker with a chip on his shoulder," said Pip. He slapped the small Bricker on the shoulder way harder than necessary.

Boost winced but didn't lose the smile.

Neither did Kavi. The lighthearted banter was a balm to his worried conscience. Keeping the smile in place was difficult. Their confidence in him felt good but if the plan failed there was no one to blame but him. A lot of lives relied on the plan working.

With their endless training, the stairs to the dock had become more of a nuisance than anything else. With the comments flying back and forth, Kavi wished the climb would last longer. When they arrived at the top, everything would get very real, very quickly.

The climb did end, of course. Most of the Ghosts reacted to walking on to the snowy dock with audible sighs of relief. The ones who hadn't been on the deck before asked all the logical questions like - how the hell did the League hide a giant airship? And why did everybody else get to use the lift for their gear?

With those necessities out of the way, the gear was transferred. Coach K yelled at the Ghosts who weren't on the Quest to get back down the stairs. Everybody knew him well enough by now to know the threats wouldn't get serious for another minute or two.

Jansen got to Pip and Kavi first. "No hero bullshit, ok? Despite what you say, this Squad needs you. Both of you." The big Krommian bumped fists with both of them.

"You keep a steady line of communication with us throughout," said Tess.

They had run several tests of Pip's new void communication skill after he unlocked it in the Pool. Tess had been able to hear him clearly from down in the courtyard when Pip was in the dormitory. Pip believed that since the communication used the void as a medium, it would work at much further distance as well.

Tess's eyes were hard as she looked at Pip. "I'm serious. We'll provide what intel and strategy we can. Use us."

Clara gave Kavi a hug. "Please be careful. I runed twelve of the fortifications you're carrying with you. I hope they help."

Coach K's hollers turned serious so the support team finished their farewells and headed back to the stairs. That left the Ghost Squadron who would vanguard the second Quest alone with the pro team and the airship crew.

Tack and White walked over to the Ghost Squadron. Tack's eyes widened when she realized Kavi would be going with them. "You make Coach K's shit list already?"

"Nope, just looking after my team."

"You volunteered?" asked Rake. The man's keen ears picked up the conversation from several meters away. "What an idiot."

"Does he know how stupid he sounds?" asked Pip. "You idiots volunteer to go on *every* Quest."

"I don't think he does," said Tack. "But he has a point. We do volunteer, but not as Ghosts." She turned back to Kavi. "Since you're here, might as well make yourself useful. Show your team to their quarters. Briefing's on the hour."

Kavi gave Pip and the rest of the Squad a tour of the big airship while the double As finished loading it. Once the rotors began to spin, Kavi led the team to their quarters.

"Ooh, hammocks!" said Pyre when they walked in.

"How long do you think we'll be on this death trap?" asked Grundle. He looked nervously out one of the porthole windows.

"Think of it this way. It's a lot less dangerous on the ship then wherever they're going to let us off," said Pip.

"Thanks, that makes me feel loads better."

"Make yourselves comfortable. Most of the time on the ship is downtime," said Kavi. "Don't talk about the plan. We have no idea who might be listening. Once Tack briefs us, get as much rack time as you can. We have to go into this fully rested."

Not long after everyone stowed their gear, White came knocking. Kavi met him. "Briefing in five?"

White nodded. The Ghosts fell in behind Kavi as they made their way to the main deck.

The pro team had been briefed that Kavi was on board. They skipped the hazing which only worked on the uninitiated. Small snowflakes swirled around them. The Ghosts tried to find a spot on the deck where they could sit or lean and still hear Team Sugoroku's tactician.

"We've only been flying for an hour. How much damn snow can make it on the deck with a giant balloon above us?" asked Pyre. He wiped off the top of one of the supply crates so he could perch on it.

The other Ghosts joined the grumbling. They had little luck in sweeping snow off the rest of the sittable surfaces. Most opted to stand. Nobody wanted to start the quest with a rash. Pyre's eyes flashed red as he danced a quartet of flames over the closest surfaces. He sat with a happy smile and a warm bottom.

"Everybody satisfied with the seating arrangements?" asked Tack. "Good, because I don't care."

"I like her. She reminds me of Coach K," said Pyre.

"Enough. Eleven, did you warn them what happens if they interrupt?" asked Tack.

Kavi looked up at the base of the balloon for a second. "Oh right. You let them get killed?"

Tack frowned and nodded to White.

The big man cracked his fingers and headed towards Pyre.

"I wouldn't," said Kavi. "I don't know if I could take all of you. But I do know you, Rake, and Tack drop first."

White looked to Tack for direction.

"By Vonn's inflated ego!" yelled Pip. "I want to survive this Quest. So does everyone on this ship. If you two can't work together, how is that going to help anyone live through this?" He turned to Kavi and put a finger in his face. "You said it yourself. She has all the information and a good head for strategy. She's the one leading this operation. So, sit down and shut up."

"I like the new Ghost Squadron tactician," said Tack out of the corner of her mouth to White.

Pip turned his finger to her. "And you! You have all the power already so quit acting like you don't. You know we're far more advanced from any other Ghosts you've worked with. Stop treating us like the snow on the bottom of your boots. That's not strategic, that's stupid. Use us."

"And how would you suggest I do that?"

"Treat us like a triple A squad. Give us access to some of the sulimite you carry. We know you're stocked for three usages."

"And how did you—"

"Never mind how we got the information. We're resourceful. Imagine how far we could push if we were suli enhanced."

Kavi kept his mouth shut. Pip was taking a huge risk. If the gamble paid off it would be a guaranteed solution to their problem. But if it didn't...their plan would be much harder to execute.

Tack considered. Both squads watched in silence as she weighed the options in her head. Finally she said, "I'll discuss it with my team. That third usage is for emergency extraction if everything goes sideways. It's hard to give up that safety net once you have it."

Kavi glared, the nerve of this woman, how she casually lorded their advantages over the Ghosts. "Wouldn't know what that's like," he muttered.

Pip elbowed him in the ribs to shut him up. "Thank you for considering it. Please, continue your briefing."

Tack looked at him for a moment as if trying to decide if he was being sarcastic. Then she sighed. "I will. Our Crackers have locked down the location to the canyons bordering the Salt Flats and the

Wastes."

Pip raised a hand.

"I know. Your hotheaded friend told me last time." She pointed to Kavi. "That's where the two of you ran into the Ach'Su. I'm not sure why the Sages keep sending us over there but it feels like something's happening in the area. I hope we're strong enough to find out what."

She pulled a map out of her vest pocket and unfurled it so it lay over one of the larger crates. The pro team immediately gathered around the crate so none of the Ghost Squad could see it.

Tack looked up and sighed again. "Ham, Plimmons, Rake - make room. You've already seen the map. At least let their tactician and the golden boy take a look."

When the big Guards backed away, Pip, Kavi and a couple of the other Ghosts squeezed in.

Tack put a finger on one side of the maze of caverns depicted on the map. "We're going to land here to the south. We're up against Senet. They should be coming in from somewhere in the north. You can see all the different entrances to the canyons. There's a good chance for interference from our mysterious third player."

"You talking about the Liberators?" asked Flask.

The small Bricker was too slow to avoid the smack White administered.

"What was that for?" asked Flask.

"No more interruptions," said the big Guard.

"And it's not the Liberators, it's the Agitators," said Tack.

"Why would they change their name to something like that?" asked Pip.

"They didn't, it's more of a....forget it. It's irrelevant to the briefing. Just be on watch for interference. If we run in to a third party, retreat back to our landing zone and wait until I contact the tactician of Team Senet. We'll work together to pinch the Agitators until the threat has been removed."

"And if there is no interference?" asked Pip.

Kavi cringed every time his friend interrupted with a question but he wasn't reprimanded. Apparently, tacticians were allowed to ask questions.

"Then we follow the original plan. The Crackers think we'll find some sort of temple or mausoleum in the middle area here." She pointed to the center of the map. "But they weren't specific about where, just somewhere in the middle."

"Did they share the actual words of the Sage with you?" asked Pip.

Tack looked to Kavi. "I pressed the Crackers this time."

Kavi was surprised until the realization hit him. Tack's competence and brusque nature was so similar to his mother's that his immediate reaction was to bristle anytime she spoke. However, like the Lioness, Tack was no fool. If she were convinced something like the Quest text might give her and her team an advantage, of course she would take it.

"Would you mind?" asked Pip. "We're going in first, it'll help if we know what to look for."

"I doubt it will help. I can't make heads or tails of the rhymey nonsense, but why not?" said Tack. She opened up a journal that looked disturbingly like the one Nettie kept with her all those months ago. "Here is the important part:

Weave the maze but beware the haze
  Prize lies deep in canyons steep
  A longing mist, a forgotten tryst
  A man lies fallen in a field of pollen
  It's here you'll find the ties that bind
  Trick three times to ring three chimes
  Speak the devotion to set walls in motion

Victory will come to those who play mum.

"You get all that?" she asked.

"None of it," said Pip. He scrawled notes in his own journal. "But it might help."

"Like any Quest, we don't know what we'll face in the canyons," said Tack. "I spent time in the red rocks when I was a girl, like most Brickers. Sure, you had to avoid snakes and maybe some spiders but they were pretty safe. But something's changed. The Quests this season are a lot more dangerous. Expect the worst. Expect more Marked. I didn't realize it until I opened up a channel with the tack from Senet before we left today. Their losses from the first Quest were worse than ours. A lot worse. He heard rumblings from one of the Senet coaches that other Companies suffered even worse than them. Be ready for anything."

Kavi paled. He was there when they lost six people - five Ghosts and a pro. He had a hard time imagining how Senet could have had it worse. For his Ghosts, that was almost a fifty percent casualty rate. If they didn't get their hands on some suli, this was going to be a disaster.

"For Ghost Squad - Senet's colors are a striped blue and brown with the emblem of an open eye. They're impossible to miss. If you see them, do your best to avoid engagement. There's plenty of canyons that lead to the middle - rather than engage, take another one. The Agitators or Liberators don't wear uniforms. If you see anyone in the canyons not wearing a uniform, attack."

"What if it's a family out hiking?" asked Pip.

Tack snorted. "No Brickers hike this close to the Wastes. If they're that dumb, you have my permission to interrupt their picnic with a fireball."

Pip nodded then pointed to Pyre. "He's our elementalist. I'm sure he'd be happy to."

"That's right. Coach Sug called you a void mage, like magick bounces off of you are something. If what we're facing has magick, I'll make sure to hide behind you," said Tack.

"I'll hold my arms out."

It bugged Kavi, but Pip stopped trying to explain that a void mage was more than a null magic zone a long time ago.

This brought a smile from Tack. "The trip's a short one. Shorter than last time so get some rest. We need you sharp."

"When are you going to make the decision about the sulimite?" asked Pip.

"I'll let you know in the morning."

40

The Accelerant

"Yeah, but what if she says no?" asked Kavi.

"Then she says no. We can still pull this off before we leave the ship," said Pip.

"But we lose the cover of darkness," said Grundle. "That's a pretty big negative."

"You've all seen how Kavi moves," Pip said. "Do you think it matters if it's dark or not?"

The Ghost Squadron huddled around a footlocker Pip and Kavi dragged to the middle of the quarters. Most of the Ghosts doubled up in the upper hammocks so they could see the map and the markers used to designate their positions on the ship.

"Stealing the suli is going to be hard either way," said Pip. "If there is a way out of this without pissing off Team Sugoroku, I'm going to take it."

"But now that you asked her, we need to assume she's got an inkling of what we might do." Kavi grabbed one of the rocks that represented one of the professional Dancers. He moved it from the pro berth on the ship over to guard the door. "We have to assume there's at least one more guard. If we surprise them, I can take three, maybe even four, but we might not have the element of surprise."

"I guess we're going to have to hope she says yes then," said Flask.

"I'm *really* uncomfortable with hope as a strategy," said Kavi.

"It's done," said Pip. "Let's take our tactician's advice and get some rest."

* * *

The day broke as gloomy as the previous. When Kavi looked through the porthole red rock canyons dusted with snow dotted the landscape. Snow was odd for this part of Grendar. From this high up, the snow on the mesas looked like icing on an overly healthy carrot cake.

He folded up the black and green blanket the Company provided. He jumped from his hammock and into the green jumpsuit he wore under his armor.

Kavi turned when the door to their sleeping quarters slammed open and Pip stormed in. The thunderclouds over his head rivaled those outside the porthole.

"You were right Kav, I shouldn't have asked. She said the team voted. Since the Quests are getting much harder, they're afraid they're going to need that safety net to make it out of this one alive."

"The subtext being Ghost Squad is already dead," added Kavi.

"That's what I said! She even apologized but her mind is made up. I asked her why she thought Sugoroku had so many fewer casualties compared to the other companies."

"And?"

"That little hyena sounding prick, Rake said, 'I guess we're just that good.' Tack laughed with the rest of them. It didn't even occur to them that Ghost Squad had something to do with their success."

"Of course it didn't," said Kavi.

"The good news is these clouds keep it nice and dark," said Grundle. His deep voice resonated like thunder from his hammock near the door. "You sure you don't want me there with you?"

"Thanks, big man," said Pip. "But this only succeeds with a tiny group - me, Kavi and Mouse. Thirty-one, you sure you can make them forget what happened?"

The small Vonderian mind mage nodded. "They have to be unconscious though," she said in a tiny voice. "And they're only going to forget for a couple of hours. I need suli to make them forget for good."

"If this goes as it should, that shouldn't be a problem," said Pip.

"Famous last words?" said Pyre with that annoying, arrogant grin.

Pip ignored him.

Kavi started to put his leather jerkin on over the green fabric.

Pip looked at him incredulously. "What are you doing? They see you in that and we give the game away. No armor. We do this quick and quiet."

Kavi grunted but set the leather down. The three of them left the sleeping quarters.

"Good luck," whispered Grundle. He shut the door behind them.

The hallways in the ship were narrow, so they had to walk single file. Luckily, they wouldn't have to pass the sleeping quarters of Team Sugoroku to get to the hold below. They would have to descend two sets of steep stairs which would be where they would be most vulnerable. Especially after they passed the privy. They didn't have permission to be anywhere else on the ship.

Kavi noticed, with some level of relief, that Grundle was right. The hallways weren't lit by mage light or anything other than a scattered porthole here and there. With the early morning storm clouds, it may as well have been night outside.

They made their way towards the privy right as one of the double

As walked out. "Sorry," the man said with a laugh. "It's gonna smell in there for another ten to fifteen minutes."

"Eww," said Mouse.

The man laughed harder and made his way up to the galley. He wasn't lying. They passed the toilets quickly as the stench had already moved into the hall.

"I don't want to know what that man was eating," said Mouse.

"Shh," said Kavi. "We're getting close."

They climbed down a second set of stairs so steep it felt more like a ladder. Kavi wondered why the sailors on the ship insisted on calling them companionways, it's not like you could fit a companion on them with you. If Kavi became an expert at one thing thus far in his time at the Nest, it was stairs. These weren't *quite* vertical, they should be able to make it up the treacherous steps with full hands.

The hold was split into two rooms. The larger room held equipment and supplies. The small room was segmented off by a short hallway which led to a door where valuables were kept under lock and key. The Ghosts hoped to exploit the only shortcoming of this room - you couldn't see the stairs from the locked door.

Mouse nodded to Pip as they crept towards the hallway. Her illusion was in place. Pip quickly peeked down the hall before pulling his head back.

He held up two fingers to Kavi and Mouse. Then he signed a W and an R - White and Rake.

Kavi smiled. This was going to be fun.

Pip shook his head. The Vonderian used his recall ability to pull a conversation from the night before. "I need your help White," said Pip in an exact imitation of Tack's voice.

"But I thought you were-," said the man. "Alright, I'm coming." The big man's footsteps echoed towards them. When White rounded the corner Kavi punched him once in the throat to silence him then moved behind him to put him in a stranglehold.

"You okay, White?" asked Rake.

"Quickly," mouthed Pip to Kavi as the big man struggled. "Hang on, I'm talking to Tack," he said in White's voice.

"I'm trying," Kavi mouthed back.

Finally, the big man stopped struggling and he slumped to the deck. Kavi and Pip pulled him deeper into the hold. Mouse moved over to the unconscious man and held her index finger and thumb over his temple.

"I don't know why Tack gave me guard duty but I could be sleeping right now," they heard Rake mutter.

They tensed as they heard Rake stand up. They didn't hear any footsteps but a moment later the man with the disturbing, blue scale tattoos materialized behind Mouse. "What did you do to him?" he shouted. Then he saw Kavi. "Oh, I'm going to enjoy this."

"Not nearly as much as me," said Kavi as time slowed. The Harpstran drew his knife but by the time Rake disappeared again, it was too late. Kavi was in motion and knew exactly where the murderer was.

He disarmed the man with a powerful punch to the wrist and silenced him with two knuckles to the throat. It took everything in Kavi not to make the strike a fatal one. The shock of the throat punch caused Rake to lose his invisibility. His eyes were wide with fear as he stared at Kavi.

Kavi refused to use a sleeper hold on Rake. He wanted to enjoy this. He punched him hard in the solar plexus followed by simultaneous strikes to the temples. Rake dropped like a sack of manure. Kavi couldn't resist and kicked him twice in the ribs.

"Enough," mouthed Pip.

Kavi backed off with a fierce smile on his face.

"Idiot," muttered Pip.

Mouse put her hand to the man's temple. A moment later she nodded.

They walked to the locked door. Pip pulled out two small metal pins he stole from the armory before they left. He inserted them into the lock.

"Don't bother," said a voice from inside. "It's open."

Pip pushed the door open. Tack sat on a chest holding a large blunderbuss, it's large cannon-like muzzle filled with Krom knew what, pointed in their direction.

"I know how fast you are Eleven. But if I pull this trigger, everything in that hallway dies. You've trained with the weapons in the armory. You know the spread of one of these things. Even you aren't fast enough to reach me before all three of you are a splattered mess on the walls."

"I believe you," said Pip holding his hands up. "It appears we are at an impasse."

"Impasse? I hold all the cards here."

Pip kept his hands up but his skin darkened slightly and a small void gate appeared in front of him. "Not entirely," he said as his eyes shifted back to their regular blue. "If you pull that trigger, the blast will kill you too."

Tack turned her head to see the other side of the gate hovering right behind her. "Neat trick," she said. "I guess we are at an impasse, at least until the rest of my team comes to check on me."

"What do we do now?" asked Pip.

"I guess that depends."

"On what?"

"On whether or not you idiots killed White and Rake."

"They're alive."

"You passed the test," said Tack with a lopsided grin. "I wanted to see how bad you thought you needed the suli and what you'd do to take it. And...," she drew out the word. "I wanted to see how good your team was." She set the blunderbuss down and stood. "If you want one usage, it's yours."

"Just like that?" asked Pip.

"Just like that. Rake and White are going to be angry but a little humility will be good for them."

"They're not going to be angry for at least a couple of hours," said Mouse.

"Really? You wiped their memories?" Tack frowned but nodded, impressed.

"It's only temporary unless I use the suli," said Mouse.

"Don't waste it," said Tack. "I'll deal with those two." She turned to Pip and Kavi. "This better pay off. My team will do what I tell them but the vote we took last night was real. If we end up in an emergency situation without a third usage of suli, they're going to blame me."

Kavi nodded. "The burden of leadership. I'm sure you can figure out some clever way to shift the blame to us." He couldn't bring himself to trust her sudden willingness to help.

Tack nodded. "I already did, but that's the wrong way to handle this. I'm not going to convince my team that you are more than warm bodies if I don't own this decision."

"Thank you," said Pip.

Tack turned to the chest she sat on. "Here it is. This has enough sulimite for your whole team as well as any applicators you might need."

"Even for the Loamians?"

"Yep. The League figured out a way to lull those terrifying insects into a dormant state while being transported. The minute you open the box, they wake up. There's only one of them in there though. My team needs only one."

Kavi cursed. They would have to decide who would get the dose between Leesta and Grundle. Kavi didn't know how that worked. Maybe they could get the bee to sting twice?

"We'll figure it out," said Pip.

"See that you do. I'm expecting you to get us to the center then we'll take over. If this works, maybe we can convince the coaches and the League to do away with the Ghost Squadron entirely."

"And then we can teach kittens to fly," grumbled Kavi.

"Quit being such a turd," said Tack. "Not only am I extending a peace offer, I'm outlining a plan for how we can change things in the League. Pessimism won't drive the change we need."

Kavi realized he was acting exactly like his mother, not willing to give anyone a second chance. "You're right," said Kavi. "Sorry. I *was* being a turd."

"Get moving. I'll let my team know I am overriding the vote, so don't feel like you need to hide it. We don't land for another four hours, get a meal in you and I'll see you on the ground."

* * *

The mood on the ground was lighter. For the Ghosts anyway. There was a lot of grumbling from Team Sugoroku as the Ghosts unloaded their own suli chest.

They donned their armor and loaded up the carts that would carry fortifications and the rest of their supplies.

"This is so much easier in the Pool," said Flask.

"Except for the part when you don't wake up alive," said Grundle.

"Yeah, except for that part. Besides, we got sulimite now, what's the worst that could happen?" said the small Bricker.

The whole Ghost Squadron groaned.

Pyre flicked the Bricker in the head. "You're really going to do us like that? Before we even start the walk into the canyons?"

"What? I'm just happy we have a chance." As Flask spoke a sliver of sunlight broke through the clouds to fall on them. "See! Even the weather agrees with me."

Kavi and Pip walked over to Tack. She looked like a crazy person as she talked and gesticulated into the open air in front of her.

Finally she said, "Fine, but we're sending our Ghosts in ten."

"What's going on with Senet?" asked White.

"The usual. They're an hour behind schedule and asked us to delay our start. I told them they have ten minutes before we advance."

"I caught that part," said White. "Did they have any new intel?"

"They didn't see anything as they passed over the site. If there is a third player, they're well hidden." She looked at Kavi. "Is your team ready?"

Kavi pointed at Pip. "Not my show."

Pip nodded. "We're ready but not planning on applying suli until first contact."

"Agreed," said Tack. She pointed to the two canyons that led north. "Right or left? According to the map, they meet up in a little over half a click. This far from the center, we shouldn't see much resistance. We'll take the other route and meet you where they intersect."

"You sure about that?" asked White. "Why don't we just have them sweep both sides?"

"Do I question how you guard this team in the field?" asked Tack. White shook his head.

"Then leave strategy to me."

Pip finished pulling on his leather vest then looked to Tack. "We'll go down the left passage. Good luck."

"Give it five minutes then roll out," said Tack.

Pip nodded and walked back to his team. "Load up, we leave in five."

41

Desert Rain

They set off at a slow but steady pace. The burst of sunlight turned out to be fleeting. The clouds beat back the advances of the sun and the red rocks took on the color of dried blood. The team groaned when the first raindrops fell wet and cold.

"I thought we were supposed to be in the damned desert," grumbled Pyre.

"I'll take this over the heat," said Flask. "My father took us to the canyons north of here in the summer one time. We ran out of water and almost died. The whole family decided we'd never come back. And...here I am."

"Cut the chatter," said Pip. "Dancers, I need you up front. Leesta, you sensing life?"

"All around us, but nothing threatening."

"Flask, how many of those spiders did Sliver give you?"

"Fifteen, but this canyon is huge. They won't be able to cover much of it."

"Can you get two of them to run zig-zags in front of us?"

"I'll try but I don't have the control Sliver does. She said they'd last five hours before running out of power so it'll be good practice."

Flask set two metal spiders on the ground then jumped back when they whirred to life. "They still creep me out a little," he said.

He flipped the machines over, flipped a couple switches and the spiders set off on an overlapping pattern of zig-zags in front of the group. Flask crossed his arms and smiled.

"What's the big deal?" asked Pyre.

"You try to get one of these things to do what you want," said Flask. He handed Pyre a spider.

Pyre shrugged then looked at the chaos of levers and switches on the thing's bulbous underside. He flipped one of them and its left legs spasmed. The metal points of the front leg stabbed into the pad of his thumb. He dropped the wriggling spider. The clockwork arachnid did circles around the group.

"See?" Flask picked up the spider and flipped the switch off before putting it back in the crate on the cart. "Sliver's incredible, these spiders are engineering marvels."

"Mind if I walk point with Leesta?" asked Kavi.

"Sure, you're playing rover anyway," said Pip. "Unless you learned to fortify this week?"

Kavi shook his head and moved to the front. He stayed a couple steps behind the spiders. They picked their way through the sand and stone of the canyon floor. He saw a couple small rodents and even a scorpion but nothing seriously threatening, which made him uncomfortable. He shook his head at this new life where a hike *without* danger left him unsettled.

They made it to the intersection without so much as a stubbed toe. They arrived a couple of minutes ahead of Team Sugoroku. Pip had Flask and Twenty-nine, a stocky Krommian by the name of Lodin, pound in fortifications while they waited. He didn't expect trouble, but better prepared than dead.

The canyon itself was smooth, formed by water eons ago. At the intersection was a clash of rocks. Large cracks ran up either side as if the gods had slowly pushed two of the larger rocks together until they began to buckle. Boulders lay near several fingers of rock which had split form the main walls many years ago.

"All quiet for us too," said Pip, sharing the little information they had with Tack.

The rain began to fall in earnest and both groups pulled out oil skinned coats. They fit poorly over armor but it was better than getting soaked through.

Kavi continued to scout ahead. They had been walking uphill since they entered the canyon. It was so gradual he hadn't noticed the slope until a trickle of water began to flow past him.

Leesta walked next to him. She stopped every fifty meters and closed her eyes to sense for life. They reached the next intersection and Leesta stopped again.

"Anything?"

"No," said Leesta. "Small wildlife and insects but that's it. No greenery to speak of save for scrub grass."

"Either direction more dangerous?"

"I can't sense a threat from anywhere." She sluiced water from her forehead and pulled up her hood. She looked to Kavi. "Why the scowl?"

"It shouldn't be this easy."

"If it helps, the animals I can sense are on edge. That's normal when humans walk by...maybe it's going to be an easy—"

"Don't say it," said Kavi. "Never say it."

"All soldiers this superstitious?"

"When the stakes are this high...don't tempt fate." Kavi looked back at the squads they'd left behind. With their hoods pulled up, they looked like a band of traveling monks. "Let's report back, Tack's got the map."

Kavi cursed as he stepped in a puddle. The small trickle of water had turned into a shallow stream down the middle of the canyon. He would have expected the dry ground to greedily suck up the water, but under the sand was only rock. The sparse foliage drank its fill within the first seconds of rain. The rocky ground offered nothing to sink into.

Tack had the map out when they returned. "We take this canyon to the right, then the one to the left. If we're going to see resistance, it'll happen soon."

"Nothing yet," said Leesta. "At least to the next fork. The wildlife is a little riled but nothing out of the ordinary."

Tack nodded. "It can't be more than three or four clicks to the center from here. Stay sharp. We'll be trailing you but only by a minute or two."

Kavi and Leesta set out. This time Lodin and Mouse joined them. Flask sent two more spiders running in front but the automatons struggled with the water. They kept getting stuck. Their legs locked up from water or dense, wet sand.

When the Ghosts reached the fork in the canyon, Pip waved the Dancers back. Kavi and Leesta had to carry two of the incapacitated spiders back. They lost sight of the other two that continued to range farther in front of them.

"Flask, no more spiders. They're useless in the rain," said Pip.

As if the clouds could heard him, the sky rumbled and the rain fell even harder.

"Maybe we can get them to pull these damn carts," said Grundle.

"Yeah, they don't roll worth a damn in the water. The further we move from the center of the canyon, the harder it gets," said Lodin.

"That's strange," said Leesta. She stopped in front of the group. "Grundle, you feel that?"

The big man shook his head. "I can't feel anything other than this bloody rain."

She cocked her head, concentrating. "The wildlife is becoming more agitated the deeper we go into the canyon."

"Keep moving but arm yourselves," said Pip. "Dancers, stay close."

They tightened their formation and continued to move.

"Something's off," said Kavi quietly, so only Pip could hear him.

"I agree. What do you think?"

"Normally, I would ask Tess and Sliver what they thought."

Pip smacked himself in the forehead. "They're going to give me an earful I haven't contacted them yet."

Kavi grimaced. "I forgot too. Better late than never."

Pip opened a void channel. Kavi listened to Pip's side of the conversation.

"I know, I forgot." Long pause. "We're talking now aren't we? Here's the situation." Pip gave Tess a quick summary. There was another long pause. He looked at Kavi. "She's explaining it to the rest of the team," he said. "No, I was talking to Kavi. I know, he's fine, we're all fine so far."

"Miss you all," said Kavi.

"A flash what?" asked Pip. Then he paled. "Shit. Ok, I will." Pip cut the connection and turned to the team. "Take the suli now."

"I thought we were waiting until first contact," said Kavi.

"Take the Vonn's damned suli now! All of you! A flash flood is headed our way. Take the suli and find high ground."

Kavi cursed. He should have thought of that. Any of them should have thought of that. They were so focused on the mission they missed the obvious regarding their surroundings. Kavi was annoyed the pro team hadn't thought of it either. They were supposed to be the experts.

"What about the pro team?" asked Leesta, as if reading his mind.

Pip turned to Kavi. "You're the only one fast enough to warn them.

Grab some suli root and get down there."

Kavi nodded. He ran to the chest Mouse already had open. Mouse, Pip and Pyre were readying three tattoo needles. That's when they heard the menacing rumbling sound.

Kavi stuck a piece of suli root between lip and teeth in the proper Krommian fashion. "Get into one of those cracks and climb it like a chimney. Take your suli. Do it now!" He yelled to be heard over the rumble. Then, he set off at a run hoping Ghost Squad would get high enough, fast enough.

The suli hit like a punch to the face and Kavi's senses enhanced. The red rocks became redder, the water became wetter and he ran fast enough to skim the top of the water. It took him only seconds to reach the pro team.

"What?!" yelled Tack.

"Flash flood!" he yelled back. "Take your suli and get to high ground. NOW!"

To their credit, Team Sugoroku didn't panic. They didn't question or disagree. Instead, they calmly and quickly opened the suli chests and distributed the doses. They left the carts and ran towards the nearest cracks in the rocks.

Kavi beat all of them. He found a crack as wide as a small chimney. He set his feet to one side and his back to the other and began to shimmy. He moved so fast his back burned at the contact. Within seconds, he was ten then twenty meters up the wall. A few seconds more and he reached the top. He pulled himself over and watched as a giant wave of water from the north cleared the canyon.

It started with a surge of black sticks and roots followed by tumbling rocks. The carts carrying their supplies went next and Kavi was certain he saw two people swept up in the wall of water. He was frantic with worry but there was nothing he could do. Mother Nature could not be stopped.

As quickly as the wave appeared, it vanished. The water level dropped rapidly from punishing force to small river, then stream, and finally a trickle. The rain tapered off and the sun once again peaked through the black clouds. It felt like an eternity, but the flood took less than ten minutes.

Kavi scaled down the wall the same way he went up. The suli coursed through his body and he was able to ignore the pain of the scratches caused by the slips as he climbed, slid and fell down the chimney.

He was first to the bottom. He didn't wait on the professional team members. He ran towards the Ghosts dreading what he'd find.

Pip and Leesta were the first down to the canyon floor. Pip extended a hand and Kavi pulled him into a hug. "Damn good to see you."

"You too," said Pip. "Who's missing?"

"I don't know yet."

They heard a loud crash and found Grundle dusting himself off from where he fell the last several meters. "Ow," he said as he looked at them.

Pyre walked over next. He looked miserable. "I reached out a hand, Pip. I swear. If I only had my staff. I couldn't think of any spells to cast, it happened so fast."

"Slow down Twenty-six," snapped Pip. "Tell me what happened."

Calling him by his number was like a slap to the face to the gangly Vonderian. It helped him focus. "Mouse and Rhaine were below me. The crack we climbed started to narrow and I couldn't move up any further. I got stuck. I tried to push but there was nowhere to go. When the water hit, it grabbed Rhaine first."

"Rhaine?" asked Kavi.

Pyre looked at him blankly.

"Twenty-five," said Pip. "Tall, dark haired Harpstran, sun and moon tattoos running down his arms. Quiet, younger than most of us."

"I remember," said Kavi.

"Keep going, Pyre."

"I reached out a hand and Mouse took it, but the water was so strong. I couldn't hang on Pip. I swear, I tried." Tears ran down his face.

"I know you did," Pip put both hands on his shoulders and forced Pyre to look him in the eyes. "Look at me, we'll grieve later. Right now you need to do what you can to help the others."

Pyre nodded and walked off to help.

"I think everyone else made it," said Leesta. "It looks like Lodin is stuck and might be hurt." She pointed to one of the cracks where the stocky Krommian was wedged. His eyes were open and his left arm was moving.

"I'll check on him," said Kavi. He scaled the rock but could tell the moment he reached Lodin that something was terribly wrong. He grabbed the man's leg. The skin was cold and damp. He jostled the arm and almost fell when the small rodent nibbling at the man's thumb bolted upwards. "Shit," muttered Kavi. He felt for a pulse but found nothing.

They hadn't even met the enemy and three were already dead.

Kavi clambered down and shook his head. "He either drowned or broke his neck."

Pip cursed. "Let's check on Tack and her crew."

Team Sugoroku stood in a circle. In the center lay Ham. He lay on his back, looking peaceful. At a glance, the man could have been sleeping if his skin wasn't waxy and pale.

Tack raised her head and her cheeks were wet. "How many did you lose?" she asked quietly.

"Three," said Pip.

"We're lucky we didn't lose everybody," said Tack. She looked to Pip. "Quick thinking, thanks for sending him."

Pip nodded. "What do we do now?"

"What we always do. Continue."

"We lost our supplies - weapons, fortifications, extra armor."

"Doesn't matter," said Tack. "Everybody's still on suli. Let's see it through."

Pip had the Ghosts take inventory. More than half had their primary weapons strapped or sheathed to their bodies but the rest were unarmed except for belt knives. The fortifications, extra ammunition and even food and armor they weren't wearing were lost to the flood.

"We need tight formations. Kavi, join the Guards and Forts in keeping the pressure off our ranged and healers."

Kavi nodded. It wasn't going to be easy. Twenty-one was their Astran Guard. A woman by the name of Piety, an excellent defensive warrior, had lost her shield in the flood. She still wore her heavy armor and managed to hang on to her mace but their defense would have to rely on speed. Grundle was the team's other Guard but he never used a shield. If he could tap into his bear form, his immense bulk would provide them with a large enough line that Kavi would only need to plug holes.

"We have to move faster. We have what, an hour of suli left? When we meet resistance, we need that power," said Kavi.

Pip nodded and shouted an order. The Ghosts began to jog in a rattle of armor and weapons that made them sound like a busy kitchen. They passed through the next intersection of canyons when Leesta held up a hand. The Ghosts came to a halt.

She knelt and put a hand to the earth in front of her left knee. "I think we're in trouble," she whispered.

The smell hit them first. It was musty and pungent like moldy bleu cheese left out at a graveyard picnic. The sound was worse. The chittering of millions of insectoid legs scrambling over rock and sand echoed against the canyon walls like a macabre drumline.

A nightmare wave of knee-high ants, beetles and scorpions rushed towards the group.

42

Agitators

"Use the rocks!" yelled Pip. "Form up between those two boulders, backs against the wall!"

The Ghosts moved quickly to form a defense before the oversized insects reached them.

"Look!" shouted Flask, pointing. Several ants ran along the side of the canyon wall. They moved slower than their brethren as the pull of gravity impeded their speed.

Leesta stood with eyes closed and a hand on Pip's arm. "I don't think they mean us harm. They're running from something."

"Ok," shouted Pip to be heard over the stampede. "Pyre, light a candle above our position to see how they react."

Pyre's skin turned blood red. A pillar of flame took the shape of an eagle with spread wings, incinerating several ants. The wave which followed swerved to avoid the heat. With the pillar active, most of the insects avoided their position. Some swerved the other direction to climb the boulders and cliff wall at their backs.

"What I wouldn't give for some of Clara's fire runes right now," said Pip.

Kavi moved to intercept the dog sized ants. He blocked a thrust from an insect before he realized it was only trying to get past him. Instead of fighting, he presented a wall of steel with the sword he managed to keep during the flood. He lopped off several spindly legs before the ants began to look for an easier way. The ants who lost legs moved forward at a stilted pace, the disability a minor annoyance.

The scorpions were the biggest threat. Even in the midst of the stampede they were on the lookout for food. When the first scorpion passed the group's defended area it paused while several ants ran into or over it. It reared on its back four legs. The rest of the insects split to either side like fast moving water around a large rock. When it's legs found the ground again, it advanced.

"I got the tail," yelled Kavi. "Guards, cover those claws."

Piety and Grundle moved in front of the large insect who probed their defenses with weak swipes of it's front claws. It didn't react when Grundle transformed into his bear form until the man-bear's large paw swiped down on the claw. There was a tremendous crack followed by a high pitched clicking shriek as black ichor flowed from the stump of its leg.

The scorpion's segmented tail arrowed towards Grundle's bear chest. Kavi was there. With a swipe of his blade he removed the stinger. He spun to stab his sword towards the arachnid's tiny brain but Piety, their Astran Guard, beat him to it. Her mace smashed the carapace protecting it's head and made a ruin of the soft tissues beneath.

The scorpion twitched twice then lay still.

The dead body became another obstacle the insects had to avoid creating a bubble around the squad. Other scorpions spied them as they passed but were not close enough to navigate their way out of the current of chitinous bodies which pulled them down the canyon.

Pyre had to create two more pillars of flame before the stampede lessened.

"Anybody hurt?" asked Pip. He nodded grimly at the chorus of nos.

"What are you doing Flask?"

"I bet I can use the venom from this scorpion tail and turn it into something nasty," he said. The small Bricker had his knife out as he maneuvered the tail.

"Do you have any flasks left?"

"There's a reason I had Boost and Sliver help me craft this belt," he said. "See, the leather is lined with molded ceramic. Even if I fall, it doesn't destroy the flasks inside." He shrugged. "It also helps keep me from exploding. Some of the things in this belt are pretty nasty."

The Squad backed slowly away from Flask.

Pip nodded once and climbed the boulder in a bid for the Squad's attention. "Assume Leesta's right. What has the power to scare a horde of gigantic insects?"

"It could be a mutated form of one of their regular predators," said Grundle after he morphed back into his slightly less furry man form.

Pip looked to Leesta but she shook her head. "I can't feel anything in the immediate area."

"It could also be something Senet cooked up from the North. Krom knows, it could be something from the Quest," said Kavi. "We don't have enough information and we're running out of time."

Pip looked annoyed. "Understood, Eleven." This brought glances from the rest of the Squad. Pip never called Kavi by his number. "But rushing into a trap, suli or not, is a terrible idea."

Kavi took a deep breath and reminded himself this was Pip's show. "You're right. Want me to keep scouting?"

Pip nodded. "Take Leesta. Piety, check on Tack's team and provide any healing they need. Let them know we're pushing ahead. Rice and Pyre, stay fifty meters behind Kavi and Leesta in case they need support."

Kavi set out and Leesta scrambled to catch up.

"What are you waiting for? Move!" said Pip as the rest of the squad stopped to catch their breath.

"What about the poison? I'm sure I can use this later," said Flask. He positioned the severed tail above the empty flask he pulled from his belt.

"You have two minutes," said Pip. "I need you backing this team up." Pip grabbed his steel tipped staff and followed the squad.

"Great idea, let's rush the extraction of a deadly poison," muttered Flask. He looked up and noticed Pip stopped to look back with a frown on his face. Flask sighed. "Don't worry, I'll get it done."

Kavi and Leesta were first to find the swept up remains of the giant ant hill. It had been flattened by the flood but some of the debris got caught on larger boulders that weren't swept away. A hole that led into the nest burbled with water. Kavi wondered what happened to underground burrows when water hit them. Several ant bodies lay on their backs near the open hole. They must have drowned. Predators wouldn't have left the meat lying around.

They saw the remains of two more enormous ant hills as they pushed deeper into the canyons. These had also been pummeled by the flood. There was no sign of ants.

The canyon narrowed and steepened as they closed on the center of the rocky maze. It was still wide enough to fit the entire team abreast but only barely. Kavi struggled to jog as the twists and turns of the unsteady path became more difficult to navigate. He began to sweat and looked up to see the sun had taken back control of the sky.

He pulled his oilskin coat off, rolled it up and tucked it into the small pack on his back while continuing to move. Leesta struggled to keep up. He hadn't realized it but he was using his skills to accelerate their pace. He couldn't overcome his feeling of urgency. Kavi *knew* that if they dawdled, he was going to lose more friends. He looked at the struggling ranger with anger. He would leave her if she couldn't keep up.

"Good," said Leesta. "I've been trying to catch you for a couple minutes."

"What is it?" he asked impatiently. He started to move again.

"Stop for a second," she barked.

"We're running out of time."

"Even if being an impatient idiot gets you killed?" Leesta said, matching his anger. "There's something or somebody around the next bend. Just because you have the most experience, doesn't mean you don't need your team."

Kavi shrugged. "You should have said something earlier."

"Sure, I could have yelled," she whispered loudly. "Because that's a great plan when you don't know what's waiting for you around a corner. Or, and here's a brilliant idea, you could have waited for me. We don't all have your speed, you know."

Kavi blinked at her. He'd never seen Leesta this angry. "Sorry, you're right. I'm just trying to keep us alive."

"Yes, because we're all helpless Ghosts that need to be rescued," Leesta said.

"You made your point. I said I was sorry."

"Did I? Make my point, I mean?" she said, hissing to keep her voice low. "Because it doesn't seem to be sinking in. This hero complex you have means you're treating us like the pro team does. Like we have no value. We worked our asses off in the Pool, Eleven. We're in this together. We all would have been here whether or not you came and played savior."

"You're right. I'm sorry. I'd be happy to take more feedback after the mission but we need to focus right now, ok?"

She nodded.

"How many can you sense around the bend?"

"More than a few but I can't give you exact numbers. It doesn't work that way."

"I'll take a look." He held up a hand before she could protest. "I promise, I'll be sneaky. Would you mind reporting to Pip and telling Rice and Pyre to be ready?"

Leesta jogged back to the others.

Kavi slowed his pace and walked with as much stealth as he could manage. He needn't had bothered. When he peered around the corner he saw a group of seven people arguing in the middle of the canyon floor. The canyons distorted the sound so he couldn't make out what they were saying.

The only thing Kavi was a hundred percent sure of was they were not wearing Senet's colors.

The Liberators were on the board.

* * *

"Of course you have to tell Tack," agreed Kavi. "I'm just saying, let's talk to them before any decisions are made. They're the only ones we know standing up to the League. How could they be all bad?"

"You said it yourself, Kav," said Pip. "We need to keep our heads down and survive the season. I don't see how talking to these people helps with that goal."

"What if they give us another way? Aren't you the least bit curious?"

Pip looked up to the sky, exasperated. "Fine, but I'm going with you. Piety, Tack seems to have taken a liking to you. Do you mind going back and filling her in?"

"I just caught up with you guys. Send Rice, he's Astran too."

"Yeah but nobody likes Rice," said Pip.

Rice nodded and rubbed his bald head. "It's true. I don't have what you'd call a sunny disposition." He scowled to punctuate the point.

"Fine, but you're going to need me if a fight breaks out!"

"According to Kavi, we're just going to have a little talk," said Pip. "Which means, yes, we probably are going to need you. Please hurry back."

"What? I can be diplomatic," said Kavi.

"Sure, that's why Team Sugoroku loves you so much," said Pip.

Piety turned around and jogged towards Tack and her group.

"The rest of you, stay hidden behind the bend. Flask, Pyre and Rice, find high ground if you can. If we have to attack, we'll need to do it quickly," said Pip.

"Clock's ticking," said Kavi. "Let's go."

Kavi and Pip cautiously made their way around the bend. They approached the group with hands held out peacefully. The group was still arguing when they approached so no one reacted until they were almost upon them.

Kavi watched as one of the women's eyes went wide. She drew her sword and the argument stopped. The man with his back to them whipped around to face them.

"Stop!" he shouted. "Declare yourselves and your intentions."

Kavi opened his mouth but Pip beat him to it. "The name is Pip Tern and I'm tactician for Team Sugoroku's Ghost Squadron."

The man sighed in relief. "Thank the Sage for small favors," he said. He turned halfway back to his group. "This is just the fodder squad. The professional killers would have attacked already."

"You're not wrong," said Pip. "Why are you here at all? Especially if you knew the League was coming." Pip craned his neck to look at the device they stood next to. It looked like something Sliver or Boost might have built. It was like a pump or something Brickers used to drill into the ground. Instead of a drill bit at the end, there was a flat, metal surface.

"We're here to prove the League doesn't have a monopoly on

Quests," said the man. He had a self-important tone that grated on Kavi.

"And we're just trying to survive," said Pip.

"Is it true they force you to come on Quests?" asked the woman who first drew her sword. She dropped the tip to the earth but she hadn't sheathed it yet

"What kind of an idiot would volunteer for something like this?" asked Kavi.

"Ever the diplomat," muttered Pip out of the side of his mouth.

"You're looking at a bunch of those idiots right now," said the man. He shifted the leather helmet he wore and moved his body in front of the device so Pip and Kavi couldn't see it. "We believe Quests are a gift to all Grendarians, not just those with money and power."

"I don't disagree with anything you're saying," said Pip. "I don't think any of the Ghosts would. We held ideals once, before we were pressed into slavery. What you need to understand is we're not here for any greater purpose. We're here because we want to live to see tomorrow. If you get in the way of that survival, we'll eliminate you like any other threat."

This brought a smile to the man's face. "You think you're that good?"

"I know we're that good," said Kavi. He moved and a fraction of a second later, he held his sword to the man's neck. "Now tell us what that device behind you is."

The other Liberators drew their weapons and looked to the man for direction. He moved his hands flat then pushed them down in the universal gesture of put down your weapons. The group reluctantly complied.

"We're not your enemies," said the man as carefully as he could with a blade to his throat. "Why don't you join us? Fight for something real. Fight against your slavers. Fight for your own freedom."

Pip's laugh was scornful. "Like that hasn't crossed every one of our minds a hundred times since our capture."

The man shrugged, then winced as the blade shifted against his neck. "Here's your chance."

"Nothing you can do can prevent the League from finding us, killing us, then killing our families. There's no easy way out of this for us," said Pip.

"Tell us what the device is for," said Kavi not moving the blade from the man's throat.

"Well aren't you the single minded type," said the man. "Before I do, let me explain how the Liberators are different. What we offer that no one else can is a Sage of our own. She can *always* sniff out when the League comes knocking. We can protect your families like we have with countless others. Give us a chance."

"Tell us what the device does, now," said Kavi in a low, deadly voice. "Last chance."

"Are you always this impatient?" He held up a placating hand when the blade started to press into his neck. "Fine, it pumps a steady rhythm into the ground that simulates a-"

"Yes, he *is* always this impatient," said a voice that rounded the corner behind the group. "He has been ever since he was a lad."

Kavi almost dropped his sword. "Carlin?"

Then a horse-sized tarantula dropped from the canyon wall and attacked.

43

Clash of The Factions

The spider dropped from the rocks and lunged at the young woman who first drew her sword. Its front mandibles scissored into her shoulder and she screamed.

Carlin had an arrow knocked to his bow. He fired as the spider struck, and the arrow sank deep into one of the beast's many eyes. It reared back.

The woman's companions pulled her into a small recess in the canyon wall to tend her wounds. Her face looked jaundiced from the poison and she shivered as sweat gushed from her pores.

Kavi pulled his sword away from the Liberator's throat and moved to engage the spider. He struck three times in rapid succession and removed the spider's back two legs.

At the same moment, Pip struck once then twice with his steel capped staff. Another of the spider's legs buckled.

It was Pyre who finished the beast. A missile of fire struck the center of the tarantula's body. After it penetrated the thick, hairy middle, the flame grew. It burned inside out and within moments created an ashy crater in the spider's center. The beast folded in on itself and died.

Rice moved to the injured woman and muttered a prayer. Her color quickly improved and a thick greenish liquid oozed from the wound. The Astran monk ripped a piece of fabric from the woman's undershirt and wiped away the poison. With another prayer, he knitted together the tissue most damaged by the puncture wounds.

The woman regained consciousness with a start. She looked at the remains of the spider and screamed. Rice covered her mouth with one hand and put a finger to his lips with the other. He pointed to the spider and gestured to the walls around them. The message was clear – do not draw the attention of more predators. When he removed his hand from her mouth she responded with a nod.

Carlin shouldered his bow and walked to Kavi. "The device is what our Brickers call a thumper. A lot of insects respond to vibrations in the earth. The Brickers set this at a frequency that's supposed to scare these enormous insects away."

"Guess that didn't work," muttered a man kneeling next to the injured woman.

"Carlin, can we not share our secrets with members of the League?" asked the man rubbing his throat where Kavi recently held his sword.

"Unwilling members of the League, Gred. Besides, Kavi isn't going to rat us out, are you boy?" asked Carlin.

Kavi shook his head. "No. Even if your damn thumper almost got us all killed."

"How do you mean?" asked Carlin.

"It started a stampede that nearly wiped out my squad."

"That wasn't the thumper. Or, at least, not solely the thumper. We used the device next to one of those hanging crystal chimes at the center of this maze of canyons. The chime picked up the beat and magnified it. That's when the bugs went nuts. We lost two of our own thanks to that stupid decision." Carlin glared at Gred.

Kavi tried to come to terms with the idea that Carlin was here, in front of him. His curiosity elbowed his survival instinct long enough to ask, "Carlin, what are you doing here?"

Carlin smiled. "Now *that* is a long story."

Kavi tried to decide which, of the hundred questions he had for the man, he wanted to ask first. Before he could ask even one, Piety rushed towards them. Kavi held up a finger to the group in front of them and walked over to hear her report.

"Tack said we're supposed to kill Agitators on sight," whispered the stout Astran woman. "She was talking with the Senet tactician when I left. As I ran off I heard her mumbling something about an arbiter. I asked her if we should wait for them before we attacked and she said it was your call, Pip."

"Then, we wait for them to arrive," said Pip. "One of these Agitators is Kavi's friend. Kavi, explain to them what's going on then give them a head start."

Kavi jogged back to Carlin and his group. "We have a standing order to kill you on sight."

"I know," said Gred. "That's why we drew our weapons when we saw you."

"We'll report to our tactician that you fled and the spider covered your trail. You've got five minutes. Maybe. Make the best of it."

"Thanks kid," said Carlin. "Next time we meet, I hope it's under better circumstances. Your mum is gonna be thrilled to hear you're still alive."

Kavi doubted the truth of that but it was nice to hear. If he had even five minutes more, he would have pressed Carlin for news of home but now was not the time.

With a nod, Carlin ushered his team back up the canyon. He gave Kavi a parting salute and disappeared around the corner.

"Now what?" asked Pip.

"Now we drag our feet as long as we can until Tack and the pros arrive."

"They're not going to like that. Best case scenario, we have forty-five minutes of suli power left."

"I know," said Kavi. His internal clock tracked the time. "Maybe Leesta and I find an alternate path that steers us clear of the Liberators while beating Senet to the center."

Pip nodded. "Go. I'll hold Tack off as long as I can."

* * *

Leesta and Kavi caught sight of the Liberators two more times and always moved in a different direction. One of the alternate paths took them up a steep incline. They followed the path for several minutes until it brought them atop a ridge above the canyons they had been climbing through all morning. To the north, lay a bowl where the striated rock formed a mesmerizing pattern in gradients of red, tan and pink. It looked like the crockery of the gods. At the base of the bowl were several spillways that led to caves. If Kavi had to guess, those caves were their Quest destination.

To the east, he caught a last glimpse of the Liberators moving quickly up the canyon paths. North and east of the bowl, Kavi blinked at flashes of light where sun reflected off armor and weapons. They were worn by the blue and brown of Team Senet.

From the ridge, there were two paths of descending switchbacks. The first dropped in to the center of the gradient bowl. The second offered high ground above a wide canyon path. With a critical eye, Kavi extrapolated that path was where the Liberators would likely encounter Team Senet.

After seeing Carlin again, he couldn't help but think of his mother.

Prioritize the threat and give me a plan of action. Her words urged him to focus on what was important. The biggest threat was whatever creatures the Quest was going to throw at them. After encountering the Liberators, Kavi downgraded them and placed Team Senet as the next greatest threat. Even if the pros tried not to kill each other, Kavi knew those tacit rules of combat didn't apply to the Ghosts. Only the Sages knew what would happen when Team Senet encountered the Liberators. Either way, the high ground would give Sugoroku an advantage in whatever happened next.

Kavi and Leesta retraced their steps. Thirty-five minutes left, he thought as they rounded the bend which brought them back to the site of their battle with the tarantula. Team Sugoroku had caught up to Ghost Squadron. Tack stood talking with Pip and White.

She did not look happy.

Kavi detailed the terrain ahead and shared his analysis of the situation.

"Yeah, but we'll be exhausted by the time we engage," said White.

"Not to mention, Cliff specifically asked us to approach from the lower canyons," said Tack.

"Of course he did," said Kavi. "That gives Senet the advantage in beating us to the Quest. Since when do we take orders from Team Senet?"

"Careful, Eleven," said Tack. "Coming from the southeast will also cut off escape routes of the Agitators."

"What's more important: beating Senet to the reward or making sure every Agitator is dead?" asked Pip.

White shrugged. "He's got a point," said the big man. "I know the League might think differently, but I don't care if these Agitators die or escape. I do care that we get to the loot first."

"That's a bad idea, Tack," said Rake. "The more Agitators we take out today, the less the chance we have of running into them next time."

Kavi looked at Rake suspiciously. "You have a personal contract on these Agitators, don't you? Another distraction which will get more Ghosts killed." Kavi shook his head in disgust.

Everyone turned to the Striker. "Well?" asked Tack.

"No," said Rake, but he wouldn't make eye contact.

"We go up the ridge," said Tack. "We'll take one minute before we descend to catch our breath. If we're in for a fight, ranged from both teams will rain fire from above while melee charges. How quick can we get up there Eleven?"

"Leesta and I did it in five. To get the whole group up there will probably take ten minutes."

"Then let's move," said Tack. Kavi wasn't the only one with an internal clock pushing urgency.

The group moved double time up the steep path. The professionals were more than happy to let Ghost Squad stay in the lead. When the two groups crested the ridge, the narrow path forced them towards the eastern descent in single file. Pip signaled his ranged Strikers to take positions above the canyon floor. They were joined by the professionals ranged warriors.

They had a view of both forces from high on the ridge. Team Senet plodded relentlessly southward. The Liberators stopped south and east of the canyon floor where Kavi expected the encounter to take place. He couldn't understand why they stopped retreating. Then he saw them fiddling with two of the thumper devices.

They were laying a trap.

Their leader, Gred, placed and turned the thumper on at the entrance to the wide canyon path where they expected Team Sugoroku to enter. The team of Liberators then moved north to the entrance through which Team Senet would arrive. They rushed to place a second thumper.

"I've got a shot, Tack. Should I take it?" asked Reaver, one of the professional ranged Dancers.

"Not yet," whispered Tack. "Let Senet engage."

The Senet Ghosts were a disorganized group. They moved liked dogs who had been beaten too many times. They tossed furtive looks at the professional team herding them forward. They were armed better than the flood ravaged Team Sugoroku however. Kavi realized that approaching from the north meant they avoided the flood. The Ghosts were led by a huge man in a full metal helm which completely covered his face.

They reached the intersection as the Liberators finished placing the final thumper. The Liberators fled at the sight of Team Senet. The giant at the head of Senet's Ghosts charged. Something about how the big man moved looked oddly familiar.

"Fire!" yelled Tack.

Team Sugoroku complied and loosed spells and missiles. Three Liberators protecting the rear fell under the onslaught. Kavi desperately hoped none of them was Carlin.

The giant who led Senet's Ghosts bellowed. He swung a titanic battle axe at the two Liberators who stood to give their companions time to escape. One of Senet's Ghosts came too close to the big warrior and the back of the axe caught him a glancing blow. It tossed the man into the air to land in a heap several meters away.

As the man flew, Kavi finally made the connection. "I'll be Krom's damned, that's Grim."

"Grim's not a strong enough word," muttered Pip. "That's a Krommian berserker. When they're in a rage they'll kill friend or foe," said Pip.

"No, I mean that's my friend, Grim," said Kavi. "And I know what a berserker is, I just didn't know Grim was one." It certainly explained a few things about the big man's past. Kavi was disappointed in himself that he hadn't pieced that together on his own. He was so caught up in his own grief. He couldn't believe how naive he used to be.

"Stay out of his way. Friend or not, he'll chop us into tiny pieces." The void mage moved to stand at Kavi's shoulder and waited for the call to attack.

They didn't have to wait long. "Melee, charge!" yelled Tack.

Kavi charged, leading the group down the path to the canyon floor. Nobody could match his speed and his feet found level ground before his companions made it halfway down the winding traverse. He took Pip's advice and steered clear of the terrifying monster his friend had become.

The last Agitator in the pass was Carlin. He had an arrow knocked and aimed at Grim. Even from this distance, Kavi could see the huntsman's eyes widen as he too made the connection. He loosed his arrow at the Ghost to Grim's right and the woman fell in a heap.

Grim advanced. There wasn't a flicker of recognition in those dead, angry eyes. Herman the golem offered more sympathy than berserker Grim.

Carlin retreated but Grim was too fast. Before he reached the older huntsman the ground exploded from all sides and ants flowed out of the earth. The Liberators must have changed the frequency of the thumpers to attract instead of repel. Carlin shot Kavi a parting smile and turned to escape in the confusion.

Grim had other plans. He threw his giant axe and it flipped end over end until the blade sunk deep into Carlin's back. The momentum of the axe carried the huntsman's body through the air to crash against the canyon wall.

"No!" screamed Kavi. He raced towards the fallen man but ants were everywhere. He slashed and cut through hardened legs and bodies like an inept woodsman with an unsharpened axe. Even with his speed, he made no progress.

Grim paid no mind to the huntsman's broken body. He pulled two hand axes from his belt and moved back into the fray. Ant bodies exploded away from the force of his blows.

There were no fortifications in place and no organized plan. The action had become a general melee with everyone fighting for their lives.

"Ghost Squadron, to me!" yelled Pip.

Kavi fought his way through the giant insects to the void mage who seemed to be doing the best of the bunch at keeping his wits about him.

"Destroy those thumpers!" yelled Pip. He pointed the devices out to the ranged fighters on the rim of the canyon above.

Flask tossed one of his remaining exploding potions at the thumper to the southeast but it struck an ant before it made impact. Ant bodies flew through the air when the flask detonated. The thumper continued its pounding on the earth below.

Pyre summoned a pillar of flame around the other one. The thumper glowed white hot before turning into molten slag. His suli-enhanced power created the unintended side effect of setting several ghosts and one of Team Senet's Guards aflame. Pyre looked at the burning men in horror, blazing eyes filled with remorse.

The assault on Team Senet was enough to catch Grim's attention.

At the base of the path, Pip assembled the Ghosts around him in something resembling a defensive formation. Grundle and Piety stood on either side of the void mage.

Piety held her mace in the air and a glowing circle of energy surrounded her and those directly around her. The ants near them bounced off the golden shield. Those Ghosts who took injury found their wounds healed within the golden circle.

The bear formerly know as Grundle swept his paws out. Every swipe threw a dead ant into the sky. One of the ants struck the advancing

Grim and Grim bellowed in rage. Grundle roared back.

"Ranged, focus your fire on the berserker!" yelled Pip. Nothing happened. He briefly looked up to the rim of the canyon but the ranged fighters had their hands full.

The mating cadence the Liberators set on the thumpers attracted more than ants. Several rock lizards were drawn by the sound hoping for an easy meal. These lizards would dwarf an elephant but somehow the creatures didn't lose any of their agility. They jumped from rock to rock and climbed along vertical canyon walls.

One of the lizards dropped into Senet's professional team, instantly killing their tactician. Its long tongue shot out and pulled in one of their Dancers in a crunch of bones. It's inner eyelid nictated twice as the Dancer's body made its way to its gullet.

Tack had more success organizing Sugoroku's defenses against the lizards atop the ridge. They hadn't lost anyone yet but Pip and his team would get no support from those above.

Grim continued his remorseless advance. All the Ghosts who once backed him were dead to ants or Agitators. With a mighty stroke of his hand axe, the final ant blocking Grim's way to Grundle flew over the defenders to land behind Ghost Squadron.

Kavi wished Mouse had survived. Her neuromancy might have been the only defense against a raging berserker that didn't end in his death.

Grundle gathered the massive muscles in his back legs and leapt at Grim with foreclaws extended.

Grim laughed and caught the bear by the throat.

Grundle struggled and his claws scored tearing strikes on the berserker's armor. They were vicious enough to soak Grim's bracers in blood.

Grim didn't seem to notice. He slashed his hand axe twice, once into Grundle's chest and once into his throat. The large bear stopped struggling and shifted back into man form as he died.

Grim tossed him aside.

Pip moved before Grundle's body hit the ground. His staff struck Grim's helmet twice in rapid succession and the Vonderian opened a huge, suli-enhanced void gate behind the big man. The strikes were powerful enough to push the berserker towards the rip he summoned. The pull of the gate did the rest. Grim howled as he was pulled away but he threw his hand axe before he vanished.

The axe struck Pip in the chest.

The Vonderian looked down at the axe in surprise and collapsed.

Kavi screamed again. All his friends were dying and there wasn't a damn thing he could do about it. The sulimite enabled Pip's team to call on their evolved powers but it wasn't enough to counter the giant berserker.

Grim fell from the other side of the void gate fifteen meters in the air above the melee. The large berserker landed on the corpses of several broken ants. Kavi stared in disbelief as the juggernaut rose and closed on their position.

Kavi moved to meet him. If time had slowed before, it practically stopped now. He would need to use his speed to knock Grim out. In the worst case scenario, Kavi would have to kill his childhood friend. There couldn't be any more deaths to his teammates.

When Kavi's sword met Grim's axe for the first time he was shocked at the power of the blow. In the hundreds of times they sparred together he knew his friend had been holding back. He never knew by how much. This was a different level altogether, inhuman. Grim had to be on sulimite too.

Kavi reeled back and tried a slightly different tactic. "Grim! It's Kavi. You don't want to do this. Please, I don't want to hurt you."

There was no recognition in the rage-filled eyes. The large man threw back his head and laughed maniacally. He roared at Kavi, and the force of the roar turned Kavi's legs to butter. The scream had to be a skill Grim discovered in his time with Senet.

Kavi found his mantra and the fear melted. *Move like wind* - Kavi effortlessly slid behind the large man who stood statue-like at the speed Kavi moved. *Strike like fire* - with the precision of a surgeon Kavi sliced his blade into Grim's unprotected hamstring. He could feel each fiber when steel parted flesh and tendon.

Halfway through the cut, the blade stopped. He couldn't fully sever the muscle at the back of Grim's leg. Kavi looked for the hand that stopped it, but there was no hand. The tendon itself wrapped around Kavi's blade. It pulsed in fiery anger. Somehow the man's rage pervaded every fiber of his being. Even his tendons fought for him.

Kavi withdrew the blade and began a new strike. This time, he aimed at the tendon above Grim's right heel. Before the strike could land, Grim's heel pulsed and a tremor shook the earth. Kavi lost his balance.

He sensed Grim's spinning strike before it began. He had plenty of time to avoid it but the shaking of the earth caused it to pass far closer than Kavi liked. The smaller man rolled to avoid it.

"You're fast, little man," said Grim in his booming voice.

"It's Kavi, but you can call me little man."

Grim wasn't listening. This was a one-sided conversation. "I'm going to enjoy this," Grim replied.

The two traded blows for what felt like hours. Kavi should have killed him hundreds of times but the man's rage found new and creative ways to counter every strike. Grim never got close to landing a blow of his own but Kavi was tiring. The suli was wearing off. Even if he could tap into his speed without it, the suli made the speed effortless. He had to try something different.

"Eleven," Kavi said, hoping Grim received the same low number Kavi did when Grim joined team Senet. Who could possibly be a better fighter than this man?

This caused Grim to flinch.

"Eleven," Kavi said again. " You are not just a ghost." It was difficult. At the speed he moved he had to speak very slowly to be understood. "You're more than a ghost, you're a man with friends and people who love him."

Grim struck again but with less ferocity. Kavi dodged the blow.

"Eleven, your name is Grimstance Broadblade. A person, not a ghost."

The strikes came even slower. Kavi landed a blow to his back with the flat of his blade.

"Your father, the general, disowned you because you left the Elites. I know now it was because you were afraid of what you'd become. You were right to be afraid. We took you in because you have always been a part of my family. You have always been a brother to me. I don't want to fight you. I'm going to put my weapon down because I can't kill a friend, a brother. If you can't see past the rage and become you again, that's okay. I forgive you if you strike me down. I love you Grim."

Kavi dropped his sword on the ground in a clatter of metal on chitin. Grim stopped. "Kavi?" he said as if waking up from a dream.

"It's my fault you're here. It's my fault you're a slave. I'm sorry, for all of it."

Rice took that moment to strike. His glowing fist passed through the larger man's helmet like a rock splashing into water.

Kavi stood in shock as the brains of his best friend ran down his face.

No. This is not how it's supposed to end.

Kavi stopped and looked at the carnage around him. Piety prayed frantically to save Pip's life but it was a long shot. White and Tack furiously fought the lizards closing in on them. There was no sign of Pyre or Flask on the rim. Kavi had to assume they were dead. Then he saw Rake, alive and fighting. The loathsome psychopath again avoided the fate he so richly deserved.

No. This is not how it's supposed to end.

Kavi accepted his own death was inevitable. He understood that risking his life to help those closest to him opened pathways to enlightenment. He even figured out how to process and deal with the death of a friend. That acceptance turned him into something else - a force with power over time - but that power didn't include the ability to choose who died and who lived.

You're almost there. The ethereal voice floated towards him. He recognized it but couldn't place it. He looked up but no one was there.

There was nothing here but death and pain. All were affected by it. Except for Rake. Somehow, he kept avoiding it. Kavi yelled in frustration until it came to him. Bad things happened all the time, sometimes to good people and sometimes to bad. So much of it was luck and circumstance. But Kavi didn't get to decide. All he could do was fight for what was right.

No. This is not how it's supposed to end.

Who was he to determine what was right? To the lamb, the wolf is evil, but to the wolf, the lamb is food. In that moment, surrounded by so much blood and death, Kavi understood. Even a monster like Rake had the same right to live and make his own decisions as anyone else. He had his role to play. Evil men made the good in others stand out.

Yes, accept it! He recognized the voice now. It was the same voice who urged him to hang on during that first, painful trip to the Nest. The voice of the woman who offered salvation to Nettie. Rose, the fifth Sage, pushed him to the edge of realization. Everyone, even those that chose evil, had the right to exist. If for no other reason than they could, at some point, see the errors in their ways.

Own it now. She spoke into his mind.

No. This is not how it's supposed to end.

So change it, tickled the voice at the edge of oblivion.

He breathed in the horror around him and accepted all of it. Maybe he couldn't decide who lived and who died but maybe he could change the circumstances.

Even a little.

Time stopped, then began to reverse.

44

Water Flows Uphill

Kavi is the only observer as time slowly backs up. The universe fights the backward motion of its most linear force like a fish on a line, pulling and jerking as time reluctantly reverses and gives ground. He has no control as he feels his body make all the same motions in reverse. It is an awkward and hideous dance. The fluidity of practiced motion is replaced by the inept movements of a novice puppeteer. It feels peculiarly similar to the dream states he finds himself in lately. But this isn't a dream, it is the unraveling of nightmare.

Rice's fist pulls out of Grim's skull and the large man's head remakes itself. The axe flies out of Pip's chest and into Grim's hand as he bounces in front of the void mage, never being pulled into the vortex gate. Grundle's wounds vanish and the bear un-pounces and turns back into a man.

Kavi watches himself backpedal up the switchbacks at furious speed. He stands atop the ridge as the giant axe slurps out of Carlin's back and lands in Grim's hands. Team Senet's ghosts uncharge from the wide canyon path. The Liberators pick up the two thumpers and shuffle backwards out of sight.

Time stops again.

* * *

He needs to keep going, back to the flood. He could save Mouse, Lodin and Rhaine. He'd even happily save Ham. Could he go all the way back and save Trixie and the Ghosts who fell in the first Quest? Kavi focused.

He yelled into the air. "I accept it! We all die! I don't get to choose!" He focused harder.

Time refused to move.

"If I can save these, I should be able to save more!"

"It doesn't work that way," said Rose. She stepped from behind a frozen Pip. He was paused with his mouth open giving orders to his ranged strikers to fan out and take positions on the rim of the canyon. She stopped to caress the handsome Vonderian's face before turning back to Kavi. "You choose your friends wisely. This one has an iron will built from years of clawing and scraping his own identity from under the weight of an entire culture's disdain."

"I didn't exactly choose him," said Kavi.

"Yes, you did." Her mysterious smile caused her almond eyes to sparkle. "Circumstances brought you together but you choose who becomes a friend."

"I didn't choose Grim."

"Poor, broken Grim." She looked down to the canyon floor where the man would soon appear. "A peaceful soul forced to do horrible things. And no, you don't get to choose family. Just like you can't choose who lives and who dies. Don't waste energy on things over which you have no control. Your choices increase when you focus on those things in your life that you do have power over."

Kavi stared down at her for a long moment. "Why do I have this power? Why can't I go back farther?"

"I don't know."

"But aren't you a Sage?"

She laughed and Kavi was reminded of summer wind rustling through wind chimes outside his father's laboratory. "Since I'm a Sage, I'm supposed to know everything?"

Kavi shrugged. "Sage. Wisdom. It's kind of in the name, isn't it?"

"You know how fickle a name is. You're a warrior, do you know everything about war? You were once a Silver Eagle, do you know how to fly?"

"I see your point, but you know more than most and speak with such certainty. By Kromm's grace, you can see the future!"

"That beast has no grace to speak of! Don't speak to me of him or the other fools this world calls gods."

Kavi blinked, shocked at the venom in her words.

She tucked a lock of hair behind her ear and collected herself. "Yes, I do speak with certainty but do not confuse confidence with competence. The more of the world I experience, the more I realize we just make it up as we go. The generals you admired at the Bastion? Making it up as they went. Your mother? Same thing. Your father? Well, that one's obvious, he'd be the first to tell you he's making it up as he goes. Sages don't come out of the womb draped in vestments of wisdom. We're like everyone else. We experience things and we learn. Then, we experience similar things and are more confident with the outcome because we've done it before."

"Nuh uh," said Kavi emphatically. "That doesn't track. For one, Sages can see the future."

"No," she said, adamant. "We see possibilities of the future, many possibilities of the future. Which is why most of us go crazy. This battle, this conversation we're having - it could have gone a thousand different ways. I experienced all of them. You might think those experiences give me the wisdom Sages are know for, but they don't. Because only one of those things *actually* happens. So, we can only learn from *one* of those things. We go crazy because eventually we try to learn from all possibilities."

"I don't understand. Shouldn't you be able to learn from the different possibilities? Don't you see what happens when people make different choices then learn from those new outcomes?"

"No! And, that is the fatal temptation for every sage. We can't learn from what *might* happen. We can only learn from what *did* happen. Choices people might have made - they didn't make them. We can't learn from possible futures. We can only learn from the past. The Sages who go crazy forget this. They confuse possible outcomes with actual outcomes. They lose grasp of the threads of reality."

"But if there's only one outcome, what's this? Look around, aren't I changing the past?"

"Yes! You are the spanner in the works. The ghost in the machine. The fly in the soup. Pick your metaphor. You are the wildcard. You are something new and brilliant that can turn this whole thing on its head. I find that fascinating and exciting."

"Turn what whole thing on its head?"

"Life, power differentials, destiny - you name it. Did you know a woman Sage is born once every three hundred years? We are harbingers of change, but if I'm the harbinger, you're it's agent. Together, we have the ability to shake things up."

"I don't want to shake anything up. I just want my friends to make it out of this alive."

"You know that's not true. You could have taken the easier path and stayed at home, followed your mother's orders, but you chose to help Nettie to try to make a difference."

Kavi looked around at all the chaos about to happen. "You really don't know why I can't go back further in time?"

Rose shook her head. "Ever since you tapped into whatever this power is, you've been breaking ground. To my knowledge, no one has ever been able to shift time. Some of the gods can slow it, like you, but nobody can shift it, turn it back. That includes the gods."

"So, what do I do?"

"What you've always done Kavi. What you think is right." She started to grow transparent.

"No, not yet, please! I have so many questions. Should I believe what happens in my dreams? Did you actually save Nettie?"

Rose ignored the first question but nodded when he asked about Nettie.

"Can you save others? Can you really stay one step ahead of the League so our families aren't threatened?"

She winked, reapplied her mysterious smile and faded away.

He took a deep breath and when time resumed, Kavi was ready.

* * *

"— and Flask. I need you up on that rim, ready to support any action on the canyon floor," said Pip, flashing back to life.

Kavi grinned. It was all real. Time had reversed. He would get another chance.

"Pip," said Kavi quietly.

"Melee, I need you-" Pip continued.

"Pip!" Kavi shouted.

"Would you wait one damned second Kavi?" said Pip, rounding on him.

"No, this can't wait. I have new information you need to hear."

Pip didn't lose the annoyed expression but could see how serious Kavi was. "Ok, what is the new information, how'd you get it and should we call Tack over here?"

"No. This is only for the Ghosts. In two minutes, the Liberators are going to place two devices on the canyon floor."

"In two minutes? How could you possibly-"

"Shut up and listen, we don't have time for me to explain, you're going to have to trust me."

Pip glared at Kavi but nodded.

"I need you to summon a void gate and send the first device on the far ridge of the bowl behind us. Send the second device north of Team Senet so it lands behind them. If possible, these devices need to land upright so they continue to function."

"Thumpers?"

Kavi nodded. "Keep our ranged from firing until after the Liberators have escaped. Come up with an excuse, any excuse for not giving the order. Actually, blame me - I'll be down there."

"Bet your ass I'm going to blame you." Pip took a deep breath. "You better be right about this."

"I am. See, there are the Liberators now. I will move the second they start setting up the second device. That's going to piss Tack off but she's not going to fire until Senet engages."

"You're going to have a lot of explaining to do."

"I know. Keep your eyes on the Liberators. They are going to set up the next device...now."

They watched as the gear shaft of the first thumper began to spin. It pushed the oscillating lever up and down in a rhythmic motion. The first two revolutions pushed the small spikes at the base of the thumper into the earth, giving it stability. They could barely make out the faint thumping sound from where they stood.

"When Reaver tells Tack he's got a shot is when I'm going to move. Act confused and yell at me like I'm disobeying orders."

"No act needed, I am confused and you *are* disobeying orders."

"See, you're good at this! No matter how bad it looks, I need all of you to stay away from the giant in the full helm."

"Sure, stay away from full helm guy."

"Promise me, Pip."

"You realize you sound crazier than a-"

"I've got a shot, Tack. Should I take it?" asked Reaver in a low voice.

Pip's eyes widened. So far everything Kavi said was going to happen, happened.

"Promise me, Pip," Kavi said again.

"Fine, I promise. Since there's no time for how, why are you doing this?"

Kavi pulled the sword from his makeshift sheath and readied himself. "Same reason I do everything, to keep our friends from getting killed. Focus on those thumpers!"

Kavi took a deep breath and felt time begin to slow. He bolted down the path.

"Damn it Kavi, where the hell are you going? I told you to wait on Tack's orders," Pip yelled after him.

"I know it's real, but even after watching it in the Pool and the recordings, the way he moves hurts my head," said Grundle. He watched the flash of movement ripple down the switchbacks. "What's he doing?"

"Besides disobeying orders and being a giant pain in the ass? I think he's trying to save us."

"What the hell is your Striker doing Twelve?" asked Tack in a far less friendly tone than Grundle.

"Good question Tack, being a hero I believe." He turned to his ranged shooters.

"Did you two plan this from the beginning?"

"No ma'am. You saw how I positioned my Ghosts, he's going off book."

"I should have Reaver take *him* out. Reaver!" she yelled, having made up her mind.

"That's a bad idea Tack. I know you two don't agree on much but you know he's special. Yes, he has a hero complex but that means almost everything he does is to protect others. It's annoying but we have a better chance of making it out of this with him alive."

"Fine," growled Tack. She turned to Reaver. "Keep your target and wait until Senet engages."

Kavi made it to the canyon floor as Gred turned the second thumper on. The Liberators reeled back and drew their weapons when Kavi appeared at full speed in front of them.

Gred turned to him and held up his hands. "It's not what it seems."

"It's exactly what it seems," said Kavi. "And it's a good plan but you're taking too long to execute. Senet gets here in under a minute and when they arrive my force will open fire. You need to leave. Now."

Kavi struck Gred in the chest with the flat of his blade to stop the man's next question. "I said now, idiots." He said it like he was taunting them. "Leave your two best fighters here. They need to help me put on a show to keep my companions from killing you."

Gred ran and Kavi faced off against the two most heavily armed Liberators. He harried them with strikes to the legs and arms.

Kavi easily dodged when they returned his attacks. "All attacks should be made off your back foot as you retreat. Do it now!" hissed Kavi. "I'm trying to save your lives."

Pip opened a void gate below the first thumper. It reappeared on the far rim of the giant bowl leaving a small hole in the rock where it once stood. Pip squinted. At that distance it was hard to tell but the thumper appeared to continue its steady beat into the earth. When Kavi pushed the heavily armored warriors back from the other thumper, Pip summoned his second void gate. This one was more precise. It scooped the second device and deposited it on the canyon floor behind the charging Senet warriors.

Kavi pushed the warriors back to the bend in the canyon path. That would put the Liberators out of range of Sugoroku's snipers. Kavi sensed his team members repositioning for a shot on the retreating force. The ridge didn't extend much farther east. Kavi was certain if he could get them back another twenty paces, he'd have saved the lives of the Sage's warriors.

The Liberators made a good show of it while steadily retreating down the trail. He heard a roar behind him and cringed. Grim had taken the field.

Carlin stepped from behind the bend with bow drawn. His arrow flew over Kavi's head to strike the big man in the shoulder.

"Damn it Carlin, let me handle Grim. You convince these idiots to run until you are no longer a threat to the League."

"Didn't know it was Grim until I heard him yelling," said the huntsman. He turned to follow the armored men who were now running. "I'll make sure they get back safe."

Kavi darted around the bend and turned to face the charging Grim. He preferred this fight to stay out of sight of the two teams.

Grim charged around the corner heedless of any ambush that might have been set for him. Kavi wanted to slap the big warrior for being such a moron. He knew the large man was in the depths of a berserker rage but that didn't excuse idiocy.

Kavi smacked him twice on the side of the helm with the flat of his blade. Each strike sounded like a muted gong. Kavi couldn't imagine what it sounded like from inside the helm.

Grim roared again and swung the giant battle axe.

"Eleven!" Kavi yelled.

Grim paused before swinging his axe again.

Kavi repeated the dance with Grim, convincing him that he had friends and family that cared about him. "I love you Grim, now stop trying to fucking kill me!"

Recognition finally dawned in the big man's eyes. Grim took off his helm. The first thing Kavi noticed was his friend had lost those scars he was once so proud of. That loss, along with the deep hollows of his eyes and the thinning of his face made him look like a remnant of the boy he grew up with. "Kavi?" The big man blinked those recessed eyes several times. "What are you doing here?"

Looking at the severe corners of Grim's once full face, the shame hit Kavi hard. "I'm sorry. I'm so sorry for getting you into this. This is all my fault. I wish you never followed me."

"No. I made my own choices," said Grim. "You're not allowed to carry that guilt. My regrets belong to me."

The words nearly broke Kavi, who hadn't realized how heavy the burden had been until now. He took a long shuddering breath before the urgency of the situation brought him back. "No. Time for that later. I'm trying to save your ass and we need to move quickly. We have to get back."

Grim grabbed him by the shoulder. "Team Senet is serious business. They'll kill you if they see you here."

"Look at me, dumbass. You see the colors I'm wearing? I'm Team Sugoroku, we're rivals in this Quest."

"Oh. Been a shitty couple of months hasn't it?" said Grim.

"Understatement of a lifetime. Besides, your team isn't good enough to kill me. Put your helmet back on, we have to report to our tacticians. Let me do the talking."

"You've changed, Kavi."

"No shit."

"Sorry I almost killed you. They pump me full of suli and point me at a target." He paused for a moment as he collected himself. "I hate it. I hate killing anything, but killing people turns me into something...awful."

Kavi pulled him into a hug. "I know," he said into the man's shoulder, which bled from the arrow still protruding from it.

They broke the embrace. Grim's eyes were wet. He let out a shaky breath. "I need a drink...thank you...for stopping me. Your form, your speed, you got better. A lot better. You've never been able to take me in the past and that was when I wasn't on suli. I can't believe you beat me."

"Twice," said Kavi.

"What?"

Kavi grinned. "Doesn't matter. Let's report back, we're going to say we killed four of the Liberators, ok?"

"Why?"

"Because we don't want to spend the rest of this Quest chasing down people who might actually be trying to help us. Besides, I don't want to hurt Carlin."

"Carlin's here too? Is he on Sugoroku?"

"No, he's with the Liberators. Enough questions, they're going to get suspicious if we don't go back now."

Grim put his helmet back on. They moved back to the wider canyon where melee groups from Senet and Sugoroku faced off on the canyon floor. Nobody attacked but both sides stared at each other warily.

Pip formed the Ghosts into the best defensive formation he could with what gear they had left.

"Eleven!" yelled Senet's tactician.

"What?" responded Kavi and Grim at the same time.

Grim turned to Kavi and offered a fist bump. "Nice," whispered

Grim. Both warriors picked their way through the defenses and walked over to Senet's tactician.

"Report," said the man.

"Do you mind if we wait until Tack makes it down here sir?" asked Kavi. "So we only do this once?"

Senet's tactician looked up to see Tack making her way down the switchbacks. He nodded.

Tack arrived moments later. "So what happened down there Eleven?" asked Tack.

"Well," said Grim and Kavi together.

"We agreed I was going to tell the story," said Kavi.

Grim smiled at Kavi and put a finger to his lips.

"You idiots know each other?" asked Tack.

"We served together," said Kavi. He kept the details of their relationship to himself. No reason to give either team a way to use them against each other. "Grim is not somebody you want to meet on the other side of a battlefield."

Tack looked the giant man up and down. "Agreed. What happened over there?"

"I took the two I was fighting down. Grim got the bowman and one other with a ridiculous throw of that axe. They set an ambush though. The rest of their force was waiting for us."

Grim nodded along.

"Why didn't you break the ambush?" asked Team Senet's tactician.

"Because we're not idiots," said Kavi.

"Watch your tone, Ghost," snapped Senet's tack.

"You're wasting your breath Cliff," said Tack. "He's an insubordinate asshole, but he's handy with a sword."

Kavi turned to smile at Tack. "You're too kind."

She shook her head but Kavi saw an upturn of lips before she schooled her features.

"Something all Elevens seem to share," said Cliff.

Grim offered Kavi another fist bump which nearly landed Kavi on his ass.

Both tacticians sighed dramatically. "So, how many is it going to take to eliminate the ambush?" asked Tack.

"Zero ma'am," said Kavi. "It was a rear guard motion. They were running as fast as they could. These Agitators aren't the best warriors but they're not idiots. They know they can't take both our teams in a stand up fight."

Tack nodded and turned to Pip. "Twelve, send two scouts – a Dancer and a Striker to make sure they've cleared out. If there's nothing to be found within half a click, let's get back to the business of completing this Quest."

Pip nodded and shouted orders. Pyre and Leesta jogged towards the canyon path Grim and Kavi had come from.

"That sound good to you Cliff?" asked Tack.

"Yeah, that's fine. We're going to have to bring that damned arbiter in to reposition us. I hate these new rules."

"Me too. Sugoroku didn't provide us with an arbiter. They give you one?"

"Yeah," said Cliff. He pointed to the group of Ghosts cowering near the canyon wall. "As if I don't have enough people to babysit."

"What? The arbiter doesn't know how to fight?"

Cliff barked a laugh. "The little prig is an administrator. Swear to Krom, if he pulls out that rulebook one more time, one of my Strikers is going to shove it so far up his—"

"Oh look, here he comes now," said Tack. "Why's he running?"

The meticulous man was running full speed, wearing a three piece suit. To a Quest. His face was pale and he looked terrified. "They're coming. My god, we're all going to die," he yelled as he sprinted to reach them.

45

Old Grudges

"Rear face!" yelled Cliff. Senet's professional team turned immediately. They placed fortifications in seconds. Their Guards and Strikers took potshots at the ants headed their way.

"They're just ants," said Tack.

The arbiter looked at her incredulously. "They're the size of small ponies. Just ants indeed."

"I see what you mean," said Tack to Cliff and they shared a smile.

"You want back up? I've got ranged support on the ridge."

"Sure," said Cliff. Neither tactician looked worried, a fact that stunned the well dressed arbiter.

"You people are crazy," said the man.

"Did you think Quests were safe?" asked Tack. "You might want to look into a different line of work."

"Where do I go, is there a place to hide?"

Tack laughed and Cliff joined her. "Sure, go hide by Team Senet's Ghosts. That big guy will keep an eye on you," said Cliff. "Stay out of the way, we have bugs to kill."

The ants died quickly. Sugoroku rained fire from above and the carcasses piled up. Within minutes, the ants had to climb over bodies of their dead to make it to their position.

"Why do they keep coming?" asked Cliff.

"I was wondering the same thing," said Tack.

"We got incoming!" yelled Reaver from high above. "Giant ant-eating lizards closing on your position."

"That sounds interesting," said Cliff.

"Two more lizards spotted," yelled Reaver. "Moving on our position from the south and west. Two minutes out."

"Twelve, White, get back up the ridge and hold that high ground."

Pip and White started shouting orders. Team Sugoroku sent their Forts up first followed by their Guards so they'd have a defense ready. Pip did the same.

Leesta and Pyre weren't back yet. "Mind if I check on our scouts Tack?" asked Kavi. "I can check in and be up that hill before the action begins."

Cliff snorted but Tack nodded. "He's got this speed skill," said Tack. "It's pretty impressive actually."

Kavi ran through the canyon at full speed. The rock walls blurred past him until he found Leesta and Pyre standing at a fork of two canyon paths.

"I told you. I can't sense anything down either path but I'm sensing a whole lot of life behind us."

"Yeah, because both teams are waiting there," said Pyre with a scowl. "We got a quarter click to go before we hit our mark."

"I know both teams are back there you arrogant prat," said Leesta. "I'm sensing a lot more life beyond what was there a minute ago. And it feels hungry."

"You can sense their moods now?" asked Kavi coming to a stop in front of the two scouts.

"By Vonn's holy...you scared the crap out of me, Eleven," said Pyre.

"Don't do that!"

Leesta nodded. "It started when I took suli."

"Let's go. We're in a world of trouble back there and we need both of you," said Kavi.

"What is it?" asked Leesta. "More ants?"

"Ants and giant lizards. Team Senet is on the ground with our squads on the ridge. We're going to take the threat together."

"Lead on," said Leesta.

"I can't wait for you," said Kavi. "Find Tack or Pip when you get back."

"We'll be right behind you," said Pyre. "We got what, twenty minutes of suli left?"

Kavi nodded. "Make it quick."

Kavi arrived back at the site to utter mayhem. Ants overran the fortifications but were only fighting the warriors attacking them. The insects were fleeing from the lizards who snapped them up by the mouthful.

One of these lizards turned it's tongue to the Ghosts of Team Senet. After the taste of Ghost, it decided it preferred eating things without an exoskeleton.

No one was surprised when the lizard ate the arbiter. His suit must have made him look elegantly tasty, like a wrapped confection, as the lizard's tongue pulled him neatly out of the crowd of Ghosts.

Grim swiped at the tongue but he wasn't quick enough. He yelled and charged the lizard.

Team Senet struggled to cut into the beast's thick hide. Their attacks strengthened when the professional team took sulimite but the lizard remained free of serious wounds.

Kavi charged in behind Grim. He hoped and dreaded his friend found his berserker rage again.

On the ridge, Pip directed his Ghosts while staying clear of Team

Sugoroku. The professionals had built an impressive defense. They used loose rocks and fragments of fortifications that didn't get swept up in the flood. Unfortunately, the defense was useless against their unconventional opponents. Gravity didn't seem to apply to these monstrous lizards. They climbed up the bowl and jumped over the defenses to find an unblocked path to the tasty humans who thought to defy them.

Defy them they did. The lizard attacking from the south got a rude surprise when his tongue was stopped by the power of White's shield.

It was Flask that proved the lizard's undoing. His timing was impeccable as he threw his final potion into the lizard's closing mouth. An explosion could be heard from deep within the beast's body. The lizard gave them a confused look, blinked twice with those disturbing inner eyelids, then fell over dead.

"Yes, Flask!" yelled Pip. "Watch the beast circling to the north."

He needn't had bothered. The Ghost Squadron and professional team had already locked on the larger beast. Reaver had impeccable aim but no matter how fast he fired his projectiles, they couldn't penetrate that hide.

The lizard's tongue darted towards an ant that tried to escape the melee by climbing the wall near the switchbacks of the path. The lizard's throat distended briefly as the snack went down. Its eyes never left the Sugoroku squads as it tried to figure out how to extend its meal.

A piercing scream shattered the air above. It was loud enough to send echoes bouncing off the canyon walls creating a resonance that sent tremors through the earth. Everyone and everything on the battlefield stopped to look up.

Kavi felt his heart drop to the pit of his stomach. He recognized that sound – the cry of a raptor fused with the growl of a lion.

The Ach'Su had arrived.

The remaining lizards took one look to the sky and fled.

Team Senet repositioned to meet this new threat.

Kavi was conflicted. Did he run up the path to fight with Ghost Squadron or stay and fight beside Grim? He looked over to see Leesta and Pyre picking their way up the switchbacks to join Pip.

The Ach'Su circled above, planning its attack.

"What is it waiting for?" whispered Grim.

It shrieked again, and another piercing call answered it from the west.

There were two of them.

"This is bad," said Grim.

"Quit the chatter Eleven," shouted Cliff. "Assemble your Ghosts in front of our line."

"That's a death sentence and you know it," said Grim.

"They die facing the Ach'Su or from my team's blades. Your choice."

"Great choice," said Grim. "Kavi, get to your squad, you might have a chance working with your own people."

"Come with me."

"And abandon my own squad? No way. Go."

Kavi nodded. Grim was right. They both had obligations. He sprinted up the hill and within seconds stood next to Pip. "Where do you want me?"

"Same plan?" asked Pip. "I'll handle the magical attacks, you handle the physical?"

"We've got an entire team behind us Twelve."

"That won't be able to scratch one of these things, even with what's left of our suli reserves." Pip turned to Kavi. "Almost feels fated doesn't it?"

"I don't believe in fate," said Kavi.

"Neither do I. But the probability of you and I standing together to face another Ach'Su is astronomically low. If it's not fate, it's something."

"Does it matter?" asked Kavi.

"I guess not. So, how do we get it to come for us?"

Kavi looked around until he saw Pyre struggling to get into position. He grinned. "We need bait."

Pip followed his gaze. "I thought you two made nice."

Kavi shrugged. "We did. It doesn't bother me to see him uncomfortable though."

"Me neither. He was such a prick those first couple of weeks." Pip looked up to the circling Ach'Su. "What do you think? Maybe a minute or two before it attacks?"

"Who knows. It's not like we're experts." said Kavi. "The only way we get some measure of control is if we piss it off."

"Which will also piss Tack off."

"Probably. She'll forgive us when she realizes we're drawing its attention."

Pip flared his nostrils and nodded. He cupped his hands around his mouth to be heard. "Pyre, get over here, we need your help!"

Pip quickly explained the plan to the man.

"You want me to do what!?" asked the Vonderian with a shriek.

"You heard me," said Pip. "Don't worry. I'll take the brunt of the attack and Kavi will do the rest."

"Fine," said Pyre. He took a couple deep breaths then muttered a fire dart spell.

Before Pyre released his spell, the two Ach'Su passed in the air above. The one who flew in from the west dove towards Team Senet from the north to strike the professional team first. Kavi could see the relief in Senet's Ghosts who now stood at the back of the attacking trajectory.

This new Ach'Su spewed its cone of darkness and the Guards locked shields and called upon shield wall skills. All of Sugoroku watched as the ghostly images of hundreds of shields formed an impenetrable line across the canyon.

The black mist struck the shield wall like a wave striking a levee. The levee held but the black mist didn't dissipate. It swirled in terrifying eddies, waiting for the shield to drop. The Ach'Su flew over the Senet warriors and wheeled around for another pass.

"Hell no, did you see that stuff?" said Pyre. "This is a terrible plan."

"This is the only way we control it," said Kavi.

"You know what Team Senet is missing?" asked Pip. "A void mage! I need you to fire at that thing Twenty-six. Right now!"

Pyre tore his gaze from the black mist swirling below and resumed his spell. Darts of fire flew towards the other Ach'Su. The Ach'Su swooped low to avoid the missiles. With the sulimite, Pyre's ability allowed him to link the darts to the creature's body heat. The darts shifted direction to stay locked on the beast.

"What the hell are you doing Twenty-six?" yelled Tack.

"What I asked him to do ma'am," said Pip. "I need to bear the brunt of that first attack. That's the only way we have a shot at this thing."

Tack stifled her protest, now was not the time. The only people with experience fighting an Ach'Su were Pip and Kavi. "What do you need from my team?"

"Don't fire into the cone of darkness. It will obliterate all missiles. Attack from behind when it wheels away. At that point, give it everything you've got."

"You want a shield, Pip?" asked Piety moving to stand next to the tall Vonderian.

"No, I need it to hit me straight on."

"We can't lose you Pip," said Piety.

"You won't. I've done this before. I'll dispel its power."

The missiles struck the Ach'Su. They were not powerful enough to penetrate its thick hide but they burned off feathers and singed the fur around the chest of the lion's body. It screamed in anger and looked for the source of the missiles.

"I hope you're ready because it's pissed!" yelled Pyre. "And it's coming for *me*!"

The Ach'Su eyes locked on Pyre but quickly shifted to Pip and Kavi. Recognition swirled in those inky pools of hatred. The bait had done its job.

The Ach'Su dived.

* * *

The Guards gave it everything but eventually the shields protecting Team Senet fell. The predatory mist struck immediately. It entered through every orifice of the two Guards who dared to keep it at bay. The Guards folded in on themselves then went rigid.

The Ach'Su who spewed the mist shrieked from high above. The two Guards gave an answering shriek, all the more terrifying coming from human mouths. When they finished shrieking they attacked their own squad.

The Astran healers who moved to help died first. They didn't even get their arms up before swords were pushed through bellies and thrust upwards to find hearts.

The rest of Team Senet backed away from the Guards, unsure whether to attack or flee. Grim had no such compunction. He struck the first Guard with the flat of his giant battle axe and the man crumpled. The Ach'Su circling above screamed in anger and lined up its next dive.

The other Guard continued her rampage and severed the arm of one of the Dancers that tried to flank her. She spun and beheaded a small Fort who tried to place a half wall to hide behind.

Cliff struck her in the back of the head with the hilt of his sword. She stumbled and a Senet Dancer struck her in the temple with her mace. She collapsed, shuddered once, and lay still.

The Ach'Su dove into the mass of disorganized Senets and grabbed a Ghost in one talon and a pro Striker in the other. They screamed as talons penetrated armor and skin.

Most of Team Senet lost sight of the Ach'Su while defending themselves from the rogue Guards but not Grim. When it dove he yelled a challenge.

The Ach'Su began to rise with its catch grasped in its talons.

Grim jumped through the air and struck with all his berserker fury. His sulimite enhanced power cut clean though the limb holding the Ghost.

The Ghost dropped two meters to the ground and groaned.

The Ach'Su screamed in pain and surprise but continued its halting path upward as blood poured from the severed limb. After a moment, the imbalance of carrying the Dancer in its front talon while missing its front forepaw caused it to drop the woman far above the canyon floor. She landed with a wet thump.

The survivors of Team Senet gave a ragged cheer as the injured Ach'Su winged back to the west.

* * *

Kavi felt a horrible feeling of déjà vu as the nightmare creature advanced. Pip stood in front, waiting for a cone of darkness that never came. The creature remembered their last encounter and the ineffectiveness of the attack on the Vonderian.

Pip summoned a void gate in front of the diving beast. Its velocity made it impossible to avoid the gate that split the fabric of space and time.

Time slowed with familiar comfort. Kavi watched Pip come to the realization the Ach'Su was not going to use its darkness. The Vonderian's eyes turned midnight black except for those disconcerting flecks of starlight. Kavi surveyed the area around him looking for where the Vonderian put the twin void gate. He smiled when he saw it. Pip was a smart one. Kavi drew his sword and ran. He knew the timing would have to be perfect. He leapt from the ridge as the Ach'Su passed through the gate.

The Ach'Su flew full speed into the canyon wall. The other side of the gate floated ten meters above the Liberators' first thumper. The massive beast struck like a bird slamming into a glass window. The Ach'Su did not have hollow bones like a bird however. The collision left it broken and bloody but didn't kill the monster.

Kavi plunged towards the beast, his blade leading the way. He timed the jump perfectly. His sword passed through the back of the Ach'Su's lion head with all the force of his falling body. Kavi felt his wrist break at the impact but the injury didn't prevent his blade from finding the creature's brain.

The Ach'Su didn't make so much as a whimper as it fell to the canyon floor.

Kavi clung to the beast's body as they fell, positioning it between him and the ground. They struck in a plume of feathers and reddish dust. Kavi staggered to his feet cradling a broken arm to match his broken wrist.

"Yes!" yelled Flask into the silence that descended after the impossible actions of the last fifteen seconds.

"You scared the crap out of me, Flask! Again!" said Pyre but then joined the rest of Sugoroku cheering from above.

Kavi limped towards the middle of the canyon path, totally spent.

"Healer!" yelled Pip and Tack together.

46

The Fifth Sage

Rice and Piety fussed over Kavi's wounds like competing mother hens. Thanks to the number of times Kavi had been healed over the last several months, his body immediately accepted it. All he needed now was something to eat. He expended enormous amounts of energy when he slowed time and when he received healing. His reserves in both areas had been spent and his stomach growled unholy complaints.

The rest of Team Sugoroku and Pip's Ghost Squadron were mostly unharmed. Scratches and sprains the extent of their injuries.

The same could not be said for Team Senet. The professional team lost nearly half its members and most of their Ghosts died in combat with the lizards and Ach'Su.

Tack ordered Team Sugoroku's healers to help Senet's survivors. Once Pyre and Piety finished patching up Ghost Squad, Pip sent them down to help heal Senet's Ghosts.

"I don't know how you fought an entire battle with this in your shoulder," said Piety. Rice used a medic's knife to dig the arrowhead out of Grim. They cleaned the wound with water and alcohol they found on a dead Senet healer.

Grim tuned them out so completely she had to repeat her statement. "Oh, they taught us how to compartmentalize pain in the Elites. If you know it'll get healed before you die, you can put the pain in a tidy little box you never have to look at."

"Until your nightmares," said Kavi.

"Yeah, haven't figured out how to get rid of those. I know what doesn't work - booze, women, fistfights..."

"The old standbys never do," said Pip. "My parents help those suffering from the mental impact of trauma. They say you have to accept the horrors before you can process them. Even magic can't heal a traumatized mind."

"Great," said Grim. He looked at Kavi and pointed a thumb at Pip. "Who's this ray of sunshine?"

Kavi introduced Grim to the rest of his squad. Most of them saw Grim fight. Some of them, like Pip, immediately treated him like a brother in arms. Others looked at him like a dangerous animal who might break into a murderous rampage at any moment.

After Grim was healed he walked over to his own group of Ghosts. Kavi watched him go. Grim looked even more broken than when he arrived at Stonecrest begging for clemency. He didn't try to hide it, openly weeping over a smaller Senet Ghost who had been killed by one of the Rock Lizards. Grim kept asking another Ghost on his squad if he had accidentally killed the fallen man while in his berserker fury.

If Grim didn't get out of the League soon, he was going to break completely. If he snapped again, Kavi feared nothing would remain of his old friend.

* * *

Tack sat with Cliff a short distance up the path from their two squads. The Senet tactician looked lost. He wiped his eyes for the third time while looking down at his dead team members. "I don't think I can do it anymore. I've buried too many friends."

"Yeah, you can, Cliff," said Tack. "You're the longest serving tactician in the League, you'll figure it out."

"I've started fantasizing about my own death...just...to get a break." He stared into the distance. "I hope when death does come, its quick."

"I'm surprised you haven't retired."

"Ha! You know that's bullshit, right? The carrot they dangle to get you to try out for the professional team - finish thirty Quests and retire. You know how many I've completed? Fifty-three. Fifty-three Quests and nothing to show for it. They always have a way to reel you back. You end up owing the bastards for some debt they dreamed up. Or, they use thinly veiled threats like *concern for your family*. We're never getting out of this alive Promo."

Tack smiled at the use of her old nickname. She met Cliff in her first season with Team Sugoroku when she was a hotshot young Dancer. "I can't believe that," said Tack.

"I mean, if we were fighting *for* something it might be different," said Cliff, ignoring the hope in her tone. "But we're not. We don't have a cause. We're not fighting for a greater good. We're toys of the League. They don't care whether we live or die as long as we keep bringing home Quest rewards. I can't do it anymore."

"You have to," said Tack nervously. "There's got to be a way out of the League. I need to believe it, Cliff. We just haven't found it yet."

"There is," said a soft, melodious voice.

They drew weapons in surprise. From his perch above them, Reaver fired several projectiles which missed the small woman with almond eyes. Her flowing black silk robes fluttered behind her in the soft wind that whispered through the canyon.

The discharge from Reaver's weapon put both teams on full alert and they moved towards their tacticians.

"A way out, I mean," she said.

"Hi, Rose," said Kavi.

She smiled at him.

Tack raised her enhanced flint lock and pointed it at the newcomer. "Who's this, Eleven?"

"My name is Rose. I'm the fifth Sage."

"But, you're a woman," blurted Tack.

"Nice of you to notice my dear. Would you mind lowering your weapons and giving me five minutes of your time?"

"You wouldn't be able to hit her anyway," said Kavi. "She can see the future."

Rose scowled at him.

"Sorry, she can see *potential* futures."

"Why should we?" asked Tack. "Do you know how much the League would give to get their hands on you? You could be our ticket to retirement."

"Let me take her Tack," said Rake. "A single strike and we wouldn't have to worry about the Agitators anymore."

Rose smiled at Rake. "I'm sorry for what they did to you, young man, but the choices you've made since are ones you're going to have to live with for the rest of your life."

Rake vanished and appeared behind Rose a moment later. He stabbed at her, but she moved, again and again. She moved just enough for each strike to miss by a hairsbreadth.

Rose turned to him. "I'm sorry." She touched his temple and he collapsed. She turned back to Tack. "Five minutes. Please."

"You haven't answered my question. Why should we?"

"Three reasons," said Rose. "One, I can offer you a realistic way out of the League. Two, as Cliff mentioned, I can give you something to fight for. And three," she pointed to the dead Ach'Su. "I can tell you the secret behind the Ach'Su and why the League insists on calling them the Marked."

"I've heard too many promises of a way out," said Cliff.

"I know," she said. "What they did to you, to all of you, is an abomination."

"Five minutes," said Tack. "Start talking."

Rose smiled. "Always the professional. Let me start with a question. Do you know why the Quests were created?"

"Vonderians believe they were put in place by the Ancients to test us," said Pip.

"Test you for what?"

"To see if we're worthy of Astra's grace?" asked Piety in a small voice.

Anger flashed in Rose's eyes at the mention of the god but she didn't release it on Piety like she had on Kavi. "No, my dear. The Quests were put in place by the Ancients to be a catalyst. They're meant to inspire and assist in the evolution of the people of Grendar. The creation of the League is antithetical to that purpose. It exploits a gift meant for the evolution of an entire species for its own, selfish gain."

"As men in power have always done," said Tack. "Big surprise, what's your point?"

Rose scanned both teams, including everyone with her words. "This created a power differential. Since only a minuscule percentage of the population gets access to this catalyst, only a tiny percentage evolves. Only you and your cohorts learn these *skills* as you call them. The rest of the world stagnates and falls behind."

"But isn't that good for those of us with skills?" asked White.

"Maybe, if you had any power," said Rose. "But you don't. The League and the entity behind them hold *all* the power. When an entity with no moral or ethical compass holds this great a power differential, what happens next?"

Tack nodded. "You're looking at it. Subjugation. The rest of the world becomes slaves too, except without the training and with no access to Quests."

"They already have too much power," said Cliff. "I wouldn't be surprised if the League bought the governments of all the Garden Cities. Who's going to stop them? Who *can* stop them?" asked Cliff.

Rose smiled beatifically. "*I* can. And, I will. You know the legend of female Sages. I'm a symbol for change, a symbol for the oppressed to rally behind. But I need your help."

Tack laughed at her. "We've seen what the League is capable of. We see it every day. We'd be idiots to help you. They'll kill our families the second we desert."

Rose took her disdain in stride. She held up a single finger. "You forget I'm a Sage. As Kavi mentioned, my gift and my curse is the ability to see all potential futures. My Liberators stand ready to whisk your families to safety the minute I give the word."

"No," said Tack, shaking her head. "The League will beat you to it."

"You misunderstand, my dear. I foresaw this conversation weeks ago. My Liberators are meeting with your families right now. All your families."

"And if we say no?"

"That's *your* choice. Let me be clear. I will not threaten you or your families. The Liberators will never work under false pretenses and I will not suborn participation. I offer you a choice, an opportunity. A chance to work for something greater without the duress of family welfare held over you. If you say no, that is the last your families will see or hear from us."

"How could you possibly protect that many people?" asked Tack. "I know the power of the League and you're saying there's another group behind them with even more power? We're supposed to put the protection of our families in the hands of one woman and a bunch of rebels? You know they don't even see you as a threat, right? You're just a gnat to them."

"That's exactly how we protect them and how we will ultimately destroy the League. Like you, the League constantly underestimates us. I *just* told you that I have my people meeting with all of your families - that's thirty-seven families, if anyone's keeping count. Yet, you still doubt me because you've been conditioned that the League is all powerful."

Tack and Cliff looked thoughtful.

"If that's not enough, let me tell you the story of the Ach'Su." She walked towards the body of the broken beast.

They followed her as a group.

"Poor thing." She closed her eyes for a moment and when she opened them, the transparent body of a man lay next to the Ach'Su. "Did any of you know him?"

"That's Wrath!" said Cliff. "The coaches told me he retired. That was in my second year as tactician. Wait, are you saying he-"

Rose nodded sadly. "I'm sorry Cliff. Something like this will be your fate if you get past the roadblocks and retire. The League endorsed transforming this man into abomination. The organization that pulls the League's strings will do anything for more gold, more weapons, more power. There are no checks, no balances on this type of greed, this level of evil. We're the only thing that stands in its way."

"Wrath was an unbearable prick," Cliff said. "He took the dirty jobs the coaches asked of only those team members who had completely bought in to the League's villainy."

Ghost Squadron turned, as one, to look at Rake's prone form. The man's blue scaled tattoos up his neck and face looked less menacing on his unconscious form, childish even.

458

"Even he didn't deserve that. To be turned into that thing. Nobody deserves that," said Cliff.

"I agree," said Rose. "Will you help me?"

"Why does the League insist on calling it Marked instead of Ach'Su?" asked Kavi before anyone could agree.

Rose looked slightly surprised by the question, almost like she didn't foresee him asking it. "Why do you think?" she asked in challenge.

It was Tack who answered. "They're going to do it again. Make more Marked. They've already done it again. There were two of those things today. They're trying to normalize it. I'm sure they think they can control it, make it a symbol of their power, the ultimate Quest solving warriors and enforcers of the League."

Rose nodded.

"Why?" asked White who had been silent until now. "Why normalize something so...horrible?"

"I don't know. Maybe to get those of us who have become so beaten down by the League to volunteer for the transformation?" said Tack.

"That's a hell of a stretch," said White. "Who would volunteer to turn into *that*?"

"They're not done yet," said Pip, his mind working overtime to sniff out the League's motives. "They're not done experimenting, refining. When they are, they want their creations to be accepted."

"Exactly," said Kavi. "But why Marked? What are they marked with?"

"The group behind the League is calling it trunite," said Rose. "It's similar to sulimite but the effects are permanent. The group calls themselves the Collective. They believe trunite gives them the power of the divine. The Collective's arrogance knows no bounds. They believe their new creations are Marked for greatness. Once they master it, they're confident everyone will want to become Marked."

"No," said Cliff, shaking his head. "That doesn't explain the other Marked we've been seeing on the Quests this season, the ones destroying experienced, professional squads across the League."

Conflict played across Rose's normally serene face. It looked like she was trying to decide whether or not to break one of her rules. Finally she said, "You're right. The Sages found out about the Marked, because of course we did. By creating something monstrous, the Collective trampled over the Sages' domain. Only Sages should create the monsters that push the heroes of each age, that drive them to be better. Only Sages can hear the directives of the Ancients."

"Not a great recruitment pitch," said Tack. "Join the Sages who have been summoning the monsters killing us."

"That's why I discouraged the other Sages from this path." Rose shook her head. "They are too deep in their anger and madness though. They loath the chains the League placed over them. They're furious the Quests aren't open to all, so they lashed out, like caged animals. They used the hubris of the Collective against them. The Sages created evolved monsters of their own, challenges so difficult that even the best League teams would fail. Only then could the Quests be free. The Sages recaptured the term Marked as a way to fight against their own subjugation."

Tack raised her weapon at Rose, again. "So, we're dying because of some argument between the Sages and this Collective?"

Rose ignored the weapon. "I built the Liberators because I wanted to free the Quests back into the world by freeing the League members who were forced to participate in Quests created by enslaved Sages. Liberate the players, liberate the Quests. The other Sages didn't have the patience for my plan."

Tack lowered her weapon and the group tried to absorb this latest information.

"Why do you think the Ach'Su had a nest near Stonecrest?" asked

Grim.

"No idea," said Kavi. "Maybe Wrath had a grudge against the Lioness? Was Wrath Astran or Krommian?"

"He was a Bricker," said Cliff.

"Huh. Maybe he had a problem with your dad," said Grim.

"You really are Kavi Stonecrest," said Pip. "We assumed, but it's nice to have it confirmed."

Kavi nodded. The Ghosts knowing his identity no longer bothered him. The reputation he created with Ghost Squad was his own.

"All good questions but ones that will have to wait for another day," said Rose. "Our time grows short to get you, your teams and your families out of harm's way." She took two steps back and looked to the entire group. "Will you help me? Will you help the Liberators?"

"Yes," whispered Cliff. "I'll help." He stood up and looked at Team Senet. "I'm sorry. I can't keep doing this for no reason anymore."

One of the remaining Senet Strikers stood up. "We're with you, Tack," he said. The others on the pro team moved to stand behind him, so did the surviving Senet Ghosts.

Grim was the last of Team Senet to stand. He looked at Kavi. "I don't want to kill anymore."

Kavi nodded to him.

"What do you think, Tack?" asked White. "This might be the way out we've always talked about."

"Maybe, but can we trust her?" asked Tack.

"We know we *can't* trust the League," said White.

"We can trust they'll kill our families if we betray them," said Tack.

Rose closed her eyes. When she opened them she looked at Tack. "Your mother says she looks forward to seeing you. She promises to bring Mittens when they come."

Tack's strong features crumpled for only a moment, just enough time to release a small gasp. She sniffed and regained her composure.

"Ok, I'm in."

"Yes!" yelled Flask into the silence.

Pyre jumped. He smacked Flask. "You gotta stop doing that."

"Sounds like Ghost Squadron is in," said Pip with a smile.

Rose whistled once.

The Liberator squad who set the thumpers came jogging around the bend in the canyon. They were followed by more than twenty others.

"Your team's bigger than I expected," said Tack.

Rose smiled. "You have no idea. The Liberators have twelve active Quest teams ready to deploy at all times. We could put a team against every one of the League's if we wanted and still have teams in reserve. We don't, because we're focused on recruitment, not completing Quests."

Tack gave her an incredulous look. "Why didn't you start with that? Your pitch would be a lot more compelling."

Rose shook her head gravely. "These decisions aren't easy and they can't be forced. If you're going to make a major change in your life, it begins with a leap of faith."

Carlin walked to Grim and gave him a big hug. "Sorry for the arrow in the shoulder."

"Didn't even know it was you," said Grim.

"Likewise," said Carlin. "Do you know how terrifying you are in battle?"

Grim's face fell. "I've heard it said."

"Nettie is going to be so happy to see you idiots," said Carlin.

"Nettie joined the Liberators?" asked Grim.

Kavi smiled. He'd seen when it happened.

The dire mood that surrounded most Quests had been replaced by something hopeful.

Kavi looked at his team and smiled. He couldn't help the bittersweet feelings rippling through him. There was more sadness than joy as he thought about how much he would miss them.

"Kavi, ready to leave this League nightmare behind?" asked Grim, his haunted eyes showing new signs of life.

"Come on, Eleven, you're normally out front on something like this," said Grundle, a broad smile painting his face.

"I'm not going," Kavi said.

"What do you mean you're not going?" said Grim.

"I can't leave them behind. Tess, Boost, Sliver, Clara, Jansen and all the rest. I'll be there as soon as I can and I'll bring the rest of the Ghosts with me," said Kavi.

"You grew up didn't you, lad?" said Carlin with a sad smile. "Your ma would be proud of you."

Even with her impossibly high standards, it was probably true. Those words would have made a younger Kavi beam. He realized, he no longer cared as much about her approval or anyone's for that matter. It still felt good to have Carlin say it.

Kavi responded with a hand on the man's shoulder. Carlin nodded in respect.

Grim wasn't done yet. "You can't go back in there Kavi. I just found you. You helped me out of that maze of rage. You helped make me, *me* again."

Kavi pulled him into a hug. "Don't worry. I'll find you again. It's going to be a lot easier knowing you're safe."

He looked at Pip. "You're not going to try to convince me?"

Pip shook his head. "Nope, I'm coming with you."

"No, Pip. This is my decision and I'm not dragging you with me."

Pip laughed. He turned to Carlin and Grim. "Has he always had this big an ego?" He turned back to Kavi. "I made my decision five minutes ago. I've been over there watching you come to the same realization. If anything, I'm dragging you along with me."

"I'll go back too then," said Pyre. Kavi could see how much it hurt the man to say it. One by one, the other Ghosts stood behind Pyre.

"We're all coming back if you two are going," said Grundle.

"That means more than you can know," said Pip, wiping an eye. "But I need to know *my* Ghost Squad made it out of this hell. It's going to be a huge morale boost for the Ghosts back home to know you're free! That you're going to be part of Rose's vision. We need Ghost Squad to build the Liberators into something we're proud of. As my final order as Ghost Squadron tactician, I order you to go with Rose."

Kavi and Pip hugged the remaining members of Ghost Squad. Grundle couldn't stop crying as he held on to Kavi. Leesta finally had to pull him away.

"We'll do Ghost Squadron proud," said Flask.

"I know you will," said Kavi.

Tack said goodbye next. "This is going to be a huge whack to the hornet's nest. You're walking into a firestorm. Keep your head down."

White laughed. "Him? Keep his head down? Who do you think you're talking to Tack?"

Tack gave a chuckle of her own. "Fine, if you're not going to keep your head down then stick it *way* up. That's how I got the tactician role. Challenge everything and everybody until they can't ignore you. Your Ghost Squad could probably take the triple A squad right now. Use that. Put yourself in a position where you can protect as many people as possible until we destroy the whole nest of evil bastards."

"Yes ma'am," said Kavi and Pip together.

The goodbyes complete, the Ghosts and Liberators made their way east. They traversed down the canyon paths to where the Liberators had their own airship docked.

Rose waited behind until everyone else was out of sight. The only people who remained at the sight of the battle were Rose, Pip, Kavi and the unconscious Rake.

"With this choice, your path gets darker," she said.

"I know," said Kavi. "But this time it *is* our choice."

"I'm going to lightly sweep your mind so when Team Sugoroku sends nueros at you, they won't be able to get anything."

"Are we going to lose our memories in the sweep?" asked Pip.

"Only about how big our forces are. You'll retain everything else. Rake, on the other hand, won't know what happened. I've wiped his memories of the Quest completely clean." She looked at the Harpstran Striker then back at them. "Kavi, Pip – be careful. You're a bigger part of this than you know."

"Yes ma'am," said Pip.

"We will," said Kavi. "And Rose, thank you. We'll join you as soon as we can."

Rose smiled sadly and followed the rest of her Liberators. Pip and Kavi watched her until she was out of sight.

* * *

When the airship captain landed he looked at the three of them waiting in the pick up zone. "Was it that bad?"

Pip and Kavi grabbed Rake and pulled him up the ramp to the airship. "You have no idea," said Kavi. "We lost almost everybody on both teams and never came close to solving the damn Quest. Let's get back to the Nest. We'll give a full debrief there."

47

Heroes Wanted

T he warehouse was a squat, unmarked brick building three blocks from the Harpstran docks. One might have thought it to be derelict but for the single guard standing outside the small door.

The inside was similarly unremarkable. Small crates piled haphazardly around the large open room. Several large crates were cleverly positioned to conceal a stairway leading into the basement. Building a basement this close to the sea took an extraordinary amount of energy and resources. It even took earth magic to manage the high water table. It was worth it. A subterranean room surrounded by water provided security from prying eyes, physical or magical.

The owners gathered for the third time in as many months. The table they sat around was small and dusty.

The majordomo was not present.

"It's time for us to acknowledge the Collective does not have our best interest in mind," said Senet. His white suit was rumpled and he had dark bags under his eyes.

"No shit, Senet," said Ch'es. He reacted to stress by eating. His tailors had been working overtime to extend his clothing to fit his bulging tomato build. "I thought you were supposed to be the smart one."

"While it pains me to say it," said Wari. "I agree with Ch'es. We knew the type of snake we were in bed with. The question is - what do we do about it?"

"I don't believe the Collective has control over the difficulty of the Quests," said Lord Go, his voice more tremulous than normal. "That power lies with the Sages."

"I've begun to doubt the veracity of that assumption Lord Go," said Senet. "I believe the Collective realized long ago that the difficulty of each Quest is directly proportional to the power of those foreseen to participate. They have pushed the League to advance, to evolve faster than what is natural. At least within the general populace. Therefore, the Quests have become impossible to all but the superhumans we created. Keep in mind, it is meant to be difficult even for them. This is not sustainable."

"I don't follow," said Ch'es.

"I'm not surprised," said Senet. "But I grow weary of dumbing things down for you. The Collective knows rapid evolution is not sustainable but they don't care. They don't care because it gives them a unique type of leverage. For us to maintain superhuman teams requires our supplication. We need to approach the Collective, hat in hand, and beg for a new technology, a new magical evolution, a new edge to stay competitive. Some of us, like Risk," Senet nodded at the man, who graciously nodded back, "have done mountains of their own research. But that research is funded by the Collective with the underlying threat of pulling the funding at any time."

"Agreed. I'll ask again, what can we do about it?" asked Wari.

"I hope you have ideas," said Mehen, her usual arrogance muted. She looked the defeated queen doing her best to put on a good face. "After I lost most of my professional team, my board of directors made it clear – one more mistake and I'm out."

"We all face the threat of replacement," said Risk. "Two Quests in, and I'm the only one with a professional team with more than half its starting roster. I don't say this to brag. My team lost its high profile Strikers and my investors are banging on my door just as hard. They want answers I don't have."

The mood in the room was as sad and dusty as the top of the table they sat around. Sugoroku and Senet were not the only Companies who lost their entire professional squads in this last Quest.

"The League is teetering on the edge of being unable to complete the season," said Ur. His voice was throaty and deep, tapping into the days he spent on the stage. "We can throw our triple A teams at the problem but what happens when we lose them too? Will we be able to field squads for next season?"

"Which leads us to Project Midnight," said Sugoroku. "Losing my entire professional team is not something I can recover from. If what the Collective promises is real, it could be a way to field a new team at the same high level."

"Ah yes," said Senet. "The Dark One's bargain. Let's continue to escalate and give more power to the Collective."

"I understand your frustration. Believe me. I share it. But, what's the alternative?" asked Sugoroku.

"What if we deescalate?" asked Senet. "What if instead of following the script the Collective pushes on us, we go back to our roots? We use our new crop of volunteers to take on Quests the old way. No skills, no Collective technologies, nothing but courage and fortitude."

"Sounds kind of boring," said Ch'es.

"Boring for us maybe," said Senet. "But not to those that will be watching these competitions for the first time. This will bring back the heroes of old. When a new skill is unlocked, the crowds will be stunned. They will be amazed. They will try to figure out how it is possible and try to learn to do it themselves. As the Ancients intended."

"You don't start a play in the third act," said Ur, rubbing his chin. "This gives the League years of storyline to take an adoring crowd through."

"Exactly," said Senet. "All of this can be done without tapping into a single Collective resource."

"But what if you're wrong?" said Ch'es. "What if the difficulty of the Quest remains and we send teams of uninitiated to their deaths? I can't imagine that's going to be very popular with betting audiences."

"Then we don't make it public," said Senet as if the answer was obvious. "We control the narrative of how these competitions play out."

"So, what do we do with the existing teams, those that have unlocked their skills?" asked Ch'es. "Rumor has it, the Agitators recruited many of our professionals that didn't die. If they keep showing up to Quests, the difficulty will remain high."

"They continue to participate but no one is allowed the use of sulimite. As for the Agitators...it may be time for us to parlay with the fifth Sage," said Senet.

"I'm not looking to go to war with the Collective," said Wari.

"Who said anything about war with the Collective?" asked Senet.

"You know as well as I that if we treat with the Sage, that's what we're going to get," said Wari. "I don't think I can handle another late night visit from the thin man."

"A parlay doesn't mean we cede to her demands," said Senet. "If this angers the Collective, we tell them we are doing our due diligence on *all* possible ways to complete the season. This is research."

Sugoroku folded her hands in front of her. "To make it more believable, we tell the Collective that if we informed them ahead of time, the Sage would have sniffed it out and would never have agreed to meet."

Senet gave her a rare nod of respect.

"What if we've already started experimenting with Project Midnight?" asked Ch'es.

"Really?" asked Mehen. "You'd subject your Company to something like that?"

Ch'es laughed. "Of course I would." The large man scowled. "Don't give me that look. And don't act like any of you haven't made these type of choices in the past. There isn't a single saint sitting at this table."

"I thought we agreed Project Midnight crossed a line," said Lord Go.

Ch'es snorted. "Says the first of the owners to condone slavery."

"How many?" asked Senet.

"How many what?" replied Ch'es.

"How many players did you send to the Collective for Project Midnight?"

"Three, all ghosts."

"This could still work as long as you agree not to send them on a Quest."

Ch'es nodded. "Agreed."

"We're going to need that in writing," said Senet.

"The real question is - can we trust Ch'es not to sell us out to the Collective?" asked Wari.

"I may not be a saint, but I'm no snitch. You know my background. You know what I've personally done to snitches."

Wari nodded.

A moment later Senet gave a single curt nod. "Who will reach out to the Sage?"

"I will," said Sugoroku. "It should be me or Mehen. This is a conversation that will go better woman to woman. I have a bit better of a diplomatic track record. No offense Mehen."

Mehen laughed. "None taken. I'm not exactly known for my diplomacy."

"Excellent," said Senet. "Final order of business. Recruitment. Are the air ships ready?"

Heads nodded around the table.

Senet smiled. "Tomorrow will be a day to remember."

* * *

Marcus looked fearfully to the sky. He had never seen anything so big. The airship that flew over Founder's Square was the most exciting thing to happen in Harpstra in his short life. And he had seen quite a few exciting things in thirteen years of growing up in the theater district.

He pulled his eyes from the ship which left a shadow as big as a cloud. He looked at the guards standing around the Square. None of them looked worried so Marcus guessed it was okay. If the people who ran the city were okay with it, it was okay with him.

Things began to fall from the sky, dumped from the airship. Marcus screamed and noticed others in the square doing the same.

One of those things hit him squarely in the head and he reflexively covered his head with his arms. It didn't hurt. He looked down at what struck him and saw something neatly wrapped in paper.

He picked it up and smiled. He opened the confection and popped it in his mouth. He smiled blissfully - caramelized honey, it was like a parade. An air parade. He liked parades. His fear vanished.

When the papers fell from the sky, he was the first to grab one. He flipped the paper over and began to read. With each word, he grew more and more excited.

HEROES WANTED

Hector the Brave, Isar the Wise and Vantrix the Valiant were titans of their generations. Men and women who moved mountains, transformed kingdoms and changed Grendar forever. What happened to all the heroes?

More sightings of fantastical creatures and horrifying monster come in from the reaches every day. Grendar needs heroes to stand again.

What do the great heroes have in common? Their stories started with a Quest. Karzak the Triumphant completed the Six Trials of Agenon. Melody d'Or defeated the Three Horned Terror of Kar'Toon.

The League has discovered six new Quests. Join us in Founder's Square at eight o'clock for more information. We need volunteers to complete these Quests. We need your help.

The League exists for one reason: to bring back the heroes of old. Will you be the next Vantrix?

Marcus grinned. This was turning out to be the best day of his young life.

Thank you

Dear Reader,

I hope you enjoyed reading Ghost Squad, the first book of the Evolution Trials. If you enjoyed the story and look forward to more stories, please do me a huge favor and leave a review on Amazon.

If you're a regular reader, I'm sure you've read this before, but that doesn't make it any less true. Reviews are the lifeblood for self-published authors and I'm no different. I look forward to bringing you the next installment of the story soon!

Thank you so much!

If you would like me to notify you when the next book is released, please visit the website: www.seanhkennedy.com and sign up.

About the Author

Sean Kennedy graduated with a bachelor's degree in physics and did absolutely nothing with it. He became a coder, an entrepreneur and now a writer. He lives in Colorado with his beautiful wife, two daughters, a rescue mutt on trial for war crimes against squeaky toys, and a German shepherd who ratted her out for a tennis ball.

When Sean's not writing, you can most likely find him outside in the mountains.

Made in the USA
Monee, IL
23 April 2023